A
Dangerous Marriage

A
Dangerous Marriage

William W. Blunt

iUniverse, Inc.
Bloomington

A Dangerous Marriage

This is a work of fiction. All of the characters, names, incidents, organizations, and dialogue in this novel are either the products of the author's imagination or are used fictitiously.

iUniverse books may be ordered through booksellers or by contacting:

iUniverse
1663 Liberty Drive
Bloomington, IN 47403
www.iuniverse.com
1-800-Authors (1-800-288-4677)

ISBN: 9781475905632 (sc)
ISBN: 9781475905397 (e)
ISBN: 9781475905625 (dj)

Library of Congress Control Number: 2012905376
Printed in the United States of America

iUniverse rev. date: 8/9/2012

To Blair, of course…

*Your patient and expert services
as reader and editor,
and your enthusiastic support,
made this book possible.*

PART 1

1

THE PRIVATE UPSTAIRS ROOM at 21 Club in New York City exuded a plush variety of elegance with its heavy burgundy damask curtains, brocade wall covering and busy, oriental carpets. As Julia Davenport and her escort for the evening entered, she saw groups of well-groomed men, most of them probably in their forties and fifties, dressed in somber colors except for the occasional flash of a yellow or red necktie, drinks in hand, engaged in serious discussion. A crowd of uniformed waiters, unobtrusive but efficient, bore platters of hors d'oeuvres and glasses of champagne on trays and filled orders for other drinks. A well-stocked mahogany bar attracted an intermittent stream of guests.

The men were joined by a few women in smart business outfits, professionals who had not had time to change after work. Then there were wives or other female companions. They seemed to be on display, like exotic, plumed birds, posturing as they hung on the outskirts of the men's conversations or chatted among themselves.

Tall and slim, with short, dark hair, Julia wore the only garment she owned that was suitable for evening: a black cocktail dress, a designer label that she found marked down twice at an upscale second-hand clothing store in Philadelphia. She hoped it would look sufficiently cosmopolitan for the occasion. In any event, in the presence of this crowd of complete strangers, she felt more like a spectator than a participant.

She had come with a man whom she had dated for a while during her last year of college. His call and invitation came as a complete surprise, but when he asked her to accompany him to a large dinner party in New York City, even though she couldn't afford to stay there overnight, she accepted with alacrity. She realized as she heard his invitation on the phone—she barely recognized his voice—that this could be the opportunity she needed to emerge from the relative seclusion she had been forced into after college.

She had become painfully aware that while she was coping with graduate school, her challenging new teaching position, and caring for her ailing mother before her mother's death, her social life had drifted into a backwater, like one of those scooped-out places she remembered along the bank of the trout stream in the woods near the house where she grew up. When she was young, she had sat for hours marveling at the objects floating there, lethargically, in perpetual circles, with no apparent means of escape. Now, she might finally have a chance to break out, to gain direction, and she became determined to do what she could, if not to catch up, then at least to push herself back into the main current.

It developed that her friend, an attorney, needed to make an appearance earlier in the evening at a business reception that was to be a celebration by a large corporation congratulating itself on acquiring a smaller company. He and the law firm he was with had worked on the deal. He was to attend to help ensure that the fairly large room looked appropriately crowded. After "showing the flag" at the reception, they were going to the dinner. She had faced the prospect of the reception with a vague sense of apprehension. But it was, she thought, a small price to pay to gain the rest of the evening.

Soon after their arrival, her escort was drawn into an earnest discussion from which she was gradually expelled by virtue of the enthusiasm of the others, men, who edged themselves toward the center to hear or be heard. Julia took the opportunity to look with mild curiosity around the room.

In a few moments her gaze came to rest on a man she had noticed earlier in passing. Now that she was free from other distractions and he was absorbed in conversation, she could take him in at her leisure. His hair was jet black and combed smoothly, straight back. His skin was deeply tanned. His imposing nose reminded her of a hawk's beak, ready to strike, and his prominent brow and well-defined, slightly pointed chin all contributed to a predatory image that was enhanced by a certain feline smoothness to his movements. What had caught her attention from the beginning, she decided later, was his aura of animal vitality.

He was confident, she could tell, even cocky, as he held forth to the circle of men that had formed around him. He might be in his late thirties, more likely early forties, which was young for this crowd of listeners, but they all seemed to be working diligently to make eye contact with him. They smiled wisely, and nodded gravely, when he spoke. He was shorter than most of them, but still seemed to dominate: a lion among a gathering of nervous water buffalo.

When her escort reemerged, Julia asked him about the man she had studied with an interest that she found had grown in intensity more than she chose to express. She learned that along with the top people of the two companies, he was something of a celebrity here. In fact, he had brought the companies together, making the acquisition possible. In doing so, he had earned a substantial commission. He had a lot to celebrate.

Later, her friend ambled off to get another gin and tonic. Julia was still working on her first glass of white wine, which had warmed to an almost cloying sweetness in the ample bowl of its glass. He left her on the edge of a small group of lawyers from his firm. Their discussion, with lowered voices, did not include her. She could hear only disjointed fragments of their conversation, but, so as not to appear abandoned and alone, with mounting embarrassment, she feigned interest.

"Hello."

She was startled to recognize, close at hand, the voice of the man who had intrigued her so much from afar. It was a resonant baritone, yet its effect was intimate, bestowing on her a flattering exclusivity. He spoke with a hint of a foreign accent. She turned. He was smiling broadly, looking directly at her. His eyes were dark brown and impenetrable, like well-polished mahogany.

"We haven't been introduced." He held out his hand. "I'm Peter Medea."

His grip was firm.

It took her a second to recover. Then she smiled back. "Hello."

"And you're Julia Davenport." He held her eyes with his.

"How did you…?"

"No, I'm not psychic," he said. "You were on the guest list. I always try to find out who it might be worthwhile to get to know. I hope that doesn't sound too calculating. Anyway, I found you by matching you with your escort."

"Well, what makes me so 'worthwhile,' as you put it?"

"My secret. For the moment, anyway. But now that I've seen you, that we've met, so to speak, I'm beginning to feel as though I'd like to get to know you with or without a reason. What do you say?"

"Sure." Julia hoped she did not betray her surprise.

"Well, we won't have much time now." Peter glanced in the direction of the bar, where Julia's escort was engaged in dialogue with another man while waiting for his refill. He pulled a slender, black leather appointment book and a Mont Blanc pencil from his inside coat pocket. "When can we get together?"

"I don't know." Julia hesitated. She was having a hard time catching up to the pace at which this man moved.

"How about dinner tomorrow evening?" Peter offered. "That's Thursday," he added, as if she might not know without her own appointment calendar in front of her.

"Here?" Julia knew she could not stay in New York.

"Here if you like," Peter smiled as he looked around the room in which they were standing, "although the atmosphere is a little more intimate downstairs."

"I'm terribly sorry, but I can't," Julia said. "I'm going back to Philadelphia tonight, and back to work tomorrow. Today was a school holiday."

"You're in school?" Peter raised his heavy black eyebrows.

"I teach. I'm a high school English teacher. In the inner city. Philadelphia. I thought you looked me up?"

"I did, but not for that." He smiled, then looked back to the appointment book. "In Philadelphia, then?"

Astonished, she tried to remember what she was supposed to be doing the next evening. Wouldn't she be correcting test papers to hand back on Friday?

"Yes," she said after a moment, "that would be lovely."

"Will you be free by, say, seven?" Peter's writing instrument was poised. His lips were full and sensual. He curled them in as he concentrated.

"Yes."

"How can I reach you?"

They exchanged telephone numbers and email addresses. He would pick her up at seven and take her to dinner. He did not say where. He would have to leave for New York by ten, so she needn't worry about being up too late.

Just then they were joined by a tall man, probably in his late fifties, immaculately groomed, swarthy, and heavy-set, filling out his well-tailored, double-breasted navy-blue business suit with an effect of solidity rather than the softness usually associated with such girth. He took Peter's elbow, as if to usher him off without further ceremony, but stopped, glancing in Julia's direction for a moment. Then he gave her an up-and-down, unhurried look, a leisurely but thorough appraisal, which brought a flush to her cheeks. Embarrassed by her instinctive dislike of this intruder, she looked back to Peter, who seemed frozen in place for an instant, his expression oddly neutral, his lips formed in a tight line.

Finally he spoke. "Julia Davenport, this is Marco DiNiro, chairman of Grendel Holdings, our host for the evening, and my valued client." He turned toward Julia. "Marco…"

But before he could complete his formal introduction, the large man interrupted him. "Call me Denny, my dear. And if you ever get tired of Peter's company, please remember to get in touch." He gave her a brief smile and an elaborate wink. He loosened his grip on Peter's arm. "Now, though, I'm afraid I need your friend here for a moment." He gave Peter a meaningful look before he walked away from them to a small cluster of men that seemed to be awaiting his arrival.

"Well," Peter shrugged, "I guess business must come before pleasure. Isn't that the way it usually turns out?" He offered her his hand. "Until tomorrow evening then?"

"Yes," she said. "Tomorrow."

At that moment, Julia's escort returned, but her gaze followed Peter Medea. She knew she was already strongly drawn to this man, so compelling and yet so seemingly manipulative. She watched him walk quickly toward the small group that had collected around Marco "Denny" DiNiro, his important client whom she had found strangely threatening. She marveled that Medea had singled her out for his attention. That she had been the subject of his research, and, apparently as a result, had attracted his interest even before he met her. Why? Still she was flattered, and gratified, and welcomed this break in her solitary routine, this opportunity to expand her horizons.

She wondered, should she have been more cautious in her response to the surprising urgency of Peter Medea's advances? But if she had been, would she ever see him again?

2

THE ANNOUNCEMENT REVERBERATED THROUGH the vast marble hall of Philadelphia's 30th Street Station as Julia, the strap of her purse slung over her shoulder, dragging a suitcase on rollers behind her, strode quickly toward the gate. The rumbling pulse of the arriving engine and the sleek passenger cars it was pulling shook the floor under her hurrying feet.

In a dark suit, chosen carefully from her meager wardrobe, that she hoped was dressy enough for the occasion, she bent slightly to the weight of her load as she rushed to board the train. She knew she had a few minutes before it was scheduled to depart, and that it would take a while to unload and receive passengers and baggage, so when she reached the platform and saw that some people were still disembarking while others waited to board, she should have felt reassured. Yet she could not quell an undercurrent of mild panic that caused her heart to race, and she knew that her unease would not subside until she was inside, with the doors shut.

After she settled into a seat next to a window, a man sat down next to her, on the aisle. Middle-aged. Like Peter, she mused ruefully. He had helped her heft her luggage onto a nearby overhead rack and was now pointedly immersing himself in the *Wall Street Journal*. Good. She looked forward to turning her attention to the surprising way her life seemed suddenly to be unfolding. Before long, she would be walking up the ramp at Penn Station in New York City, to be, once again, with Peter Medea. She wanted this, had anticipated it often in her thoughts since she had seen him last, when he had taken her to dinner, but she knew that the stakes for her could be much higher this time than before.

The events that had led up to her being where she was at this moment—on the Metroliner, reaching its cruising speed toward her destination—had rushed past her too quickly. The demands of her work this close to the end of the school year and preparing for her summer job, had not left her enough time to contemplate them. To savor them, yes, but also to understand their meaning. Because, even as she looked forward to this next episode in what had come to seem to her as an exciting adventure, she could not shed the uneasy feeling as she embarked on it that she was not doing as much as she should to control her own destiny. As she turned away from her traveling companion to look out the window, she realized that this was her first real opportunity to sort out these conflicting feelings about Peter, even though she knew that by being here in the first place, she had committed herself to taking the next step.

In spite of her good intentions, though, she found herself distracted by the voyeuristic glimpses the view from the moving train afforded her of the back yards of tenements, a woman hanging clothes on a line, a courageous effort at a communal vegetable garden, the rear of a scruffy auto shop. The zoo magically appeared, only to glide swiftly out of her line of vision. Then a more suburban kaleidoscope—tree-lined streets, garden apartment complexes, town squares, and low station platforms fronting parking lots full of commuters' cars, SUVs and pickups—sped past.

But soon, her thoughts were relentlessly drawn once more to the purpose of her journey. She still stared out of the window, but now with unseeing eyes. She realized that she had become strongly attracted to this man, much older than herself, who had come bursting into her life, virtually from nowhere. She wondered what his desires might be. She tried to understand her own, and what the possible consequences, good or bad, might be of her trying to attain their fulfillment.

She pondered the outcome of their evening together in Philadelphia, such a short time ago. Even though it was he who had suggested it, she had still been surprised, and flattered, when this obviously busy man, drove (was driven, in a limousine, to be accurate) all the way from New York in the middle of the week to have dinner with her, as he had promised. At first she was on her guard. Their conversation had been easy, but light. He professed to be interested in her thoughts on various topics, her opinions. Maybe he was. Or maybe it was simply a technique he employed to put his companion of the moment at ease, one reason he was so successful (she assumed) in his business dealings and, she imagined, with women. In a short while, though, his companionable manner won her over. She found that when he spoke she was interested in what he had to say. She had been pleased, too, and relieved, that after all his effort in coming there, he maintained respect for the distance that she instinctively kept from him this first time they were together.

It seemed to her almost as if the two of them had stepped out from the party in New York for a while for some fresh air, away from the noise and frivolity inside, each to learn who this other person was in whom they had seemed to become so interested. In retrospect, though, she realized that he had learned far more about her than she had about him. Beyond his gracious manner, and his apparent feelings for her that were evidenced by his being there at all, and the interest he showed in her, she knew little more about him at the end of the evening than she had before she had first greeted him at its beginning.

Before they parted, he had asked her to spend a weekend in New York as his guest. He would arrange for her travel. He did not suggest that she stay in his apartment. Instead, he offered to put her up in a nearby hotel. It was with only a hint of apprehension, an unidentifiable, and therefore presumably insubstantial, concern that she had accepted his invitation. But now she was overcome with an ennui born of confusion. Was it wise for her to be spending a weekend alone with Peter so soon after their first meeting? What message would it convey to him? What did he want of her? What, indeed, did she, whatever she might like to admit to herself, want of him?

The announcement that the train was approaching Trenton startled Julia from her reverie. As it pulled into the station, it moved slowly along the platform, passing clusters of people gathered where they hoped the doors would be when the train stopped, readying themselves to board. She realized that in spite of the line of inquiry her mind was taking, she was impatient with the speed of the train's progress. Trenton seemed so close to Philadelphia, and New York so far away from Trenton!

Persons occupying seats vacated them and new passengers shuffled down the aisle of her car to claim them. When the train began to slide along and away from the platform she saw that her quiet neighbor had stayed put. Again, she turned to stare out the window. This time she was surprised by thoughts of another man—the only other person in her life who had affected her this way. From her perspective now, after all these years, she was sure that she had been truly in love with Danny Johnson, as young as she was when he came into her life. A year ahead of her in high school. Tall, blond, on all the teams. Every girl's dream. It had been amazing to her that he had singled her out, had returned for her graduation, taken her to the senior dance.

Then it had ended so strangely. After all this time she was still visited by vivid images of her first timid response to his advances in the fragrant shadows inside the hay barn where he had taken her after the graduation picnic. Of their kiss, and her mounting desire, and his. Of his forceful, almost violent, effort to consummate with her what he thought they had begun. And finally, of how, with equal force, she had pushed him away in spite of the desire that she still felt for him. To this day, when she least expected it, she was caught unawares by the ineffable sadness she had felt as she witnessed his stunned reaction and then his sulky retreat back into his own world, a place into which she had been admitted, in uneasy awe, for such a short period of time.

Now, whenever she thought of Danny, which she did more often than she liked to admit, even to herself, she marveled that her life must be so bereft of incident that she was still, after so many years, drawn to dwell on her feelings for him. Was it her loneliness? Was it out of desperation? Or could it simply be that having Danny was a dream she could afford because there was virtually no risk that their relationship could ever be rekindled. Because there was so little chance of her having to actually decide whether he was the one. To commit herself to him.

She smiled wanly. In spite of the incident in the barn, he had called her once while she was in college (how did he find her number?). She had not responded. Looking back on it, she was not sure why.

Julia leaned her forehead against the cool glass of the window. Danny wasn't perfect, she reflected. He had certainly demonstrated that to her before they parted so long ago. But neither, she suspected, is Peter.

When the train glided into the station at Newark, the last stop before Penn Station, Julia looked down on the nearly empty platform. Hardly anyone, it seemed, was getting off. Like Julia, they all were intent, as quickly as possible, on getting to New York City. Then it quietly began to move, pulling away, picking up speed as it crossed the trestle bridge over the Passaic River and headed out onto the Meadowlands. Soon they would be in the long tunnel under the Hudson River. She couldn't be more than a few minutes away from her arrival. Suddenly her mood lightened and her excitement mounted in anticipation of the weekend.

3

To stay within her budget for her trip to the city, Julia ventured from the light, open space of Penn Station's main terminal, where she emerged after disembarking from her train, into the tunnel that led her toward the subway to Times Square. She pulled her suitcase with one white-knuckled fist and held her purse, its strap around her neck, firmly against her with the other. Once committed, she was swept along by the flood of people who had made the same choice.

On more than one occasion she had taken this same route with her mother as her guide, to get to Bloomingdale's and places further uptown, but she had forgotten the claustrophobic grunge subway travel in New York could offer up, particularly as summer approached. It came to her with force as she began the walk through the underground passageway at Times Square to the platform for the shuttle to Grand Central.

The stale odors of frying food from stands along the way and the accumulated fragrance of filth and sweat seemed to be drawn out from the pavement and walls by the heat and steamy humidity. All around her people were rushing to get through. Taking the route of least resistance, she gravitated toward the faster-moving center of the river of humanity.

To each side, a stream of harried commuters heading for the station struggled to pass by in the opposite direction. Like spawning salmon they worked their way doggedly upstream, surging forward, then wriggling and dodging to find places where a slacker current could help them mount another burst of speed toward their contrary goal.

On the fringes lingered a collection of strange-looking souls. Clothed in eclectic miscellany, many of them guarded soiled blankets or bundles of rags. They languished on the pavement along the now-grimy white-tiled side of the tunnel, gathering in alcoves that had once housed fast food stalls or tourist trinket counters like the animals in the small, decrepit cages she remembered from the old zoo in Central Park she had seen as a child. Some paced wearily. Others stood, leaning against the wall, or lay on newspapers, staring blankly out at the passing frenzy. A number drank from containers clutched inside crushed brown paper bags. A few concentrated on wrinkled, frayed fragments of reading material. One held an open bible close to his face, lips moving silently to the sacred text.

A wild-looking man with thick black pointy hair thrusting angrily in all directions harangued the transient congregation, shouting and gesturing at them. Julia averted her eyes and stared ahead of her until she was past, but could not shed a vague, uneasy residue of guilt that settled on her as she hurried on.

At the end of the shuttle ride she spilled with her fellow passengers out into another long subterranean cavern that led to the Lexington Avenue line. She took the local train uptown. It was even more crowded.

Crammed into the car she found a place near the door with enough room for her suitcase. Positioned next to it, grasping a handle hanging from above her for support, she found herself forced into alarming intimacy with the passengers standing beside her. Dressed in thin, light clothing blotched by stains of perspiration, their warm bodies brushed and bumped against her as the frantic train swayed and lurched along its course. With them, and to avoid staring around her with an appearance of unwonted curiosity, she gazed intently at the strip of miniature billboards above the windows. She read one message after another, over and over, a litany that helped subdue her panic while she waited tensely for the platform at her stop to glide up to the door of the car. "U cn lrn to wrt fst." "Why suffer from acid indigestion?" "Need a high school education?"

Finally, with a grateful sigh, she emerged, lugging her suitcase, from the steep-stepped subway exit into the marginally fresher unseasonably summery air of the city's noisy streets during rush hour. She walked from 77th Street down Lexington Avenue to 76th Street, then cross-town to Madison Avenue. Her arm grew weary. Her feet ached. Strands of damp hair clung to her forehead. Sweat trickled into her eyes and the corners of her mouth. She tasted its salty tang as she forced a steady pace toward the hotel.

At last she arrived. The doorman immediately took her burden from her tired grasp and carried it inside. She stepped across the threshold.

She remembered the Carlyle from long ago. Her parents had taken her there once, to the piano bar—the Bemelmans Bar—as a treat after a chamber music concert in a nearby church. Now the lobby seemed a cool, magical oasis.

To avoid the cost of a tip, she took the key from the man at the front desk, waved off the startled bellman and found the room Peter had engaged for her—her room—on her own. It wasn't large, but seemed like the height of luxury, with its apple green carpet and peach wall covering hung with watercolor paintings of flowers. A vase of white carnations stood on a round table. It was a different world to her, or, at least, one she hadn't seen since she was a little girl.

She lingered in the bathroom. She examined boxes of soap—opening one and lifting the small cake to her nose, breathing in its pleasing floral fragrance—and miniature containers of lotion, powder and shampoo that were nestled in a wicker basket that sat on the counter near the sink in front of a huge mirror. A bud vase holding a single pink carnation stood on the other side.

When she looked up, her reflection caught her eye. She reached for one of the fluffy face towels that were stacked on top of a rack next to her and patted away the moisture that lingered on her forehead, at her temples and above her upper lip. Then stepped back and checked herself in the mirror, wondering as she did what Peter Medea might see in her.

She was a little too lanky, skinny she felt, her figure not quite full enough by conventional standards. Her facial features favored character, with prominent cheek bones, a sculpted nose that was larger than she would have liked, and a strong chin. Her mouth was too wide. She did like her eyes, mainly because they were her father's: large, a complex sort of grey with hints of green radiating out from black pupils, framed by dark lashes and brows.

Her hair was dark brown, cut short and curling inward below the line of her cheek bones at a length that showed off her long neck, another of the few of her features that she was truly fond of.

All said and done, not so bad, she thought as she gazed evenly at her own image staring back at her. Not great, but not so bad. She smiled.

Julia's clothes were damp with perspiration. She shed them even before she unpacked. Then she walked to the tall windows at the end of the room, flanked by floor-length curtains. The sunlight, friendly now, streamed into the room. She was on a floor just high enough for her to be able to see fragments of Central Park, one block away. She knew that Peter must be in one of those buildings that partially blocked her view, preparing to see her.

Later, at the appointed hour, refreshed by a nap between the silky sheets of the comfortable bed and revived by a soak in the bathroom's long, deep tub, she went down to the lobby to wait for Peter. He was late. At last, she saw him walking across the plush carpet to greet her. She realized that she had been afraid she would be disappointed, let down by the image she had built of him in her imagination since he had climbed into the limousine and driven away from her in Philadelphia. But as he came toward her, smiling broadly, with a smoothness of motion that at the same time betrayed a suppressed physical tension—the controlled animal energy that had caught her attention at the beginning—the sight of him was exciting to her.

He took her to dinner at his club on Fifth Avenue. It was elegant in its way, but not the romantic setting that she had been anticipating. Then they went to a concert at Carnegie Hall. In Philadelphia she had told him how much her family enjoyed classical music, about her mother's teaching piano, and how she, Julia, enjoyed playing. She hadn't practiced when she should have, and so hadn't advanced beyond picking her way through the easier of Mozart's Piano Sonatas and the like. Now, as they moved through the throng of concertgoers, she was flattered that he had remembered. The performance they attended was a touring European chamber orchestra. The featured work was Mozart's 23rd Piano Concerto. It was one of Julia's favorites.

Afterward, Peter said that he had business he needed to attend to the next morning, Saturday, and wanted to attack it early so as to get it behind him and begin his weekend—their weekend— in earnest. They were back at her hotel well before midnight.

When they reached the bank of elevators just off the lobby, they stood, waiting, with two or three other people close by. Their conversation trailed off to an uncomfortable silence. Her earlier apprehension about whether she would be willing to fulfill Peter's expectations had, in some subtle way, been replaced by a vague feeling of deflation as she let her eyes drop and prepared to wish him goodnight, to depart alone for her room. It was not until a bell announced the imminent arrival of the elevator that he stepped closer to her. Without embracing her, he reached to brush her face gently with his fingers, then lifted her chin and kissed her. Julia responded, but under the constraints he imposed. In a moment, he withdrew.

This intimate contact, their first, as brief and controlled as it was, stirred her. His kiss seemed full of promise, revealing, she sensed, a passion held in check by him which, if she desired to do so, she had the power to release. She was almost grateful that he had kissed her in such a public place, and that his apparent concern for discretion made it impossible to carry the moment further. She wanted an opportunity to get her footing on this new terrain.

4

I T WAS JUST A short walk from the hotel to Peter's apartment house. The next day Julia arrived at the entrance close to noon, as Peter had directed. Guided by the doorman and accompanied by the elevator operator she ascended to the small lobby in front of the doors to his and one other apartment. Peter was waiting for her there.

He showed her quickly around before leading her through the dining room to a terrace where they would be eating lunch. They stood by the waist-high wall at its edge. Flanked by other tall buildings, they were high above Fifth Avenue, looking out over Central Park.

The cloudless sky, a deep inverted bowl of blue, defined with clarity the jagged horizon of the city that stretched around and past the far edges of the park. Its trees and lawns looked from where they stood like an undulating sea of green, washing up against the base of the vertical cliffs of the apartment towers that rose in regular ranks above it. The reservoir in its midst was an immense oval eye reflecting the sky at which it stared. Peter pointed across at the steeple of Riverside Church on the distant edge of the visible city, and, nearer, above the north corner of the park, the dark bulk of St. John's Cathedral.

They sat down to lunch, which was already set out for them on a glass table under a striped awning.

Now it seemed to be Peter's turn to talk about himself. Julia asked him about a photograph she had noticed standing in a simple frame on a small table in a corner of the hall. It showed an older couple in some sort of traditional costume. The man resembled Peter, although he was heavier. His skin had that same dark, healthy look. Peter told her that those were his parents. He had been born in Greece. His family had immigrated here when he was still young. The photograph evoked in Julia's mind travelogue images of villages with small white houses scattered along a rocky shore, nets drying on racks, women in black, children playing on the beach, and strong, swarthy men in colorful wooden boats fishing in an azure sea, all under an achingly bright sun. Peter told her that it had been taken at a wedding anniversary, in Brooklyn.

He said that he had started with virtually nothing. He won a scholarship which, combined with the life savings of his parents and jobs on the side, got him through Yale. After a few years in a bank training program, with the help of his employer, he worked his way through business school. He stayed with the bank for two years after he got his degree. His department handled secured financing of large corporate projects. He saw a future in mergers and acquisitions, moved to an investment banking firm, and was launched. A few years later, he went out on his own.

"You really have something to be proud of," she said when she thought he was through.

"Yes," Peter looked away from her. "I suppose I do."

"What do you mean?" Julia said. "Look at me. My family. My grandfather was successful, but he was still young when he lost practically everything. My father was doing all right when he and my mother lived here in New York and the suburbs, but after we moved to Libertyville, where I grew up, he didn't make much at all. That's why my mother taught piano. To help keep things together. Now I..."

Peter turned his gaze squarely on her. His voice took on an edge that she hadn't heard from him before. "Let's just say that I've gotten off to a good start, but I still have a long way to go. I'm not complaining, but even today, in my business, there's still an 'old boy's network' that can help, or hurt, depending on who you are, or where you came from. Something your father, or your grandfather, didn't have to worry about the way I do."

Julia looked down.

"Anyway," Peter said, returning once more to his relaxed, inclusive, tone, "it hasn't been easy, but I'm glad things have gone well for me. Thank you for not taking it for granted."

He looked away again and smiled. "I've been told that I'll never be satisfied."

He rose from the table, all at once the businessman.

"I'm afraid something more came up this morning that I have to take care of. One more meeting. I'm sorry."

He gave her a key to the apartment and took her down with him to reintroduce her to the doorman so that she could go and come as she pleased. He hoped to be back by four. They should have time to go for a walk, he told her. Maybe they could stop for a cup of coffee before she would have to return to her hotel to change for the evening.

Julia did not follow Peter out of the lobby. Instead, she waved to him, returned to the elevator, took it up to the small vestibule on his floor, turned the key in the lock to his front door, and walked in. Perhaps his apartment would provide some sort of window into this man toward whom she seemed to be moving at such speed—a pace he was setting for both of them.

However, whatever message the place may have held for her was difficult to decipher.

The furnishings were opulent, but bland. Mostly expensive copies of English and American antiques, she decided. Two large Audubon elephant folio engravings of long-legged shore birds—sumptuous reproductions—hung in the living room. There were English fox hunting and sailing ship prints that could have been originals, or not. As Julia explored, she decided that Peter had simply given over the entire apartment to a "correct" decorator who chose, bought and arranged everything. Even the kitchen seemed hardly lived in.

With an edgy excitement she systematically turned every knob and opened every door. A guest bedroom with a small attached bathroom was sparsely furnished. A few of the same type of English-style prints hung on its walls. A door at the back of the main hall led to a closet stacked high with cardboard moving boxes.

What appeared to be his study or office did betray Peter's presence. A desktop computer sat on a Chippendale style table desk. Office equipment and file cabinets were in evidence. A mobile telephone was cradled on a base that displayed numerous buttons for direct lines or extensions.

To the side, a smaller table was home to stacks of papers and file folders. Along the back edge of the table stood a row of various reference books. A linear forest of bookmarks fashioned from torn bits of paper— white, pink, and yellow—grew raggedly from their tops.

Julia recognized the black spine of *The Social Register*. Her mother had gained some kind of hollow satisfaction from their family's being included in its listing. It seemed superfluous and oddly out of place here. A small knot of excitement, a spirit of adventure tinged with guilt, built quickly in her chest as she picked it up. She saw that it was a few years out of date. She opened it to the only marker between its leaves, a yellow "sticky" torn from a note pad. Midway down the right-hand page she read "Davenport, Julia Vandenheusen" and her address and telephone number, and abbreviations for the college and graduate school she had attended, and her degrees. They were under an entry for her mother, her father having died before this edition was published. She smiled. Her mother had kept the information there current right up to the end. Carefully she closed the book without moving the marker and slid it back in place.

A paperweight held down a stack of pink telephone message slips that lay next to the laptop on top of the desk. She did not look at the messages, but she did pick up the paperweight. It was a clear, three-or-four-inch solid Lucite cube. Suspended inside was a miniature printed sheet of paper. She turned the cube so that she could focus on the tiny print. At the top was a date in the previous year, 1990. Below the date it said: "Grendel Holdings, Ltd. has acquired all of the capital stock of Hammerschmidt-U.S.A. Limited," followed by a paragraph that was in writing, if they were real letters, which was too small to read. It was a commemoration of some sort. That name, "Grendel Holdings," seemed familiar. Then she remembered the large man who had come up to Peter when he was talking with her at the reception at 21 Club. Peter identified him as the head of the Grendel company. She couldn't recall his name. But she did remember that his apparent effort at casual humor had seemed to her to be too personal and strangely out of place. Almost sinister. Almost threatening. Smiling nervously at what seemed now, as she thought about it, to be an overly dramatic reaction on her part to this man whom Peter seemed to hold in high regard, she returned the paperweight carefully to its exact previous position.

Passing back through the hallway toward the living room, she stopped at the one door she had yet to open. She contemplated it for a moment, then reached for the crystal knob, turned it, and pushed gently, as if someone might be asleep in there whom she did not want to disturb. She stood at the entrance and peered inside. Indeed it did appear to be Peter's bedroom.

The difference in décor from the rest of the apartment was startling. The walls were painted a glossy black enamel. The thick carpet was white. A huge bed dominated the room. It was covered by a spread with a checkerboard design of large black and white squares. The low headboard was plain, black and shiny. Past the bed, flanking a tall, Chinese-style dark red lacquered dresser, French doors with white curtains led to another terrace. Through them, filtered daylight illuminated the room with its glow. A rectangular mirror hung above the low headboard. Facing it along the wall opposite the foot of the bed were four tall mirror panels which appeared to be the doors to a bank of closets. As her eyes moved back to the bed she became aware of something above the plane of her focus. She lifted her gaze. A huge mirror, almost the area of the bed and roughly the same shape was fastened to the ceiling directly above it.

She stared up, momentarily perplexed. Then, as she took in this bed enveloped with reflections of itself, she caught her breath and blushed deeply. Her eyes lingered there for another instant before she backed away, pulled the door shut and retreated quickly to the terrace where they had eaten lunch.

The view was spectacular. Despite the far-away traffic on Fifth Avenue, and a tiny, distant airplane crawling, it seemed, like an ant, across the ceiling of the sky, the scene before her seemed still—devoid of the frenetic movement that she thought of as being an immutable part of the city's personality.

She could not hear the plane's engines at all, and the normally intrusive commotion of honking horns and roaring engines from cars and buses on the streets within earshot was, here, magically reduced to a distant cacophony, almost a hum. It reminded her of the time she had stood one afternoon long ago with her father in the nave of a great church. The vast hush was given substance by the low chorused mutter of the voices of the other people there in muted conversation and in prayer.

Gazing out at this scene, she had a giddy feeling of unreality, reveling as she was in the scope and grandeur, and the beauty, of everything laid out before her, with no reference to the myriad concerns of all the people which the panorama encompassed, engaged in the constant, mundane struggles of their daily lives. It was exhilarating. Powerful. Heady stuff, she thought, for Peter Medea to have at his beck and call.

As she left the terrace and started for the front door, she stopped in the hall for a moment and peered once again into the living room. She tried to understand her feelings about this place. Peter lived here but in many ways it was more like a model apartment than a home. As she paused there it came to her. It was as if she was looking onto an elaborate stage set for a play that had just begun, waiting for her entrance.

5

ON JULIA'S LAST EVENING with Peter, he took her to dinner at 21 Club, to commemorate, he said, his good luck in meeting her there in the first place. Then to a musical in a theater just off Broadway. They sat near the front of the orchestra. He suggested that they finish off with supper or dessert at the Algonquin Hotel. He had picked her up in a limousine, and it had been waiting for them in each instance to convey them to the next stop on their itinerary. Now they pulled up in front of their final destination.

Peter walked briskly through the lobby. Julia trailed him, gazing with interest around her. At the entrance to the legendary dining room, without looking to either side, Peter strode past an elderly couple waiting in resigned attendance for the maître d'hôtel and led Julia toward a vacant table. As she followed him, she glanced sidelong at the small, gray-haired woman, neatly dressed for the evening, who stared back. Julia looked away.

The room was full, but the ceiling was high and their table was well spaced from the others, so the noise of conversation and laughter was stimulating without creating an overpowering din.

Her mother and father had talked nostalgically about the Algonquin and Julia had been there once for tea when she was a little girl. She knew that it was frequented by writers, actors, musicians, and their friends, as well as by theater and concert goers who enjoyed basking in the former's presence even if they could not be in their company.

While her father was a bachelor he used to meet some of his oldest friends here for drinks. Also, when her parents had lived in Greenwich Village before she was born, many of their friends and acquaintances had been performing artists. She knew that after her mother and father had moved out of the city it was here that they had kept in touch with these people. The Algonquin and its ambience had gained mythic proportion in Julia's mind. She was thrilled to be here, with or without the cultural celebrities whom she suspected she would not recognize anyway.

As they sat down next to each other, Julia looked around the large room with wide-eyed, shameless curiosity. "The last time I was here," she said, "I was so young that later I couldn't remember exactly what it looked like, but now that I'm here again, it all seems familiar. I do know that my father said he liked that little bar we passed just inside the entrance better than the one at the Estuary Club. He loved their martinis."

Peter glanced at her quickly.

"The Estuary Club," he repeated quietly, as if to himself.

Then he resumed his own survey of the room.

She found herself gazing again at the people sitting at the tables in front of them. "My parents came here a lot with their friends. I can only think of a few of them that I might recognize, because they visited us when I was older. They were close friends of my father even before he met my mother. Let's see, there were Grannie vanDamm, and Squeaky Strothers."

"Squeaky?" he asked.

She settled back and returned her attention to Peter.

"Archibold Strothers. My father said he used to sing bass in the choral society in college, and his friends thought Archibold sounded pretentious, so everybody called him Squeaky."

"Founder and senior partner of Strothers and Cole," Peter said.

"He's very musical," she said, "and I think he's still a director of the Metropolitan Opera."

"He is." Peter's tone was matter-of-fact. Then, "vanDamm…"

"You might know his brother, Sandy," Julia ventured. "Granville—Daddy said that no one ever called him that—was the music critic for…"

"Sanderson vanDamm." Peter recited. "Former Deputy Secretary of the Treasury, now with The Whetstone Group. A partner. One of three."

"My father knew him, too, but more from work. They were in the same sort of business, I think…"

"I interrupted you."

"That's O.K." she said, "I shouldn't be rattling on like this anyway. I'm sorry."

"Who else…" Peter started, then seemed to check himself. He reached for the menus that had been placed on the table by the maître d' while they were talking, offered one to Julia, and smiled.

"I hope you left room for something more to eat."

She looked at the menu. She had not finished her dinner before they left the restaurant for the theater, and was hungry again. She scanned the entrees.

Peter glanced at his menu and put it back on the table.

"Let's take a look at dessert."

"Great!" She hoped she did not sound disappointed.

The waiter materialized at her side with the dessert cart as she spoke. She agonized over her decision, but soon pointed to a pastry tart filled with sliced apricots arranged around the edge and three small, plump strawberries in the center, set in custard.

The waiter turned to Peter, who shook his head, "No."

"Please bring us some coffee, too," Peter said. "Espresso."

Then he looked over at Julia.

"Is that all right?"

"Sure, I love espresso. Decaf, please. But I wish you'd keep me company having dessert. I hate to be eating alone."

"Not tonight." Peter smiled. "We both have big appetites, but you seem to be able to satisfy yours without hurting yourself. I'm not so lucky. I'll stick to coffee for the time being."

He looked away for a moment. "You know, in a way, I'm in the same sort of business as Sandy vanDamm."

"An investment company? Like my father was in before we moved away? I'm not sure what..."

"There's a difference though. His group invests in companies, gets control. Of course they can make a lot of money. But they've got a lot at stake, too, so they have to make sure the target company's managed well. They do try to protect themselves. Set up different entities to isolate any damage, that sort of thing. Even then, things can go wrong. Key people can leave, the market for their products or services can go south. Are you following me?"

Julia nodded.

"As I see it," he continued, "the mistake people like him make, that is, people who approach things the way he does, is that they get too involved, take too much risk. What I do is help companies get financing. You know. Money..."

"I know," Julia said.

"Yes, well, I find financing for a company, people to invest in it or lend to it, to help it out at its time of need or to take advantage of an opportunity, for which I get paid a healthy fee. Then I'm out of it. No more worries. If I think the company has promise, I try to get some stock as part of my fee, a kicker so to speak, but since the stock doesn't really cost me anything, it's not the end of the world if the company goes down the tubes. If they do well, then so do I, and without all of that responsibility."

Julia was listening carefully when the waiter brought them the tart, along with the coffee. Peter paid no attention to their arrival. Seeing this, she gave her dessert a longing glance, but did not pick up her fork.

"Take the TryCo acquisition. You know, the deal that the party at '21' was about. I did something for TryCo Corporation awhile back and took part of my fee in stock. I could see they were going somewhere if they played their cards right. Then they needed more funding. They went to an old line investment banking firm, but when things didn't seem to be moving fast enough with them, I found someone I knew to buy TryCo out: Grendel Holdings. DiNiro. You met him there."

That was his name, Julia thought. The large man with the unpleasant sense of humor she had thought of when she was alone in Peter's apartment. She tried to suppress her negative thoughts about him. "Yes," she said. "I remember."

"When Grendel exchanged its stock for TryCo's, I made, well, a lot. On paper, anyway. But the point is, now I have the Grendel stock—its price isn't doing that well now, but it'll come back—and I can wash my hands of TryCo."

"You must be very pleased," Julia said.

What Peter was saying fascinated her. As far back as she could remember, her father did not seem to care about making money, although she knew he had been successful financially at one time, before they moved away from New York. Its absence in the Davenport household when Julia was growing up had caused friction between her parents, as well as hardship for her mother after her father had died. Still, the delicious-looking tart was beginning to compete for her attention. She gestured toward it, her fork now poised in her hand.

"May I?" she asked.

Without waiting for a reply, she cut into it, trying not to disturb its appearance any more than was necessary to separate her first bite.

Peter continued. "Law firms like Strothers and Cole are important sources of information for me, help me keep on top of who is looking for what out there." He swept his hand through the air in the general direction of the world beyond the confines of the hotel. "Outfits like that could refer companies to me.

"Venture capital groups like Whetstone are a potential resource. Any client I have would give a lot for that type of equity partner. That is, someone who will give a company money for its stock."

Julia had become wholly engaged in consuming the last morsels of the tart. She glanced up and saw that Peter was looking at her—watching her eat, she thought with embarrassment. As she met his eyes she saw in them an opaque impenetrability that had become familiar to her, that made it difficult for her to be completely relaxed with him despite the attention he gave her and the graciousness of his manner toward her.

She smiled nervously, lowered her eyes, and put down her fork. Strangely, she felt as she had as a child when she had eaten too fast, or made slurping noises with her soup. She had earned not a reprimand, but a certain look from her mother or father, which served the same purpose.

She started to raise her napkin to her face, to remove any shreds of evidence of whatever transgression she might have committed. At the same time she was annoyed by her own feeling of submissiveness.

"I wish I could get as much pleasure out of eating as you do," Peter said.

Julia looked up again. He was smiling at her.

"It's time for a toast! Wouldn't you like some cognac?" He turned to find a waiter before Julia could answer.

"Two cognacs, please," he said to the waiter. "Remy Martin. And two more espresso."

The waiter nodded to both of them, almost imperceptibly, and backed away.

In a few moments the snifters and coffee arrived. Once they had been served, Peter reached for her glass of brandy and held its bowl in the palm of his hand with the stem between his fingers, swirling the amber liquid gently around the inside. He gave it to her and did the same for his own.

They both inhaled the pungent vapors that rose from the liqueur as it was warmed by their hands. He closed his eyes and smiled, but the strength of the fumes made Julia start back. Her eyes began to water.

She quickly blinked to diffuse the tears before he could see them, and glanced back at him. He was just looking up.

"Great, isn't it?" he asked. He raised his glass before drinking, looked at her and said, "To you, and your courage in accepting my invitation to come here without really knowing me, or knowing what to expect when you arrived."

She lifted her glass. "I can't drink to that, but I can drink to you, and your asking me. I've had a wonderful time."

Julia touched her glass to his and looked at him. Now she saw in his eyes something different: an intensity that seemed to reflect the way he applied himself to everything he undertook, and at this moment, she realized, it was concentrated on her. It struck her that the curtain which often seemed to be drawn across his eyes, screening his emotions from view, was a product not of a lack of depth or any intent to hide, but rather of focus. It was like a beam from a searchlight in the night. You can only see its full brightness during the moment when it is turned directly at you.

She was flattered, but it made her uneasy as well. Her emotional responses were not keeping pace with the demands she read in those eyes. Yet he had neither said nor done anything that required a reaction beyond what she felt comfortable giving.

After a sip of his brandy, he seemed content to cradle the snifter again, breathing in from it occasionally, while she finished hers, along with her coffee.

She picked up the small curl of lemon peel from the bottom of the drained espresso cup. It had come on the saucer and she had twisted it once and placed it in the coffee. She held the tip of one end between her fingers, chewed on the rind for a moment, and then, sealing it between her lips, sucked out its essence. The lemon's oil tinged with the flavor of the dark, slightly bitter coffee was pleasantly tart on her tongue. When she looked up she saw that Peter had again been watching.

"You do try to get the most out of everything," he said, smiling again.

"And you don't?"

"How observant! But you're more eclectic in your appetites. That's something I have to learn from you."

Her eyes lowered. She stared at the brown-stained rind lying in the bottom of her empty cup.

He started to rise. "I begin to get restless sitting in one spot for too long. Are you ready to go?"

It was less a question than a veiled command, she realized, but she was getting used to this side of him. Besides, she, too, needed to stretch.

"Yes." She reached for her purse. "I'm ready. But I'm really glad we came here. Thank you."

Peter helped her with her chair.

"You're welcome," he said.

He guided her ahead of him as they moved to the door.

6

THE LIMOUSINE WAS WAITING for them when they emerged from the hotel. As Julia stooped to negotiate the door into the cavernous back of the car and take her seat on the far side, she was apprehensive. They were moving inexorably toward the end of the evening, the last night of her weekend there. She anticipated that they were approaching a turning point and a need for decisions by her which she was not sure she was ready to make. Behind her façade, her self-assurance began to crumble.

She managed a smile as Peter sat down.

The car door closed behind him with a muffled "chunk" that shut out the world behind it. Julia had not been particularly aware of the closeness of this quiet, protected setting when they had been conveyed in it from place to place earlier in the evening, but now, suddenly, she was struck by its extreme intimacy. Small lights in the bottom of the doors stayed on, dimly illuminating the interior. Heavily tinted windows and the partition between their cocoon and the driver preserved their privacy completely. The floor was covered with deep plush carpeting and the rest of the interior with velour, all a soft gray. A sizeable cabinet of what appeared to be polished, grained wood housed what might be a bar. There was also a small television served by a futuristic-looking aerodynamic aerial she had noticed on the outside of the car. A mobile telephone rested in its cradle next to the cabinet. Unobtrusive reading lights perched on flexible necks at the corners of the shelf in front of the rear window like small, attentive birds.

As the car moved away from the curb, Peter reached for her hand, and held it in his. He looked at her.

"Julia," he said, "I've had a good time this evening. Thanks for being here."

His eyes were obscured by the shadows cast by the dim lights near the floor, but she imagined them as she had seen them a few minutes earlier: intense and consuming.

"I don't think we should go back to the apartment," he continued, his mouth betraying the hint of a smile. "So I've asked the driver to take us to your hotel."

Julia absorbed what he said, and tension she had not even been aware of drained from her in a rush. But it left in its place a curious sense of disappointment, almost of loss. Then concern. Was there something she said? Or didn't say? Did she seem too naïve to this man of a world so different from hers?

He leaned toward her, still looking into her eyes.

"Before we get there, Julia," he said, "I very much want to kiss you."

At his words, her distress vanished. She reached behind him to pull him closer. As their mouths touched she closed her eyes.

His lips were warm, but firm at first. They softened as she explored them with hers. She felt the hardness of his tongue, then responded with hers.

Her need became an aching. Surprising herself, she surrendered to a wanton attempt to draw from this kiss all that she had missed during the years of her distraction and, she now realized, deprivation. Her concentration was complete.

Peter moved his hands to her shoulders and gently, but firmly, pulled back. He smiled, watching her silently.

As they moved apart she met his gaze for a moment before she looked down. She was exhilarated, but felt strangely shy with him. She knew her eyes still betrayed the depth of his hold on her when they had kissed. Her lips felt swollen. When she looked up again she saw his smile.

"Well!" he said.

"Yes," she said.

As he reached again for her hand, she glanced for a moment beyond him at the parked cars, nearly empty sidewalks and dark, shuttered store fronts that glided darkly past the tinted window like ghosts of a world she barely remembered as she felt his touch.

The limousine drew smoothly up to the front of the hotel. The driver opened the door for them. Peter walked with her inside. They passed the subdued gaiety of the piano bar into the hushed brightness of the elegant lobby and stopped in front of the bank of elevators. When Peter pressed the button, the doors of the elevator in front of them slid quietly open.

Peter turned to her. "I'll pick you up tomorrow morning. We'll have breakfast at the Plaza. Is that all right? How does nine-thirty sound?"

"Great." She looked up at him and smiled. "I guess it's time to say 'good night.' I've had a wonderful time."

Then, before she could turn to enter the elevator, he pulled her toward him, his hands holding her shoulders, and kissed her on the lips, but with restraint, even though there was no one in sight. Still, there was something in this kiss that brought their encounter in the limousine back to her, and reminded her of what it could be like again.

She waved to him awkwardly as the tall doors of the elevator started to move together. Through the vanishing space between them she saw him turn away and stride out into the lobby.

7

I T WAS SUNNY AND bright when Julia walked with Peter from the
lobby of the hotel to his cab, Julia sensed a freshness in the air that she
hadn't noticed during her visit until now. Traffic on Fifth Avenue was
light and the drive to their destination went by quickly.

The high ceilinged main dining room at the Plaza Hotel was formal,
paneled in dark wood, but with its generous, tall windows overlooking
the plaza at the hotel's entrance in one direction and Central Park in the
other, it seemed full of exhilarating light, designed to raise the spirits of
all who entered. Peter had been prompt, and she knew there would be
plenty of time before her train was scheduled to leave Penn Station. So
she should have felt relaxed and ready to enjoy herself.

Instead, Julia was anxious and confused. Their kiss had kindled a
fire in her that had burned into the early hours of the morning. The glow
of its embers had caused what sleep she finally found to be fitful and
restless. Yet by the time she awoke, its ashes had cooled enough that she
found herself concerned about the nature of its source.

After they were seated, Julia gazed across the table at Peter while he
talked of the weather, of the show they had seen, of the concert earlier.
Did she know what she felt for him other than the strong desire he had
stirred in her with his kiss? He was so much older. What did he really
feel for *her*? He hadn't said, but if he had, could she trust his words?
Without true mutual affection, did she want to expend her emotional
resources on any man at this point in her life? Her mother would have
told her that she needed to invest her energies, to begin to build for the
future. That she needed to be cautious.

She remembered Rita Craig's words when she had confided in her
friend and fellow-teacher, before she decided to accept Peter's invitation
to see him in New York. She told Rita how she felt so attracted to this
powerful, compelling and apparently successful man who had suddenly
come into her life, forcefully pursuing her, but without seeming to force
himself upon her. While Julia's mother was in the hospital, and after
she died, Rita, with her husband Calvin, had provided Julia with a
reassuringly domestic safe haven when needed, and with companionship
and support. Now, after sharing Julia's wonder at how her relationship

with Peter had moved forward at such a fast pace, Rita, always down to earth and ever the pragmatist, had said, simply: "It almost seems too good to be true." Of course, she hadn't meant to be entirely serious, but could she be right?

Distracted as Julia was, sitting across from Peter in these elegant surroundings, she must, she thought, be a poor, unresponsive companion. When they first sat down, her appetite had seemed ravenous and she had ordered a full breakfast. Now, as she studied him, she hardly touched her food, nor did she participate actively in the conversation.

"Is something the matter?" Peter broke in on himself.

She hesitated a moment.

"No."

"Are you sure?"

She nodded, smiling weakly.

"Good." He rose, reaching for the cell phone in his coat pocket. "I'm terribly sorry, but while you're finishing up, I need to make a telephone call. It'll only take a few minutes, I promise. When I get back I have something I want to talk with you about. And we should still have time for a walk, if you'd like. We can leave your suitcase here."

She watched him pass through the entrance of the dining room and out of sight.

She had begun to loathe these intrusions: at least twice the first evening she was with him, then yesterday when he put off seeing her in the morning for business, again when he ran off after lunch, and now here, while they were spending their last hours together before she had to leave for Philadelphia and home. During her wakeful night she had wondered, among other things, how anyone could really have that much business to conduct. This time, though, she found that she was grateful to be left alone. At last she would have a chance to organize the confusion that plagued her—to make decisions, to chart a course for herself with confidence, to go over what she would say to him. She had a lot to accomplish in this brief respite from the compelling dominance of his presence.

Turning, she gazed out the window. Across the street a line of horse-drawn carriages waited in the fresh morning sun for customers. While the drivers gossiped, standing or leaning in casual poses against their vehicles, their steeds stood with patient resignation, shifting occasionally from one foot to another, necks sloping down to drooped heads, muzzles buried in worn feed bags attached to their bridles.

Couples dressed for church strolled past a scattering of disheveled people huddled with their backs to the gray stone wall that separated the sidewalk from the park, some begging, others simply staring disconsolately in front of them. Bicyclists, roller skaters and skate boarders of all ages sped past the end of the wall and onto a roadway leading inside. Over the weekend, the park was closed to cars. Under the casual eye of parents and nannies who sat in the shade on a long curved bench facing the entrance drive, children cavorted on the grass and pavement of a small traffic circle at the corner that she was sure must be a busy intersection during the week. Two teenagers played catch with a Frisbee.

Julia noticed a woman who looked to be about her age crossing the street diagonally in front of her to avoid the traffic light, glancing both ways for cars. She walked with an air of purpose toward the park's entrance. She wore sneakers, tights and an oversized T-shirt that hung below her waist. She carried a pair of roller blades slung over her shoulder. With her free hand she grasped the handles of a small, brightly colored athletic equipment bag. Her arm and the bag swung in easy arcs as she strode with evident determination toward her objective. When she passed through the entrance and into the park, Julia was surprised at the momentary surge of envy she experienced as her eyes remained at the spot where the woman had disappeared from sight.

Was there a message here that could help guide her through her labyrinth of doubt? This thought bought her back to the task at hand: to sort out her emotions about Peter and to chart a course for herself before his return from his call. Too late...

"I'm back!"

Julia caught her breath. She turned from the window. Peter was already settling into his place across from her.

"I told you it wouldn't take long," he said, filling the momentary silence. "I hope I didn't interrupt something important." He was smiling.

Her throat tightened. "Peter, we have to talk." Her heart began to pound, its beat reverberating in her chest cavity with such force she thought he must be able to hear it.

"We have been...we *are* talking, aren't we?" Traces of Peter's smile lingered, although his tone was serious.

"No!"

She hadn't meant to sound so forceful. She started again more evenly.

"What I mean is..."

Peter interrupted. "Before we talk, as you say, may I ask you something?"

She knew he was not looking for a reply. His ironic tone sounded slightly patronizing. She bided her time in silence. Her hands rested, palms down, on the table in front of her. Without conscious command from her, a forefinger began to tap the tablecloth.

He looked at her.

"Julia."

He reached across the table for her hands, covering them with his, then holding them, stroking the backs of them with his thumbs, over her knuckles, down the crevices between her fingers, gently massaging.

Her tapping finger was stilled, but Julia was too distracted to fully register the pleasant sensations his ministrations began to arouse in her, the message from him they seemed to convey. Instead, she decided to use this pause as an opportunity to resume delivering her message. While she was trying to marshal the right words, though, he continued.

"What I want to say is that I have grown very fond of you. I was attracted to you from the beginning. I guess you could tell."

He smiled.

"Each time we're together, that attraction seems to get stronger. I don't know exactly what forces brought you to that party at 21 Club, but..."

"Peter..." she began.

"Please," he said, preempting her still another time. "I have an important question for you."

He withdrew his hands slowly, and took a sip of water. She pulled hers back a little, but otherwise let them lie as he had left them.

"I have engaged a house, the home of friends of mine, the Vardamans. Call it a villa. On an island in the Caribbean. St. Maarten. Beginning less than two weeks from today. Would you come with me?" He paused.

Julia stared at him.

"I'm sorry to spring this on you with so little notice, but then we haven't…well…been acquainted with each other very long.

"It's really delightful there. Beautiful beaches, small mountains in the center of the island, great walking, terrific snorkeling—have you done that?—not much excitement otherwise, but an excellent place to relax. A favorite spot of the rich and famous. It's off-season, but maybe we could find a party or two if we're so inclined."

"Yes." She was grateful that her voice had responded when she called on it, in spite of its momentary flight. "That is, I'm sure it's beautiful, but…"

In her new state of agitation, she could not pin down exactly why she had reservations about taking advantage of this amazing opportunity then and there. She searched the corners of her seemingly vacant mind for a plausible excuse to delay her decision.

As her voice trailed off, Peter took over again. "I know this comes at the last minute, and you might have a conflict, might have something else going. Unfortunately I have some business I must conduct there with Rob Vardaman in the middle of the following week—you will have to fly back on your own, I'm afraid—so my timing can't be very flexible.

"This is an unusual opportunity. There are only a few real hotels, and besides, it wouldn't be the same. So if you know someone, you usually have to put your bid in early, a year ahead sometimes, even off-season, like now, to get this kind of deal."

She had not stopped looking at him, and she sensed a change. He was still smiling pleasantly, but she saw a greater intensity in his look, the same focus on her and her response to him that she had seen the previous evening. And his voice had taken on a new tone of determination.

Hers, in contrast, seemed to her to be tentative. Weak and unconvincing. "Peter, as you can see, I'm overwhelmed by your invitation. I know it must be wonderful there, and heaven knows I could use a break." She struggled to gain a feeling of conviction. "I do have commitments, though, which I'll have to see if I can work my way out of. The summer session of school begins soon and I've promised I would help everyone else get things ready, and…" She stopped, resolved not to get into details that could make the reasons for her hesitation seem trivial.

Peter still held her eyes with his, but he had stopped smiling. He reached again for her hands.

"I asked you to New York because I wanted you to be with me here. I've greatly enjoyed our time together. I hope you have, too. Now I hope you want to be with me in St. Maarten. I know you'll tell me your decision as soon as you can."

Julia absorbed with a hint of irritation what sounded to her uncomfortably like an ultimatum. In a moment, though, this reflexive reaction gave way to concern.

"Yes," she said, "I will."

8

JULIA GAZED DOWN FROM her window in the huge airplane that was well on its way to San Juan, Puerto Rico. Peter had business there on his way back, so he booked it into the itinerary for the round trip. They would connect with a smaller plane for the flight to St. Maarten. Below her stretched an infinity of low-lying cumulus clouds arrayed in regular ranks like a flotilla of ships with billowed sails suspended over the ocean and stretching to the horizon in all directions. The sea, remote and vast, shone sky-blue back up to her through the intervals between them. Staring down at it induced the giddy sensation that she was looking up, past the clouds and into the heavens, instead of at the earth.

Could it be that her going off to an island hideaway with a man she had known for such a short time, and whom she realized she may not really know at all, was an illusion, too? She glanced furtively past her shoulder and saw that yes, Peter Medea was dozing in the seat next to her. She smiled at her foolish momentary need for reassurance, and sighed, sinking back into the soft, leathery upholstery of first class cabin luxury.

Her thoughts were interrupted by the flight attendant. He offered her a glass of champagne. The cool liquid tingled past her lips, over her tongue and down her throat, suffusing her perversely with a soothing warmth. In her other, ordinary, life, she hardly drank at all, so that now, almost immediately, she felt the effect of even this small amount of wine on her state of mind.

She remembered what Rita had said when she told her about Peter's invitation, and that she would be alone with him for the entire stay. Rita had congratulated her with appropriate enthusiasm, and then provided what she called "some practical advice." "I know he's swept you off your feet, and that you'll be having a great time (doing what I can't guess!), but don't forget, this is just for fun. You've really got to know him a lot better before it can be anything more than that. I'm not kidding, Julia!"

Rita was right, of course, Julia did need to get to know Peter better. But, just as Rita had said, Peter had "swept her off her feet." How had that happened? What was it about him that she felt so attracted to? He was forceful and exuded power. In that sense he was charismatic, seeming to be respected by and exerting influence over the people that she had seen him with—unlike so many other men she had been acquainted with. And he seemed directed and ambitious, unlike her father, whom she had loved and respected, but she knew was not assertive, nor had he been ambitious in the way Peter was. She was sure that her father, as sweet and kind and wise as he had been, had not provided her mother with the life she had been used to and had expected when she married him. As much as her mother had loved her father, Julia knew that she had been disappointed in him, in the life as a writer he had chosen instead of pursuing his seemingly successful investment banking career in New York.

But at the same time, Peter was thoughtful about her sensitivities and psychic needs. Unlike Danny Johnson, Peter was restrained with her when he sensed that was what she needed. Too restrained in a way, which she realized now only served to help whet her appetite for him. For more of him. He was sexy. His taut, muscular build that was imperfectly hidden by his conventional clothing—even just the way he moved—acted like an erotic magnet to her. He often did not seem demonstrative with her, she mused, but then she thought of how his tender words at the Plaza, and the gentle touch of his hands when he was talking to her there, had caught her off guard. She paused, closing her eyes, to savor once again the intimacy of their kiss in the limousine, the sense of urgency she had drawn from someone who had seemed so self-contained. She remembered his studied determination not to follow up his advantage then, which she had reacted to with both frustration and relief.

She realized that none of this was really "knowing" Peter the way Rita had meant, but did there always have to be logic in a woman's feelings about a man, or the other way around? Weren't there times when things just clicked? Just fell into place? The way it had been with Danny. In fact, with Danny, she had been indecisive, had not followed her instincts when, perhaps, she should have, and what might have become a love story for her turned into nothing but hollow disappointment.

In most ways, she acknowledged, Peter remained a mystery. But mysteries had always intrigued her, hadn't they? The unknown was full of potential, wasn't it? She remembered how her father had let her sit in sometimes when he and visiting friends from New York got up a friendly poker game after dinner. They had laughed at her standard method of play: staying in, no matter what. Now, novice player that she was, presented with an interesting but possibly dangerous hand, she again determined to stay, despite a raise in the ante, to see what might develop. After all, couldn't she always fold her cards? Leave the game?

Of course she knew that coming on this trip with Peter involved an implicit commitment on her part—one that could prove distasteful. But she doubted it would. In fact, she found that she was looking forward to fulfilling her part of that unspoken bargain. She smiled. Was that the real reason she was here? Her mother, she thought, would not have approved.

She remembered Rita's earlier words. Was this all, indeed, "too good to be true?" She again looked over at Peter next to her. He was in a rare moment of repose, sound asleep.

She took another sip of the champagne. This trip was neither an illusion, she decided, nor was it a mistake. It was an adventure, with someone she was attracted to and who desired her. It carried with it the promise of elevating her life to a new level of fulfillment. She had not dreamed these things possible just a short time ago. She looked out of the window. They were soaring high above the expanse of clouds, hurtling away from her familiar world, toward the distant horizon beyond which lay...what?

Peter's hands were resting in his lap. She reached over and stroked the closest one until he lifted it. As he woke, she held it in hers and grinned at him.

"You look like you're enjoying the flight," she said.

He smiled and returned the pressure of her grasp.

9

WHEN THEY FINALLY ARRIVED at St. Maarten's airport, Peter and Julia descended the steps that were pushed up to the exit of their plane. Immediately, she sensed a difference in the air. It was softer, with a distinctive sweet fragrance, perhaps in part from flowers, but it seemed to her that it must as well be drawn by the humid heat from the subtropical vegetation that seemed so exotic to her as she looked at the setting of the small terminal.

Later, as she walked through the front door of the villa Peter had talked so much about, where they were to stay, the same ambience pervaded her senses. She came to think of it as a medium for all that would happen while she was there, giving those events a special significance, as though experienced vividly in a dream.

A man who seemed to be in charge in the absence of the owners ushered them into the villa. Managing to be deferential without a loss of dignity, he introduced himself to her in a Jamaican lilt as Simon. He took their suitcases to their rooms while Peter walked her around the precincts of this place that would be the setting for the next act of the drama of which she had begun to feel she was a part.

It was impressive. The house was set on a hillside, back from the top of a cliff of volcanic rock that plunged into the sea below: pale yellow stucco, red tile roofs and, facing the sea, large windows. Two wings jutted from the main house out to the edge of the steep incline. The master bedroom and a small sitting room were in one. Two connected guest bedrooms, with separate baths, were in the other. Small, walled terraces graced the end of each wing. The courtyard around which the house stood, its open end toward the sea, was filled by a large terrace. Below it a fresh water swimming pool completed the pleasing arrangement. Sizeable palms, palmettos and lime trees, were set in large planters in the corners of the terrace and the area around the pool. A steep footpath cut through the volcanic rock led down to an inlet where she could see a small, crescent beach that was tucked against the base of the cliff.

The high ceilings of the guest rooms where Julia and Peter were staying gave them a feeling of spaciousness. Their tall doors leading onto the courtyard were backed up by inner ones equipped with great wooden louvered shutters, so that an occupant could open the outer doors and enjoy the sea breezes without sacrificing privacy. When they returned from their tour, they found Peter's bags in the larger room on the end. Without discussion they accepted Simon's assignment of their accommodations.

Peter suggested a swim in the pool before dressing for dinner. She changed in her own room, behind the closed connecting door.

By the time Julia started down to the terrace, a towel over her shoulder, Peter was waiting for her, standing in a monogrammed terry cloth beach robe, a hand resting on a chair. Rope sandals with plush straps protected his feet. When she approached, he removed the robe and kicked off the sandals. The effect was dramatic. In his skin-tight, brief swim suit he was muscular and compact, with a uniform dark tan. His body hair was black and abundant. Compulsively, she glanced at the assertive line that ran from his navel to the top of the skimpy trunks, pointing down like a bold directional sign.

As he approached her, she could not help feeling self-conscious in the one-piece bathing suit her mother had helped her choose years ago, like a clothed visitor in a nudist camp. Peter made a point of looking her up and down slowly.

"You are beautiful!" he said, stepping back. "You know that, don't you?"

"Thank you!" Her pleasure, and relief, at his words were profound. Color rose to her cheeks.

He took her hand and they walked together down to the side of the pool.

10

IT WAS TIME FOR dinner. Only a little later than promised, Julia emerged from her room onto the terrace. She was in the same black cocktail dress—her only dress suitable for evening—that she had worn to the reception where she met Peter. She walked slowly down the few steps to where he stood. Her eyes glistened brightly in the evening light.

She stopped to look at Peter as he came toward her. He wore a navy blue jacket, subdued red pants, shirt open at the neck—but in her mind's eye she saw him as he had been earlier, his body taut despite his easy carriage and smooth gait, and powerful.

He took both her hands and greeted her with a kiss on her lips that lingered deliciously for a moment before he led her across the terrace.

"I asked Simon to serve us dinner out here," he said.

He gestured toward a table which was set for the meal, complete with a white table cloth, candles, and a vase of white flowers. A longer table, set at the back of the terrace, was arranged to hold a buffet.

"In the meantime, how about a glass of wine? Something else?"

"Everything is beautiful!" Julia took it all in as she spoke. "I'd love a glass of wine. Maybe a spritzer would be better. Is there any soda?" She realized at once the absurdity of her question in the midst of such plenty.

Peter smiled and walked to a small bar set up near the door to the main part of the house.

She remained standing by the table, her eyes following him. He moved away, stood over the bar for a short while, turned, holding a glass of wine and her drink, and started back to rejoin her with measured, seemingly relaxed strides.

This is a mating dance, she thought as she watched him. *We bathe, and oil and perfume our bodies. With painstaking care we clothe ourselves to impress. We strut slowly in front of each other with whatever grace we can muster, elegant birds showing off with stately movements. We eat because the process of consumption is part of the ritual, too. But food cannot satiate the appetite we feel. So, soon, with a frenzied hunger we shed our garments in an unruly heap, and...*

Peter handed her the glass of wine and soda, interrupting her curious reverie. His eyes were fixed on hers. She dropped her gaze, and blushed.

The sun was low on the horizon. It shone with a deep golden light on the buildings in dramatic contrast to the darkening indigo of the sky, burnishing the red tiled roofs to incandescence, as if the fire that had ignited in her had leapt to her surroundings. Bathed in this light, her skin seemed kindled by it as well.

"You look lovelier by the minute," he said.

She looked up at him again and broke into a shy, crooked smile.

He took her hand and led her to the table that was set for dinner.

They put down their drinks and moved to the buffet where food was now laid out for them in red clay serving dishes. Behind it, in attendance, stood Simon and a young woman. The sarong in which she had wrapped herself, a colorful African print, revealed a pleasing figure. Her face was round, her large, dark eyes solemn. Her hair was arranged in long dreadlocks. She wore dangling brass earrings.

"This is Melanie." Peter glanced in the woman's direction. "She's in charge of the kitchen."

"Hello, Melanie," Julia said. "It looks delicious."

Melanie responded with a demure smile. Her eyes lighted momentarily on Julia, then came to rest on Peter.

Simon and Melanie stepped back and waited.

"Thank you," Peter said dismissing them graciously, but with finality.

Absently, Julia lifted small amounts from each platter and bowl onto her plate with the silver serving utensils. When she was finished, she waited for Peter. They sat down at the dining table so that they were facing the sea and the embers of the setting sun. For just a few moments its rosy afterglow spilled over them and everything around them before draining away over the water into the darkened sky.

A bottle of champagne rested on ice in a wine cooler that stood by the table next to Peter. Its neck protruded at an angle from under a linen napkin that had been laid over it, the swelling of the cork at its end wrapped in foil. Peter peeled back the foil and protective wire mesh and worked at the cork with his thumbs. When it sprang free, first foam, then the frothy liquid welled up and pulsed from the opening. He quickly guided the flow into their glasses. He raised his toward Julia.

"To you!"

She raised her glass in return.

"To you," she said, and paused. "To us."

As they ate, and Peter made conversation, Julia somehow kept in touch, but her mind was in a different sphere.

How will it be with him? She wondered. Will I please him?

She thought of the other times, all while she was in college. The first, she admitted to herself, was, more than anything, simply to be initiated into the rite. The few others were desperate efforts to keep the interest of men whom she had not loved, but whose companionship she had sought to insulate herself from loneliness. But more than that, she realized now, she had been seeking to find something transcendent in such an intimate act of giving and taking, of surrender, of faith in another human being. Her search had been in vain. So each of these encounters, in its own way, had ended for Julia in a disconcerting emptiness that seemed to her, in retrospect, to be a subtle form of humiliation. Afterward, in this respect at least, she had been grateful to be able to withdraw into preoccupation with her mother's decline, with graduate school, and, later, with her demanding new profession.

Then, for a moment, she was surprised by thoughts of Danny Johnson, with whom she had *not* made love. What would it have been like with him?

"I'm not sure you're listening to me, darling," she heard Peter say. He reached over and stroked her knee through her dress, resting his hand there for a moment, then squeezing her leg gently before he took it away.

His use of the endearment, on which she dwelt as he spoke it, gave his touch an intimate, almost possessive quality—a message dispatched to her senses, telling her of things to come, that lingered on her skin and sent a pleasurable shiver up her spine.

Julia recited, "You were saying that it was too bad I had to leave, that you had to stay alone to work with Rob Vardaman on an acquisition." She was surprised that she could concentrate at all, even though the sharpest of the sensations he had set in motion had subsided. "But do you have to talk about my leaving?"

"You're right," he said. "I was just thinking that it was bad luck you would be missing the Vardamans. Vicki will be here, too, later on. And DiNiro."

"DiNiro? That man at 21?"

Once again she forced herself to suppress the unease that the man's manner had, no doubt beyond reason, generated in her during their brief encounter at the reception.

"Yes. Denny DiNiro. He's an important business partner of mine," Peter said.

"I could arrange to stay another day," she said.

"No, I don't think that would be..." he looked away for a moment "...wise." He turned back to her. "I'm sorry."

She reached for his hand. "Just a thought."

He refilled their glasses, although she had barely touched hers, and resumed his conversation. Her mind continued on its own wayward course.

After she had accepted Peter's invitation she had bought condoms to bring with her. She assumed he would provide for himself, but what if he didn't? She pictured the shiny blue box, with its thin foil packets, their contents rolled tightly, waiting. It was tucked into a corner of her suitcase.

She had not thought that she was hungry, but little remained on her plate.

"I'm sorry," she said, "I've let you do all the talking and you haven't had a chance to eat."

"Maybe it doesn't always show, but I don't mind hearing my own voice." He smiled. "Besides, I must have taken more than I wanted. I'm sure they have ice cream or sherbet. Would you like some? Or coffee?"

"Not right now, thanks, but everything was delicious."

Neither spoke immediately, shaping a moment of uneasy contemplation. Poised in the silence, Julia was surprised by a small chill breath of anxiety, like an unwanted draft in winter, leaking around a window frame or through the cracks between the floor boards of a house she had thought to be tight and snug. Looking down at her hands as they rested in her lap, she worked to dismiss it.

Peter ended the break that had intruded into the rhythm of the dance.

"Why don't we walk down to the beach?"

They blew out the candles. Lanterns placed at the corners of the terrace kept it softly illuminated. He took her hand once again, and they walked past the pool to the head of the path. There he reached behind the low wall to a switch and hidden lamps threw dim lights on each of the descending steps in front of them. They started down together.

At the end of the path, Julia slid her arm around Peter's waist. He held her as well, and they walked this way, side by side, across the shallow beach to the water's edge.

The expanse of the night sky was littered with stars. It seemed cool after the mildness of the day, but even so she felt a delicate zephyr of curiously warm air breathe on her bare skin. This cove was protected from the surf she heard breaking on the cliffs in the distance. Here, small wavelets gurgled as they broke at their feet and sighed, draining through the fine gravel the short distance back to the sea.

As if on cue, the two of them separated and turned to face each other. Once her eyes adjusted, she could see Peter clearly outlined against the sand, the sea and the starry sky, but could barely discern his features. They both smiled at the challenge of confirming the other's corporeal integrity in this new, darker world. She saw the white of his teeth in the light of the stars. Traces of that light were reflected in his eyes as he looked into hers.

She reached up to his face and for the first time touched the features that she found so sensual and compelling to look at, learning their essence through her fingertips.

Finding her shoulders with his hands, he guided her to him, moving his arms around her as she came. Their lips met. They kissed softly and tentatively at first, each searching for the other uncertainly in the darkness, but soon she became lost in their kissing, carried away by its force.

At the same time, his kisses were reassuring, even calming. All at once the troubling undercurrent of doubt that had been tugging at her as she moved along the course that had led her here seemed to be resolved. It drained from her like the spent waves hissing over the sand back to the sea.

She realized now how often she had returned in her memory to the last time they had been together like this, in the limousine in New York, wondering if it could possibly have been as she had thought. As she had then, she parted her lips in invitation, seeking again the forcefulness of his tongue. Once more this intimate exploration fueled her craving. But this time she felt no frenzy as before, no need to drink the cup dry at once to slake her thirst. Instead, she savored each moment as it led to the next, allowing her desire as they kissed to ripen like fruit on a tree, to swell into fullness, tender and sweet, trusting that it would be plucked and eaten when its time had come.

Her hands moved to the back of his neck and his head. She ran her fingers through his hair to get as strong a grasp as possible to pull herself to him and press her mouth to his.

They stepped back, each finding the other's hands so they still would be touching. She looked at the glimmer in the shadows that were his eyes in the darkness. She was full of feeling for him.

They turned together, and as she walked with him toward the steps leading to the house, and to his room, she knew that the real dance had just begun.

11

THEY STEPPED INTO THE dusk of Peter's room. It was illuminated only by the lights around the terrace and pool outside, filtered through the louvered slats of the shutters on the doors and windows. Peter flipped the switch for the lazy wood-bladed overhead fan and left her side to turn on a low table lamp in the far corner. She was glad. She wanted there to be enough light to see him, and be seen by him.

Yet standing alone, waiting for his return from across the room, she was suddenly hesitant. Despite moments of doubt, she had looked forward to being here, to making love with Peter, ever since she had accepted his invitation, with its clear, and desirable, implications. Her expectations were fueled even more as they had moved through the evening toward this moment: his flattering compliments, his apparent pleasure in her company, the subtle electricity of his hand on her leg before they walked down to the little beach below the pool, their kiss at the water's edge just minutes ago. But this was the first time in her life that she cared deeply about the outcome of having sex with a man, and once again she was surprised by a welling up of anxiety about the adventure on which she was about to embark. Would she do the right thing? Make the right moves? Be good? Would he?

But when he returned and he took her in his arms and kissed her, with more feeling, if that was possible, than with their last kiss, her unwanted doubts and inhibitions seemed, finally, to evaporate. Then he withdrew gently to take her hand.

As he led her toward the bed, she wished that she could shrug off her dress, and slip, and underclothes, so that they would simply fall from her easily, like a silky, diaphanous gown, breathing on her as it drifted down her body to pool at her feet, leaving her to feel the softly moving air on her skin and hair, free and clear of all impediments, for Peter's eyes and his delectation. But she knew that the reality would be different. Her dress zipped up the side, most of the time not smoothly. She had worn a bra, not because she sought to hide from Peter's gaze the manifestation of her breasts, her nipples, under the fabric of her dress, but because she always did. For the same reason, under her slip, she wore pantyhose. Dealing with all of this would be awkward and embarrassing. She longed to excuse herself to undress for him in private, in her own adjoining bedroom, to emerge in a few minutes covered only by her silk nightgown, or, perhaps, by nothing. To present herself to him, for his enjoyment, and hers, as a finished product, ready to use, batteries included. That would also have given her the opportunity to root in her suitcase for the foil packet that contained the protection that even in her heightened state of need she knew was essential to her wellbeing.

Before these distractions could cool her ardor, as she felt in spite of her best intentions they were threatening to do, she found Peter holding her at arms-length, looking into her eyes. He was not more than a few inches taller than she, but he projected to her an image of benign power and control that arrested her mind in mid-thought and commanded her full attention when he spoke to her softly, but firmly.

"Julia, darling," were his only words. Then, as he led and she followed, they undressed together and each other, as if they were participating in a leisurely, tender ritual, each lingering on their own discoveries, he with kisses on each part of her as it was revealed, until the ceremony was complete, and they were once again in each other's arms, this time on the bed.

It was then that he took charge. He lavished attention on her, with his hands, his fingers, his lips and his tongue, even his teeth, until she became an engine of pure desire, of almost frantic need. And yet he set a pace and exercised a control that denied her the release that seemed to be so near to her grasp, which only served to make her yearning stronger. Even as she rode this wave, she was astonished at the contrast between this entirely new experience for her and the way it had been with the others, before.

To the extent that she could think at all, she found herself focused on, almost mesmerized by, his erection. She had never been given the time, the luxury, of contemplating at her leisure this unique expression of male desire and wanting. Her other partners had simply used their penises as a tool for attaining their satisfaction, dispensing to her whatever pleasure might be available as incidental to their primary purpose in having sex. Its stiffness, its curiously velvety feel to the touch, its heat, its ruddiness and its apparent eagerness, fascinated and flattered her. She marveled that she, her body, the prospect of uniting with her, had caused such a curious and exciting phenomenon. So it was to this place, this organ, on which she instinctively lavished her attention—the same kind, using the same means, which he had used on her. And she drove him to the same sort of low moans that had been issuing from her lips since he had begun on her. Finally, he handed her a condom which he produced from the bedside table and guided her so that she unrolled the moist sheath down over its rigid length.

When Peter entered her, filled her, stretched her, she felt as though her nerve endings, her receptors, were stretched too, as tight as the strings of a violin, and that she was as sensitive to his touch as those strings would be to the subtlest texture of a taught bow being drawn across them. She was amazed by the sharpness of the waves of pleasure his invasion triggered as they spread quickly from her core to the surface of her skin. His sensuous ministrations to her before, and the anticipation generated by her new, intimate familiarity with the instrument of this benevolent assault, and his gentle, but increasingly firm, maneuvering of that instrument in the depths of her, combined to work their magic. She was surprised, almost immediately it seemed, by a shattering release of the exquisite tension that had been building in her since his caresses had begun.

At that moment, she was overcome with a feeling of sexual ecstasy that was totally new to her. But Peter was far from finished, and as she was soon to learn, neither, by far, was she.

12

JULIA WOKE SLOWLY. SHE felt supremely content. With her eyes still shut she tried to pick up the thread of a marvelous, sensuous dream that, sadly, drifted away from her as she gained consciousness.

She opened her eyes to sunlight glowing warmly through gauzy white curtains that billowed lazily in from the windows facing the sea. She reached for Peter. He was gone. Startled, she looked around quickly, only to find him standing by the bed in his terry cloth robe with a towel draped around his neck, looking down at her. She smiled.

"Good morning," he said, smiling back at her.

He greeted her as if it were just another morning, the beginning of just another day. But when Julia looked up at him—the great wooden ceiling fan beating its leisurely rhythm in the soft air above him—she felt the languorous fingers of desire stir her once again.

"I didn't want to wake you," he said. "I'm going for a swim. In the ocean. The salt water's refreshing at this time of day."

"*We* are going for a swim." She got up quickly. "You can't get rid of me that easily."

She scampered from the now-sacred precincts of his room to her own, splashed some water in her face, and brushed her teeth. Then she picked up a comb from the dressing table and strode to the full-length mirror on back of the closet door.

When she raised the comb to her hair, she caught sight of her reflection and stopped. There she was as Peter had seen her, in the softly lit room, last night. Intrigued, she moved closer to the mirror and scrutinized herself with care, looking at her lips, which had been used with such force, at her nipples, which had been given so much attention. She thought she sensed a change, but she could not be sure. The only thing clearly new was a small bruise on her shoulder at the base of her neck. She touched it fondly.

No time for this, she thought, as she pulled on her bathing suit, threading her arms through its thin straps, adjusting its top so that it didn't bind. But even as she prepared for her swim, she was flooded with images of their time together just a few hours before. Of Peter. Of seeing the effect that wanting her had on him as they gazed on each other's nakedness for the first time. How it had charged her with an irresistible yearning to touch him there. The delicious suspense. And then, his mastery of an art at which she was such a novice. His mastery of her senses. How he had made her feel. The intensity. The ecstatic release she had never known with a man before, had not even thought possible.

A light, cooling breeze gently ruffled the broad expanse of the sea. She held his hand as they walked back down the path cut through the lava to the beach in the small sheltered cove.

When they stepped off the bottom of the path and onto the sand, Peter shed his robe. To her surprise, he stood naked before her, now in the delightful clarity of the day. Laughing, she quickly peeled off her bathing suit and went to him. They embraced before splashing into the water. It was cool without being cold, and refreshing. She was engulfed by the light, foamy feel of the sea.

After their dip in the ocean, Melanie served them breakfast on the terrace. Coffee in a thermos was accompanied by a pitcher of hot milk. Everything else was on one large tray, and each plate or bowl was covered with a white linen napkin that Melanie removed for them once she had set the tray on the table. There were rolls and thin, flat wafers, thick butter patties wrapped in gold foil, chunks of different cheeses, and two kinds of jam in jars with quaint foreign labels. Prosciutto and salami in the center of a small platter were surrounded by slices of mango and papaya and wedges of limes.

"This is beautiful, Melanie," Julia said. "Thank you very much."

The young woman bowed her head slightly and offered her little smile, again looking directly at Peter, who glanced at her while he unfolded his napkin. Julia was surprised at how much this insignificant rudeness annoyed her, again, but the feeling passed as soon as Melanie left silently and Peter's attention was fixed back on her.

Julia was famished, and once they served themselves, she began to devour her breakfast with such unguarded enthusiasm that Peter started to laugh.

"You'll get another opportunity to eat, you know."

"I've been pretty active since dinner." She looked at him and smiled. "Swimming always makes me hungry!"

She laughed.

"Peter, I'm so glad I came!"

"So am I."

He reached for her.

Julia looked down at her hand in his. "You know, at one point I thought seriously of refusing your invitation. Why? Because I wasn't, well, sure of myself, I guess. Of my feelings. Of yours. It was here that I came to my senses. If I hadn't come to St. Maarten, would I ever have found out how I felt about you?"

"I imagine I'd have tried to see you again," Peter said, "just to give you another chance."

"It didn't seem that way to me at the time. Somehow, the way you put it, made me think I was making a final decision. That's probably why I came, in the end."

She looked up at Peter. He was gazing out over the water, smiling.

"You'd better eat something, too," she said.

As he began his breakfast in earnest, and they talked of trivial things, she became totally absorbed with him. She hung on his words—not their substance, but how they sounded as he spoke, the movement of his lips when he was saying them. She gazed at his face, seeing nuances of line and color and expression she hadn't noticed before.

She took in tiny details, like the clusters of fine, black hairs that sprouted from the backs of his fingers, and the incongruous smoothness of his hands, with hardly any visible veins showing, despite their obvious strength.

Her thoughts returned to their time together, to where those hands and fingers had been when she was with him. Then in her mind's eye she saw Peter's robe fall from him on the beach, and felt again the softness of the water on her skin as if its caresses were his touch.

She stopped eating and waited with muted impatience.

As soon as she thought that Peter was through, she took him by the hand and pulled him urgently back inside, to partake once more of the headier fare on which they had gorged themselves the night before.

13

THE HOUSE AND THE place where it stood, the vegetation everywhere, the people on the island and the island itself seemed exotic and mysteriously foreign to Julia. Peter helped her explore. They ventured on bicycles to a picturesque village and navigated along narrow roads to vantage points over the sea. Nearby they found a lighthouse that reminded her of one she had seen when she was small, on a family outing to the New Jersey shore.

For refreshment, they swam. Peter favored laps in the pool. Julia liked the ocean.

Once Peter took her snorkeling. He drove them to a wide beach separating a small grove of tall coconut palms from a quiet, crystal clear lagoon that was protected from ocean waves and predatory fish by a coral reef. He showed her how to use the equipment they had found in the house. Then he retired with his laptop to a folding chair in the shade of the trees.

Julia soon learned to clear her face mask and to puff incidental water out her breathing tube like a blowing whale so that she could concentrate on the extraordinary world below the surface of the calm water. At first she simply floated face downward, gazing at the undulating vegetation and the colorful creatures nurtured by the shelter of the coral. A school of small fish moved through the water like a miniature *corps de ballet*.

Then to get closer she held her breath and dove. As she descended, the sunlight, filtered by the water above her, seemed to illuminate the realm she was entering like light shining through tall stained glass windows inside a great cathedral, but constantly changing with the movement of the gentle waves on the surface.

Julia reveled in the sensuous embrace of the sea, warmed by the sun in this sheltered place, and in her surprising discovery of such elegant vitality teeming there. She visited Peter once, urging him to join her. He demurred, returning her kiss before she waded back into the water by herself.

So, even in this extravagantly romantic setting, Peter worked. He spent many hours each day in a small room in the main house that was packed with a desktop computer, a printer and a telephone. Walking by, she could see him in the midst of his papers, laid out on the table that served as a desk and on the floor. When Peter shut himself off from her, absorbed with his unnamed tasks, Julia luxuriated in this unaccustomed found time, reading paperbacks she had brought, pausing once in a while to take a refreshing dip off the small crescent beach. He did not encourage her to be with him in his office and kept the door locked when it was not in use.

Too soon, the day arrived for her stay with him to end. Her plane was to leave the island shortly after eleven in the morning. Peter had gone into town in a car borrowed from the house on what he said was a short errand that could not be accomplished conveniently on the way back from the airport, leaving her to prepare for her own departure.

Reluctant to go, she had put off packing until well after breakfast. When she began at last, it quickly became clear that she had left too little time. She had not brought a great deal with her but had kept track of nothing, so in addition to the relatively simple task of fitting her things into her suitcase, she was required to track down various belongings scattered around the compound. At last, with less than half an hour to go before they planned to drive to the airport, she felt confident she had gathered everything together, and started to pack.

The telephone rang.

Simon or Melanie always answered, unless Peter thought it was a business call. And wasn't there an answering machine to step in when needed? She had not touched a telephone since she had been there. She waited.

The ringing was insistent. Was it Peter, stuck somewhere? How would she get to the plane? Finally, she picked up the receiver, holding it cautiously, as if it might strike out at her in retribution for her temerity.

"Hello?"

"Hello," said a man's voice. "May I speak with Mr. Medea, please?" The voice had the relaxed, intriguing lyrical qualities she had heard in the speech of Jamaicans on the island, like Simon.

"I'm sorry," she replied, "Mr. Medea is not here. May I take a message?"

"Well, is Mr. Simon Marlowe there?"

"He doesn't seem to be around." She did not have time to search for Simon.

"Miss Melanie Kingsley?"

"No."

"Well then," the pace of his voice was still measured, "I would like to give you a message for Mr. Medea. Will you be seeing him?"

"Yes," she said. An edge of annoyance had crept into her tone. Precious minutes were passing. "Please give me the message!"

"Well," he said carefully, to be sure it was understood, "I am at the airport." He paused. "I work for the airport."

"Please!"

"Yes," the man said, "well, Mrs. Vardaman, Mrs. Vicki Vardaman, asked me to tell Mr. Medea that she will be arriving here at the airport, by plane, Tuesday—tomorrow—afternoon, at three."

"All right," said Julia, concentrating. She did not have a pad or a writing implement within her reach. "That's Tuesday at three," he said. "I'm not sure why she did not call him herself, but what does it matter? She said I was to give this message only to Mr. Medea personally, so it is very important that *you* do so. Thank you. Goodbye!"

"Goodbye," Julia said.

As she hung up, she went over the simple message in her mind once more. She had been confused while the man on the telephone was speaking, because Peter had said that it was *Mr.* Vardaman, Rob Vardaman, whom Peter was going to be doing his business with, and Mr. DiNiro. But she was sure the man had said *Mrs.* Vardaman. Hadn't Peter said that Vicki Vardaman wasn't coming until later?

Julia glanced at her watch and realized that she had ten minutes before she was supposed to be leaving the house.

"I can't believe it," she muttered to herself, and turned furiously to the task at hand. She reached for her toilet kit and shoved it down unmercifully on top of whatever else she had already stuffed into the bag. "Where *is* Peter, anyway?"

As if her words, like an incantation, had summoned him, Peter emerged through the terrace door of her room.

"Anything I can do to help?" He was unsuccessful in masking his concern at her state of readiness.

"I thought you were lost!" Julia hardly looked up.

She zipped her suitcase closed, scooped some miscellany from the dressing table into her purse and slung it over her shoulder, picked up her raincoat and turned for the door. He was already starting to leave with the suitcase.

"Wait a second," she said to him. Dropping the purse and the raincoat on the bed, she ran the few steps to him. She threw her arms around him and pulled him against her. He put down the suitcase and joined her in the embrace.

She kissed him firmly. "I've had such a wonderful time!"

"I have, too," he said. Then he reached for the suitcase. "But we'd better get moving if we're going to make it."

Julia shook hands with Simon and Melanie, both of whom materialized on the front steps of the house despite their apparent absence earlier. When she thanked them and said goodbye, Melanie's eyes were directed at the ground in front of her.

"Goodbye, Miss," she said, and performed a hint of a curtsy. "Safe journey."

With Peter behind the wheel, they raced to the airport. When they ran out on the tarmac, the movable steps were being rolled away from the small plane's entrance. An attendant took her bag to shove up into the cargo hold and the steps were pushed back. She waved to Peter from the top of the stairway, blowing a kiss and stepping back inside just as the flight attendant closed the door in front of her.

The passenger compartment was only half full and she was able to find a seat next to a window facing the terminal. She saw Peter standing by the gate, which was simply an opening in a hurricane fence in front of the low terminal building. She supposed he could not see her, but she waved anyway. His arm made a wide arc in the air before he turned his back on the plane and walked quickly toward the terminal.

The message, she thought suddenly. I forgot to give him the message!

The plane started to move. She peered out the window at the small building that was gradually moving out of sight, and sighed.

There was nothing she could do about it then, she realized. She would have to remember to tell Peter on the telephone. Maybe from San Juan if she had a chance. Failing that she would call him that night. She rummaged in her purse for a scrap of paper and a ballpoint pen.

She wrote: "Peter—Tomorrow. 3 p.m. Vicki Vardaman."

14

SINCE THEIR TIME ON St. Maarten, Julia was drawn to Peter's company, it seemed to her, as water is compelled by its very nature to flow downhill. But like the water in the stream where her father taught her to fish when she was growing up, flowing over or around boulders, its path turning this way and that, plunging suddenly in free fall only to splash happily into a pool, each moment of Julia's adventure with Peter seemed to bring her new excitement and a new appreciation of this man who had become her lover. She made the trek to New York City every weekend that he was not traveling, so that over the course of three months she had stayed with him often, occasionally having to amuse herself and keep house while he was away for some of her precious time there attending, he said, to his business.

And so it was that she found herself once more alone in his apartment, again looking forward to a weekend in New York City with Peter, awaiting his return. Her mind travelled back to her first visit, before St. Maarten, when he had been called away to fulfill a last minute business obligation, and she had been left to roam its rooms and halls, speculating as she did so, based on what she found there, about the nature of this man whom she hardly knew then but to whom she had found herself more and more strongly attracted. By now, though, this place of his had become familiar to her. She knew the doorman and she had her own key, so she was able to settle in by herself before Peter's arrival from an out-of-town business trip.

Peter had told her that he planned for them to have dinner in a certain low-key Upper East Side restaurant where he had taken her before. However, on the train from Philadelphia, she conceived of a different type of evening—one that would start with drinks and a candle-lit dinner in his dining room, and quickly proceed next door to the bedroom that had intrigued her so much on that first visit. There she hoped to enjoy with Peter a wholly different repast and, she thought, the less time spent between dining and the rest of the evening's activities the better.

Peter was scheduled to arrive at LaGuardia airport at four-thirty. He had told Julia to expect him a little over an hour later, allowing for baggage handling and traffic. Luckily, she had taken a much earlier train than necessary to make sure that any unexpected delays in transit would not interfere with her leisurely preparation for him, so she would be certain to be at her best when she greeted him. Since she experienced no such delays, she had plenty of time to carry out her plan to surprise him.

Having committed herself to this project, she was concerned at the expense it might entail. As always when embarking on a journey, she had tucked some extra cash into her purse for emergencies. Now that she was safely ensconced at her destination, she felt comfortable reallocating it to dinner so long as she expended it wisely. She stopped at a specialty grocer on Lexington Avenue and the butcher a few doors down, both of which she had discovered on earlier visits, to gather together the ingredients. On the way back she passed a liquor store (self-styled as "wine merchants") on Madison Avenue, and with a clerk's help, chose a suitable but inexpensive red Bordeaux. A florist shop she passed on the way home yielded a modest bouquet for the center of the dining room table. Later, she was familiar enough with Peter's kitchen and dining room to be able to arrange the ingredients for preparation and set the table, all within the short time allotted by Peter's declared schedule, without serious difficulty. Each task as it was completed heightened her excitement in anticipation of his arrival.

A few weeks earlier, Peter had taken her to a stylish boutique on Madison Avenue where they had looked at dresses. More than an hour before she expected Peter she laid out the product of that shopping expedition, which she kept hanging in Peter's closet rather than taking it home, where she knew it would never see the light of day, or night. It was an elegant cocktail dress, a dark green velvet, but still a thin fabric, its lines simple but subtly responsive to the shape of her body in a flattering, sexy way. Its thin straps left her shoulders virtually bare. Then, in the large bathroom next to Peter's bedroom, she settled into the huge bathtub, filled with warm water spiked with lavender scent that had been a present from Peter. She would like to have washed her hair—she'd brought her dryer for the purpose—but was afraid there wasn't enough time.

After she toweled herself off, she put on her half-slip, pulled a soft, warm sweater down over her bare top, and donned her old, tan raincoat and wool-lined slippers. She took the alarm clock from the bedroom to make sure she would start to dress in fifteen minutes and ventured out onto the terrace overlooking Central Park, her favorite spot in the apartment. It was late September, and there was a chill in the air, but it was calm, and she was sure she would be comfortable. First she took in the expansive view, and then lay back on one of the lounge chairs to stare at cumulous clouds building in the late afternoon sky.

She tried to imagine Peter standing in front of her, holding out his hand, leading her inside. She closed her eyes. She visualized him and the times they had been together. She thought of her yearning for him when they were apart, and the thrill of her happiness when they were together. Then it came to her like a revelation. The feelings she had for him must be love. She doubted that she had ever loved a man before, really. She thought for a moment of Danny Johnson, but it wasn't the same, and couldn't be. She hadn't been with him enough, or at all in any meaningful way. And she had been so young then. Now she was certain: she was in love with Peter. Maybe she had been all along—she must have been—but was afraid of being hurt and hadn't wanted to admit it to herself. Such deep, full feelings for him. Such a need. She grinned as she mouthed the words: I love you, Peter.

"Hello!"

She thought she was awake when she heard his voice, but wasn't sure.

"May I join you?"

She opened her eyes just as he kissed her gently on the lips.

"Peter!"

She sat up.

"I look awful! What time is it?"

"You look fine. My plane was early, and the traffic was light. It's not five yet."

"Oh, Peter. I wanted to be all dressed and pretty for you."

When she stood, he kissed her again, pulling her against him. She raised herself on the balls of her feet to talk softly into his ear.

"I've missed you so much. Why do we have to live so far apart?" She kissed his neck and his cheek. "I thought it would be fun to eat here tonight. Everything is practically ready. I just need to broil the lamb chops and steam the rest for a minute or two. There's a bottle of wine for dinner, but we can cheat and have a little now. While you're washing up,

I'll get dressed. Then, with a little luck, I'll be undressed again before I even set foot in the kitchen."

He smiled at her. "I guess you didn't notice the champagne in the fridge. I was going to break it out later, but I'm sure it won't mind. I'll bring you a glass. I'll need to cancel that restaurant reservation, but I have to say your program for the evening is hard to resist." He brushed her lips with his. "Don't be long."

He turned and walked toward his office and the telephone.

Dinner would have to wait.

The champagne bucket had moved to the top of Peter's bureau. He sat on the bed in his shirtsleeves, leaning back on the pillows arrayed against the headboard, one leg stretched out and one dangling to the floor, holding his glass as it rested on the sheet. Julia sipped from hers and set it on the bedside table, next to the lamp, the only one that was lighted. It cast a soft glow that disappeared in shadow in the corners of the room.

She stood erect before him and, with provocative deliberation, slid the straps of her dress first from one shoulder, then the other. They had begun this ritual in the villa on St. Maarten, in his bedroom, which had become their bedroom, after their first night together. She reveled in the sensuous feeling it gave her, both to perform for Peter's pleasure and to draw out her anticipation of the even greater intimacy to come. As he watched, she eased the dress down to her waist, gradually revealing her breasts, then pushed it past her hips to fall in a pool of soft, dark green folds at her feet. Next came her slip.

She felt the intensity of his need in his gaze. It caressed her with almost as much tactile effect as his hands might have if he had reached out to touch her. Feeling his look and anticipating his touch hardened her dark nipples and prickled the skin along her arms.

At last she removed her shoes slowly and stood still before him. Then he rose and she reclined, without their touching still, and in front of her, at a measured, tantalizing pace, he unclothed his nakedness, and the manifestation of his desire.

In this way they began.

Their appetites were undiminished since that first time, but it seemed to her that every time after that they came to know each other more. To understand the other's pace and rhythm. And each time it was better. Her agonizing absence from him seemed to have built up in her a reservoir of even more unspent passion. Their making love had become for her an event of profound consequence.

This time was no exception. She was frantic to have him.

When at last she did, lying underneath him, she felt, for a moment, a wonderful relief—here they were again! Then a familiar, exquisite tension began to mount in her.

Without any thought except to dwell on this tension and to strive with Peter toward its resolution, Julia's eyes drifted past him to the ceiling, and to the huge mirror suspended from it. She became aware of the bed, as seen from above. She saw an unfamiliar creature lying there in the light of the single lamp, staring back at her, pale and wide-eyed. Like a strange insect, it seemed to be pinned helplessly on its back, struggling against a dark animal presence that moved on top of it. The insect's mouth was open in surprise, its legs were flung out, knees and feet raised, writhing. Startled, she forced herself to focus. Yes, it was her own body she was looking at, embraced by her lover, shining with sweat, lunging to receive him. Excited by this vision, she raised her hands to Peter's shoulders and watched their reflected image as she moved them, fingers spread, over him, down his flanks to his buttocks.

"Yes," he breathed as he moved on her.

She closed her eyes.

"Oh, Peter!" she said.

"Yes, yes...

"Yes!"

15

JULIA GAZED ACROSS AT Peter after they had finished their dessert. She had slipped back into her dress. He wore slacks and a silk shirt open at the collar. Bathed in the rich light of the candles, his face, with its dark complexion and strong features, his large nose, his sensuous lips, reminded her of a man in an Italian Renaissance portrait: successful, worldly, powerful. And, as she knew so well, passionate. She reached to him past the centerpiece she had arranged from the bouquet of flowers. He extended his hand and squeezed hers before she withdrew it and sat back in her chair.

She was not sure why she thought of Vicki Vardaman just then. From Peter's conversation while Julia was with him at the Vardaman's villa on St. Maarten, she knew that Rob and Vicki were close friends, that Rob was involved in Peter's business affairs, and that Peter would be seeing them, along with Mr. DiNiro, after her departure. Vicki's message for Peter, received by Julia just before the end of her stay on the island left her with the impression that Vicki might have been arriving before the others. That Peter would be alone with her there. Julia hadn't thought about any implications that turn of events might hold for her when she made a point of delivering the message to Peter by telephone from the airport in Puerto Rico. Or later. Until now, after almost three months, when, out of any context that their conversation here seemed to provide, she spoke.

"Did Vicki arrive on time after I left you on St. Maarten? Did everything work out?"

"As far as I can remember. Yes." Peter looked up. "What made you think of that?"

"I'm not sure." In fact, she was surprised herself that she had even begun this conversation. Without thinking, she lowered her voice. "Of course, I have no hold on you. No right to..." She hesitated, troubled by how to phrase her thought, and its implications.

In the ensuing moment of silence, Peter reached for the bottle of wine and glanced at Julia's glass. When she waved him off, he poured some for himself. Then he raised his eyes to hers.

"There is something I want—no, I need—to tell you. That I planned to talk with you about while you're here, with me, this weekend. But first, since you brought her up, and I guess it's just as well that you did, you need to know about Vicki. And me. It's important that you find out from me rather than," his fingers curled around the stem of the wine glass and he lifted it, looking into the clear, deep red liquid, "some other way." He sipped the wine and raised his eyes to hers.

"Vicki and I . . . that is," he put his glass down, "we were quite, well, close at one time—before you and I… Before you, of course. Before I realized how much you mean to me."

Julia looked away. "Quite close," she repeated without being aware of having spoken. "But…" She turned back to him, searching his eyes for any message they might hold that was not conveyed by his words.

"That's past," she said at last, not daring to ask it as a question.
"Past." He smiled.

How far in the past? Julia wondered. Again she remembered Vicki's message. The time she must have spent with Peter, however short it might have been, before the others arrived at the villa. That was certainly after he had met Julia.

She took a deep breath. Only then did she realize how tense she had become while they were talking. She kneaded her neck with her fingers. Taut muscles hurt to her touch. With her other hand, she clutched her napkin in a tight ball. She was perspiring even though she had thought it was too cool in the apartment when they sat down.

"And I very much want you two to be friends," Peter continued. "I just didn't want you to be surprised, that's all."

"And her husband, Rob?"

"He knows. It's all done. Finished." He leaned forward. "Are you all right?"

"I think so." His eyes were dark in the yellow light. She could see the flicker of the candles burning there. Hers were filling, and as they did, her vision of him became blurred and indistinct.

"I love you, Julia," he said. "Only you. You must believe that."

"Yes," she blinked back her tears, "I do."

She could see him clearly now, and she met his concerned look head on. "I love you, Peter," she said, "very, very much."

As if on cue, they both rose, and in a moment were in an embrace that ended with a lingering kiss.

When they separated, Peter smiled, but his expression, shared by his eyes, became one of focused intensity. "Which brings me to what I really wanted to tell you. To talk about with you. But not here." He picked up his wine glass and the bottle and led her into the living room. He set them on the coffee table in front of the sofa. Empty glass in hand, she followed his lead. Then he took her hand and helped her settle down next to him. He fixed his gaze on her.

"What is it, Peter?" she said, her voice betraying concern. "You look so serious. I understand about Vicki. I'm glad you told me, but it doesn't mean anything now, does it?"

Peter shook his head. "It's not that," he said and took her other hand in his. He shifted so that he faced her squarely.

"You know, I think that I'm a great business negotiator. If I want something from the other side, I can usually ask for it in a way that makes them think that I'm making them an offer that they can't refuse."

"I know," she said with a wry smile.

"But this isn't the same."

He paused and looked down at their hands, clasped together between the two of them, before he raised his eyes once more to hers. Julia caught his tone and his expression and a curious new thought came to her even before he spoke again.

"I know I can't make anything like that kind of offer here, to you. All I know is that I need you more than anyone or anything I've ever needed before in my life. And I'm in love with you. Passionately, irrevocably in love. And I want you to be my wife. While I was away from you this time I realized that I had to talk with you. To tell you. To ask. To plead, if necessary. I haven't even had time to pick out a ring to tempt you with. I should be giving it to you now. But Julia, will you marry me?"

"Oh, Peter!" Even though, she had sensed at the last minute what he might be about to say, his words seemed literally to take her breath away for an instant, or at the very least to rob her of the ability to speak and formulate a reasoned response. When she regained her equilibrium, she clasped their hands together and kissed the back of his before she looked up at him again.

"Peter, I've missed you so much every time we're apart, every time I have to return to my other life, my life away from you. I love you. I love you so much. But…"

"I know this must have surprised you. Too soon. Too abrupt. If you need time, I'll understand…"

"Will you? I know it may not seem this way to you, but it has come on me so suddenly. I'm not sure what I want to think about, but I know I should. Think. It's such an important decision. Your happiness. Mine. That you have even considered it, have asked me, is so…so beautiful. But…"

His expression softened into a smile again.

"I know. It's important to me, but I *have* been thinking about it. A lot. So it's only fair that you get a chance, too. You've told me that when I ask you to do something with me, it always seems like some kind of ultimatum to you. That it's now or never. When I asked you to come with me to St. Maarten…"

"Yes. When you asked me, that's what I thought. At the time. But it was so perfect. You were so right about going there."

"I think we agree about that!" he laughed. "But please believe me that I want to marry you now, and will tomorrow, and the next day. Will I be impatient? You know me well enough to know that I'd be lying if I said wouldn't. But only because I want you so much. Want to march with you down to Tiffany or wherever you desire to get that ring. Want you to live with me for the rest of my life."

Blinking back new tears, she reached for him, wrapping him in her arms. Even as she cried she managed a smile.

"Peter, darling, I love you so much. You won't have to wait long. I promise."

Then she glanced at the bottle Peter had set on the table when they had walked in from the dining room.

"I guess maybe I'll have a little more of that wine after all," she said.

Julia was determined to think about the prospect of marrying Peter carefully, objectively to the extent that was possible, before she made up her mind and gave him her answer. She knew, now, that she loved him. What else was there? What questions required answers before she should reach her conclusion?

She consulted Rita Craig, her sole confident, again. Rita's advice was virtually the same as when she had talked with Julia about whether to accept Peter's invitation to St. Maarten. "Of course you love him.

Otherwise you wouldn't be bothering with all this. But what's as important is whether you really know him. Whether the person you think you love is the whole person, or just the part of him you see, that you want to see, when you're with him." Then with a smile, but somewhat ominously she added: "Remember to take off those rose-colored glasses."

Yes, Julia knew that in many ways she still did not know Peter Medea. Of course she enjoyed being with him, but she realized that he could seem private and mysterious, and sometimes unaware of others and their concerns. He did have a sense of humor. It was on the dry side, but so was hers. He was not absorbed in cultural pursuits, as she tried to be, consistent with her limited budget. But he had taken her to concerts and the theater, and seemed interested in her observations and guidance in that department.

Each time she stayed with him, they cherished their selfish isolation, devoting every minute to each other, so she was not surprised that she had met none of his friends and knew nothing of his social life. Not that she required that he be gregarious, or even socially active. She had never needed a large social circle herself, as her mother had. After her family moved to their isolated nest in rural Pennsylvania her mother, in spite of her piano teaching and PTA activities and book club, had been terribly lonely, while Julia, with only two or three other girls from high school as her friends, had been perfectly content. But, she supposed, knowing the types of people Peter enjoyed outside of his business would be a window of sorts into the type of person he was himself.

From what she had experienced so far, the milieu that he seemed most at home in was that of business. His business. She knew little about the nature of his business except what he had told her at the Algonquin during her first visit to New York at Peter's invitation: the role he said he played in the transaction that had been the subject of the reception at 21 Club where they had met and in similar situations with other companies. He had made it clear that he would consider some of her father's friends as good contacts for him. The only business associate of his she knew in person was Marco DiNiro, whom she had met at the same reception at 21 Club and to whom she had taken an immediate dislike. But she felt that she should not, and would not, judge Peter based solely on this unfortunate connection.

Then it occurred to her that indeed this universe of his, the one outside the private enclave she and Peter had constructed around themselves when they were together, was one with which she was familiar, by reputation at least, because at one time it had been her parents' milieu as well. Each of them had told her, from a different perspective, of their world before her father became disillusioned with the competitive arena of finance in New York City. One where power and money were the essential social currency. When her father abandoned his Wall Street career and took up writing and promoting conservation causes in rural Pennsylvania, moving there with his family, her mother had sorely missed the life that her father had chosen to put behind them. According to her, she had thrived in it. But would Julia?

At the same time, she asked herself, should she be disturbed that Peter sometimes seemed obsessed with his business, and was obviously very ambitious, if his apparent financial success was the result? Whatever else, she was confident that he would provide for her.

Besides, wasn't she "obsessed" in a way with her own career? By her desire to teach? It wasn't the same type of ambition, but ambition it was: to improve her ability to impart knowledge to young people, particularly those whose access to such knowledge was limited, and, if it came down to it, to be recognized as being good at what she did.

She knew, because he had told her, that Peter had been married, briefly. His willingness to share this information when he seemed reticent generally in the rare instances when his past became the subject of their conversation, somehow added credibility in her mind to his explanation: that he had simply made a naïve, a terrible mistake. He assured Julia that his feelings for her fell into a wholly different category than any he had ever felt for the unnamed woman whom he had been mistaken about.

Finally, she posed to herself this challenge: how could she come to know Peter better, as Rita had suggested she should? She couldn't say that she knew him as well as if, say, they'd been able to live together for a period of time before they decided whether to marry, but even if she wanted to, that was not a realistic option. She certainly could not just quit her job and move in with Peter, in New York, without knowing what her future with him would hold, could she? Anyway she was sure that no matter how acceptable such an expedient might be in some circles, Peter would see it as projecting the wrong image to the business contacts and associates, and to the world at large, that he wanted so much to impress. And she was sure that just visiting more weekends for months on end would not yield any more information than what she knew already.

In the end, she came to believe that all this analysis, evaluation and speculation, circling in her mind like a cat chasing its tail, was totally ignoring the most important consideration: that she knew now that she was deeply in love with this man, that she missed him terribly whenever they were apart, and that she felt fulfilled and complete whenever they were together. Would she learn anything from waiting that would alleviate this pain of separation? Why should she subject herself to further torment? Finally, she posed this dilemma to Rita. Her friend, when pushed, had to agree.

Julia telephoned Peter and accepted his proposal long before her next trip to see him. When she did see him, they began to celebrate the moment she crossed his threshold.

PART 2

16

PETER'S APARTMENT—THEIR APARTMENT, NOW—WAS perfectly suited for giving parties, but entertaining was not conceived of by Peter as an opportunity for them to enjoy the company of purely social friends. Instead, Peter saw it all as a function of his business. He wrote off the costs of most parties as an expense for tax purposes. Some were paid for by clients.

Their first large reception set the pattern. Peter and his secretary, Brenda Thornton, assembled lists of potential guests and monitored the success of invitations at luring them into appearances. All of the invitations were handled by a social secretary firm retained by Brenda. Brenda also engaged the caterer, and even, at Peter's direction, arranged for flowers. Julia, as Peter's wife, was the hostess. That was all. Her personal involvement began only when Peter coached her about the reasons each of the guests had been invited, their relationships with each other, and their relative importance to his or his clients' purposes. With one exception.

At Peter's request, Julia was to provide to Brenda, to add to the invitation list, the names of those of her father's friends that she felt she knew well enough to approach for this purpose. If any responses weren't received promptly, she was to follow up the invitations by telephone or a note to encourage them to accept.

When the time for the much-anticipated event arrived, more than a hundred guests attended over the course of the evening. Most drifted in for a drink and hors d'oeuvres and to see who else might be there, then left after a polite interval. A few business associates arrived early and stayed for the duration. Marco "Denny" DiNiro, Chairman of Grendel Holdings Ltd., whom she had met at the 21 Club reception, was one of these. Peter had told her that tonight DiNiro would be picking up most of the tab and the party was being staged for his benefit.

Again Peter introduced him to Julia. DiNiro's appearance and manner were much as she remembered. Tall, quite heavy-set, but suave, he was immaculately groomed. The kind of person who makes a strong first impression in a group, like Peter but more so. Like a public figure.

He greeted her with a smile and the same appraising look she had found so disturbing before.

"Good to see you again, my dear. So now you have become Peter's latest acquisition. And such a pretty one, at that." He held her hand in the two of his while he glanced at her just a moment more before surveying the setting of his party with a critical eye. "I'm sure you'll prove to be a most valuable asset." He bestowed his exaggerated wink on her, and moved off to greet a new arrival.

Julia came away from this second, fleeting, encounter with Denny DiNiro unsure of whether or not she had made a good impression, or any, on this obviously important business associate of her husband. She worried that her lack of empathy had shown through her polite smile. His manner seemed to her to be more calculating than genuinely friendly. Watching him later from a distance, she noticed that while he smiled often, his eyes, small in proportion to his large face, but intense, were constantly on the move, probing among the gathering of guests. She imagined them assessing, analyzing, planning, dismissing. Like a predator sizing up potential prey. They seemed to be on a different track entirely. She vowed to herself to make more of an effort, when the occasion arose, to please this man for her husband's sake, in spite of an aura emanating from him that she found to be disconcerting at the least, if not actually menacing.

Rob and Vicki Vardaman were among the early arrivals. Rob, she came to learn, was ambitious and smart, but otherwise quite different from Peter. He was older, his hair silver-gray. Tall, slim and angular, in a business suit that was cut fuller than current fashion dictated, a white shirt with a starched collar, and a wide patterned necktie, he looked as if he had stepped out of a news photo from the 1930s. In company he was quiet, almost retiring, as he listened to others patiently, with demonstrated attentiveness. He seemed thoughtful and, therefore, knowledgeable.

Of course, the principal object of Julia's curiosity, mixed with a large portion of apprehension, centered on Rob's wife. "Vicki is straight from Hollywood," is the way Peter had described her to Julia before the party, without any reference whatsoever to his revelation the night he had proposed to her of his previous relationship with this woman. And when Julia saw her sweep through the entrance to the living room, the sight was not reassuring. Vicki was loud, forthright and charismatic.

Her figure, tightly sheathed, was generously endowed but in pleasing proportion. The kind, Julia felt certain, that men salivate over. Her animation and vitality made her white-blond hair coloring and her lavish use of makeup, which exaggerated her already-large features, somehow suitable and right. Julia tried desperately not to think of herself as in any way engaged in a head-to-head competition for Peter's attention with Vicki Vardaman. And she remembered Peter's last words when he had talked to her about Vicki: "I want you to be friends…"

Vicki did not join the women at the perimeter of the room, but dove instead into the cluster of men surrounding Peter. High-powered conversation—business talk—seemed to Julia to fly around Peter like angry hornets, yet in the midst of it all, Vicki was perfectly at home. Her boisterous voice rose above the masculine din in the center of the room.

Later in the evening, Vicki took Julia by the arm, guided her to the study, which was out of the main stream of the party, and hugged her. Then she held her at arms length.

"You're so pretty. So much style." She let go and stepped back, her arms out, her hands spread, like someone in a Renaissance painting viewing a miracle. "How did he ever find you? I didn't think he was that smart." She smiled, her eyes seeking Julia's and holding them.

Since she had married Peter, Julia's usual self-assurance had been under siege. Without the psychic rewards she had derived from her teaching, in spite of its frustrations, and without even the casual social encounters that had been part of her life in her old neighborhood in Philadelphia, a new form of loneliness had already pulled at her even as she was embarking on this adventure with him. Now she was presented with the vibrant spectacle of Vicki Vardaman, seemingly confident to the point of intimidation, whom Julia knew from Peter had been, in important ways, on as familiar a footing with Julia's husband as she was herself. So, at this kind and supportive greeting from Vicki, Julia found tears threatening to embarrass her as she responded.

"Thank you," she said. Her voice was choked. She blinked and regained her composure. "How nice you are."

"I won't ask what you expected," Vicki said, motioning toward two chairs in the corner of the room. "Peter must have talked to you about Rob and me. We've known him for an age. You were with him at our place in St. Maarten, I know."

They sat close to each other and away from the buzz of the party.
"We had a lovely time," Julia said. "I should have thanked you before
now. We. . .that is, I missed you by a day. Peter stayed over. I remember
he had business with Rob. You left a message."
She felt heat rising to her cheeks and looked down for a moment.
"Ah, yes." Vicki, too, looked away.
Then she took Julia's hand in hers and turned to her again. Her eyes
were surprising. Gray and cool. Incongruous, like icebergs floating in the
Gulf Stream. Julia returned her gaze.
"I shouldn't monopolize you," Vicki said. "You'll want to get to know
everyone. You can be such a help to Pete. And we'll see a lot of each
other. I'll make it my business.
"But I want you to promise me something. Pete is so wrapped up
in his work, and you already know, I'm sure, how intense he is. If ever
it gets to you, talk to me. Put your head on my shoulder. We know him
and love him, and we'll straighten him out. Promise?"
"Thank you," Julia said. "Peter has a lot on his mind, but he's sweet
and considerate. We're very much in love."
"Of course you are. I've been presumptuous and too direct, I suppose.
But that's my way." Vicki rose, lifting Julia up as well with the pressure
of her hand in a regal sort of gesture. "Please, don't be offended. And
don't forget."
Vicki turned to look down the hall toward the wet bar off the living
room. It was hidden behind closed doors because it was not being used
by the caterers. With an air of familiarity she opened it, found glasses
and reached into the small refrigerator for some ice. She surveyed the
bottles at the back of the counter. "Now," she said, "let's find something
good and strong to help us celebrate our wonderful new friendship."
After Julia's encounter with Vicki, Rob Vardaman broke away from
the congregation of males to talk with her. Soon he caught the eye of
a small, agile man who walked across the room and joined them. He
was shorter than Julia and slightly bent. Ears protruded almost at right
angles from a large head. Curly grey hair and long sideburns framed a
square, creased face. He looked to her a little like a large, dignified organ-
grinder's monkey. The effect was humorous, and he seemed to enjoy it
himself, as if he had adopted this form for other people's amusement.
Joshua Adams' whole countenance smiled when Rob introduced him
to her.

"We met when you came in, I think," Julia said.

"Josh is an M.D. and a PhD." Rob continued, "and runs a company—TryCo. Practical applications for chemistry, right Josh?"

TryCo, she thought. The name was familiar.

"Research," Adams said to Julia. His expression became almost somber. "And it's a division. A division of a company that's stock has gone to hell." He glanced across the room at DiNiro. "Remember, Rob?"

DiNiro turned in their direction and she was sure at first that he had caught Adams' look. But his expression never changed, and, apparently without the intensity she had observed in him before, he swung his gaze around the room with the languid sweep of a person who is searching a crowd, out of curiosity, not need, for someone he does not find there. She could not be sure in the end whether he had even noticed Adams at all.

"Those problems will be behind us before long," Rob said to Adams, his hand moving to the other man's back with fraternal familiarity. Then he said to Julia, "Josh is a very interesting man."

"Pete tells me that your father was Harold Davenport." Adams broke in before Rob could elaborate. His smile returned. "I enjoyed his musings from time to time. The Wilderness Council's magazine carried some of his articles. He was my type of person. Had the right priorities."

Julia smiled while she sought words to express her happiness at this unexpected recognition.

"Unfortunately, I'm on my way to the door. We'll have to talk some other time."

"I'd love to," Julia said. "Do you have to leave so soon?"

Adams glanced at his watch. "It's not soon for someone my age," he said, and his face crinkled into a broad grin. "We'll meet again. I'll make a point of it."

Julia was pleased, and flattered, that many of the persons she had added to the list of invitees attended the reception. She was gratified that while personal intervention by her had not been necessary for most, the calls that she did make had yielded a number of positive responses from people that Peter seemed to feel were important to him. Those reminders were embarrassing for Julia. She felt that if someone she knew had decided to pass, they must have good reason and should be allowed to do so in peace. But, to please Peter, she persevered, and now she was glad that she had.

Her greatest triumph, it seemed, was Sanderson vanDamm's appearance, although he did not bring his wife. Julia was surprised when he had accepted since it was his brother that her father had been closer to. His presence seemed important to Peter and for the short time vanDamm was there, after he had paid his respects to Julia, many of the other male guests, including DiNiro, gathered in his presence, all trying, it seemed to her, to impress.

One of those that Brenda reported had not been heard from was Archibold Strothers, the attorney in whom Peter had shown a keen interest when Julia had mentioned him before as an old friend of her father's. Happily for her, Strothers rescued her from the need for any follow-up by calling her directly (not the social secretary) to announce that he and his wife from his second marriage, whom Julia did not know, would not be able to attend.

"Unfortunately, we have a previous commitment."

"I'm sorry," she said.

"So am I," he said. "So is Amelia. She is anxious to meet you. I watched you grow up you know—mostly at a distance, I'm afraid, but I can remember when you took me to your favorite place in the woods behind your home in Pennsylvania."

"I know. You were sweet to me."

He had been out to their house at The Colony, near Libertyville, after her family had moved there from New Jersey, only once that she could recall. She must have been around fourteen. She remembered liking him, but she knew his face more from a photograph with her father taken at a party at the Estuary Club than she did from her own memory.

"One other thing," Strothers said. "Thank you for including us among the select group to be sent your wedding announcement."

"Of course! I know you were one of my parents', my father's, closest friends."

Julia had not invited the Strothers to her wedding, or anyone else for that matter, except for Rita and Calvin Craig (Calvin couldn't make it). With both her parents gone, and no close relatives alive, she had been content with the private civil ceremony that Peter suggested. Peter's parents and Rita were the only persons in attendance. They were married by the Justice of the Peace in his office downtown, in the basement of the Municipal Building. Announcements were sent to friends.

The Strothers had given Julia a set of elegant champagne glasses. She hoped that her note had shown how touched she had been. But even so, she felt uncomfortable.

"It was a small, civil ceremony. We decided…"

Strothers broke in. "We understand completely, my dear." Then he seemed to hesitate, and when he did speak his voice was low, almost as if he was talking to himself rather than the person he had called.

"I'm just sorry I didn't know before…" He seemed to stop in mid-thought.

"How could you have?" Julia said. "It all happened so quickly. But I'm not sure what you mean…"

"Nothing, really." His voice was strong again. "Or I guess what I really mean is: Congratulations! I know your mother and father would have been happy for you, and proud."

Then he paused still again.

"I hope you know that we want to help you in any way we can."

"Thank you."

"Will you let me take you to lunch sometime soon?"

"That would be wonderful."

Something in his tone, or perhaps the care with which she sensed he chose his words, left her feeling deflated. As she replaced the receiver she wondered whether he would ever follow up on his suggestion about lunch. When, if ever, would she see him again? And what kind of "help" did he think she would need?

17

JOSHUA ADAMS CALLED. HE was in the city to see some people for business. He had tried to reach Peter at the office but encountered instead a voicemail announcement, "So I thought I'd try his home number."

"Peter's in Chicago," Julia said.

"That's where I came from," Adams said. "Funny. I talked with him a couple of days ago and he didn't mention he'd be there.

"It doesn't matter, though, because I really just planned to use him to get a chance to see you. Would you let me buy you a drink this evening? Of course, if Pete's coming back tonight, I know you two will want to be alone. But if he's still away, let me relieve your boredom. I *am* a dirty old man, but I'm really harmless. I'd like to learn more about your father."

"Of course," Julia said. "Peter won't be back until tomorrow, and I need to get out. I'm getting a little stir-crazy."

Adams said he would get back in touch after his meetings that afternoon, when he would have a better idea about his schedule. Julia was pleased. She had liked Josh Adams when Rob Vardaman introduced them, and she felt lonely with Peter away still again. She looked forward to this unexpected break in her solitary routine.

First, though, she wanted to get hold of Peter. She needed to know if there was anything in particular he wanted her to say, or not say, to Adams. More important to her, she wanted Peter to know before the fact that she would be alone socially with a man, "harmless" or no, and why.

Peter usually called her when he was travelling. He had discouraged her from calling him. He could never be sure, he said, that he would be staying in the hotel that was listed on the typed summary that Brenda prepared for her, or even be in the designated city, for that matter. And, he said, he wanted to keep his cell phone clear for business calls, except late at night. This, however, was a special occasion.

With some trepidation she dialed his cell phone, but Peter did not pick up. Peter had not given her an itinerary for his trip. He was only scheduled to be away for two nights.

Julia decided to call his office. Brenda would know the number of his hotel so that she could leave a message there in case she missed him. It was at least an hour since Adams must have tried to reach Peter, and long after lunchtime, but Brenda Thornton's smooth British voice still apologized in a recording that "we cannot answer the telephone at this time" and urged Julia to leave a message after the tone. "While the cat's away..." Julia recited to herself. She told the machine that Peter should call her.

She had one more chance of reaching him. He had told her that the entire first day he would be meeting with someone at Crouch Partners. She remembered because he had referred to the company before and the name had amused her. She had her own access to the computer in the study (not, of course, to Peter's files and documents) and searched the Chicago white pages on the internet for Crouch Partners' number.

"Crouch," said a woman's voice.

A command? Julia smiled.

"May I help you?" the voice continued.

"I understand that Peter Medea is meeting with someone there today. This is Mrs. Medea. If he is free, I'd like to speak with him. Otherwise, could I have the secretary of the person he is with?"

"Just a minute, please."

Baroque orchestral music replaced the voice when Julia was put on hold. Bach, she thought. The piece was familiar, but before she could place it with certainty, the voice broke in.

"I'm sorry, but Mr. Medea is not here."

"Are you sure?"

"We log in all visitors. He is not in the log. I have not seen him and I've been here since nine this morning, except for lunch."

Suddenly Julia was concerned. It was not like Peter to be late for an appointment, let alone not to show up at all.

"Can you tell me who he was to meet with? When was he supposed to be there? Did he call?"

"Please hold."

The Bach sounded annoyingly cheerful. Now she recognized it: a gavotte from an orchestral suite. In a short while, though, the woman's voice returned.

"We know Mr. Medea," the woman said. "The person who was at my desk during lunch did not see him come in, either. We keep a composite calendar of all scheduled appointments with outside visitors. We do not usually disclose this information, but just so you don't worry, I can tell you that he did have a meeting with one of our principals scheduled for today, but this shows that he called two days ago to reschedule. He is not on today's calendar."

"I see," said Julia.

"Please hold," said the voice.

Bach had been replaced by Vivaldi. One of the Four Seasons concerti. Was it *La primavera? L'autunno?* She could never get them straight.

She hung up.

18

WHEN JOSHUA ADAMS CALLED, he suggested to Julia that they meet at the bar on the ground floor of a nearby hotel. "I don't think the live music starts until much later," he said, "but I like the atmosphere."

"That would be fun," she said. It was the Carlyle, where she had stayed during her first weekend in New York with Peter. "But Mr. Adams..."

"Josh, please."

"This may seem silly to you, Josh, but I'm not sure when Peter's calling from Chicago and I don't have a cell phone. He could leave a message, but he's so busy that sometimes there's no way for me to call him back. Would you mind terribly coming here instead? For dinner? I'd love to have an excuse to cook for somebody."

It was after seven when the doorbell rang. Julia had changed, but was still in the kitchen, in her apron, getting dinner ready.

Adams made drinks for both of them at the wet-bar—bourbon on ice for himself and a white wine spritzer for Julia—and brought them into the kitchen.

He sat on a tall stool at the breakfast counter.

Julia poured a trickle of white table wine over the two trout she would be poaching. "I know this sounds crazy, but cooking dinner for someone is a real treat for me." She cut a wedge of lemon and squeezed it into the wine, retrieving stray seeds with a teaspoon. "We eat at restaurants nearly all the time—which I like, of course, but I have to admit that I pictured myself as more of a domestic person when I got married." She picked up a small container of dill and shook some on the fish. "Particularly since I'm not working. I seem to have a lot of time on my hands." She twisted the pepper grinder and watched the black grounds dot the silver skin of the trout. "I had to outfit this kitchen almost from scratch. Pots, pans, utensils. Herbs and spices. I can't imagine what Peter did in here. Practically nothing, I guess. Do you mind a little garlic?" Even as she asked, she dusted the fish lightly with garlic powder. "There!" She stepped back, undid the apron and laid it over the other high stool. "Ready to go." She looked at Adams. "I never asked you if you like trout."

She laughed nervously. "I'm not sure what we'd do if you said 'No.' We could order in. That's the other thing we do. Gourmet meals. Catered. I should be grateful. I am. Anyway, let's go and enjoy our drinks for a while. Dinner will only take a minute to cook."

She started for the living room. "I really must be wound up. Blah, blah, blah. You'd think you were the first person I'd talked to in a year. You must wonder if I ever stop."

She sat on the sofa, he on an upholstered chair next to it.

He smiled at her. "Do you have many friends in New York?"

Such a question might have seemed offensive to her. Prying. For some reason, coming from him, it did not.

"My parents lived here," she said. "My father had New York friends from before he met my mother. Even after they moved to a small town in Pennsylvania..."

"Libertyville?" Adams laughed. "I always wondered about that by-line: 'Harold Davenport, The Colony in Libertyville.' He seemed so cosmopolitan, I suspected him of putting us on."

"It was real. I grew up there. I remember my parents' friends from New York coming out to the country. We haven't actually seen many here except in a formal sort of setting. Peter encouraged me to call them. We've invited them to parties. You've met a few. But of course, they are a lot older..."

"My age," Adams said. "Gray beards."

"Even if I saw more of them..."

"It wouldn't be the same as knowing some people in your own age group," he broke in again.

She looked at him. Just as she had remembered from the party, he was almost elf-like—an aged pixie—in appearance. Short in stature. Large head and broad brow. His eyes were round and nearly black and his features craggy. He smiled readily, and when he did he seemed somehow to be helping you see the humor in himself.

Without thinking about it, she trusted him implicitly. Watching him smile at her, seeing his concern for her happiness, she thought of her father and of the times long ago when he had teased her into telling him about her problems, somehow making them seem to dissipate as she talked. She pictured her father in the woods he had taught her to love, sitting on the ground next to the little brook near the house, his arms clasped around his knees, while she sat on her rock and unburdened herself.

She shifted her gaze away from Adams to hide her emotion and forced her voice to be strong. "I'm O.K.," she said as she stared past him across the room. She rose, "Would you like some cheese? I'll be right back," and fled to the kitchen to compose herself.

She returned with a wedge of brie she had left out for a while and a handful of crackers.

"Vicki Vardaman, you know her, has been a great friend. Even though they spend a lot of time out of the city, she calls me, talks with me. I'm planning to go to an aerobics class twice a week. I'm sure to meet people there. And we give parties for Peter's business associates and prospects, and go to benefits, receptions."

Julia spread a few of the crackers with the soft cheese.

"I've kept in touch with a friend in Philadelphia, Rita Craig. She's married—I like her husband, too—but she hasn't been able to get away to come to New York yet. I'm working on her, though.

"I go to museums and galleries. I read a lot. I love fiction. That's what I teach—taught, I guess I should say. But I have a real weakness for biography, too. It gives the reader a kind of human-scale, intimate look into history, doesn't it? Life and times sort of thing, I guess. That fascinates me. And I play—practice, really—my piano."

Julia took a deep breath, and let out an audible sigh.

"Whoops! There I go again. Talk, talk…"

She held the plate out to him.

Adams looked at her. "New York can be a rough place. It takes time here to fit in, more than with a lot of other cities I imagine." He accepted a cracker. "So, you're a teacher. What about your profession?"

"I taught high school English, and courses in the summer to disadvantaged kids. I'm not working now. Peter doesn't like the idea of my going back to it. He says I could help him with his business, but other than keeping in touch with my father's friends, he hasn't given me much to do."

Adams got up. He began to walk around the room, looking at various objects, and back at Julia. "This place—I see you haven't changed it much—is wonderful. A little on the formal side for me," he smiled at her, and she felt further kinship with him. The impersonality of her new environment struck her the first time she had seen it, when any suggestion that she might soon be living there would have seemed ludicrous. Now its sterile message of materiality and propriety intimidated her. It was perfect, and cold. She could not seem to come to grips with altering that perfection, nor could she understand how it should be changed to transform its club-lobby look to that of her home, unless she were to scrap it all and start from the beginning. That, Peter had made clear without actually saying so, would be unthinkable. "It's marvelous, nevertheless," Adams continued. "Beautifully decorated. Well equipped kitchen, thanks to you." He winked at her. "Incredible view." He gestured vaguely toward the terrace. "Great location." He stood in front of her. "But it could be a prison to someone with vitality and imagination who doesn't have a sense of purpose, a cause in life beyond keeping it," he swept his arm around to take in the apartment, "in order."

"Actually, Peter has me use a cleaning service," Julia said with a trace of a smile. Once every other week, Julia stood aside or left the apartment for three hours while two burly men in white coveralls vacuumed, scrubbed and polished their way through it with alarming energy and speed, leaving her to level a picture or make a fine adjustment in the placement of a table lamp or an ashtray.

Adams looked down at her. "I hope you don't mind a little home-spun philosophy, and that you don't think I'm intruding, but I'm so old, maybe I can get away with it. Anyway, my feeling is that in the best of relationships—for me, at least—love by itself is not enough. Even if you *were* allowed to cook and clean house." He laughed briefly at his little joke. "Your marriage? Of course, you have to judge. That's none of my business.

"I don't know Pete well. I imagine he can be quite forceful when he has made up his mind. But I really believe that, as we used to say in New Hampshire, where I grew up, a person belongs in harness. Of course, working with Pete, if you find that fulfilling," he smiled again, "but I'm thinking more of something of your own making."

Julia stood, looking at Adams. Teaching, she knew, had been her "cause in life," as he had put it, as well as her calling—until she had married Peter. For a moment, her mind was absorbed by a compelling recollection of a recent telephone conversation with Rita. It struck her how similar Rita's message had been to the one he had just delivered: how important resuming her career would be for Julia's state of mind as she embarked on her new life as she had described it to Rita. "At least until you have to think about putting everything on hold for a while when you have children." Rita's voice had risen a little. "I can't imagine just dropping your teaching cold like that when you're so young, and you put so much into it, and you were making so much progress." Rita was not one for indirection.

Julia started toward the kitchen. "I have a little more work to do before we can eat. Please, stay here and enjoy the view."

"I'll keep you company, if that's okay with you," Adams said, and followed her out of the room.

19

DURING DINNER, JOSHUA ADAMS talked about Julia's father. "I don't know how big a following he had—it must have been considerable, I suppose—but I know I was a fan. Even a disciple, you might say, although of course I never laid eyes on him, or talked to him."

"I'm embarrassed," Julia said. "I was just out of high school when he died. He didn't talk about his work much and I didn't read all of his writings. He loved the outdoors, wildlife, the woods, wildflowers, everything like that. Conservation as opposed to development. He did take field trips on assignments, I guess, but most of all he used our home as a sort of local base for communing with nature. We were on the edge of state forest land and, farther away, a protected wilderness area. He was an admirer of Thoreau."

Adams nodded, encouraging her to continue.

"As soon as I was old enough, he brought me into this world of his. What I took to most, when I got a little older, was fishing. Fly-fishing, although I started out with spinning tackle. He was a dedicated fly fisher. I know he wrote about that. There was a small trout stream within a short walk from our back yard. He would spend hours fishing, watching the fish, watching me try to fish. Of course all the fish went back into the stream. To be caught again, I guess.

"I know he wrote columns, worked on assigned articles, did a lot of free-lancing. My mother kept the manuscripts that he saved, and some of the published articles he clipped, and tear sheets that magazines sent him. But she never appreciated his writing. It's not that she didn't like it as such. It was more that she didn't like it as his occupation. Once he began to write he never made much money, you know. I think it bothered my mother that it didn't bother him. Does that make sense?"

"I can understand where she was coming from," Adams said. He shook his head. "It must have been a terrible blow for her, and for you, when he died so suddenly."

"And at such a young age," Julia said. "Of course he didn't seem young to me when it happened—that awful car accident—but he was. My mother never really got over it.

"Did you know that he wrote poetry? It's beautiful. He was accumulating a collection for publication. Or at least to try to publish. Do you read poetry? Before you leave, let me give you his manuscript. On loan. I'd be curious to hear what you think."

"I'll go one better than that," Adams said. "I'll see what I can do to help get it published, if you would like that."

Again, Julia was overcome. "Yes. Thank you," was all she could manage without betraying herself.

It was only a little past nine when they finished dinner. She urged him to stay for a while, and served them coffee in the living room. They sat together on the sofa, their cups and saucers and a small silver tray with a few sugar cookies left over from dessert on the low table in front of them. Adams spoke.

"You haven't asked me what I 'do,' which shows how well brought up you are, but it's on my mind anyway, so I'll tell you. I'm a research scientist who has been dragged into the business world by his own avarice, and finds that he doesn't much like what he sees there. It's getting to me.

"My wife died years ago, so I can't burden her the way I used to. I've tried talking to myself." He laughed. "It doesn't work. So I'd like to try you out. Besides, I want you to know some of this because… Well, I'll explain later. But maybe business talk doesn't interest you."

"Please, I'd like to hear about it," Julia said. "It may seem odd, but one of the things that attracted me to Peter—I know we've come a long way since then!—was how competent, no, more than that, how powerful he seemed, how much in charge, when I saw him in his business environment. I feel the same way now when we entertain his business associates and prospects. It's exciting to me. Can you understand that?"

"Of course, although if that's the case, you wouldn't be very excited by me. I'm a lousy businessman."

"I don't believe you. It doesn't matter anyway. But I *am* interested. Please go on."

Adams took a sip of coffee. "Well, in a way it may be quite simple. It looks as though a few of my colleagues and I have been taken, and it hurts. I won't end up on the street, but a lot of what I have been working for, have built up over the last few years—my last fling, I imagine—seems to be going down the drain.

"A small group of us started a company—it was based in a rural area near Hartford, Connecticut—around some progress we had made in research. We called it TryCo. 'Try.' Get it?"

The name was familiar to Julia. Peter had told her something about the company. She remembered that he had found financing for them or something like that, and had been pleased with the results.

"Our first targets were chemicals to enhance agricultural production," Adams said. "We convinced some money people to grubstake us. Pete helped us find them. That's when I first met him. If it weren't for Pete, we never would have gotten off the ground. To help compensate him, and to keep him interested in us, we gave him some stock. So he became one of us, in a way. We asked him to serve on our board, along with one of our investors, but he declined.

"After that we were lucky. We hit on some solutions that sold well— licensed, really—to some huge chemical companies. International stuff, too. We all thought, hey, this is fun, but without our own production facilities, we weren't making as much on our patents as we could be. Plus, our investors, and Pete, too, I know, felt that we should be doing more research. All of that takes money, of course.

"The investment banker in New York we went to didn't seem to be getting anywhere, and again, it was Pete who pulled our chestnuts out of the fire. Or at least so we thought at the time. He found a company that was willing, even anxious, to help. But—and this was a big 'but'—they wanted to buy us out to do it. That wasn't what we had in mind at all, originally, but to shorten the story, we were persuaded. They would put in all the money we needed, they could finance our future capital needs and would treat us as a stand-alone entity. They said they didn't believe in fixing things that weren't broken.

"There was one other big 'but.' They said that they wanted to conserve their cash, in part to make sure it was available to put into our company, so instead of paying us money for our stock, they offered to pay us with shares of their stock. They would give us stock that at the time—and there's the rub—was supposed to be worth the amount of the purchase price. In the end, we agreed."

Suddenly it came to her.

"I met Peter at a reception at 21 Club that had something to do with TryCo. Later he told me about what he did for them, for you, I guess. I don't remember it all. But you must have been there, too!"

Adams smiled. "Well, I must have been, although I can't believe I didn't make a beeline for a pretty girl like you! As to what Pete did, if it weren't for him, the acquisition never would have happened. Which, as it turns out, might have been a better result."

He shifted his position, the better to face Julia. "Anyway, since then, we feel that they haven't provided the financing that TryCo—I should say the TryCo *division*—has needed. They moved our headquarters to Chicago, which led two of us original guys—not me—to quit. They're micro-managing me (I'm the president of the operation) to death. Other things. But the worst is that their stock has gone to hell in a hand-basket. Through the floor.

"Well, our original investors and some of us have nosed around and we think we've found that this company that bought us out failed to disclose some pretty important circumstances. Important enough that if they had told us back then we would have known that their stock was way overvalued.

"We're still in the dark about most of this, but if any of it's true, it's serious business, because they're a public company, and these may have been things they should have been telling their own stockholders about. But closer to home, it means that they out-and-out lied to us. Really, stole from us, because they got TryCo for a song, based on what we know now about the value of the stock they gave us. We never would have agreed to the deal if we'd known.

"Pete doesn't think things are as bad as some of my partners, and former partners, do. I hope he's right, because if they're right and he's wrong, my group will want to sue."

"That's terrible!" Julia said.

"It's a real dilemma for me," Adams said. "I hate confrontations and disputes, and I always try to believe—the eternal optimist—that they can be resolved without going to court. I think Pete agrees with me on this one. In any event, the whole business wears me out. It's bad for my digestion. And my sleep."

"Peter never told me."

"I'm sure he's got a lot on his mind. Anyway, his fee was paid in cash, but he got our stock as kind of a bonus, and he already owned some shares, and the stock of the company that bought us out that he received in the exchange has gone down, too, of course. I know he is concerned for us. I suppose that's one reason I unburdened myself at your expense, other than for the therapeutic value. So that you know that Pete has been a huge help to us. A real friend. Completely supportive. If something happens, a lawsuit or whatever, I want you to know that at this point we have no quarrel with him, personally. At all."

Mostly to show that she was following him and interested in what he was saying, she asked, "What was the name of the company that did all this to you?"

"Grendel Holdings. A guy named Marco DiNiro. 'Denny' to the cognoscenti. He was here when we met—at your party. Not one of my favorites. Certainly, not now."

"Grendel?" She remembered Peter's praise of Denny DiNiro, and the less-than-positive impression DiNiro made on her when they met, first at that same reception at 21 Club and later here. And there was something else she could not quite bring to mind.

She hoped her voice sounded appropriately casual. "Peter's mentioned Grendel, I guess. And I remember meeting Mr. DiNiro."

"Well, now we're all mad at those guys."

"It certainly sounds as though you ought to be," she said. She gestured toward the tray. "Another cookie?" she asked him. "More coffee?"

Adams stood up. "Thanks, but it's almost ten and I've got an early meeting tomorrow. I'm not as much of a night owl as I used to be."

"I'm afraid I haven't been very helpful," she said.

"But you have. You've been a good listener. That's all that the formula calls for." He smiled.

They walked together to the front hall and the door to the vestibule and elevator.

"Everything was perfect," he said. "It's not often that I get to spend an evening with a beautiful woman, but that didn't distract me from appreciating the dinner you prepared, or our conversation."

"Thank you," Julia said.

"I hope you still intend to lend me your father's poetry manuscript," Adams said. "I'll return it, but maybe you'd better send me a copy instead of the original. I'd feel privileged to read it, and I might have some useful contacts when it comes to publishing it. I might want to send it somewhere—but I won't do anything without checking in with you first."

"Yes," Julia said. "I'd completely forgotten." The truth was that she was still pondering Adams' account of his problems with Denny DiNiro. "I'll make a copy and send it to you."

He gave her his card. "Remember what I said earlier about your teaching. I think it could be important to you, and to Pete, for that matter."

"I will."

They shook hands.

"May I?" He kissed her on the cheek. "You're a wonderful girl," he said. "I hope Pete realizes how lucky he is."

While Julia was finishing in the kitchen, cleaning the pans and putting everything else in the dishwasher, Peter called. He was sorry he had not been able to get to a telephone sooner. Even then, he was in the middle of an important dinner meeting and could not talk. He had forgotten that the Crouch meeting had been on the schedule that Brenda had prepared for her, and so he had not bothered to tell her that it had been postponed. The man he was to see had been called out of town. Brenda would have known, of course, but unfortunately she was out sick. She had not been able to find a temp. That's why Julia got a recording at the office.

He thanked her for making Joshua Adams happy. In a way Peter was glad he wasn't there, he said. The old man was a complainer.

During their conversation, Julia remembered that the receptionist at Crouch had said that Peter himself had postponed the meeting, but in the rush of the call she didn't think to bring it up. After she put down the receiver, though, she was struck by the contrast between Peter's dismissive tone when he talked about Adams, and Adams' expressions of faith in her husband in spite of his concerns about the way he believed that he and his associates had been treated by DiNiro and his company. During this part of her evening with Adams she had felt that there was something she knew, had discovered much earlier, that might bear on his disconcerting conclusions. Now Peter's remarks served to arouse her curiosity about what it was that had troubled her as Adams was relating his disturbing story.

Before she started to get ready for bed, she went to the study. She looked for the Lucite cube she had seen on Peter's desk on her first visit to the apartment. She could not find it. She remembered that it contained in miniature a notice of some kind. "Grendel Holdings, Ltd.

has acquired..." the notice said. She could not remember the name of the other company. It was a German name; it was not TryCo. In her mind's eye she could see the tiny date in the upper left-hand corner. It was, she thought, August 15. But more important it must have been nearly a year earlier than when she picked up the cube during her tour through Peter's apartment after he had left for a meeting her first time there. So the party celebrating the TryCo acquisition, where she met Peter, occurred well after the transaction described in the announcement.

Adams didn't seem to know it, but Peter had been working with DiNiro long before he worked for TryCo and Joshua Adams.

20

ONE SOCIAL EVENT THAT Julia always looked forward to, even though the men inevitably ended the evening in deep discussions that centered on their common business interests, were the occasional dinners she and Peter spent with Rob and Vicki Vardaman. Sometimes the Vardamans came to their Fifth Avenue apartment, with its views of Central Park, but more often she and Peter ventured across town to the Vardamans' spacious duplex living quarters on the Upper West Side. This was just such an occasion.

The conversation about a trip to St. Maarten began after the delicious meal that Vicki freely admitted had been delivered by a caterer because "I've never learned to make my way around in that kitchen, and I certainly don't want to start now!" Brandies swirled in large snifters. Rob made espresso with a machine that gurgled and hissed importantly, to everyone's amusement. They sat facing each other on a casual arrangement of sofas and comfortable chairs.

At first it had seemed to be Vicki's idea that Peter take Julia with him to the Vardamans' villa on St. Maarten while he, with Rob's assistance, met with a group of international investors. "We insist," Vicki said to Peter. "Don't we Rob?" Then to Julia: "While the men do whatever they do to keep us in diamonds and furs, we'll do the island. I admit that it's not the liveliest or the biggest, but I know that when you were there before you were so wrapped up with Peter—to put it discreetly—you couldn't have done it justice. And whenever they," she waved at Peter and Rob, "decide they want to be with us, we *may* let them." She stood up. "Shall we drink to Julia's reunion with paradise? Pete?"

Julia did not crave travel for its own sake—to see new places, or for a change from New York City, which she had come to appreciate as a fascinating, if not particularly friendly, venue for her day-to-day existence. Consequently, she was not disappointed that Peter never took her with him on his trips, where she knew he would be as preoccupied as if he were at the office, despite her presence. Rather, she dreamed of basking in his attention for more than half a day or a night at a time, and of winning the opportunity to lavish hers on him undistracted by his seemingly omnipresent business concerns and obligations. She wanted him to break away for a while, to dedicate time to himself and to her, to be alone with her in every way. It did not matter where. So she tried not to betray her ambivalent feelings.

Rob seemed to sense her hesitation. Before she could voice any concern, he held a hand up to Vicki, and turned to Julia. His demeanor, never particularly animated, was unsmiling. Not threatening, but serious.

"Let me explain." He put down his brandy and leaned toward her as Vicki returned to her place on the sofa. "Of course we'll have time to enjoy ourselves, but essentially, this is going to be a business trip. And we'll be looking to you, Julia, to participate."

Julia was thrown into confusion. Suddenly she felt that everyone seemed to be waiting for some sort of response from her, one that she didn't feel equipped on such short notice to provide. She glanced at Peter, who smiled at her, but not with humor—more, she thought, like a studiously patient adult trying to encourage a small child to behave in front of company. Then Peter looked back toward Rob, and following his lead, so did she.

"I'm not telling tales out of school," Rob continued, "when I say that we think that Denny DiNiro seems to have great plans for you, Julia. He wants you to be involved, as all the rest of us already are, in helping him, and therefore all of us, attain an even greater level of financial success than we have already managed. Peter, of course, has other clients, other things going on, but sooner or later most of them seem to end up benefitting from his close association with Mr. DiNiro. Vicki and I have tied our futures to DiNiro entirely, with gratifying results. And now, you."

Julia's gaze had dropped to the intricately patterned oriental runner at her feet. She tried absently to understand its labyrinthine design, and Rob's message, neither with much success. When Rob seemed to be finished, she looked up at Peter. Her voice betrayed a resentment that surprised her as she began to comprehend Rob's meaning.

"So my going is, well, like a command performance?"

Rob broke in. "I know all of this should probably have come to you from Peter, and I've intruded. But he and I talked about it, and we thought that if I was the messenger, it would help convey the importance of your involvement to all of us. To the team, if you will."

Peter rose and came to her, his smile broadening.

"Well now, darling, it can't be as bad as all that. I told you before that I thought you could help me, and now you get a chance to help out all of us and our esteemed Denny, too, by coming with me and your best friends to a certain tropical (well, almost) island that I happen to know you are very fond of."

He pulled Julia up from her chair, encircled her with one arm, and raised his glass with the other.

"I'm with Vicki. Let's drink a toast," he called out in what struck Julia as an uncharacteristically boisterous voice: "To Julia and her glorious, and worthwhile, expedition with all of us to the magical Vardaman villa by the sea. To St. Maarten."

Peter resumed his position on the sofa and leaned toward Rob. The men settled into their usual after-dinner conversation, catching up on business matters of mutual interest. Vicki glanced at them, then turned to Julia. "Don't you think a nightcap for the girls would be a good idea?"

Without waiting for an answer, she picked up the bottle of brandy, took Julia's hand and led her into the kitchen. They both brought their snifters with them. Vicki sat on one of four tall stools ranged around an island set in the middle of the spacious room. "Actually, there's hardly anything to do in here. I was really looking for an excuse to get you alone for a minute." Julia put her hand over her glass, but Vicki poured herself a refill. "After that talk by Rob about DiNiro and our futures, and how you can fit in, and the like, I want you to know where I'm coming from about all this—about Denny more than anything. As you know by now, I'm not one to keep my feelings to myself."

Julia had begun to feel the lateness of the hour, and was not looking forward to the task of cleaning up that retiring to the kitchen would most likely have led to, so now, with relief, she perched gratefully on another of the high stools and gave herself up to listening to Vicki instead.

"I know that Rob and Peter seem to worship the ground that DiNiro walks on, but I can't help it. He bothers me."

Julia looked startled. Vicki countered with a smile. "Don't worry, Rob knows exactly how I feel and, no surprise here, disagrees. He says that Denny's been successful beyond the bounds of imagination, and that's enough. All I should care about is the bottom line. Well, maybe he's right, but I can't help how I feel, and I guess, in spite of what the guys say, I just have a hard time trusting him." She stood. "I'm not sure why

I'm telling you this. Because we're friends, I guess. But there's something else, too. It always seems like DiNiro's about to make a pass at me…"

"I know," Julia interrupted without thinking, relieved for a moment that she wasn't alone in her reaction to this man whose presence seemed to be insinuating itself into her life whether she liked it or not.

Vicki stood. "You, too?" She put her hands on the marble counter of the island, and leaned toward Julia. "I can tell you this," she said in a sotto voce whisper. "If that man ever lays a hand on me, I guarantee he'll get a swift, hard knee where it really hurts!"

She looked over at the dishes and glasses that were still piled in the sink, but contented herself with swiping a dish towel over the top of the island and throwing it onto the counter. "Rob tells me to stop worrying. He says that business is business. And Rob's right, we've done well since Rob's been in with DiNiro. Denny's done a lot for us. So I guess as long as he keeps his hands off you and me, we both should play along. And I do know Pete thinks you can be a big help to him." At that, she turned and started out of the kitchen and back through the dining room to the living room where the men were already standing.

As Julia followed, Rob's statement earlier in the evening, repeated now by Vicki, left her with a vague feeling of foreboding. What did everyone expect of her? What if she didn't want to help Denny DiNiro in the way they wanted her to? Or at all?

21

Julia sat at a round white pedestal table shaded by a large white beach umbrella set in its center. Tassels decorating the umbrella's circumference danced above her in a temperate breeze that cooled her despite the force of the midday sun on the world outside her sanctuary. The fringe swayed, then fluttered, on subtle cues given by the moving air. Beyond this gay distraction the ruffled blue-green waters of the bay in front of the Vardamans' villa stretched past small, hunched islands of gull-stained rock to meet a cloudless sky. The elegant house with its terraces and pool hung in the brightness like a solitary pearl pendant on a necklace strung with small crescent beaches and dark volcanic cliffs that lay on the breast of the sea.

She sat alone. The others reclined, partially submerged, on the steps at the shallow end of the pool, not far from the table. Their voices provided friendly reassurance of their presence. They were not talking to her, and she did not try to make out words or meaning. Rather, the murmur of their conversation, the ocean's dialogue with the sand and sharp lava rocks below the terrace, and the gentle blustering of the wind, blended to create a soothing tonic of sound that washed over her.

It was near the end of March when Peter and Rob flew to St. Maarten, before their wives, to use the house for a meeting with some potential investors who were involved with off-shore companies based there. After the men were gone, Vicki guided Julia on a shopping expedition in New York City. She insisted that Julia have a bikini, a beach robe and at least one stylish tropical-weight outfit for the trip, none of which Julia would have purchased without the other's prodding.

The women arrived on St. Maarten in a festive mood. They found that Rob, and even Peter, it seemed, were ready to relax.

Julia was infused with romantic nostalgia as she toured the familiar house and grounds. It had been less than a year since her life had changed so abruptly. Now, on this terrace, this beach, in these rooms, Peter indulged her fancy, joined her in retracing their progress through it all, and seemed to be amused by her sentimentality. When, at last, they were together on the bed in the guest room on the promontory over the sea, with the music of the ocean and its breezes in their ears, he too, she thought, was moved by the special significance of the act of love in this place.

While they were on the island, Julia, in conspiracy with Vicki and Rob, contrived that she and Peter would be alone much of the time. Yet the Vardamans—Vicki in particular—had become her closest, in fact her only, real friends in her new life, and she found that the social ambience of their presence was gratifying as well.

Her enjoyment of each moment there was such that she had become completely unaware that those moments had accumulated quickly into hours and days. She was surprised and dismayed when she realized at breakfast that they were to fly back to New York the following afternoon. Now, though, sitting by the pool, she drifted into a reverie, belied by her open eyes and erect posture, in which she discarded thoughts of future or past and became absorbed totally in the immediate, in all of the pleasurable sensations her surroundings offered.

"Julia?"

Preoccupied, she fought off this attempt by Peter's voice to intrude.

"Darling." He kissed her forehead and took one of her hands in his.

"Earth to Julia!" It was Vicki.

Julia recognized the greeting her mother had used to penetrate her occasional trances of self-absorption. Amused, she focused on her three companions.

Vicki smiled broadly in her surprising, heavy makeup. She could never have been fully immersed, Julia thought, because her carefully attended hair looked the same as it had in her initial appearance of the day, at breakfast, miraculously unaffected even by the persistent breeze.

Her shiny, metallic-copper bathing suit clothed her voluptuous figure more in a technical sense than otherwise. Those few parts of her that were denied access to the world seemed to be struggling with the flexible material for their liberty, pushing out against it with exuberant vitality. By then, Julia was no longer startled by the effect. In a sense, and despite a twinge of jealousy, it was comforting. At the start, she had been apprehensive about her virtual nakedness in her own, her first, bikini. In Vicki's company, though, her attire felt quite conservative.

Rob, tall but slight of build, seemed almost frail in his full-cut boxer-style trunks, and prim. He had dried himself, combed his hair and put on a white linen Panama shirt, his trademark. He wore a shirt on the island for all occasions, it seemed, except when he was submerged in the water.

Peter glistened from tanning oil he must have rubbed on before his swim. Residual droplets of water beaded on his shoulders. His dark skin was smooth but taut, gracefully containing muscles that seemed to lie in watchful readiness. Julia realized that she was gazing at him longer than the occasion called for and forced her eyes away.

The scene struck her as almost surreal while she struggled from her meditative state to rejoin them, peering from her shade to make them out in the harsh brightness on the other side of the table. Peter and Vicki, sitting next to each other, projected charismatic images to her. They seemed to go together. Bigger than life. Rob looked out of place with them, like a dutiful lawyer or accountant who had been forced by his client's requirements to be available for business in this decidedly un-businesslike setting.

All of them wore opaque, reflective, electric blue-tinted wrap-around sun glasses with racy lines and no frames along the bottoms. Space goggles. She found it difficult to relate to these people without being able to see their eyes, as if she were looking at them from a distance, and listening to their voices on the radio.

A gaggle of empty highball glasses stood on the table. Pinned beneath them, restless paper cocktail napkins were goaded by the wind into fruitless efforts at escape. Simon appeared with a tray. He walked quietly down the steps to the lower terrace where they were seated, cleared the table and served them ice in fresh glasses and more of the light rum punch they had been drinking.

"This O.K.?" Vicki asked. "Anyone ready for some serious stuff? We'll be having lunch soon."

At Vicki's direction, Simon left the ice bucket and pitcher and slipped back to the house.

Vicki faced Julia. "With us now?"

"It's beautiful here," Julia said to no one in particular. She turned to Vicki. "What a terrific idea it was to come."

Rob spoke to her. "We," he seemed to glance at Peter, "are setting up a new company. It will be an important part of our business. We'd like you to be its chief—really, its only—officer of record. You get a bunch of titles, but you don't have to do anything except sign a few papers once in a while. I'll guide you through that when it comes up. How about it?" He sipped his drink and turned away from her, to Peter.

Julia worked to shift the focus of her mind still again. Her eyes flicked over to Peter. She couldn't see his eyes, of course, but his look seemed to rest on her, his expression neutral, the way she had seen him with others sometimes when he thought he was not being observed by them. Quickly his face began to work into a smile.

Finally she said to Rob, "I suppose so. But why me? I don't know anything about your business."

"You're one of us," Rob said. "You're in the circle." His head did not move, but she sensed that behind the shield of his sunglasses he could not help looking again at Peter. "We know we can trust you."

Peter's smile was perfected now. He seemed relaxed. "It's Denny's idea. And you need to understand, it's important not just to us, but to him. But it's not a big deal," he said. "Nothing to think twice about. A formality, really. It's just," he hesitated, "convenient." His expression did not change, but he lowered his voice, his tone became serious, and he directed his words to her as if the two of them were completely alone. "It's a way for you to help," he said.

So, she thought, this is it—or the beginning, at least. How I'm going to help. What I'm going to be doing for Marco DiNiro. Her eyes found Vicki.

"Why not?" Vicki said with an exaggerated shrug, and smiled back.

Julia looked at Rob again. "I suppose you're right."

"Let's drink to it." Vicki raised her glass. "And then let's eat." She looked at her wristwatch that lay on the table, then rose. "Lunch is ready."

The others followed, but Julia remained in her seat, pondering the role for her proposed by a man she not only disliked, but found strangely sinister. Why did it worry her that she was being pressured to become associated with this man in one of his… What? Schemes? But is that what it is? Or is it simply some sort of clever, but innocent, business strategy the purpose of which simply had not been explained to her. Vicki, whom she knew seemed to have no grand illusions about DiNiro, had nevertheless urged her to take the leap. In response to Julia's looking to her, to Julia's hesitation, Vicki had said "Why not?"

As she gazed out again across the water, her eye caught a distant hubbub. A flock of sea gulls, startled by an unseen threat, was exploding in all directions from one of the rocks in the bay, a flurry of flapping wings. But they soon regrouped into ordered formations in the air and returned to their former perches like planes to an aircraft carrier after a mission at sea.

Suddenly Julia rose and strode after the others toward the house, and lunch.

"Yes," she said to herself. "Why not?"

22

THEY SERVED THEMSELVES FROM a buffet in the spacious dining room rather than on the upper terrace, to avoid the heat of the sun. Melanie stood by, looking after the food and clearing the table, while Simon presided over the wine.

Julia noticed on this trip, as on her first visit, that Melanie, while not exactly sullen with her, did not seem focused when Julia spoke to her. Although she could find no fault in Melanie's services at her behest, neither could she detect any of the enthusiasm that Peter generated in the other woman simply by his presence.

"I don't think Melanie likes me," she said once to Vicki when it seemed to fit into a conversation between them. "I hope I haven't offended her in some way."

"She's never mentioned anything. Besides, she's the same with me." Vicki laughed. "Melanie's just a girl, that's all. Like us. She's more interested in the men than the women."

When they had all finished eating, Peter and Rob, coffee mugs in hand, escorted Julia into the office which Peter was using as his work area, the same room he had used when he and Julia were there alone. They had already prepared various legal-looking documents for her to sign. Julia sat at the desk. They told her that she was to be the sole officer (president, treasurer and secretary combined) of the nascent company, Finance ServiCo, Ltd., which was to be based in St. Maarten. Vicki and Rob, both legal residents, and a lawyer, not present, who was a Dutch citizen, were the incorporators and directors. Peter's name appeared nowhere.

"But this isn't right," Julia said when she saw what was typed under the first place they pointed out for her to sign. It read "J. Vandenheusen Davenport." Her maiden name. Her voice rose. "My name isn't 'Davenport!'"

"We know," said Rob.

"Of course you know," said Julia, her voice quieter now, but still taking on an edge. "That's not the point." She looked at Peter, holding the offending piece of paper out to him. "What does this mean?"

"Darling," he said, taking the document and putting it back on the desk in front of her. "Lots of women keep their maiden names as a matter of principle. There's nothing strange about that these days."

As she absorbed his words, Julia was surprised by the seemingly incongruous image of Joshua Adams, his expression earnest and somber, telling her of his concern about Denny DiNiro's ways of doing business. Then she remembered her discovery that Peter must have been involved with DiNiro well before the events occurred that Adams was so concerned about. These thoughts, in turn, reminded her of the uneasiness she had felt earlier at her becoming involved at all with DiNiro in this way.

She started to speak, but Peter held up his hand, as if he were a trainer, she thought, dealing with a disobedient dog. It was a familiar gesture, and one she had come to dislike.

"You don't happen to use your maiden name *usually*," he continued in a soothing tone, "but *here* we need to differentiate *you* from *me*. Can you understand that?"

She knew he was trying, although without success, not to sound patronizing to her, and she did not want to confront him. She hated the way she felt when she got into an emotional argument, a fight, with him, and the way he responded. Her strident tone, and the cold rancor, or disdain, it incited in him, seemed to expose—to exaggerate—differences between them that she knew shouldn't matter. The disquieting aftertaste was always a sharpened awareness of a void that lurked for her just beyond the outer border of her love for him.

They had not quarreled this way more than a handful of times, she was sure. But for each there had been a point, a boundary, she could feel herself passing when the emotional content of her reaction to something he said, or did, to her reached an irrepressible level. Then she would, in a way, leave herself—watch herself as if from a vantage point apart, an audience to a drama played out by someone else over which she had no control. Her desire to please him and to make him love her because she loved him was overwhelmed by a need to express herself that suddenly seemed absolutely essential, and right. Then, always, came the regret.

So she said, "Sure. I guess it doesn't really matter anyway. To me, I mean. It just looked odd at first."

As she signed the various documents, with Rob guiding her through the process, the telephone rang. There was a separate line for the office. Peter picked it up.

"Hello."

Pause.

"Yes, good to hear from you. We're still on for next week?"

Pause.

"Oh, I see. Where are you calling from?"

Pause.

"That would be fine. Great. I'm sure it would be O.K. with Rob." He looked over at the other man and shrugged. "There's a morning flight that leaves San Juan at eight-fifteen and arrives at nine-twenty. I'll pick you up. Look forward to seeing you."

After a pause, "Goodbye."

Rob had stopped working with Julia and was looking up at Peter. So was she.

"Denny!" said Peter, exhaling, after he had replaced the receiver on its cradle. "He's in San Juan and wants to see me. Here."

"DiNiro? Tomorrow morning?" Julia did not try to hide her disappointment at the intrusion on their last day.

"No, the next day." He turned to Rob. "I hope that's all right with you. I don't think he would have taken kindly to being put on hold." He smiled. Rob nodded. Peter spoke again to Julia. "We were scheduled to do this in Chicago, but that's the way it goes. I need to see him alone. You go as we planned with Rob and Vicki."

"You can't come back with us? With me?"

"I'll come up after he leaves."

Peter dealt this blow in a matter-of-fact tone that annoyed her. She worked to keep her voice steady.

"If it's that important, I suppose." Again the edge crept in. "How long..."

"What?" Peter looked at her evenly. "As long as it takes."

She managed a smile. "I'm just disappointed we won't be together on the flight home. And tomorrow night. It would have been a perfect end to the vacation."

"So am I." His voice was gentler. "I'm sorry."

Then he looked at Rob and the small pile of documents in front of Julia. Rob was pointing to the last place for Julia to sign her unfamiliar signature.

"What a coincidence!" he said. "He calls, and here we are in the middle of putting together his company."

The two men laughed.

The following afternoon Julia found herself once more at the window of a plane that was to take her away from St. Maarten and from Peter, who, again, would be staying on. Peter stood on the edge of the tarmac. When the engines of the plane started up, he waved. As soon as it began to move, he stopped, turned and walked back toward the car.

Vicki sat next to Julia. Rob was settling in across the aisle, his briefcase open already, arranging his laptop computer to begin work.

The plane turned on the taxiway and the terminal passed out of sight. Julia sighed.

"It'll be all right," Vicki said, and patted her knee. "In a night or two he'll be back in your arms, and in the meantime, don't worry. Simon and Melanie will take good care of him."

Julia was not sure why Peter's staying made her uneasy. She knew she should have been used to his absences by then. She smiled to thank Vicki for her thoughtful words, but hearing Melanie's name brought back to her once again images of the girl's bold glances at Peter when she had been serving them. So, in the end, Vicki's effort at reassurance only served to trouble her more.

23

JULIA STARED OUT OF the window of the luncheon club's dining room on the top floor of the Equitable Building on Broadway, near the center of New York's financial district. After their meal, Archibold Strothers had left her to take a call. She was enjoying her time with him, a diverting interlude in what had developed as the uninspiring routine of her life since she had moved to New York City after marrying Peter. Still, she could not help wondering why he had summoned her to meet with him with such urgency.

Taking in the view, she remembered how this building had seemed to soar above her as she peered upward at it from the sidewalk. Now she saw that it was matched in height by many and dwarfed by others in her line of sight. Far below her, thin ribbons of streets, tiny vehicles and minute dots of human inhabitants seemed delicate and ephemeral in contrast, coexisting warily with the behemoths that stood over them. She felt as though she was set among a gathering of great granite and steel and glass giants that towered above a Lilliputian world. Of that fragile world, only the sharp spire of Trinity Church at the end of Wall Street, in the midst of its grassy churchyard, was prepared to challenge the army of monoliths, but from Julia's vantage point its bold attempt looked sadly futile.

Glimpses between the skyscrapers of the world beyond them were more reassuring. The Hudson River gleamed in the early afternoon sun, a bustle of ferries, tugs, and barges suspended in its brightness. The city did spill over to the far shore, in New Jersey, but there its islands of industrial and office buildings amidst a sea of landfills, railroad yards, and dingy rows of houses at least seemed to subsist on a more human scale. And the hazy wooded hills that rose up behind them and stretched to the western horizon told of a vastness of nature that even these ranks of man-made Goliaths could not intimidate.

The decor of the reception area for Strothers' office had been comfortable and understated, with a turn-of-the-century look: quilted leather sofa and chairs, a hardwood floor setting off a large antique Turkish rug, and a roll-top desk against the wall for the use of those who were waiting. When they met there, Strothers took immediate pains to put her at ease. "Please," he said, just as he first had urged her on the telephone when he responded to their invitation to their party (it seemed so long ago, now), "not 'Mr. Strothers'. If 'Squeaky' doesn't come easily, try 'Archibold'. That's what my business friends call me."

Before they ascended to the roof for lunch, he took her on a short walking tour of the area outside the building. The sidewalks and many of the narrow streets themselves were crowded with a frenetic, democratic hodge-podge. Smug, professional-looking men and women competed with secretaries, office clerks, messengers and vagrants for freedom to pass. A few clustered around the large, colorful umbrellas of wagons tended by hot dog and polish sausage vendors, waiting their turn for service. Others stood against the walls or in the entryways of buildings, eating from their fingers, talking with companions or standing alone, staring out at the passersby, seeking relief from the noonday sun. But most were on the move, many with cell phones to their ears or seeming to talk to themselves as they conversed through nearly invisible headsets, jostling and darting toward what they perceived as important destinations with unrelieved intensity. Like Peter, she thought with a thin smile.

Strothers took Julia to the front of the old Sub-Treasury Building, an edifice of classic repose, a Greek temple, small but dignified in the shadow of its soaring neighbors, with George Washington's statue on its steps. They visited Fraunces Tavern, a simple two-story red brick structure with yellow-painted wood trim, incongruous and small in the company of the office buildings around it, where Washington said his goodbyes to his officers in the Continental Army after the fighting had stopped. They sat for a minute in the diminutive park at Bowling Green, a gathering spot for the original Dutch settlers. They strolled through the cool neo-gothic majesty of the interior of Trinity Church and, outside again, into its quiet cemetery with its thin, worn tablets and modest monuments marking graves, some more than 200 years old, with quaint simplicity.

It was pleasing to discover these serene old places tucked in amongst brash symbols of modern financial power, holding their own there, surprising Julia when they came upon them around a corner or at the end of a narrow street. They intrigued her. In contrast to their surroundings, they conveyed a message she thought she understood: of simpler values, of a pace in life that was sensible and more to her liking. As they left the churchyard and headed to lunch, she felt a momentary pang of regret for the loss of those times that had passed so many generations before she was born.

The club reminded her of the living and dining areas of Peter's, and her, apartment. After they were shown to their places and the waiter left their menus, Strothers had leaned toward her. "This is called a club," he confided, looking around the room and then back at her, "but it's really just another place to do business. Lots of deals are cooked up here, and not a few destroyed." He smiled, settling into the leather-backed chair. "But I don't believe in mixing a good meal and business. That's what offices are for."

After this introduction, they had talked of her family, especially her father, and of Strothers' wife and his grown-up children from his first marriage, where they lived and what they did. When she told him that she had put her teaching career on hold, at Peter's urging, he had raised an eyebrow, but made no other comment. It was pleasant for Julia, and disarming, in contrast to her apprehension about this reunion with one of her father's closest friends after the words he had used on the telephone when he had invited her: "It is most important that I talk with you. As soon as possible." They had seemed to carry such dire portent.

She turned away from the window and saw Strothers returning to the table. He looked preoccupied as he moved in her direction, but from time to time he slowed to greet other diners with a smile along the way. It was an expression of his favor that flashed on as he approached each recipient and disappeared quickly when he had passed; as if for their benefit, by sleight of hand, he had pulled a life-like mask of approbation over his pensive, almost grim visage, and then removed it when it was thought to be no longer of use.

Tall, white-haired, looking completely at home in his double-breasted, dark blue pin-striped suit, he was impressive, intimidating, almost overbearing in appearance. She thought of Peter—how he had reacted when she first mentioned Strothers' name long ago at the Algonquin, and how disappointed he had been when Mr. and Mrs. Strothers had not been able to come to their first party. Or the second. The Medeas had received no invitation in return.

"Sorry, my dear." Strothers touched her lightly on the shoulder before he sat down. "I'm afraid I'm going to have to run off sooner than I'd planned. But let's do have another cup of coffee first." He motioned to a waiter, who broke off whatever mission he was attending to and brought the silver-plated coffee server to their table. She refused with thanks. Strothers took half a cup.

Julia saw that her time with him was about to end. In the momentary silence she leapt in. "We're sorry we haven't been able to get together. That you haven't been able to come to see us," she said. "Peter would very much like to meet you. It would mean a lot to him." She felt herself blushing. "That is, after everything I told him about how good you had been to me when I was young," she added quickly.

"Yes," he said. His tone seemed flat even though he smiled at her. He took a sip from his water glass and shifted his gaze to the window.

"I'm not sure he would find me very useful to him."

Julia reddened again and looked at the table.

He turned back to her. "My law practice has changed, you see. I started out as a litigator. For a long time I tried civil cases having to do with corporate transactions, usually ones that went sour. Somehow from that I drifted into helping put deals together. A litigation client got me into it, and one thing led to another, as they say. I built quite a good practice that way while my partners continued handling lawsuits. But I'm afraid I've drifted backwards. For a while now I have been representing companies and people who have been hurt in their dealings with others. Breach of contract, fraud, and so on. I guess that was really my great love all along. I just allowed myself to get sidetracked. So, you see, I don't have the contacts any more that I used to—that Mr. Medea probably thinks I have."

Still flushed, Julia looked up at him. "Please. That's not what I meant. Not at all. And it's Peter, not Mr. Medea. He's my husband. You haven't met him yet, but I know you will like him when you do."

"But," he seemed not to hear her, "there is something more important that I feel I must tell you." He leaned forward, as if to give his words added emphasis.

"Julia, I have truly enjoyed seeing you, how you've grown into such a delightful, and beautiful, young woman. I know Amelia will love you. As I said when I first talked with you, we both want to help you in any way we can—to be as good friends to you as I know your father would expect us to be." His tone changed as his eyes shifted away from her for a moment. "I do wish I'd known about… that we'd been in touch before you decided to…" He looked back at her.

Julia shifted in her chair under his gaze.

"But that can't be helped, and as it is, now, I find myself in an extremely touchy, difficult, situation. The reason I told you about the type of law practice I have been getting into is..."

He reached for his coffee cup, but evidently changed his mind, pulling away his hand and looking at her again.

"Because of my ethical responsibilities to a client, I'm afraid, for the time being, it is going to be impossible for me to be in social contact—any, really—with your husband, or you. But there are some important things I need to bring to your attention, even though I can't speak as freely with you as I would like.

"First, as I assume you know, your husband is working with a man named Marco DiNiro. And what I *can* tell you because it is historical fact, although my staff was only able to unearth some of this by extensive investigation, is that Mr. DiNiro himself has been the subject of civil lawsuits for fraud in his business relations with others, and violations of the civil remedies provisions of the U.S. securities regulation laws. In addition, in at least one instance he was charged with criminal violations of the securities laws. The lawsuits were settled out of court, and the criminal charges were dropped, apparently because key witnesses either recanted at the last minute or, literally, disappeared.

"Right now, there is a rumor on the Street that Mr. DiNiro is under investigation by the U.S. Attorney's office and the Securities and Exchange Commission, the SEC, for alleged new securities crimes—charges that, if proven, could land him in jail for a long, long time given his past problems.

"As I said, all of this is information that is available to anyone who works hard enough to get it. What's trickier for me to get into is that I have reason to believe that some of Mr. DiNiro's current business dealings may be subject to question—that is, on legal, maybe even criminal, grounds." He leaned toward her and fixed her with a gaze that betrayed his concern. "You must believe me, Julia. I'm in a position to know."

Julia continued to look across the table at Strothers, and to hear him, but she felt a numbness building up in her, a fear without knowing what to be afraid of. She knew she should try to remember what he was saying, to be able to determine his meaning later when she felt more up to the task, but instead she wanted to reject the words as he spoke them, not to hear them or, failing that, to discard them as if they had never been uttered. Then, too, they seemed to be reaching her from a great distance. He seemed to be drifting farther and farther away from her as he spoke.

"I don't understand." She heard herself try to span the gulf that was widening between them.

"I'm sorry," he said.

He reached for her hands. She pulled them back and held onto the edge of the table lightly with her fingers, the way a frail old woman might touch a wall as she walked next to it—not just for support, but to give her confidence in her own place in the world, in her own corporeal existence.

"I'm telling you this to put you on the alert. Stay out of whatever business activity he and your husband are engaged in. Don't get drawn in. Innocently, you could be hurt. I'm sure you've read in the papers of such things happening, a wife being implicated.

"Beyond that, it's important for you to know that DiNiro generally has a reputation as a rough customer. Ruthless. He could even have connections with organized crime. Not a savory character. I don't want to sound overly dramatic, but I can't help believing that he could be dangerous to anyone who gets in his way."

As she listened, Julia was visited for a fleeting moment by the image of Vicki Vardaman in her amazing copper bathing suit and opaque, racy sun glasses, sitting in the blazing sun across the table from her at the pool in St. Maarten, with Rob and Peter looking on. Again she heard Vicki's almost raucous voice rise above the sound of the wind and the sea. "Why not?" Vicki had said to Julia and shrugged. "Why not?"

Then Julia's numbness in the face of Strothers' words closed in on her, like a bank of chilling fog, its fingers wrapping around her brain. The distance that separated them had become an impossible barrier. She stared incredulously across the void.

Strothers leaned forward. "I really shouldn't be talking with you at all, but I feel I must, for your sake. It's hard for me to explain now. As soon as I can, I will. I wish I could tell you more. But I truly hope that you will take me seriously about all this. Otherwise, we'll worry about you, Julia."

She dropped her hands into her lap and looked at them. They seemed far away, too. She could not feel them as they slowly worked her napkin into a ball and then carefully spread it again, smoothing out the wrinkles as best they could.

"What are you trying to tell me?" Julia asked.

"The last thing I want to do is to hurt you, but I don't want you to be hurt either. You must believe that."

"I don't know what to believe."

"Please. Think about what I have said."

"Yes," she said. She was not talking to him, though, but to her hands.

He sat back. "Also, it would be a great help to me, and possibly to you as well, if you were not to tell your husband about this conversation. I know I have no control over that, but I am asking for that consideration."

Julia pushed her chair back and rose. "I have a crowded afternoon," she said as if to herself. "I must be going."

"Of course," he said. He moved around the table to help her. Before he reached her, she started to walk toward the entrance to the room, past the stand for the maître d' (he was no longer there), and into the lobby of the club. Strothers followed her out.

The express elevator to the ground floor opened as she entered the foyer. She turned and held out her hand.

"Thank you for lunch."

He took her hand in both of his.

"I'm sorry you are angry with me," he said. "You'll understand in time."

She withdrew and stepped quickly into the elevator. Her view of the anxious face of Archibold Strothers was cut off abruptly by the door sliding closed in front of her. The elevator accelerated so quickly from the eating club down toward the building's lobby far below that it felt as though its floor was dropping away, out from under her, and along with it, she felt, the secure, certain world she had assumed she would be living in as the wife of Peter Medea.

In spite of Archibold Strothers' request that she not do so, Julia's first thought as she stepped out onto the street was to go to Peter at once. He should know that people were accusing him with vague, threatening charges, mostly relating to his relationship with Denny DiNiro. Besides, she was hurt. Even though from the beginning she had felt uneasy in the presence of DiNiro, and she knew that Vicki did too, she felt violated somehow by the attack that this man, a friend of her family who had seemed by the end of their conversation to become a stranger to her, had mounted against her husband and his business associate. It made her feel weak and insecure. She needed the strength of Peter's consolation. But she did not go then. It would be an intrusion to walk into his office unexpected, and she did not want in any way to betray the nature of her concern to Brenda Thornton.

And she did not tell him when he came home from work that night, tired but still wanting her. She hungered for him and was afraid that her story would irritate him and turn his attention away from her.

She remembered again in the morning, but he was leaving early on a trip out of town and, she thought, there would not be an opportunity before he had to go for the kind of discussion that her news would precipitate. She needed enough time to explain to him and make sure he believed that she was simply passing on what she had heard and that she was not herself part of some conspiracy against him. And she decided for the same reason that the subject could not adequately be dealt with on his telephone call from a distant place. Besides, she hesitated to distract him from giving her the reassurance she craved of hearing him tell her how much he missed her, and the opportunity she needed of telling him how lonely she was in his absence.

When he returned a few days later, her conversation with Strothers did not seem so immediate, nor her need to convey its substance to Peter so urgent, although she knew he should know and she did intend to bring it up on the right occasion. Also, enough time had elapsed since then that she began to fear that Peter would wonder why she had not brought it up earlier unless she believed it herself.

So, in the end, she carried the unwanted secret like a small but vexatious wound inside her. Despite the increasing discomfort its festering engendered, she allowed herself to hope that, somehow, it would cure itself.

24

JULIA DID HER GROCERY shopping at a small supermarket on Second Avenue. It was a long haul, from Fifth Avenue across town and down a few blocks, but it was the closest place she could buy food and house supplies without conscience qualms about expense and latent fears of sinking into a degenerate, spendthrift, lifestyle. If she had talked about it with Peter, he would have told her to order over the telephone from the upscale grocer on Lexington and have everything delivered, leaving her simply to tip the delivery person and unpack the box of groceries. At the least, he would say, she should take a cab. So she didn't bring it up.

Instead, she walked over after breakfast on her shopping day—after Peter left for the office, if he wasn't traveling—carrying a fold-up cart and pulling it back to the apartment laden with most of a week's provisions in brown paper bags. She enjoyed the exercise and the chance to see the street life of that part of the city. She marveled at the muscular dance of cars and trucks jockeying for position no matter how light or heavy the traffic, eclipsed from time to time by the drama of an ambulance, fire truck or police car on a frantic mission, siren wailing and emergency lights flashing. Then there were the people: all sizes, shapes and apparent means, or lack of them, moving at a run, or at an amble, or not at all. And, finally, their dogs, of equal variety, some obviously loved, some respected, and a few barely tolerated, dragged impatiently away from a sniff at a hydrant or a rare patch of dirt so as not to delay the progress of an officious owner.

Different cross-town routes, allowed her to take in the ambiance of a variety of tree-lined rows of brownstone townhouses, small, almost intimate, apartment buildings and a surprising number of neighborhood businesses tucked discretely between residences and at the ends of blocks: Chinese laundries, shoe repair shops, narrow, high-aisled convenience stores, a hole-in-the wall "We Fix Everything But Broken Hearts" presided over by an old man who seemed to spend most of his time sitting in the well of the basement entryway on a kitchen chair, reading tattered newspapers. The front of a private school, really four townhouses fused into a single entity, or, depending on the cross-street she took, its playground, separated from the sidewalk by a tall, sturdy cyclone fence, always caught her attention. She was often tempted to simply stand and stare, to absorb the vitality, the abandon, of the young students, in their early 'teens or younger. Some lingered outside, near the steps to the entrance to the school. Others, behind the fence in the back, participated in various sports and games, or urged on those who were playing with shouts and squeals. She imagined herself as one of the two or three teachers who monitored all this frenetic activity, gossiping in a corner of the playground, or striding into the fray to settle a dispute, or helping to organize the choosing up of teams, or comforting a younger player over a scraped knee.

This routine gave her a window on her corner of the world that she cherished. Because she was there, she became a part of all of it herself. She came to believe that she belonged. These expeditions also provided Julia with welcome opportunities for casual contact and, sometimes, interaction with others. Check-out clerks, cashiers, sales clerks, the man or woman (depending on the day of the week) at a newsstand where she bought a magazine once in a while, and even passersby like herself, became anonymous nodding or speaking, acquaintances, as the occasion warranted.

Now, Peter was out of town, again, but for longer than usual. Still, she felt buoyed as she set out on her journey when the daytime doorman for the building next to theirs gave her the tilt of his hat and a broad smile in response to a wave of her hand as she walked north on Fifth Avenue before turning east at the next cross street. The first time she had noticed him as she passed, shortly after she began to venture out from the apartment when she had taken up residence there, she was impressed with his posture, tall and straight, and his obvious, unembarrassed pride in his uniform and his job. He looked Irish, with an agreeable face and a frank, open expression that flattered her as she noticed him following her with his gaze. Ever since she had caught his eye one day and smiled, they had developed a pleasing, if mute, bond of communication.

It was sunny and warm. Spring was deferring to summer. She knew that baking heat was around the corner, and along with it the malodorous fragrances of close city living, and health warnings to the elderly and the short of breath. Now, though, the atmosphere still retained a soft, sultry clarity. So when she returned, after she put the groceries away and folded the bags for reuse, instead of warming up a cup of coffee and flopping into a chair in the study to sip it while she finished reading The New York Times, she allowed the sensuous air to pull her back outside.

Folded newspaper in hand, she set out for Central Park, with its winding, wooded paths and its quiet places among the trees and rolling lawns lush with young growth. There she began to stroll. She came to a bench in a place that was speckled with shade, looking out on a bright patch of grassy slope that ended in a grove of trees. Behind these rose a line of tall buildings, offices, apartments, hotels, reaching into the sky, as if to remind her of the fragility of this tranquil outpost of nature in the midst of the urgency and power of the city that was now her home. Here she settled, laying the paper down next to her.

It was, she thought, just such days, at this time of year, that had been the worst for her in Philadelphia. Most of the time there, her determined regimen had successfully crowded out any awareness of the vast empty spaces in her existence. Her tasks and responsibilities had monopolized her attention. They had seemed all-consuming, first college, then graduate school, and finally the even more demanding schedule of her teaching. And, of course, caring for her mother's needs, and striving to anticipate her expectations.

Toward the end, her life with Nan, her mother, had been frantic and confining. In part this was a product of Nan's psychic and physical dependency and the jealousy with which she protected her access to every free minute of her daughter's time. In spite of Julia's efforts and sacrifices to please Nan and make her more comfortable, Julia had become the unwilling lightening rod that attracted crackling bolts of complaints and irritability hurled by Nan, in her frustration and pain, at the forces that had shaped her life and the cruelly inequitable gods of chance. There had been this and, simply, Julia's despair at her helplessness in the face of her mother's decline.

But in the early summer, while she strolled in a park near their apartment or walked along the Schuylkill River, the new warmth of the sun, a soft breeze brushing her skin, the exotic scent of the linden trees in bloom, the chaotic melody of a mockingbird's song to its mate tumbling gently over her—the rest of the world exalting in the seasonal process of birth and regeneration—would pierce Julia's armor of routine and preoccupation and flood her with a disturbing sadness.

She smiled ruefully. Now, she thought, I have no crowded schedule, practically no responsibilities at all, and still, in spite of being married to the man I love, the ache of loneliness.

After almost half a year of living with Peter Medea as his wife, she was often assaulted by the same feeling of longing that had caused her such anguish when she was living with her mother, or alone—not vague as it was then, though, but defined, focused, and therefore far more intense: a yearning for Peter that had become almost as familiar to her now as his presence, but this time almost totally unsullied by the kinds of distractions that her work had provided her in the past. This time he had been away for five days, and would be gone for another week. In Europe. Working to put together something for an unnamed client with international operations. For all his late hours and traveling, this would be the longest she had been separated from him since their marriage.

She closed her eyes. Peter was thousands of miles away. Yet she could see him as if he were standing close to her. She knew the touch of his skin as she put her arms around him. She felt the warmth of him against her.

Her eyes flicked open at the sound of approaching footfalls, not loud, but persistent. Someone running. A fair-haired man, broad-shouldered with a rangy-but-muscular build, was jogging past. She followed him with her eyes, his torso and buttocks powerfully revealed to her imagination beneath a sweat-soaked T-shirt and his skimpy running shorts, his arms and legs pumping, his body working to the rhythm of smooth strides.

Without thinking, she rose from the bench to watch him as he began moving out of sight where the path dipped. Just then he slowed for a moment and turned his head back toward her. Before she could shift her gaze, he caught her eye, and smiled.

Abruptly she turned away. Embarrassed, she reached down for the newspaper lying on the bench, still folded and unread, and began to walk briskly back to the apartment.

She had thought many times since Joshua Adams' visit for dinner of his forceful words urging her to resume her teaching career. To "stay in harness," is how she thought he had put it. She had pondered Rita Craig's many admonitions on the same subject, and Archibold Strothers' arch expression when she told him that she was idle. She knew that when she allowed herself to think about it she did miss the challenge and sense of achievement teaching had given her. Until this moment, though, she had been inhibited by Peter's distaste for the subject, let alone his predictable reaction to her acting on their advice. He had made it clear soon after they were married that he envisioned his wife as a woman of leisure, except when she was, occasionally, able to help him. Now, though, for some reason she could not fathom, the incident in the park had suddenly brought her face-to-face with a deep sense of loss to her psyche, to her own sense of identity, that was being exacted by her failure to pursue her calling, her "cause in life" as Adams had called it, her career in teaching.

She knew she had to move rapidly. May was surely too late to get any full-time summer work, but there might still be substitute jobs available, and time to find something for the next school year. She knew she should obtain New York State certification as soon as possible, to expand her options. Toward that goal, she sat down at the computer and began to search. She identified licensing procedures and requirements. She called the city school system.

At the same time, though, she decided to explore possibilities through an association of private schools she had heard about when she had first been looking for a job in Philadelphia. Its members might not require her to hold a state license to teach, at least on a part-time basis. So she set about tracking it down, too.

She spent the next few days traipsing around the city picking up brochures and directories describing summer schools and other programs. She learned employment solicitation procedures, and collected job application forms. She completed some of the applications and went back to the streets to deliver them. By the time Peter returned, she had set up exploratory interviews with two private schools.

"Why?" he asked. They were sitting on the sofa after dinner. His face was a study in pained self-control. "Didn't we talk about this a long time ago?"

They had, of course, when she had been dreaming out loud about her life after marriage. She had wondered how long it would take to qualify in New York. He had dismissed the issue as irrelevant and she had acquiesced without much thought. Now, however, was different.

"Teaching is my profession, my calling."

"What about *my* business? It's that career that's keeping this ship afloat. That makes it all possible. I need you to help me, Julia. I told you that."

"You haven't needed me all of the days, and nights, when you've been away, or working late, have you?"

He turned toward her and reached for her hands.

She was surprised that a smile seemed to be working at the edges of his mouth as he paused before continuing. Was he pleased with himself? Or embarrassed? She couldn't tell.

"Julia, listen to me. As you know by now," he continued, "before any social event I plan to attend, whether or not it's intended strictly for business, I find out as best as I can who will be there, and take stock of the guests. Do some basic research to see who I might want to cultivate as a business contact or who might lead to other contacts, and the like. Well, the reception at 21 for Tryco, where we met, was no exception. Remember, I told you then. That's how I found you."

Julia's back stiffened. She pulled her hands away from his grasp.

"Don't get alarmed. It's just that before I realized how great you are—even before I knew what you looked like, how ravishing you would be—and certainly before I fell hopelessly in love with you, I knew a little about you."

Julia smiled. "I like 'ravishing'." She folded her arms in front of her and sat back to listen.

"My point is that almost from the beginning I've had this hope, this vision, that you would become involved with me in my business, as sort of a partner. Not on the numbers or administrative side, of course, but in other ways. Helping me expand my contacts and keeping them active. The role Denny has given you, with Finance ServiCo is another way. These things are important to me, and they should be to you."

At this, Strothers' words, his disturbing warning at the end of their disorienting luncheon together, came back to her. She tried not to show it. As Strothers had requested, but not for that reason she was sure, she had not told Peter, and now she was not confident, after such a long interval, that she could explain her omission to him.

Still she had not forgotten. It was because of Strothers' expression of concern that she was uneasy during the occasional sessions that Rob Vardaman had already begun with her, usually after dinner at Rob and Vicki's or occasionally in her and Peter's apartment. Rob would take her aside and hand her Finance ServiCo documents to sign: minutes, authorizations, and even checks (all to other companies) in her capacity as treasurer. She took pains to read them and asked Rob questions if she had any. When payments were indicated, she knew that she didn't know who the payees were or why they were owed the funds that were to be paid out—she had to trust Rob and Peter—but on their face, the actions she was told to take seemed innocent enough, and so she complied. When Rob first approached her, as Peter had said he would, she reasoned that allowing herself to get involved with Finance ServiCo in the first place, before Strothers had talked with her, may have been a mistake, if Strothers was right, but that simply fulfilling her obligation once it had already been undertaken was in the nature of an inevitable consequence of her initial misstep. She had agreed to act as the company's officer, albeit in ignorance, when she signed the papers on St. Maarten. For her to refuse to fulfill that obligation would seem like an affront to Rob and Peter, a challenge to their character, a repudiation, none of which did she intend. Still, even as she complied with Rob's instructions, she could not suppress an undercurrent of apprehension.

Julia leaned toward Peter and took his hands in hers, just has he had held hers a moment earlier.

"Peter, I want to help you, any way I can. But I don't want to be helping DiNiro. I know I've only met him a couple of times, but I don't like the way he looks at me, and I can't help it, but I don't trust him. Everything that I hear…" She thought of her conversations with Josh Adams, and with Strothers, but brought herself up short. "Do you need to keep working with him? Can't you leave him?"

Peter looked startled. He pulled away from her and began to speak. "Hear? About him? Who…?"

Quickly Julia cut him off. "It was just a thought. Anyway, you sound as if you think teachers live in another world. As if I'm going into orbit and will never come down. It's just a job, like any other job. Better in one way. When I'm teaching I'll usually be able to organize my time away from the classroom to make sure I'm free when it's important.

"I'll always have time for my sessions with Rob. They're short, and so far they've been in the evening or over weekends."

She gave him a thin, twisted smile. "I'll be around a lot more than you've been recently!"

"It's not just that," he said. "It's image. You help me sell myself to a bunch of people who wouldn't give 'Medea' the time of day, but who might just listen if I come to the party with a 'Davenport' on my arm. And none of *their* wives even work, let alone teach."

Julia dropped his hands and crossed her arms in front of her again. "I've met some of these women you're talking about. Is that what you want me to be like? Their only job is to wear the right dress to the next party and not spill their drink on the host's rug. Oh yes. It helps to remember a few names, too. Their idea of an intellectual conversation is to critique the latest Neiman Marcus catalogue!"

Peter stared at her in silence.

"I really need something to do," she said. "No, that's not it. I *do* things. I read books, go to museums, galleries. I putter around, find tasks for myself. I practice the piano. It's that I need to have, must have, something more in my life. *To* my life. Something more than making work for myself, or staring at the wall. Sighing over you when you're gone."

Her eyes shifted away for an instant. "Getting horny."

She looked back at him. "I just don't see any role I might have with you and your business as taking up the slack. When I need to work with you, I will. Anyway, I have a right to a career just as you do. A challenge." Josh Adams' words came back to her. "A cause in life. A feeling of satisfaction."

"And I don't give you satisfaction?"

"Of course you do. That's not it exactly either. Maybe the word is 'accomplishment.' The kind of thing *you* seem to get from your work most of the time."

"Julia, let me tell you something," Peter said. "I would do anything to make you happy. You know that. My father worked all his life to try to make it so my mother wouldn't have to work. He never succeeded. Now I have, and I'm damned if after all that, my wife's going to work anyway! It makes it look as though I can't provide for you."

Despite, or possibly because of Peter's outward show of relative calm, Julia found that her voice was rising. It began to sound shrill.

"So my idleness is your badge of success?"

"If you want to look at it that way, I suppose so," he said. "My father was embarrassed. I would be too. I guess I'm just old-fashioned."

"Not 'old-fashioned'." Julia was close to shouting. "Antediluvian!"

Two days later, she accepted an offer from a private school uptown, in the nineties—only a bus ride, or a moderate walk, up Madison Avenue—that had lost a day-camp counselor to a broken leg. A few days later she had developed at least two decent leads for full-time positions with private schools in the fall. Meanwhile she would work on earning her state certification.

25

Low, dark clouds rolled through the summer sky, obscuring the tops of the taller buildings. The wind carried the rain to Julia at a slant, pelting her with large, warm drops as she walked across town and down Madison Avenue.

She had brought waterproof foul weather gear with her to New York, dating back to her college days, yellow, hot and shapeless, but it did not seem suitable for the city. And since it was just sprinkling when she left the apartment, she chose not to use the only umbrella in the apartment, a large affair designed for golfers. So she was left with her stylishly short, "water resistant" tan raincoat and a baseball hat Peter had bought for her when he had gone to a Yankees game to entertain one of his clients. These were not adequate to the task.

It was like being sprayed in the face by a hose. Her hair was flattened against her cheeks and neck and rivers ran under her collar and down her back and front and through the light fabric of her black leotard, chilling her when the water reached her skin. Her legs, sheathed in tights, were soaked to above her knees as the raincoat, short enough already, was blown up and around her by the wind. It was blotched with wetness. Her feet squished in the sneakers she used as walking shoes as if she had just stepped out of a stream.

After a few blocks, she had been tempted to hail a cab, but none were in sight. Madison Avenue's traffic moved one way uptown, so a bus was out of the question. She decided that she could not get any wetter and settled into a steady long-strided pace, virtually the only person along her route not huddled under an awning or staring disconsolately from inside a store front.

Twice a week now, after work and before dinner, Julia trekked to the second floor loft over upscale art galleries and antique shops in the mid-sixties for her aerobics class. She had discovered the place through a card she picked up from a stack on a counter at the hair dresser she had begun to use. Her hair cutter recommended it. He knew one of the instructors. "Brad. Tell him I referred you. Maybe he'll send me a bunch of roses or something." He paused. "I'd be more interested in the something."

Long walks in the city had been her only form of exercise. Peter suggested aerobics as more likely to keep her fit. He worked out on weights in a small gym in his office building and even in his hotels, he said, when he was on the road. At first, though, she took to the idea of organized exercise mostly as a vehicle for getting to know women her own age, or at least some with a few of the same interests.

As it turned out, it was not the meeting ground she had hoped for. The participants took their classes very seriously. They arrived just before the sessions began, unpacked their professional-looking aerobics shoes from their sporty athletic bags, laced them up quickly, and laid claim to the most advantageous location they could find on the lacquered hardwood floor in front of the leader's raised platform. Also, most seemed to be preoccupied with the other events of their apparently-busy days: when the music for the last set was turned off, they invariably changed their shoes quickly, threw on their coats or jackets, and reached for their cell phones, which had to be turned off in the precincts of the exercise room, starting to talk as soon as they hit the stairs to the exit.

At first, Julia had felt shy about exposing herself in her black skin-tight outfit. Her reticence fell away once she saw the others. They donned a blinding variety of colorful, revealing, designer costumes with blatant disregard for peculiarities of figure that surely must have been thought an embarrassment anywhere else.

Some, of course, had something to show off. They arched and reached and stretched and pranced for maximum visual effect. But despite the general enthusiasm for movement at the beginning of the fifty minutes, fatigue that threatened many, and a numbness to the blasting decibels of rhythm rock and hip-hop that must have afflicted everyone, acted in time as effective equalizers. Before long, none but a very few were standing out except the instructor. His or her energy, authoritarian manner and unfailingly cheerful demeanor, despite the rigor of the program, inspired, during the session, admiration at first, then a growing envy in some and toward its close an antipathy bordering on hate in others—whatever emotion was necessary to keep each participant actively engaged.

When Julia arrived, still a few minutes early, she dug into her thoroughly soaked carryall for a towel she had stuffed with her shoes into a plastic bag for protection, patted her face, and rubbed the sides and back of her head vigorously to get the worst of the wetness from her hair. She was sorry there was a mirror across the front of the room.

She would have to look at herself whether she wanted to or not. She sat down to change her shoes.

"Ms. Medea! A call for you! Ms. Medea."

Since active cell phones were banned there, customers had to rely on the telephone at the desk for emergency in-coming calls. So while paging for these calls was not common, it was not surprising, either. Julia, however, was startled. The only persons who could know her whereabouts were Peter and, possibly, Brenda Thornton.

The woman who had paged her held the telephone receiver in the air. Curious, and a little worried, Julia walked toward the desk in her bare feet to take the call.

She arrived at the same time as a platinum blonde, trim, with a generous bust, in white denim hot pants over a one-piece aerobics suit splashed with a Pucci look-alike pattern in electric pastels. The woman stared at Julia for a moment as they stood at the desk.

The person holding the telephone looked at them. "Ms. Medea?"

"Yes," said Julia.

"I'm Gina Medea," the blond woman said briskly. "I'm expecting a call." She reached for the receiver and began to talk.

Julia had noticed her among the Wednesday group. It was hard not to, with her stylish costumes, her bright hair and aggressive front. She was one of the show-offs. She seemed older than Julia and looked like someone from a chorus line—one of the Rockettes?—just past her prime.

After he had told Julia, before they were married, of his marriage, Peter had spoken little of his first wife, Eugenia Kviess—pronounced "kiss." Gina. Julia had asked him about her but did not press him when he demurred. "That's all behind me," he said, without further elaboration. It had not seemed to matter.

Vicki had volunteered once that Gina was a model for a department store and had made it at least as far as some nationally distributed catalogues, she thought. Gina had been a company-supplied hostess ("legit" Vicki had added with a reassuring smile) at a business reception where Peter met her. Their marriage lasted only a year. Vicki did not know, she said, exactly why they fell out except to say that Gina "changed" somehow and they ceased to "get along."

Julia returned to her station to finish putting on her shoes. Then the session began. It was eerie for Julia to realize that she was going through the day's exercises in the same room with Peter's former wife, someone with such an intimate shared experience who was nevertheless a complete stranger. Julia was in the third row on the right, Gina in the front row on the far left. Julia could not see her directly from her vantage point, but through the controlled activity in front of her she could spy on her in the mirror. Even as she did her best to follow the instructor on the platform, her eyes were mostly on Gina.

She was hard to miss. Technically she was executing the same routines as everyone else, but, magically, she transformed the mundane movements into a sinuous, erotic ritual. Julia was fascinated.

During a break, Julia checked on the weather. Shades were drawn over the line of windows that looked out on the street. She walked to one and peered behind it.

The blustery downpour had settled into a steady drizzle. People with umbrellas were back on the sidewalks, as was the display of fresh fruit on a table in front of the miniscule grocery store where she sometimes bought an apple to eat on the way home. It was loosely covered with a sheet of clear plastic. She decided she would walk back unless it was raining harder when she was finished.

She pulled away from the window to find Gina Kviess Medea standing just a few feet away. She looked at Julia with ice-blue eyes framed in heavy black liner and mascara that Julia had not noticed before, and held out her hand. She really *was* blond once, Julia thought irrelevantly.

"You're Julia," Gina said, her gaze steady, "Peter's new possession."

"And you're Gina," said Julia. "Actually, we've been married for quite a while, if that's what you mean."

"I'm sorry," Gina said, "I'm not really bitter. I got over that a long time ago. And I don't want to put you off, because I'd like to talk with you. Coffee after this thing is over? There's a place across the street."

Julia knew it—a small café with white tables and dark wallpaper, and a shiny, marvelously complex-looking espresso and cappuccino machine on the small counter near the front. She had thought of going inside more than once. Yet somehow it did not seem right to Julia for her to sit down now for a chat with this woman who, because of Peter's reticence, had turned into such a mysterious figure.

"O.K.," she said. The weakness in her voice annoyed her.

"I don't bite." Gina smiled.

Julia tried again.

"Yes."

"Great." Gina said. "Meet you at the desk."

26

THEY BROUGHT THEIR LATTES from the counter to a small round table in a corner of the room and sat on two of the four fragile-looking black chairs with bent-wire backs that were arrayed around it. Julia had forgotten to bring a sweater to the class and after she took off her raincoat, she pulled it back up around her shoulders to moderate the air-conditioned chill that seemed to be mandatory for all indoor public spaces. Gina unbuttoned the thigh-length, glossy white coat she wore over her aerobics outfit and left it on. She hooked her umbrella in the back of the unoccupied chair next to her.

"Well." Gina put down her mug and looked directly at Julia. "We're here! I'm surprised I had the courage to talk to you in the first place. I was scared to death."

"Why are you talking to me?" Julia had ordered cappuccino and warmed her hands around the mug as she met the other woman's gaze.

"To be honest, I'm not sure."

Julia's eyes dropped. "I'm not sure I should have come."

"Afraid of Peter?"

"Of course not." Julia looked up. "Why should I be?"

It was Gina's turn to glance away. She picked up a small box of matches from the unused ash tray and studied it. "I've been going to these aerobics classes since before Peter and I broke up. A true veteran." She struck a match and watched it burn. "Good therapy," she said.

She seemed to relax a little, which put Julia more at ease, too. As they sipped from their mugs their eyes met again and they both smiled.

"The instructors are usually good," Gina said.

"My hair dresser knows Brad."

"He's one of the best."

"I noticed you as soon as you started coming." Gina's eyes surveyed Julia. "There's something about you. You are, well, a nice person. I can tell."

"What do you mean?"

"I didn't know who you were until this morning," Gina said. "The telephone call. When I found out, I knew I had to talk with you. I know you've been coming regularly, but how could I know for sure whether you'd show up again next week? Or at all? So I had to do it now.

"The funny thing is, I don't know exactly what I want to say. What I should say. What I shouldn't. Particularly now that I know I like you. It's kind of sad that we'll probably never talk like this again."

"But we've only just met," Julia said.

Gina lit another match and stared at it as the fire exploded, then burned evenly, consuming the match stick. She flicked it out just before the flame reached her fingers.

Julia was drawn in to fill the void that threatened their conversation.

"I told you I had doubts about coming here with you." She swirled the milky liquid in her cup. "It *does* have to do with Peter, but not with being afraid of him. What a strange thing to say! It's that meeting you this way is sort of like sneaking behind his back. He hasn't talked much about you or your time together.

"Anyway, now that I know you better it doesn't seem as wrong to me for some reason. I'll tell him. Why should he care? We're in the same aerobics session. Why shouldn't we enjoy each other's company if we want to?"

Gina sipped her coffee. "I'm a model." She put her cup down and rested her elbows on the table gesturing with her hands.

"I know," Julia said.

"I started out when I was still in high school. Good money for a kid. All of us who were old enough had to chip in for the family. When I got out of school, I studied dance, but nothing ever came of it. Never made it big as a model, either, but it's a living. I quit modeling while I was with Peter."

"I'm impressed. That explains the great way you move in class."

"Thanks." Gina smiled. "And you?"

"I teach school. English, in high school," Julia said, "Or at least I did until..."

"You married Peter." Gina looked down as she spoke.

"Yes, until then. But I'm getting back into it, if I can find something at the last minute for the fall term. Or substituting at least. I used to do work with underprivileged children in the summers. Right now, I'm a counselor at a day camp uptown."

"And that's O.K. with him?" Her eyes searched Julia's face.

Julia shrugged.

Both women fell silent. Julia shook the contents of one of the little brown paper pillows of "all natural Turbinado sugar" to one end of the packet, then to the other. Gina took a sip of her coffee. Then she looked back at Julia.

"He's sexy, isn't he?" she said. Her eyes seemed to lose their focus.

An image of Gina the model, the dancer, writhing with Peter on the bed in Julia's and Peter's bedroom, reflected in the huge mirror on the ceiling, burst into Julia's mind, fleeting but vivid. Strangely, it stirred her. She felt hot blood surging through her, into her face, and looked away.

"See," said Gina, her attention on Julia again, "you *are* nice. You're blushing."

Again they laughed.

"I'm sure you'll be happy. Both of you." Gina's tone was serious. "I had my fling, but I'm from nowhere. My father was a poor German immigrant, my mother a Czech."

"I grew up in a little rural town in Pennsylvania," Julia said. "No place at all."

Gina smiled. "You're too much," she said.

"Peter's parents were immigrants, too." Julia pressed her. "Greek. He was brought up in Brooklyn."

Gina laughed. Then she looked away. Her expression faded to a thin smile. "That's exactly the point. He wanted to get away from that. To escape. I couldn't help him. You can."

"How about another?" Gina glanced toward the counter and the shiny espresso machine.

"I don't think so," Julia said. "I have to get back soon."

"But first, would it bother you to talk about what happened between you and Peter?" She felt her heart begin to pound. "Not that I can complain about the result." She giggled, and blushed again. "Is that a rude question? It doesn't matter if you'd rather not."

"Don't worry about it," Gina said. "The fact is, I'm not sure why, but that's one reason I wanted to talk with you." She settled back in the small chair. "There's a lot I could say, I guess. It's good you didn't ask me when it was going on. I would have given you an earful then."

"When *what* was going on?" Julia leaned toward the other woman.

Gina seemed not to hear her. "The thing is… It will be a lot different for you. It will be."

Gina fell silent. Julia thought she was finished. She was about to get up when Gina spoke again.

"It had to do with ownership, in a way." She was looking past Julia toward the window and the street and the rain that washed the gray day. "A time came when I realized that I belonged to him," she shifted her eyes to Julia, "but he didn't belong to me. Not one hundred percent." Then she stared past Julia again. Her voice lowered, almost as if she were talking to herself. "I guess some people would be satisfied with that. I wonder once in a while if I should have been, now that I look back on it…"

Finally she turned again to Julia. Julia's attention to what Gina was saying was rapt. Absolutely still, without being aware that she clutched a crumpled paper napkin in one hand and the edge of the table with the other, she listened.

Gina held Julia's gaze and her voice was firm again. "I fell totally for Peter when we met. When he hit on me at some business meeting he was attending. And that didn't change. I have to be honest: even after everything that's happened, I'm still trying to get him out of my system. I guess you can relate to that.

"But I really believe, now, that he just looked on me as a good lay— we were great in bed—and married me to make sure I was available when he wanted me. Maybe back then he thought that's what marriage was all about. Then he got tired of me, I guess, or began to realize that I couldn't serve his purposes. When that became obvious, it suddenly dawned on me why I was there, which was not easy to take. And when he got bored with me, or whatever, it seems like he just went out and found other outlets, you might say. Finally, I couldn't take it any more, so I left. By that time, I think he was just as glad to get rid of me as I was to leave."

As if she was waking from a trance, Julia's lips began to move silently, seeming to try, without success, to speak. But Gina raised her hand and Julia stopped. She recognized an annoying gesture of Peter's, but maybe because at this moment she was completely at a loss for words, she didn't seem to mind it coming from Gina.

"Remember," Gina continued, "that was me. And as much as I hate to admit it, I can see where Peter was coming from. Not that he was right to use me that way, but I understand why he did. What I know now that I've met you is that I'm not the only one who learned something from our marriage. It's obvious that he has, too. From his perspective, at least, it looks like he acted a lot smarter."

She stood up. "I hope I haven't told you too much. You did ask, and I did want to talk with you about it, once I recognized who you are. But I'm sure now that it'll be different with you. I'm not bitter about it. Really. It's just the way it is. You bring more to him than I did. Period, end of report."

As Julia rose from the table, she caught Gina's eyes on her. "We're very happy," she said to this woman who thought she knew Peter so well. She could hear that her voice was a little too loud. "We are very much in love."

Gina smiled at her. "I can see that."

They walked together to the cash register near the elaborate coffee maker. Gina fumbled with some bills she pulled from her purse. "My treat," she said.

Julia smiled. "Thanks, but I get to take you the next time."

"Sure," Gina said.

When they reached the sidewalk they stood for a moment looking at each other. The rain had nearly stopped and the sun in the early evening was strong enough, shining through the dispersing clouds, to cast faint shadows. Wisps of steam rose from the blacktop street.

Julia shifted her weight to one foot and swung her canvas bag in a short arc, back and forth. "I've really enjoyed getting to know you." She took a step toward Gina. "I'm going to walk. I'd better get going." She offered Gina her hand. "See you next week."

Gina took it, then leaned forward and kissed Julia's cheek. "Good luck," she said.

Julia watched the other woman. Gina did not look back as she walked smartly to the intersection and waved at a cab that had just let off a passenger. She climbed in. The cab turned and disappeared around the corner.

At dinner that night Julia did not tell Peter about her encounter with his former wife. She did tell him that she would like to have the mirror over their bed removed. She said it wasn't suitable for their guests to see and did not project the image he was trying to create. She supervised the workmen who took it down the next day. A painter recommended by the building management came and repainted the ceiling so that the spackling where the fixtures for the mirror had been would not show.

Gina was not in the class the following Wednesday. Nor the week after. At the end of that session, Julia asked about her at the desk. The woman there looked at the appointment calendar in her computer. Then she reached in the desk drawer for the enrollment book. Gina had cancelled her current subscription, she said, and was not scheduled for any more sessions.

"I didn't realize," the woman said. "She must have talked with someone else. It looks as though she isn't coming back. Too bad. She studied dance, you know."

"Is there some way I can reach her?" Julia asked.

"We don't give out telephone numbers," the woman said. Then she looked at an entry in a file in her computer. "But we don't seem to have one here for her anyway. I'm sorry."

Dejected, Julia descended the dark stairs to the street, turned up town, and walked slowly back to the apartment. Why, she wondered, would Gina be moved to make such a clean break, almost to run away from her, right after their first meeting? Then she remembered a fragment of what Gina had said to her when they were huddled over coffee in the little café. She hadn't thought much about it at the time, but now for some reason she found it troubling. She tried to recall its context. But in any event, she could almost hear Gina's voice as she was speaking to her: *To be honest, I'm still trying to get him out of my system.*

27

THE BED WAS STREWN with Peter's clothes. Suits, still on their hangers, a few neckties, and shirts, briefs, socks and handkerchiefs folded and in piles lifted from the drawers of his dresser. He had called from Boston to say that he had just learned that he would need to leave for Minneapolis on Thursday, after spending only one night at home. Would Julia mind having a suit—her choice—cleaned, and make sure he had shirts and ties ready to pack for what he hoped would be just a two-day turnaround in the Mid-West?

When she surveyed Peter's closet she realized that it had been months since she had taken any of his suits to the cleaner, except in one instance when there had been a spill that spotting couldn't cure. So she decided to use this occasion to take them all and start with a clean slate. She would have to accomplish this project in halves because there were so many. She picked one for Peter to take with him, and added half of the rest to it for the first trip to the cleaner. Before bundling them up to haul the three cross-town blocks to her destination, she checked the pockets of each for stray possessions.

Of course she could not see the stiff, rectangular paper objects sequestered in an inside coat pocket of one of the suits when her fingers first touched and then closed around them, but at that moment, she experienced a comforting sense of discovery and satisfaction. She couldn't remember the last time she had found anything when she checked before handing clothes over to the cleaner. These felt like things of substance. Finally, adhering to her ritual had saved something important from certain theft or destruction. Even when, triumphantly, she pulled them out into view, she was fooled.

Airplane tickets, she thought. Hundreds of dollars that he would have lost. Why hadn't he mentioned that they were missing?

In a moment she knew. They were not tickets, but vouchers for tickets that had already been tendered, used on trips taken long ago. One was for Peter, and one was for B. Thornton. Brenda. On the same roundtrip flights. To and from Chicago. First Class seats next to each other. In February, almost five months earlier.

Absently, Julia sat down on the edge of the bed. The suit jacket slipped from her hand to the floor. She laid the two vouchers, one above the other, facing up, in her lap. Peter had never told her that he took Brenda on trips with him. She wished he had. Then it would have seemed of such little consequence to have found these now.

She thought about the dates of the flights. What was the trip for? She shut her eyes. What did it matter? Still, she gathered up the vouchers, rose, and walked listlessly around the bed, out of the bedroom, and toward the study. As she moved through the hallway that had become so familiar to her she felt removed from her surroundings. Disengaged. And drained. She remembered the feeling—once, just after college, when she was dialing the telephone to make an appointment to see the doctor about what she thought was a lump she had discovered in her breast. And again, walking down the hall from the waiting room to his office. After a mammogram and an examination the doctor told her that she had been mistaken.

Julia found Peter's current appointment book where he usually kept it, in the top drawer of the desk in his office. She sat there, with the vouchers laid out at her right, and leafed through it. There was one page for each week. She found the right week and saw the entry, "Chicago," along with the times of departure and arrival, in Peter's strong hand. The dates on the ticket vouchers matched those on the calendar perfectly. There was no mention of Brenda, nor were any meetings listed, but there was a smudge where some words had been erased.

Then it came to her. This trip must have been around the same time of year when Joshua Adams had called on her. That was an event she would not forget: her initial concern about seeing Adams alone, and the empathy she felt with him after he had been there for only a few minutes. Peter was in Chicago then, too.

She thumbed through the weeks, starting with the beginning of the year. As she worked her way to the end of February, she found that Peter had been to many places—Atlanta, Los Angeles, Boston—in that short period. Seeing it laid out before her made her realize again just how much he was away from her. When she was finished she knew that during that time Peter had traveled to Chicago only once.

Brenda had not been in the office when Adams called, Julia remembered, nor when Julia had tried to reach her much later in the afternoon. Peter had given Julia an explanation. What was it?

She touched the tickets, moving her fingers over them, as if through gentle stroking she could coax out from them the secrets they had been party to. What had Peter and Brenda talked about on the plane as they started on their journey? What had they looked forward to?

That's silly, she thought. Business people take their assistants and colleagues of the opposite sex with them all the time. She had accepted it in others as a testament to the strength of their marriages—that their wives or husbands trusted them, that they were able to keep their relationships with their associates on a strictly business basis despite the imposed intimacy of traveling together. She strode back to their bedroom to complete her tasks there, then trek to the cleaners.

It was cruel, she thought, that he wouldn't be home until a day and a half had passed. A long time to live with doubt, however speculative it might be. To brood. But when she did sit down with him, though, and tell him her fears, calmly, he would explain. He would reassure her.

Peter did not call. Brenda did, late in the morning, to tell Julia that he would be home late, and should arrive by six-thirty or seven that evening.

Julia had hoped she would not have to hear Brenda just then, and she was frightened by her thoughts when she did, by the temptation to ask what city Brenda was calling from. But other than "Hello," the only words Julia spoke to her were "Thank you, Brenda" at the close of their brief conversation.

After six, she sat on the sofa, perched tensely at the leading edge of the center cushion, and waited for Peter to open the front door. He would leave his briefcase, laptop and overnight bag in the hall, walk into the living room and kiss her in greeting before he strode into the study to pick up his messages from his answering machine and his computer.

She could not think of what to say to him, or when. Perhaps, she thought, the passage of so many long hours of anxiety since her discovery—minute-by-minute it often had seemed—had numbed her, had dulled the intensity of her concern. Yet she noticed that she anticipated his reentry into the quiet, secure-seeming world of their apartment with the same uneasy apprehension that had followed her into the study the previous morning and looked over her shoulder as she had leafed through his appointment calendar.

Before sitting down she placed the vouchers in full view on the low table in front of the sofa. They looked incongruous there in the midst of the carefully appointed and arranged environment of the most formal room in the apartment, like ketchup stains, or blood, on a starched white shirt.

She stood when he finally entered the room. His kiss was perfunctory, but she expected that. He was usually still preoccupied when he first arrived home from a trip. What did surprise her was the difficulty she found in meeting it with warmth of her own. He did not seem to notice. Nor did he look down at the coffee table before he started to move away.

Her heart began to pound so heavily that she thought it must somehow affect her voice. "Haven't you missed something?" she called to him.

He turned. She gestured with her hand toward the table. He took the few steps that were necessary for him to see the objects there clearly.

"What?" He did not reach for the vouchers.

"I found them in your pocket before I took your suit to the cleaner. Look at them." As she spoke, she could feel the emotions of the last day and a half galvanize her resolve. She picked up the vouchers and handed them to him. "Here," she said, and stared at him.

He glanced at them, then looked back to her. "So?"

"What do they say?"

He slipped them into his pocket. "Why should I read them to you? You already seem to know all about them." He started away from her again.

"Please, Peter!" She touched his shoulder.

He turned to face her. "What is this all about, anyway?"

If his tone had been even, or even angry, it might have been different. But what she heard was an impatient adult talking to a foolish child whose questions were keeping him from something much more important.

"I have to know what's going on, Peter." Her voice rose quickly. "What was Brenda doing with you in Chicago? Or before? What is she doing now? Did you drop her off on the way home from the airport today?"

She paused to suck air into her lungs.

"You want to know what it's 'about?' One thing it's about is that I'm not going to live with someone who is cheating..." She stopped. "Someone who is fucking his secretary. Dear, efficient, officious Brenda."

She was shouting at him. "Is that what you are doing, Peter?"

Peter shed his mask of indifference. His face flashed into anger. He grabbed her upper arms with both hands. His grip was harsh, causing her pain, but she felt a momentary flush of relief, grateful that she had finally engaged him.

"Stop," he said. His voice was rough, barely under control. He shook her once as he spoke.

"Let go of me!" She tried to keep her voice firm, not to plead, as she worked to wrench herself free. Suddenly she seemed to have succeeded, because she felt his grip on her release, but at the same time she realized that he had propelled her, thrown her, into the sofa. She landed sitting, heavy with the momentum of his push. As she started to rise she saw that he was seating himself in the chair next to her. She sank back.

"Damn it, Peter. How could you do this to me?" She was distressed that her voice had taken on a plaintive tone. She rubbed her arms where he had held her and felt tears begin to rise. She fought them back.

"But darling," he said almost quietly, leaning forward, his face calm now, focusing on her, "I haven't done anything at all."

She watched him, crossing her arms in front of her.

"I remember the trip. Brenda was familiar with the deal we were discussing in a board presentation, and we wanted to have our own minutes, so to speak, to help us debrief afterwards. She took notes for us. She was really the only one who could. Did a great job."

Julia sighed. "There was nothing about a meeting in your calendar."

"You looked in..." he started. Then, "Well of course you did. You were concerned. I understand." He glanced at the ceiling. "I only use my desk calendar as backup. Sometimes it's helpful to have something written down, open in front of you, to remind. My full calendar is in my computer, darling. You should know that. And that far back it must have been deleted long ago." He smiled.

Suddenly she remembered what Peter had said to her about Brenda's absence then. "You lied to me." She did not raise her voice. She felt tired. Her anger seemed spent. She was hugging herself, rocking slightly, back and forth, on the couch as she spoke.

His eyebrows lifted.

"When I asked, you said that she wasn't in the office because she was sick."

"Did I? Your memory is a lot better than mine. I guess I was afraid that you might get the wrong idea about the whole thing." He paused. "Brenda has helped out a few other times, too. It shouldn't be any concern of yours, but I suppose I could tell you beforehand. That time I didn't, though, and when you asked, I didn't want to disturb you."

He reached out his hand to her. As she looked at him, she caught a fleeting recollection of a conversation with a receptionist at some company in Chicago when she was trying to locate him the day Adams called. He hadn't been there. The woman said that Peter himself had postponed a meeting he had scheduled. Later, he had told Julia something different. What? She moved her hands to her lap, one clasping the other.

He let his hand drop to her knee and squeezed it gently. The pressure of his touch through the light fabric of her skirt stilled her rocking.

"I should have had faith in you," he said. "I know that now. I'm sorry, darling."

She was crying when he stood and reached for her. She rose.

"I love you so much," she said. She wrapped her arms around him, clung to him, buried her face in the suit that smelled of him and felt his warmth through his shirt.

He smoothed her hair with his hand.

"I know, darling."

28

J ULIA AND PETER STOOD on the balcony of their hotel in Salzburg. They looked across the river at the dome of the Baroque cathedral and the spire of St. Peter's church where, Julia knew, Wolfgang Amadeus Mozart had performed and conducted his own sacred music when he was still virtually a child.

Peter had let Julia plan a short vacation for them around his business obligations in Germany. They had landed in Frankfurt, the site of his first meeting, followed by a dinner, in which Julia was included, with Denny DiNiro. Then they drove to stay in Salzburg for the few days before Peter, with DiNiro and Rob Vardaman, would be attending business meetings in Bonn. She told Peter that she would prefer to be with him in Bonn, too, but he discouraged her, saying that he would be totally occupied with the others and in other business meetings so that she would hardly see him, and, he implied, be in the way. Besides, he said, Bonn is "all corporate and government office buildings—nothing that you'd be interested in," and she should put together a sightseeing itinerary elsewhere that would enable her to rejoin him in Frankfurt for their departure for home. She decided that after he left for Bonn, she would stay in Salzburg.

As they gazed at the scene before them, they saw the fronts of a row of elaborately ornamented houses that rose above a line of linden trees that marked the far bank of the Salzach river. The roofs, towers and steeples of the rest of the town crowded in back of them and up the base of the mountain that towered above the town. A brooding medieval castle fortress on a shoulder of the mountain overlooked it all: a jealous old Teutonic baron keeping an eye on the antics of his pretty, flirtatious young bride.

It was early evening. In a few minutes they were going to dinner and afterward, at Julia's urging, to a concert at the Mirabell Palace on their side of the river, where Mozart had also performed. They stepped back into their room. Julia sat on the edge of the bed. Next to her, tossed there carelessly by Peter when he had taken his clothes from the tall wardrobe that stood in the corner of the room, was the jacket of the suit he was wearing that evening. It was the one Julia knew he had worn when he was returning from Chicago earlier in the year, with Brenda. Its inside pocket had held the airline ticket stubs. The thought rippled the surface of her mind for just a moment, like a large fish in dark waters rising to feed, then sinking silently back to the cold, gloomy depths.

Now she, not Brenda, was traveling with Peter.

To make constructive use of the pause between dressing and going out, Peter had picked up that day's edition of the Financial Times. He settled into a carved wooden chair he had pulled up in front of the open French doors leading to the balcony, and read. The summer air was clear and the lowering sun lent objects in the scene behind him a richness they had not enjoyed just a few minutes before.

As he concentrated on the world of business, Julia lavished her attention on everything about him: the intensity of concentration in his features, the strong hands that now manipulated the newspaper with habitual facility but that had the facility as well of giving so much pleasure to her, the hint beneath the soft, open shirt and full-cut trousers of his powerful body, not relaxed entirely, she knew, but rather, like a cat's, poised even when in repose.

And, like a cat, he seemed somehow remote. She wanted to enfold him, to absorb him as she was absorbed by him. But as she looked at him there, she felt, strangely, that she could not.

"What are you staring at?" he said. He spoke without raising his eyes.

She smiled wistfully.

Later they descended the carpeted staircase to the dining room. It seemed as though the rococo demeanor of the town had marched, or danced perhaps, through the lobby of the hotel and, with a grand flourish, settled happily into this elegant space. On the walls, curling ribbons of plaster appliqué bordered huge, elaborately framed mirrors with a delicate flamboyance. Heavy curtains tumbled from swags to frame high windows that faced the tree-lined river across a busy street. Two immense chandeliers flaunted slender arms that reached in flowing curves to hundreds of electrified candles suspended under the pale blue ceiling like so many stars shining miraculously in a day-lit sky. Above them putti, suspended in flight among the clouds, gazed down at the diners below. All but the painted ceiling and the shiny parquet floor seemed to shimmer in white and gold.

Julia stopped and stared around her like a small child walking into a wonderful toy store for the first time. They were seated and left alone to interpret the large menus. Peter picked one up.

Julia did, too, but soon put it down. "I can't get used to this place," Julia said. She tilted her head to take in the ceiling again at greater leisure. "It certainly is different from the restaurant in Frankfurt."

Peter peered at her for a moment. "I'm glad you got a chance to get to know Denny better, and vice versa. It looks to me as though he's quite taken with you." He smiled, and then returned to his task of assessing the offerings before interpreting likely choices for Julia (he had spoken German to the waiter, and so they had been given the version that did not include translations).

Julia stared across the table at the back of the menu Peter held in front of him. She was surprised by images from her disturbing encounter on the day of their arrival in Germany, with Denny DiNiro. She felt a cold shiver run through her entire body even though the air in the restaurant was warm, if not a little stuffy.

29

PETER HAD ACCOMPANIED DENNY DiNiro to a meeting in Frankfurt that lasted most of the afternoon. Afterward, DiNiro took both of them to dinner. He brought a friend—a svelte, stylishly dressed dark-haired woman, certainly not older than twenty-five. Julia was not surprised to learn that she was a fashion model. She spoke little English, apparently, and remained quietly aloof for the most part, viewing them as might any spectator to a drama played out in a foreign tongue, pouting lips and large eyes providing no window to her thoughts.

In contrast, DiNiro this night was voluble. Even though Julia had first been introduced to him at the reception at 21 Club where she met Peter, and later when he had been their guest at their first effort at social entertaining, which he had apparently underwritten, she had not spent more than a few moments with him on each occasion. Her impressions in both cases had not been positive, as she had shared with Vicki Vardaman, who herself expressed concerns about him. Now, for the first time, she let her eyes dwell on him. As she was already aware, he was a tall man, and heavy. His large frame rescued him from an appearance of obesity, but his face and hands were fleshy. His tanned skin was stretched smooth in its task of containment. The young woman was not short and was anything but willowy, but she looked almost insubstantial as DiNiro rested his arm possessively across her bare shoulders and introduced her to them.

His full lips formed a small mouth which seemed to stand in opposition to his apparently open, gregarious manner. The contradiction was partially corrected when it stretched into a smile, except that his lips had a curious way of curling over his teeth, hiding them, so that his open mouth seemed hollow, like a Halloween jack-o'-lantern or the maw of an old crone in a fairy story. She noticed, too, for the first time, that his eyes at those moments retreated into his flesh, away from the recipient of his attention.

"What an honor," he said in the lobby of their Frankfurt hotel. He took the hand she offered while his gray eyes, flat, impersonal, traveled over her with the same clinical thoroughness that had made her uneasy before. He bowed slightly, presenting to her his head of slick, black hair, oiled and thinning at the crown, and raised her hand to his lips, European style. Instead, though, of brushing the backs of her fingers, or not touching them at all, he gave them a full, wet kiss. As she withdrew it, she wondered fleetingly if she could wipe the residue off on something without attracting attention. He caught her eye, and smiled. His eyes disappeared.

They dined in a private club. The room was lighted principally by candles. The décor was modern, but its simplicity was warmed by the rich colors of the polished, dark hardwood paneling and deep magenta carpeting. The chrome of the furniture mirrored the richness in which it was set and glinted with points of candlelight. The flesh of faces, and the women's shoulders and arms became lustrous beacons of pale gold radiating from the velvet twilight of the room. Eyes were dark receptacles of reflected fire.

"Please," DiNiro said as they sat down, "call me Denny. Everyone does. Even my enemies, of which I have just a few." He erupted in a mirthless sort of laughter.

A squat bottle of Dom Pérignon was waiting for them, iced, in a wine cooler next to the table. The wine steward popped the cork and filled their glasses. But after a toast ("To success!") and a celebratory gulp, with which he downed the entire contents of his glass, DiNiro started in on a clear drink poured over ice, with a lemon twist, that he must have ordered before they sat down.

He gestured toward his drained champagne glass. "I love that stuff," he said to Julia, "but it gives me indigestion. This gin," he raised the glass with the ice cubes, "treats me much better." He waved to the waiter to bring another before the one in his hand was empty. "Peter never joins me," he nodded across the table, "but I forgive him."

As they waited for their food, then ate, DiNiro drank, ordering one gin and ice after another. Peter and DiNiro talked of business affairs. Julia was left to make conversation as best she could with DiNiro's reticent companion. The language barrier between them made normal communication impossible, so the two women were forced to content themselves with staring silently at the scene around them and trading uncomfortable smiles with each other from time to time. Julia did not hear or understand everything the men were saying, but it was apparent that they were discussing the meeting in which they had participated that afternoon, how recalcitrant the Hammerschmidt people had been—pig-headed really—and what DiNiro might do about it. Joshua Adams' name came up, along with others whom she guessed must have been with Adams' company. At length she grew determined not to be relegated to the periphery. During an apparent lull in their tête-à-tête, she plunged in.

"I've talked with Josh Adams," she said. "He *is* interesting, isn't he? You must feel lucky to have him working with you." She looked at DiNiro and smiled.

He turned to Julia with what she took as an expression of concern. "You were listening to our little conversation? Heard us touch on a few what you might call 'sensitive' subjects, I imagine?" Then his expression relaxed. "Of course. Why shouldn't you?" He raised his glass toward her. "This is the first time we've been together like this, and I forgot to welcome you as a member of our little team. To Julia. One of us!" He took a substantial swallow. Ice must have blocked and dispersed the liquid in his glass when he tilted it, because some dribbled off his chin and onto the front of his shirt. He dabbed at the dampness with his napkin as he glanced at Peter. She saw him compress his left eye in an elaborate wink. Peter's expression seemed frozen in neutrality. His eyes alone moved, from DiNiro to Julia and back again, but they conveyed no message to her that she had the power to read. Then he reached for his glass of champagne and raised it, without drinking from it, but finally responding to DiNiro's look with a smile.

"In any event, my dear," DiNiro took still another large draft from what seemed to her to be his third or fourth gin and ice and wiped his mouth with his napkin, "I'm not sure how long Adams will be working with us." He glanced again toward Peter and his expression seemed to harden. "As I've told Peter, here, often enough, I should have gotten rid of that man before he started to become so troublesome."

"Get rid of him?" Julia tried to mask her surprise. "What do you mean?" At the same time she noticed Peter out of the corner of her eye looking at DiNiro with a new intensity, shaking his head slightly, but firmly.

DiNiro turned back to Julia, his face relaxed once more, and smiled. "Just a manner of speaking my dear," he said, "but Mr. Adams has become a problem."

"It's such a shame, too." He settled back in his chair and reached still again for his drink, a new one even though the other glass was still almost half full. "We took good care of Joshua Adams." He laughed and held a smile as his eyes shifted away from her for an instant. "Didn't we, Peter?" The black shadow in his seemingly toothless mouth and the slits where his eyes had been looked macabre in the yellow light. "As it turned out, things didn't go quite the way he had hoped. I'm not sure he appreciates us now. Here he is in business—a businessman—but he doesn't seem to understand that in business, life doesn't always treat you fairly. Treat you the way you want. And that in business, a person, each of us, has to look out for himself. I have to admit, things were rigged against him a little," he laughed and again looked in Peter's direction, "but still, he's just not being a good sport. As you might have guessed by now, I'm a little put out with him, to be truthful."

He leaned toward Julia. "And one thing you'll find out about me sooner or later: I am very good to my friends, but very hard on my enemies. On people who get in my way." At that instant it came to her that Archibold Strothers had used practically the same words to warn her against getting involved with this man. Then DiNiro's voice took on a harsher tone. "Very hard." At that he slapped the palm of his free hand down on the table, causing a thump that might have turned heads. But Julia did not look away to find out. She was suddenly transfixed by the change that seemed to have come over him. He looked to be agitated, almost enraged by the image he had conjured up of such a person. Perhaps of Joshua Adams. "So if you're smart, you'll stay on the right side of Denny DiNiro, my dear." His voice moderated a little as he spoke these words, but his look into Julia's eyes, over the glass he was raising to his lips, was steady, almost threatening, she thought. Then he bestowed his elaborate wink on her, smiled once more, and turned back to Peter to resume their conversation.

By the time they were finished eating it was nine-thirty, which was not late by continental standards, or even by Julia's under most circumstances. But this was Julia's and Peter's first day. They had disembarked from the airplane early that morning after what had been, for Julia, a nearly sleepless night. Peter showed no signs of fatigue, but the combination of wine, rich food, the comfortable chair and the dimly lit ambience seemed to shift an almost irresistible weight onto Julia's eyelids. She fought to keep them from closing, and herself from plunging into the sleep that by this time she strongly thought she deserved. So, when DiNiro rose, she felt a surge of gratitude and relief. She pushed back her chair and started to stand, too.

DiNiro raised his hand in the same gesture of control that she found disconcerting in Peter. She half-expected him to command: Stay!

"Please," he said instead, looking at Julia, "we must celebrate your joining us, and our first opportunity to get to know you," he tipped his head in a little bow, "with some cognac. Meanwhile, I shall return in a moment."

His gait was ponderous as he walked away. He seemed to need to concentrate carefully on the location for each footfall, depending on the accuracy of his step to keep his balance. By the time he reappeared, his three guests had been served snifters of Remy Martin. The bottle stood on a round silver tray next to DiNiro's place. But for him, still another frosty gin over ice awaited his return.

He sat heavily. Relaxed, his large frame seemed to fill out as his flesh settled, like rice in a giant gunny sack. He reached out below the edge of the table and his meaty hand came to rest on Julia's leg, well above her knee. She could feel the humid heat through the sheer silk of her dress and steeled herself against wincing or pulling away. He leaned toward her.

"Julia, my dear," he said, patting her once with the offending hand, then leaving it where it lay, "I want to thank you for something."

Julia glanced at DiNiro's female companion who seemed to be staring into the middle distance during the entire conversation.

"The girl? She can't understand a word we're saying." DiNiro turned to her. "Greta?" The young woman's eyes moved to him and seemed to come back into focus. DiNiro talked to her in soothing tones. "Do you know what the fuck we're talking about?" The woman offered a tentative smile back.

DiNiro grinned. As he leaned even closer to Julia, his eyes scuttled into hiding, like two snakes that preferred to strike from the dark safety of the rocky crevices where they lived. She felt an added pressure from his fingers on her flesh through her dress.

"I want to thank you for helping to make me rich."

He broke into a slow, lumbering laugh that must have again attracted the attention of the other diners in a room where the general conversation created a sound no louder than a quiet hum. Julia dropped her eyes, forcing herself not to focus on the hand that rested on her leg.

"Eh, Peter?"

"She doesn't know, Denny," Peter said. "Perhaps..."

"Well, that's hardly fair, is it? How can I thank her properly if she doesn't know what she's doing?" He laughed again.

Julia shifted her position, crossing her legs. Forced to move his chair closer if he was to keep his grip on her, DiNiro withdrew his hand and straightened.

"I'm not sure I know what you're talking about," she said, trying to avoid anything in her tone that would reflect her annoyance.

"Of course not," DiNiro said, his humor apparently undiminished. He finished off his drink, tilting his glass high. Again ice cubes tumbled against his mouth, and the liquid overflowed the rim of the glass at the edges, splashing down, this time staining his wide silk necktie with dark, wet blotches. He did not seem to notice. "And Peter's trying his best, without words, to tell me not to enlighten you. So to make him happy, I suppose I won't."

"But I must at least let you know that your company, Finance ServiCo, has been extremely useful to me, personally. A resource. It makes money for me—for us, you might say—without really doing a thing, even though it appears otherwise. And it wouldn't be possible without your doing such an exemplary job as its president and treasurer. *Especially* as treasurer!" He glanced at Peter and emitted a quick explosion of laughter. "It may seem like magic, but it isn't. No. Not magic at all. It's taken a lot of work, and you, my dear, have helped."

DiNiro wagged a finger in Julia's face. "I'm going to make sure that Peter rewards you accordingly." He leaned toward her again and put his hand to his mouth as if to shield the others from hearing, but without lowering his voice. "You are a beautiful girl, my dear, and I would reward you myself, in my own way," he winked at her again, "but I think Peter would get terribly angry with me if I did." He sat back and laughed until tears gushed from the creases of his eyes and washed down his cheeks.

After dinner, they returned to Julia's and Peter's hotel in DiNiro's hired Mercedes limousine. On their arrival, when the driver opened the door, Julia and Peter climbed out and DiNiro followed, steadying himself by placing a hand on the driver's shoulder before shaking hands with Peter. Then he slapped Peter heavily on the back, and turned to Julia.

"Thank you," she said quietly, making a conscious effort to meet his eyes. She extended her hand.

He ignored the gesture, but instead reached out with both hands and held her by her shoulders. His eyes darted through another quick survey. "You *are* nice, my dear," he said. "I'm sorry we hadn't really gotten to know each other until tonight." He glanced at Peter. "I feel now as if we are old friends." Then he stepped closer and kissed her on her mouth.

Julia was too surprised to do anything that would embarrass Peter as it was happening, but when DiNiro turned away from her for a moment she wiped away the wetness of his kiss from her lips with the back of her hand.

The limousine door remained open, and while DiNiro said a last word to Peter, Julia leaned down to look in. The young woman remained sitting there, pressed back into the corner where she had been forced by their crowding in for the drive to the hotel. In the shadows, with her large, wide eyes and elegant bone structure, she looked like some sort of hunted animal. A delicate doe, gone to ground.

"Good night," Julia said to her, and smiled. A response flickered across the other's face before she disappeared when DiNiro pushed past Julia and slumped heavily into the car. "And good luck," Julia said, almost to herself, as the driver stepped in front of her and closed the door.

The car's occupants merged into a dark bulk behind the heavily tinted glass. It pulled away from the curb and sped off around the circle in front of the hotel and out of sight.

30

Focusing again, Julia looked across their table, past the small vase of fresh flowers, at Peter. "DiNiro is a horrible person."

He seemed to ignore her. His eyes did not leave the menu.

Julia shook her head. "I know he's important to you, but the way he kissed me. And the scared look on that poor girl's face."

Peter looked up and smiled. "I'm sure she isn't 'poor,' and if she is, she'll be a lot less so if she keeps in Denny's good graces for a while."

"You know I'm not talking about money."

"Maybe she thinks he's delightful company. Anyway, she probably cut a deal with him beforehand. Besides, Denny isn't so bad."

"You actually *like* him. I still can't believe it!"

Peter cocked his head. "I told you. In some ways, he is my type of man. Knows what he wants. Goes for it. Doesn't let things, or people, get in his way."

"Well, I think he's sinister. What did he mean about wanting to 'get rid' of Josh Adams? And then the way he talked to me. Threatened me."

"Don't worry." Peter's expression was serious. "You're safe from Denny as long as you stick with me." Then a smile formed on Peter's lips. "Besides, you shouldn't take things so literally. I'm sure that Denny's bark is much worse than his bite. But he does have to be tough, and it's important in the kind of dealings he gets involved in to have an image that matches. Appearances do count, believe me."

"What kind of dealings? And why is he so down on Adams?"

"Adams has become something of a pain. Maybe Denny's going to do something about it."

"Isn't Adams your client?" Julia said. "Can't you help him in some way?"

"He was, but he isn't any more. He's just an employee of Denny's now. Or former employee. After what Denny said. I'm not sure which."

"But isn't he your friend?"

"He talks too much," Peter said. "He's a bore. And he's pushing Denny. That's not smart. I admit I made some good money off his company, TryCo, for awhile, but that's past."

151

It wasn't until she had mentioned Adams to DiNiro at dinner in Frankfurt that she recalled how angry Adams had been with DiNiro during their talk in the apartment. But he hadn't blamed Peter.

"You've been working with Denny for a long time."

"A lot longer than Adams!" His eyes shifted back to the menu again.

"Really?" She remembered discovering that before, after Josh Adams had left her that earlier evening. She wondered again if Adams knew. "I wish you weren't."

He gave her a quizzical look. "Weren't what?"

"Working for DiNiro."

"Hey." He turned his attention back to the menu. "Why is Adams so important to you all of a sudden? Or DiNiro, for that matter? We have a concert to go to. Don't you want me to explain some of this stuff to you so we can order?"

Despite his abruptness, Julia was grateful to be diverted. "Thanks. I wouldn't want to embarrass you by bringing out my phrase book." She laughed. He looked up and smiled.

The concert program was short. It was not late when they stopped at a nearby café for dessert. Then they walked back.

The summer air was cool. A low, waning moon hovered behind a tenuous curtain of clouds. Its light seemed to envelope the town, replacing the substance of reality with ghostly forms cast in paleness and deep shade. The gray bulk of the hotel, its façade brightly lighted, greeted them as they made the last turn before their arrival.

When they entered their room, Julia opened the doors to the balcony and gazed across the river. The indistinct jumble of treetops, roofs and spires seemed threatened by the mountain's gloomy presence, about to be consumed by its black shadow.

She turned back to Peter. Clung to him. Burrowed against him for his warmth, seeking the reassurance of his strength.

The eerie pale light from the veiled moon penetrated into the intimate recesses of the room, and in that uneasy glow, they made love.

31

JULIA WAS LOST DEEP in early slumber when the telephone rang. "I'll get it." Peter's voice sounded quickly from the darkness.

But the telephone was nearest to her. Before she was fully awake she reached to turn on the table lamp and at the same time picked up the receiver.

"Hello?" Her voice was husky with sleep. Struggling to clear her mind, she tried to ready herself for the task of translating the reply. None came. She decided to hand the problem over to Peter, who spoke German fluently. Just then she heard a voice on the other end of the wire.

"Hello. Julia?"

She recognized it at once and kept the receiver.

"Vicki!" she said.

"It's late," Vicki said. "I tried to reach you earlier, but you were out."

"You didn't leave a message, did you?" Julia glanced at Peter, but he was already climbing out of bed and did not look at her. Vicki said nothing, so Julia rushed ahead. "Anyway, your voice is so clear. You sound as though you're in the room next door, or at least here in Salzburg with us. Are you going to be in Bonn with Rob?"

Vicki did not respond immediately. Then she said, "I need to pass something on to Peter. I'm afraid it might disrupt your plans a little. I'm sorry. Could I speak with him for a minute? I promise I won't be long."

"Of course." Vicki's words caused Julia a pang of disappointment. She motioned to Peter, who by now was sitting on the edge of her side of the bed. The air was chill, and he had wrapped his robe around himself. "We've had a great time. I'll tell you all about it when we get back."

Peter took the receiver from her, cutting her off from saying good-bye to her friend, and began his own conversation with Vicki, cryptic in his concise responses to whatever Vicki was telling him.

Julia lay down, curled herself around him as he sat, and closed her eyes. Through the silk material of his robe she felt the warmth of his nakedness on her thighs and stomach. As he spoke, she reached inside its folds and stroked his leg. But Peter pulled away and stood, his back to her, talking quietly into the phone.

Her eyes flicked open. Soon, though, even as she tried to listen to his end of the conversation, to decipher the meaning of his words, they faded to an intermittent murmur in her ear, and she fell into a half-sleep, waiting to learn the outcome of the call.

She woke when Peter sat on the edge of the bed and put his hand on her shoulder.

"Bad luck." His tone was matter-of-fact. Almost businesslike. "I'm going to have to fly up to Bonn early tomorrow morning."

"It's DiNiro, isn't it?"

"I'm going there for him, if that's what you mean, but he doesn't have any control over the schedule. If you need to blame someone, blame the Hammerschmidt people. They're the ones that have pushed up the timing."

"But why Vicki?"

Peter raised his eyebrows.

"Why was it Vicki who called?"

He sighed. "DiNiro called Rob, it seems, to ask him to make the arrangements." His eyes drifted away from hers. "Rob wasn't there."

"Don't they know you're taking a vacation? Tell them. Surely you've earned that much respect."

Peter shrugged.

"I'm disappointed, that's all." She sat up. "I know! I can go with you. I won't be in the way, I promise. I'll just be a tourist and see the sights on my own. Maybe we could fly home directly from Bonn."

"We already talked about that." Peter looked at the ceiling for a moment "Besides, there are no direct flights from Bonn that we could get on, and we should really drop off the car in Frankfurt."

"Of course." She sagged against the headboard of the bed. "I understand. I'll stay here and drive it back, as we planned."

"That's more like it," Peter said. "We won't have a lot of time, but we can work out the details in the morning." He turned off the light before he walked around the bed, climbed in and lay down, his back to her.

"Good night," he said.

She settled down again too, put an arm over him and pulled herself close to him. She kissed the back of his neck.

"Good night, darling," she said.

32

In the hope of distracting herself from her loneliness, Julia had sought the formal, impersonal atmosphere of the hotel dining room, with the quiet buzz of the other guests' chatter, in contrast to the intimate breakfasts that Peter had ordered to their room. So she sat at one of the smaller tables, nursing her coffee and nibbling on a croissant. As it turned out, the elaborate décor and the size of the room, peopled by a desultory scattering of quiet diners, only served to intensify her distress. She felt cheated. In part she was irritated at the man with whom her husband worked. Also, she could not help feeling that, somehow, she had been betrayed. Peter was not, it seemed, willing to stand up to DiNiro. Worse, in spite of his expressions of concern earlier that morning, before his departure, she had sensed Peter's enthusiasm for his coming journey. Most of all, though, she was acutely aware of the vacant space left by his absence.

She pulled her travel guide from her purse, leafed through it to the description of Salzburg, and held it open on the table. She had their tickets to a concert that evening at the Mozarteum, an intimate eighteenth century setting near the hotel that she had seen with Peter on a walking tour. Now she wanted to organize the rest of this day, and also her final days here alone, to maximum effect. She ordered a refill of her coffee and lost herself in her reading.

The clear, sunny sky, the crisp air with its occasional gentle breezes, just enough to give cheerful movement to the leaves on the trees along the river, lifted Julia's spirits as she set out on her first day of sightseeing. She decided she would walk to a few of the many attractions where she and Peter had not been able to linger on their quick tour of the town the day before. Tomorrow at breakfast she would look into possible routes for a scenic drive and find out what nearby towns and villages might have to offer.

Her first stop, Mozart's birthplace, a walk-up apartment in a modest townhouse, with a store at street level at the time the Mozart family had lived there, was the perfect antidote to thoughts of Peter that had dominated her at breakfast. Instead of Peter, here Julia thought of her mother, who had taken so much pleasure from playing Mozart's music on their piano. She wished her mother could be with her to see the clavier that, as shown in a family portrait, Amadeus and his sister played while their father accompanied them on the violin and his mother sang. She imagined him as a precocious boy, impatient at having to pose with the others for the artist whose painting showed what was no doubt a true likeness of the young prodigy, and not the bewigged, dignified personality found on album covers and the like today. She would have liked to have been able to share with her mother the delight Julia knew she would have taken in these things.

After a pleasant, light lunch in a sidewalk café, Julia hiked up the hill to the Hohensalzburg Castle, the forbidding medieval stone fortress she had seen at a distance that dominates the town below it. She toured the rooms that in a long bygone era had been occupied by the rulers of the little state of which Salzburg was the capital, and visited a church located within the castle's walls. Then, she found a bench on a terrace with a beautiful view of the town below and of the nearby mountains and sat down to rest for a few minutes before descending.

She had hoped that spending much of the day as a tourist in this fascinating place would allow her to forget, or at least not mind so much, that she was alone. Even without such distractions, she thought, Peter was away so often that she should be inured to the experience.

It was no use. Julia was suddenly flooded with memories of the short time they had been together here, memories that only served to revive her intense longing. After all, she thought, this stay in Salzburg was to have been the high point of their first real vacation together after their marriage, not counting their weekend excursion to St. Maarten so many months ago. Now it had been shortened to little more than a day. Since they had been married, she had been left to fend for herself for days on end in New York (her working on weekdays didn't make the nights or weekends any easier). Now here she was fending for herself in this city that she herself had chosen because she thought it would be such a romantic place to be with her husband.

She looked out over the spires and domes of Salzburg's churches and the lively texture of myriad rooftops and their decorations, with the wide, dark swath of the tree-lined river dividing the oldest part of the town from the grand palace and parks beyond it. The afternoon sun gave drama to storm clouds gathering behind the mountains in the distance and a richness to all she saw below. It was a view to be shared with a lover. With Peter. Or at least she could have gone with him to Bonn.

Her eyes began to fill. She blinked back her tears and stood. She turned and strode quickly toward the castle gate and, ultimately, their— now her—hotel. If she could not have Peter here, she must, at least, be with him on the telephone. She had to talk with him.

By the time Julia reached the hotel and her room, it was late afternoon. First she tried reaching Peter through his cell phone, but could not get a connection. In the early morning rush of his departure, he had not given her the name of his hotel in Bonn or told her of any other way to reach him there. So she was forced to try to find him through DiNiro's office in Frankfurt. Peter had given her that number, for emergencies, before they left home.

The receptionist there spoke English and directed her to Mr. DiNiro's secretary.

"The reservations I made for Mr. Medea were for two days from now," the secretary said in response to Julia's question.

"But wasn't the schedule changed? Weren't the Hammerschmidt meetings to start earlier?" Julia asked.

"Mr. DiNiro is still here. He plans to be in Bonn with Mr. Medea in two days. I can give you the name of the hotel where I reserved a room for both of them and Mr. and Mrs. Vardaman. It is the Maritaim. If he is in Bonn, he may be there. The other hotel where Mr. Medea stays occasionally, when he is not with Mr. DiNiro, is the Dorint Venusberg. It is smaller and I doubt that he would be there since he would have to move when Mr. DiNiro arrives."

So, she thought, Vicki will be there. Why, then, was Peter so set on my not even planning to go to Bonn as part of our original itinerary? Or now.

"Didn't Mr. Medea talk with you—your office—about the new schedule?"

"He talks with Mr. DiNiro frequently. He uses a direct line. Would you like to talk with Mr. DiNiro?"

"That won't be necessary," Julia said, perhaps too quickly.

The secretary gave Julia the telephone numbers for each hotel.

"Should I cancel the room in Frankfurt the night before your departure?"

"No," Julia said.

"He ordered a limousine to the airport."

"Please keep that as well," Julia said. "Thank you."

But with the telephone numbers in hand, Julia hesitated. Peter would probably check in only after he had attended to his business matters. The early evening, just before she left for the concert, would be the safest time to reach him. She didn't want to be forced to leave a message.

She kicked off her shoes and stepped out of her dress, tossing it over the back of a chair. Then she lay back on the bed and closed her eyes.

Her thoughts drifted again to Peter's sudden change in plans. He usually seemed to her to be so forceful, so much in control. But not when DiNiro was involved. Earlier she had resented his failure to stand his ground to protect their vacation. Now she felt concerned for him. It must be hard for someone like Peter to be at another person's beck and call all the time.

What a surprise to hear Vicki's voice last night, sounding as close as when she called Julia at home in New York City from the Vardaman's apartment on the West Side just a few blocks across town. Julia could tell that Vicki was distressed at having to be the messenger bearing the bad tidings. That was sweet of her, although it hadn't softened the impact of her news. Strange that she—or Peter—didn't say anything about her being in Bonn while Rob was at the meetings that were originally scheduled.

She looked forward to telling Vicki about the things she and Peter had done and seen on her first trip to Europe, to compare her reactions to those of her friend, who was such a seasoned traveler.

Suddenly, Julia realized that she was tired, physically and emotionally. There was time to take a nap before getting ready for her lonely dinner and trek to the nearby concert. She turned on her side, curled up, and fell asleep.

It rained during the concert. Julia had heard the muffled rumble of thunder while she was listening to a chamber orchestra play some of Mozart's amazing musical confections on original instruments. Now as she walked home the sky was still heavily overcast. The lights of the town reflecting off the low clouds created a glow bright enough to give definition to objects not directly illuminated by the street lamps or floodlights. Puddles still lay along the curbs, but the sidewalks and streets were already drying in a fitful breeze. It was humid and sultry, not cool as it had been the night before.

Earlier, she had slept so soundly and for so long that she had barely been able to take a shower, dress, and walk quickly to the concert hall to be seated for the beginning of the performance. No time for dinner. So now she was hungry. Still, she was not in the mood to tackle on her own one of the cafés or restaurants that she saw when she emerged with the crowd after the performance. The lively animation and loud conversation, the aggressive good cheer that she saw and heard as she walked by seemed intimidating. It might not have been under other circumstances, but as a lone, married woman she did not feel comfortable about entering into that scene. A couple at a table near the window of one place held hands and seemed to gaze into each other's eyes as they talked. Julia looked away.

As she neared the hotel, she veered off onto a paved walkway leading through the trees that lined the river to a row of low park benches along a gravel path that followed the river's edge. The air had become still. A light mist hovered, suspended above the water. The reflected images of the lights along the far bank and the lighted fronts of the tall houses behind a row of trees there undulated in the blackness of the smoothly flowing stream as if they were moving resolutely against the current. It was quiet except for the muted gurgling of the dark water passing along the bank of the river below her and the occasional drip from the leaves of the trees into puddles that remained on the sides of the path. Standing where the paved walkway and the gravel path intersected, she looked for a dry spot to sit.

In the shadow cast by a light above the path shining through a large tree that sheltered a nearby bench she could just make out two figures, joined in an embrace. They were kissing. One, a girl, was facing Julia, her eyes lost in darkness. Julia turned abruptly back the way she had come. Quickly she retraced her steps toward the hotel.

She had not been able to call Peter before the concert as she had planned, but now, no matter how late it would be when his phone rang in his hotel room, whether he would be sleeping or not, she needed badly to hear his voice.

Of course, the hotel's restaurants were closed. Julia would have to go to bed hungry. On her way to her room, she asked for messages at the front desk when she picked up her key. There was one from Peter. He was sorry he missed her and would call again early tomorrow morning. He left no call-back number.

In spite of clear evidence of her presence—one of her suitcases on a portable rack and another against the wall near the wardrobe, a vase of flowers she had bought for them on their one walk standing on a table surrounded by its sad detritus of fallen petals, a program for the earlier concert on the mantle of the fireplace—the room looked oddly vacant to her now without the prospect, even, of Peter's presence there.

It had begun to rain again. Dull explosions of thunder and the urgent rush of a downpour came to Julia from the window she had left partially open for ventilation. The tattoo of hard-driven rain on the French doors to the balcony and on the window alarmed her. The curtains at the window billowed into the room. She looked behind them. Water glistened in widening pools on the sill and dripped from it, staining the rug behind the curtains with dampness. With an effort, she pushed the sash down. As she was replacing the curtains, lightening struck somewhere close behind the hotel. The trees and the river and the town beyond flashed before her eyes like an eerie afterimage of the gay, bright scene she had relished in the daytime when she had been looking from that same window with Peter at her side.

Momentarily forgetting her resolve to call Peter, she sought sanctuary from the violence of the storm that beat against the closed windows of the room by crawling into the bed. Like a little child seeking its protection, she curled up under the duvet, pulling it up to her chin in spite of the still, humid air around her. But as she lay there, alone in the bed where they had been together, she realized once again how much she longed to be with Peter, how she craved the affirmation of his embrace. Her yearning for him became a palpable hunger.

Sweat beaded on her forehead and coursed in tiny, cool rivulets over her eyelids and temples like the rain on the window pane, and onto her cheeks, like tears. She looked at the clock. It was nearly one. She swung over the side of the bed and reached for the note pad she had left on the table after her call to DiNiro's office that afternoon. Then she picked up the telephone.

Through her own hotel's switchboard, she reached the hotel in Bonn where DiNiro's secretary said Peter was already booked to stay with DiNiro. The operator there put her on hold before she recited a litany that Julia did not want to hear: Mr. Medea was not registered now, but was expected in two days. Would she like to leave a message?

The process seemed interminable. She sighed with impatience and started over, asking the switchboard operator in her hotel to call the other, smaller hotel. Its name was familiar to Julia. She thought she had seen it on one or another of Peter's itineraries prepared by Brenda. She was confident, now, that he would be there, but if it was so small, would anyone be stationed at the switchboard at this hour? If they were, would they speak English? At last the ringing stopped. A man answered, and she made her inquiry.

"Oh, yes. Mr. Medea is here," the clipped voice said. She caught her breath. "It is late. Would you like for me to put you through to his room?"

"Yes, please."

"Very well. Thank you."

The telephone at the other end buzzed quiet dashes. Once, twice, three times. At last she heard the receiver being picked up. The initial clean click was followed by thumps and taps. It had been dropped. Finally someone spoke.

It was a woman's voice, sleepy and irritable.

"Hullo?" it said.

Julia could hear heavy breathing on the other end. She felt her throat constrict.

"Vicki?" Her own voice sounded high and thin to her, and the whole conversation seemed removed, as if she were listening to it spoken by others in a strange, improbable dream.

"Vicki?" she said again. "Is that you?"

"Shit!" Vicki said, away from the telephone, and then in a whisper that was barely audible, "It's Julia!" The thumps and taps began again as Vicki struggled to seat the receiver in its cradle to disconnect the call.

Just before she succeeded, Julia heard a man's voice in the background. The words were growled in low tones, a heavy whisper barely controlled. Yet they were quite distinct.

"That was goddamn stupid," the man said.

It was Peter.

161

33

J ULIA HAD BEEN DISTRACTED by the stress, the exhilaration, of making her escape: re-booking her plane reservation from Frankfurt and her one-night hotel stay there, canceling the balance of her hotel reservation in Salzburg, packing, and driving to the Frankfurt airport where she turned in the car. All of this had been costly, but uncharacteristically she felt no guilt at all when she charged to their credit card the expenses she incurred by this abrupt change in her itinerary. She left a terse telephone message for Peter at the desk of the hotel he would be moving to the next day, when his originally scheduled business in Bonn was to begin, informing him of her early departure for home.

Now, though, sitting back in her roomy, comfortable seat in the first class cabin, staring out the window at the hazy view of land and water below (was it Germany? The North Sea?), she was revisited by the shock and distress and fury that had almost overwhelmed her before her hasty departure. Against her will, she was drawn into a vortex of anxiety, reliving her dramatic discovery in the middle of the night in Salzburg of Peter's betrayal, and Vicki's. Then her mind turned to Brenda Thornton. In spite of some inconsistencies in his story, Peter's explanation of Brenda's presence with him on the trip to Chicago so long ago was perfectly logical. It *was* logical, but at the same time she was struck by something that until that moment she had not permitted herself to see. She was jealous of Brenda and had been from the beginning. Brenda. So protective of Peter. So accessible to him. And, from what Julia could tell from Brenda's tone and manner with her, so jealous of Peter's wife!

Next came Melanie, the cook at the Vardaman's house on St. Maarten, her eyes fixed brazenly on Peter while Julia spoke to her. How often had Peter and Melanie been alone together?

Finally, there was her talk with Gina, Peter's first wife. What had indeed been "going on," in Gina's words, that had led to the break-up of their marriage? And why did Gina not want to continue what had seemed to Julia to be a promising acquaintance?

And all the while these thoughts tormented her, she drank.

Her previously underdeveloped taste for wine had been sharpened during the course of this abbreviated trip under Peter's tutelage, so that her initial swallow of the Rhine offered to her by the flight attendant was disappointing even though she had enjoyed the same label, decorously sipping her one glass (along with a glass of champagne) on the way over. Now, after she started on her second refill, though, it seemed to taste just fine, and, as she felt its warmth course through her, she began to feel ready to take stock, to try to understand, and to think ahead, at least for the immediate future. To develop a plan of attack.

As she sipped her wine, and continued to gaze, unseeing, out the window, she came face to face with the reality that even apart from his work, Peter inhabited a private world that spun in an orbit that was totally separate from the one she shared with him. And she became determined to take advantage of Peter's absence from the apartment to find out whatever she could about this world of his before his return would give him the opportunity to revise or obfuscate history. Obsessively, and oblivious of the luxury of her first class accommodations, she planned her research, step by step, with morbid satisfaction.

By the time she had polished off her fourth glass of wine, and her meal had been served, she had begun to feel soothingly distant from the shattered self-esteem and bitterness that had become the totality of her existence since hearing Vicki answer Peter's telephone in Bonn. She also became aware of a steady ringing of some kind that was generated from within and that only sounded worse when she put her hands over her ears to shut it out. Still, she reasoned as she started on her fifth, or whatever, glass, Vicki regularly drank as much or more without apparent effect, and, anyway, it was a small price to pay for deliverance, however temporary, from her anguish.

Even after she switched, finally, to coffee, and then plain water, picking at her food, and came down from the high that the alcohol had taken her to, her anticipation of her invasion of Peter's privacy was intense. She did worry. By delaying his receipt of her message until he reached his second hotel, had she left herself enough lead time? If she had envisioned her plans then instead of on the plane, she wouldn't have warned him until she reached home. Would he now accelerate his own departure? Or, with no need for a ruse to hide behind, would he simply enjoy a few extra days with Vicki—a windfall provided by the victim of their attempted deception? But under any scenario she could imagine, she should have at least twenty-four hours to herself. And after that, maybe she would track down Gina, to find out what Gina could add to her dark compendium of knowledge.

When she finally reached the threshold of the apartment, it was early evening. Hunger pangs reminded her that she had hardly eaten anything from the decent-looking airplane dinner and, later, the snack offered an hour before landing, distracted as she had been and unable to muster any appetite for food. She had not slept and felt tired as well as weak, almost dizzy, her head dense and aching. When she turned the key to find that the door, while locked, had not been bolted she suddenly became alarmed, giving her a quick pulse of adrenaline. When she opened the door, though, seeing nothing amiss, she forgot her momentary concern and her excitement at the prospect of the journey of discovery that lay ahead for her while she followed Peter's undisturbed tracks sparked in her a new and even greater surge of vitality.

But immediately after Julia entered the apartment, Brenda Thornton, smart-looking, fresh and energetic, stepped from around the corner of the hall like an apparition from one of Julia's worst nightmares. She carried a stack of notebooks and papers and a bundle of compact disks in the white envelopes that Julia knew Peter used for their storage. She looked irritated at Julia's intrusion.

After a stunned pause, Julia understood. Avoiding physical contact despite the narrow passage, she strode past the other woman to the study, Peter's office. Peter's desk was clear, as it had been when they left. She opened the middle drawer. He had not changed his habit of leaving his appointment calendar there even after, a couple of months earlier, it had provided a clue that helped lead Julia to first suspect the use he made, with Brenda, of at least some of his business trips. Now it was gone. But most significant, Peter's personal computer was on, displaying part of what she suspected was his more detailed appointment schedule.

In a moment, though, Brenda was behind her. She leaned over in front of Julia and quickly worked the keyboard to exit the file displayed on the monitor and turned the computer off. Briskly she picked up her purse from the floor next to the desk without relinquishing her other cargo and strode toward the front door. She brushed past the elevator operator, who had brought Julia's suitcases into the front hallway. He turned and followed. With the appointment books and the envelopes securely in her grasp, Brenda stepped into the elevator and departed. She must have had her own key, and the doorman, Eduardo, who was new, must have known that Brenda was there first, since presumably he gave her access to the elevator. Mysteriously, he had failed to alert Julia. Had he warned Brenda of Julia's imminent arrival?

All the while, no word had been spoken.

34

PETER ARRIVED, AS SCHEDULED, four days after Julia. At that time he said nothing to her about her early departure, or the events leading up to her decision to leave so soon for home. She assumed that he had braced himself for responding to an attack by her, and was not prepared to introduce the subject of his transgressions himself because it would be hard for him to apologize to her, even though he might feel genuine contrition. But she did not attack him, or berate him, or dissolve in tears. At first, by the time he returned, she was simply numb from mourning—not so much his sins against her, but what she feared would be the loss of him, just as, years ago, she had lost Danny Johnson because of her forceful rejection of his advances. Peter's betrayal had not engendered hate so much as deep disappointment. Mysteriously, to her, she realized that she still loved him, and wanted him, and was unwilling to do anything that might lead to her losing him more than she already had.

And, too, by then, and as the days passed after his return, her image of his treachery had become cloudy. Everything had happened so quickly. How many words were spoken, five or six, a dozen, before it was over? The fumbling noises, the clicks of a receiver being clumsily seated, silence, then a buzz. It all seemed so unreal. And, really, the only transgression she positively knew of was this one, which might, she dared to hope, stand in isolation. By his own admission to her, he had once been intimate with Vicki, before he met Julia. Now couldn't he have succumbed again to Vicki's temptations in just this one moment of weakness? And she certainly had no proof of whether any of her other suspicions were justified, did she?

So she did not question his silence on this most important of all subjects, nor did she break that silence herself.

And, of course, she avoided Vicki.

Then, late one morning, unannounced, Vicki came to her.

"I hope you weren't on your way out," she said, sweeping past Julia into the apartment before Julia could voice any objection. "I just felt we should visit for a while. It's been so long since we've had a chance to chat.

I don't believe we've laid eyes on each other since you came back from Europe, have we?"

She walked directly to the wet bar, filled a highball glass with ice and poured vodka over it until the clear liquid reached the rim.

"Don't you want something?"

"No, thank you," Julia said out of habit, although it had not escaped her that she was being offered her own liquor by an uninvited guest.

But when Vicki found an open bottle of white wine in the small refrigerator, poured a glass and held it out, Julia took it. She followed Vicki into the living room and sat on a chair near the sofa. Vicki remained standing.

"Peter would be shocked if he knew I was here, with you," Vicki said. She took a long swallow from her glass.

Julia was silent.

"He knows I don't lie very well. He doesn't trust me."

"Should he?" Julia asked.

"No."

"Should I?" Julia looked into her glass of wine.

Vicki walked to the sofa and sat down.

"There are some things about Peter," she said, "that I think you should know."

When Vicki left, an hour later, Julia, in a daze, decided to take a drive. Peter hired limousines or rented cars rather than own one in the city, but she had persuaded him to keep her mother's old Volvo in a garage in the Bronx, where storage was cheaper. When he was away, she sometimes took the subway to Van Cortlandt Park, walked to the garage, and drove into the country for recreation and peace of mind.

It was already mid-afternoon by the time she reached the garage. She headed north along a winding parkway, crossed the Tappan Zee Bridge over the Hudson on the Thruway, then left the interstate at the first exit on the other side. It took her back south, and with another turn she was curling down through woods to a cluster of tree-shaded cottages: a little town friends of her family had lived in long ago that was bypassed by the din of human traffic usually so dense in most places this close to the city. There she pulled up next to a small, grassy park at the river's edge, where a ferry used to dock. She did not even leave the car.

By the time she got back, after midnight, Peter had long since arrived home. He was in bed, reading. He must have heard her in the kitchen but did not get up. When she came into the bedroom, he put down his book.

"I was worried," he said.

"Why?" she said, "You have so many others to take my place."

"What do you mean?" Peter reached for her to lean over the bed and kiss him.

Julia stopped, woodenly, just inside the room, numbed by the implications of her resolve. "Vicki came over this afternoon."

"Oh?" He retracted his arms.

"We talked. Or, I should say, she talked. I listened."

Naked, Peter flipped the covers out of the way and headed for the closet. His partially-tumescent penis, protruding hopefully from its copious nest of black pubic hair, betrayed his thoughts when she had first appeared in the doorway. She looked away. He emerged in a terry cloth robe, the one he had worn their first time together on St. Maarten, at Vicki's pool.

He sat on the side of the bed.

"So, what did dear Vicki have to say?"

"Why don't you tell me? You seemed to be involved—intimately—in everything she talked about."

"I told you a long time ago that Vicki has a big mouth, and an imagination to go with it."

"You told me that because you were afraid that she was going to expose the truth about your relationship before we were married, not because you thought she would lie to me. Unlike someone else I can think of, Vicki just has a conscience, that's all."

Peter rose and moved to the door. Julia stepped aside, then followed him. At the bar he poured himself some vodka on ice. She shook her head when he looked to see if she wanted something.

"I've never seen you drink anything hard before," she said. "Vodka?"

"There's a first time for everything."

"Vicki's drink."

"Is it?"

In the study, he sat on the arm of the overstuffed leather settee. Julia stood. Her eyes ran over his working area, clean of any loose paper now. Even the pink telephone message slips that he had moved to a Lucite dispenser had long since been removed. For an instant she could see Brenda switching off the computer and escaping in harried dignity with Peter's appointment books clutched under her arm, like a thief on an inside job interrupted while closing the safe of her employer. She smiled to herself.

"Look, Julia," he said, "I'm not perfect. I'd be the first to admit that."

She laughed. Mirthless, it felt to her almost like crying. He didn't seem to hear.

"I did meet Vicki in Bonn. I don't know what she told you, but I can assure you it was the first time I was with her that way..."

"Fucked her," Julia corrected, her mouth dry. She walked away from him to get a glass of water at the bar.

"...saw her," he continued when she returned, "since before I met..." he hesitated, "that is, since our marriage. And I'm telling you—I told her this then, too—it was the last time. Ever. I don't know what got into me."

Julia started to pace back and forth in front of Peter. "Now I know that you fucked her the day after you fucked me on St. Maarten when we were first there. That beautiful romantic time, when I was so full of love, and filled with the milk of your manhood. I don't know why I hadn't figured that out before. She practically told me by mistake when she left that message. I've been so blind!" She slammed the meat of her fist on the top of the file cabinet, as if she were trying to drive it into the floor.

"That was before we were married."

"*That* was before, but what about..."

"Whatever else Vicki said was bullshit." Peter was on his feet, too, shouting, brandishing his fist at Vicki despite her absence. He stopped, looked at Julia and smiled quickly. His voice became quieter. "You can't believe everything Vicki says. You know that already. She'll do anything she thinks she needs to do, say anything, to get what she wants. That was the first time since before our marriage, and I told her that I was never going to..."

"Fuck her..."

"Yes, whatever. Again. That I love you. And now she's trying to drive a wedge between us. Don't you see? That's the way her mind works."

Suddenly Julia's legs began to fail her. She sat heavily on the edge of the desk, holding onto it at the same time with both hands, leaning on her straightened arms.

"Peter," her voice sounded hoarse to her, "I think you are lying to me." She raised her voice and stood again, leaning toward him as if to focus her whole body in accusation. "You are a liar!"

He leapt at her, shouting, too. "You..." He grabbed her shoulders, pulling her up from the desk, and shook her. "Damn you!"

She felt the pain from the pressure of his fingers biting into her muscles. She could still move her arms, though, and, with all the strength she could muster she pushed at him with both hands as hard as she could. "Stop that!" she said, the way she would to a large strange dog that had jumped up on her, commanding, but not with complete confidence in the outcome. He let go.

"What about Melanie?" Julia's voice was dull. She resented the physical strength that seemed to give Peter an element of superiority in spite of his moral corruptness. But it became animated again as she alluded to the Vardamans' comely servant on St. Marten. She began to pace front of Peter, brandishing her fist at him as she spoke. "Vicki told me about you and Melanie. So I guess you must have had an exciting interlude before DiNiro showed up after the rest of us left you alone with her that last time we were there. Or maybe the two of you shared her. That would have made Denny happy, I'm sure."

She stopped in front of Peter and looked him directly in the eye. "And Brenda? Vicki said that you..."

"Of course," he interrupted with a stage laugh. Abruptly he started pacing back and forth in front of her, gesturing dramatically with his hands.

"Vicki on Mondays, Brenda on Tuesdays..."

"On trips..." Julia interrupted.

"Someone else on Wednesdays. Then, I suppose, there's Gina. She..."

"Gina?" Julia's legs started to go again. She leaned against the file cabinet. "I didn't say anything about Gina!"

He turned to look at her, his expression blank.

"Now I believe you're finally telling the truth!" she shouted. She stepped toward him and with a wide, arching blow, slapped him on the side of his face with all the strength she could muster.

His reaction was quick, almost reflexive. In a short, powerful movement, like the stroke of a piston, he hit her full on the front of her shoulder with his clenched fist.

Julia stumbled backward, her surprised body slamming against the file cabinet. She felt no pain at first, but she desperately needed to sit down. She settled in a heap on the floor of the study. Peter whirled and stalked, without rushing, to the bedroom. He did not close the door.

Then the throbbing came. Quietly, she cried.

It was not made up, but without changing her clothes, she slept that night on top of the covers of the guestroom bed.

35

J UST AS JULIA'S ATTENTION had been temporarily diverted from the trauma of Peter's betrayal with Vicki by the demands of pulling off her hasty departure from Europe, now she was too busy arranging for her departure from their apartment, and from Peter, to be overwhelmed by the enormity of her decision to leave him. She reached that decision, finally, a little more than a month following their confrontation over his infidelities, while he was out of town. She was determined to act on it immediately, before his return might undermine her resolve, or interrupt her hurried preparations. Only a short interval remained in which to pull everything together before his scheduled arrival, if he did not come back early! She had just two days to transfer her savings (she was determined not to use the credit card he had given her), to find a temporary place in Philadelphia to stay, and to pack the luggage she would take with her and a few boxes, some of which she would need to mail to herself because there wouldn't be room in the car. Also she had to retrieve her car from the garage in the Bronx.

Late the last night that she would be sleeping in Peter's bed, in Peter's apartment, she was congratulating herself on the progress she had made and reviewing her tasks for the morning when she recalled again her uncomfortable meeting with Archibold Strothers, and his parting words to her. "Don't get drawn into it, you could be hurt" was the gist of it. Had she done anything that could lead to her getting "hurt," even though at the time she had not been aware of the implications of her actions?

There were records, documents, which she knew Peter kept in the apartment, rather than in his office, where, she guessed, he might be worried because of Brenda's access. She suspected that they must reflect most, if not all, of what she had done in her capacity as an officer—*the* officer—of Finance ServiCo. Peter had thwarted any previous effort to look at his files by keeping them locked, but just a few weeks before, he had unthinkingly given her access to this source of what she hoped would be important information. To relieve her boredom one evening when he was away, she was aimlessly leafing through a reference book he kept at the back of his desk and a small envelope with a thin, flat key inside literally fell into her lap. Strangely, she had not been moved to take advantage of this surprising discovery immediately, although curiosity did lead her to try the key in the file cabinet lock, successfully, before she replaced it and the envelope in their hiding place. Now, though, she found it again. It was after midnight when she opened the lock and searched the drawers, flipping the folders toward her quickly, one by one.

She found it: "Finance ServiCo, Ltd." The files were pressed together at the back of the bottom drawer, three or four of them, manila folders except for a stack of papers hole-punched at the top and held by two rivets, and a bound book of ledgers. All of them together (if she had found them all) made a substantive, but manageable stack. When she removed them, she pushed the remaining file folders back to try to fill the space.

Then she remembered Joshua Adams and his conversation with her when he had been there, and DeNiro's and Peter's concerns about him. She skimmed through each drawer again and took out the two fat files labeled "TryCo" and a thinner one marked "Adams."

All of the tabs on the folders, including those for Finance ServiCo, were hand-written by Peter. Not even Brenda, she realized, would know the contents of these files.

She was sure that there was not enough time left for her to analyze all this material, this potential trove of information, even if she understood what she was reading. Of course, it would be best to copy them and replace them before she left, but she knew that even an express service would not be able to get the job done in time to meet her schedule. So she piled them in one of the boxes to be mailed to the post office closest to her temporary place of residence in Philadelphia, and picked up by her there.

She arose the next day with hardly any sleep behind her after her late night bout with the files. She had been kept awake by a high level of anxiety, not so much because of her decision to leave but rather her fear that she would not have things together in time to leave when she felt she needed to. But food, coffee, and a strong sense of urgency gave her the energy for the flurry of activity that was required. Late in the afternoon she was relieved to find herself ferrying those boxes that needed to be mailed down the elevator and to the car which she left standing in the loading zone in front of the building. When she returned from the post office, she dealt with her luggage and the remaining boxes, loading them into the car for her exodus.

The doorman, Eduardo, and the elevator man, both helped, managing to hide their curiosity about the events that were, with their assistance, transpiring before their very eyes. After she had thanked them both with modest tips and a handshake, which without her announcing it, was her goodbye—to them, to the apartment that had been her home for nearly a year, and to her life with Peter—she climbed into her car and slowly drove off. She glanced back to see the two uniformed men standing by the entrance to the apartment house in bleak surroundings: gray pavement under a gray sky, leafless trees, and dust blown up by a chill late October wind. The dreariness of the scene was relieved only by a short evergreen hedge that ran along the base of the building, but she suspected from movement she had noticed walking past it from time to time late at night, and evidence of tunnels dug into the dirt among the bushes, that it was likely infested with rats.

Before she brought her mind into full focus on the journey ahead of her, she thought for a moment about the files she had taken—borrowed—from Peter. She knew he would be furious, but her conscience should be clean, she assured herself. She wasn't taking them to hurt anyone, but just to protect herself and, possibly, Josh Adams. One of the first tasks she would take on after the boxes arrived at the post office in Philadelphia was to have the files copied and then send the originals back to Peter.

Once that was behind her, she thought, no harm done. She would be free and clear.

PART 3

36

T HE ATTENDEES AT THE Eastern Pennsylvania Association of
Public School Teachers regional spring conference, held this year
in Philadelphia, began to move into the cavernous meeting room toward
a buffet table piled high with hors d'oeuvres. Two bars off each end of
the long table beckoned with colorful arrays of liquor and wine bottles,
beer bottles and soft drink cans sunk into coolers packed with ice,
and stacks of glasses on trays. Round, white-clothed tables ringed with
folding chairs waited on the perimeter. After the last scheduled meetings
of the day, held in smaller conference rooms at the facility, the teachers
began to straggle through the entrance in groups of twos and threes. The
trickle quickly increased to a steady flow. Some chatted, some giggled or
laughed, some were simply quiet and determined.

Julia stood to the side, trying to spot Rita Craig before her friend
was sucked into the room by the momentum of the crowd. The wall next
to her was covered with a huge mirror. She turned to it. She liked the
sophisticated look of the fitted silk dress she had chosen for the occasion
from the small wardrobe she had accumulated over her year with Peter
Medea, but something about it bothered her.

Rita appeared in the reflected scene before her. Like most of the
others, she had not changed her outfit from the working dress she had
worn all day.

She was framing Julia with her thumbs and the palms of her hands,
a fashion photographer, as Julia turned to greet her. "Wow! You belong
in 'Allure'."

"Hardly." Julia was aware nevertheless of the color that rose in her
face. "Anyway, it doesn't look right for here."

"That depends on whom you want to impress," said Rita.

Rita was a redhead and almost as tall as Julia, but bigger. Solid,
Julia thought, not fat. This, along with an air of irrepressible, directed
vitality, gave her a formidable presence among most other women and
men alike. Outgoing and well-liked, she was at least ten years older than
Julia, although she did not look it. The summer after Julia had married
Peter Medea and left Philadelphia, Rita moved from the school system
where she had taught with Julia to a more rural area, and a teaching

position at the Ironton High School. Julia had called her in distress from her tiny short-term rented apartment in Philadelphia where she had taken up temporary quarters after her escape from New York City. Rita encouraged her to apply to fill a vacancy at Rita's school, starting in the middle of the school year, on an interim, trial, basis. She was accepted, and rented a small house in Ironton that was an easy commute to the school, her new employer. Then, while Julia worked to settle in, her friendship with Rita and Rita's husband Calvin, whom Julia had rarely seen in Philadelphia, promised to provide her with important collegial credibility at the school, and a sense of belonging in the town, at a time when Julia had neither the energy nor inclination to seek these for herself in this new and unfamiliar setting.

Julia and Rita walked across the foyer, which had almost emptied by then, and into the crowded reception.

"We'd better hurry if we want something to eat." Rita grasped Julia's upper arm firmly and guided her toward the table of hors d'oeuvres. "This crowd'll clean the platter in a minute or two, and what you see is what you get. No new supplies. We can meet people later."

Julia was disappointed to find that the fare was less lavish than it had seemed at a distance. Most of the canapés were crackers or bread rounds smeared with different colored processed spreads. Any meats such as salami or ham, if offered at all, had already been swept away. An empty bowl sat in a container of melting ice chips, garnished only with scraps of cracked pink shells and hollow tail fragments to betray the identity of its former contents.

Around the two friends the feeding frenzy continued unabated nevertheless. Hands clutched for short lengths of celery stuffed with the same processed spreads piled on a platter in front of Julia. An arm thrust past her toward one of the last pink-topped crackers on a plate nearer Rita. A person reaching from behind apologized as she jostled Julia with an elbow. Julia picked three or four grapes from a stem, added a couple of cubes of cheddar cheese to her modest cache, and backed out of the thick of the action, leaving Rita to triumph in what Julia knew would be an unequal contest with the others for the remains of the carcass.

She stepped away to take in the rest of the room. The only people she was likely to recognize were some of the other teachers from Ironton and those to whom Rita had introduced her during the day, whose names she did not remember. She smiled at one of the latter, a woman who was walking by with a companion. They did not stop.

By now, many had settled down at the round tables. Empty chairs were tilted against them to show where places were saved for others.

"I hate sitting down." Rita had withdrawn from the competition holding a plate piled with her spoils and was following Julia's gaze.

"You get stuck with the person who happens to park next to you." Rita was warming to her subject, gesturing with her free hand. "Or suppose you want to talk with someone who's already sitting. If *you* sit, then you have to talk with them all night, or get up and leave, which can be embarrassing."

Julia nodded her assent.

"No way to get to know anyone across the table…"

Over Rita's shoulder Julia's glance rested on a man standing at the edge of a nearby group, facing partly away from her. She had not seen him earlier at the conference. Tall, blond hair that had darkened, a good deal thicker through the waist and neck than she remembered. Of course he might be here. He started to turn in her direction. Quickly, without thinking, she looked back at Rita, moving so as not to face him. Even as she did so, she was aware that their eyes had met. She pretended she hadn't noticed.

"Do you lean in front of the person next to you?" Rita was saying, "Or just shout across the table…"

"Julia Davenport!"

His stentorian greeting, spoken from a number of yards off as he strode toward them, turned nearby heads and cut Rita off in mid-sentence.

"Speaking of shouting…" Rita muttered in *sotto voce* as he arrived. They both looked at the newcomer.

"Hi, Danny," Julia smiled weakly when he stopped in front of them. "It's Medea."

"What?"

"My last name. Medea. I've been married for a long time now."

"Rita," she turned back to her friend, "this is Danny. Danny Johnson. We…knew each other in high school." Then, still looking at Rita, "Danny, this is Rita Craig."

"Hi," Rita said. She extended her hand.

Danny was looking at Julia, smiling broadly. He did not see Rita's offering.

"Great dress!" he exclaimed with some vehemence, looking Julia up and down. Then he made a show of glancing quickly around the room. "A pearl before swine," he announced grandly, cocking his head in a gesture that Julia recognized, and opening his arms toward her.

"I'll try not to take that personally," Rita muttered, and withdrew her hand.

"You're really looking great," Danny's voice sounded louder than necessary to reach his small audience. "Isn't she?" He turned, finally, to Rita.

"Yes," Rita said. "She is."

Danny had a glass in his hand. It was empty except for a few ice cubes. He held it up.

"Can I get you ladies anything?"

Julia opened her mouth to respond.

Rita spoke first, looking at Julia. "It's a cash bar."

"Oh..." Julia exhaled. "I'd love some plain soda, please."

Rita rummaged in her purse and came up with some bills.

"Let me get you something," she said to Julia.

Danny broke in. "Nothing doing. This is my treat."

"Soda would be fine." Julia spoke more firmly in the face of these offers.

Rita held out three dollars.

"This *woman* would like a glass of white wine, please."

Danny took her money, spun away from them on his heel, and walked quickly toward the nearest bar.

Rita turned to Julia.

"Danny Johnson," Julia said. "He was a class ahead of me in high school. I haven't seen him since."

"Maybe so," Rita shrugged, "but he seems to want to make up for lost time."

"He went to State," Julia resumed quickly. "He wanted to teach in the town where I grew up. Maybe he is. Maybe that's why he's here."

"I love these meetings," Rita sighed elaborately. "You never know who you're going to see here, or," she winked at Julia and smiled, "what seeing them will lead to. True, he may not be Prince Charming, but you could do a lot worse."

Julia looked toward the bar. Danny was returning.

He held out their drinks, keeping for himself a glass filled to the top with what looked to Julia like bourbon, displaced by a few ice cubes. He caught her glance.

"At these places I always get a double. Saves wasting time in line." He raised his glass. "Cheers!" He smiled at Julia. "Here's to our reunion."

"Cheers!" Rita held her glass up before taking a sip.

Julia seemed to be preoccupied with the task of drinking her soda. She stared at her glass. As she raised her eyes she saw Rita looking at her.

Rita leapt into the momentary silence. "I've got to give a message to someone." Her tone was bright and cheery. "I'll track you down when I'm finished." She glanced toward Danny. "Good to meet you." Then she moved away.

"Don't be long," Julia called after her. As she heard her own words she realized how strange they must have sounded to her friend, who had just gone out of her way to leave them alone together.

Rita did not look back.

Slowly, Julia turned to face Danny.

37

Late Sunday afternoon, Julia and Rita set off for home. Rita guided her car from the city streets near the railroad station up a ramp and onto the expressway that followed the Schuylkill River out of town. The road was elevated. A short while later, Julia looked from the passenger seat across the small valley at the classical style columns and façade of the art museum, a dominating presence on its high promontory. Crouched below it in the park on the bank of the river were the pumping station decorated as a Greek temple and the line of neat, crisp-looking rowing club boat houses, like chicks clustered under the watchful eye of their mother.

The water of the river was smooth and black. The lawns of the park were already verdant and lush, its trees washed with the pale green of spring. The scene was placid and restful in the clarifying golden light and darkening shade of the lowering sun.

Julia thought of her walks and picnics there with her mother—poignant memories—as she had watched Nan move inexorably toward death.

Rita broke into her reverie. "I still can't believe you turned down a chance to go to dinner with that guy. Why?"

"I'm not sure myself," said Julia.

After Rita had left them alone at the reception, Julia told Danny that she was living by herself in Ironton and teaching at the high school. Danny told her that he had taught for a couple of years, but had turned to selling text books to school systems—the compensation was better and he met so many interesting people—and how successful he was at it.

She was surprised by his invitation for dinner. Her negative response had been reflexive. She felt the same internal conflicts then that had surfaced when he had left a telephone message for her in college and she had not returned the call. This time, when she declined to go with him for dinner after the reception, she was startled to see in his eyes and his body language that he was keenly disappointed. Even hurt.

Still, he gave her his card. She could call his cell phone, or she could leave a message at the other telephone number there, he said. He was on the road a lot, but would get back to her. Without looking at it, she put it in her purse. He wrote her number down on a small pad that he fished out of his coat pocket.

"I don't have a cell phone," she told him, without explaining that she felt more comfortable with an ordinary "land line" and couldn't afford both.

"Anyway," Julia said to Rita, "I had a great time with you. Meeting your friends. The meal was terrific. Didn't we have fun?"

Rita refused to be distracted.

"You've been living like a nun for months, ever since you got here."

Julia remembered when she had first come to Ironton, launched, it had seemed, on a glassy, featureless sea of loneliness, with no confidence left in her internal instruments of navigation.

"I can handle it," she said. "I've been through it before. Living with my mother after my father died. And by myself after my mother died. You know about it."

She looked at Rita as she spoke, then turned to gaze again out the car window. They were on the Interstate. The calm sanctuary of the park on the river was far behind them. Rita's words led her to think again of her social isolation when she was subject to the all-consuming demands of living with her mother, and later when she was fully immersed in her new teaching career in the city. From that she had shifted into the intensity of her involvement with Peter, then to her life as his wife, with its own brand of loneliness, only to be betrayed by the man with whom she had fallen so deeply in love. And in a way, long ago, Danny Johnson had betrayed her, too.

"Don't worry about me. I'll know when I'm ready."

For an instant she saw Danny's face before her, and the disappointment written there.

"I just don't think it's now."

38

JOSHUA ADAMS HAD CALLED Julia once at the apartment on Fifth Avenue to talk with her about the difficulties he had encountered when he submitted her father's poetry manuscript to acquaintances of his in the publishing industry. He pledged to try some other avenues he thought might have a better chance of success. With that exception she had not been in contact with him since his visit for dinner with her, when Peter had been in Chicago—as it turned out, with Brenda Thornton. Before he left he gave her his business card, and his home telephone number. Mainly because she was still interested in Adams' attempts at getting her father's work published, but also because she had truly enjoyed his company, she sent him her address and telephone number once she was settled in Ironton. But with the passage of time, her hope of hearing from him had faded and she had not thought of him, or the fate of her father's poetry, for months.

So when she stopped on her way out the door to answer her telephone after a few rings it was a pleasant surprise to recognize his voice and hear him identify himself to her after such a long time.

"I should have called long ago," he said. "I've been thinking about you. Worrying a little, I guess. How are you doing?"

She knew that his question expressed a genuine interest and concern. She wanted to be honest with him, and so was forced to think about herself, her own well-being, something she had shied away from for a long time for fear of what she might find. In fact, he had caught her at a stressful moment. She had been heading out to attack a number of important errands, more, she knew, than she had time to complete. As pressing was the load of last minute work she faced, generated as a matter of course toward the end of any school year. Hovering in the background of these immediate challenges was her concern about her future at the school, since she would not be told whether she would be hired full time until after an evaluation that presumably would rely in part on her students' performance through the end of the year, including the scores on their final exams. But more disturbing, as she heard this voice from her past, images of Peter and the end of their marriage began breaking to the surface of her mind as well, like dark objects lost at sea, long ago forgotten, but now dislodged from the ooze at the bottom by the surging of a distant storm to rise and lurk among the waves.

All of these thoughts flooded her mind in response to Adams' deceptively simple question. But at the same time, when she heard him speak, and pictured from her memory of their scant meetings the earnest expression on his highly animated face, she smiled. Just as when he came for dinner, she mused, this man, with only a few words, had soothed her ruffled state of mind, had put her at ease.

"As well as could be expected, I guess," she responded to Adams' expression of concern. "Relatively speaking, I'm quite happy. Happy, that is, to be here rather than the alternative."

"I'm glad. I was sorry to hear of your separation."

"Don't be," she said. "It was for the best. Certainly for me. Probably for Peter, too, although he doesn't seem to see it that way yet."

"When I learned about it, I was surprised," he said, "but I think I'm beginning to understand."

Here she was, Julia thought, for the first time since she had fled from Peter—shocking him, and herself, by packing up and moving out while he was on what he had told her was a business trip (how could she be sure?)—moved to talk to someone other than Rita about how she felt then, and why. As if Josh Adams was her mother and Peter had been a date who had failed to show. *Come here, darling. Let me give you a hug. If he's that kind of boy, you aren't interested in him anyway, are you? Of course not.*

Adams cleared his throat.

"To change the subject slightly, do you know about the lawsuit? My partners, and I, against DiNiro? And Peter? The papers were served a few weeks ago."

"No. No one told me." Julia felt a pang of apprehension, but not surprise. She thought of all of Adams' complaints to her when they had talked after dinner, and the state of his relationship with DiNiro as she understood it from Peter and, for that matter, from DiNiro himself.

The fingers of Julia's free hand began to work at the springy coils of the telephone cord, vainly trying to smooth them into straightness. She sat down.

"Well, I didn't know how you would feel about..." He stopped.

She sensed his discomfort.

"Julia, we thought you might have been exposed to things while you were with Peter that could be of use..." He stopped in mid-sentence again.

Julia's mind raced. Of course there were the files she had copied. What else? Peter never discussed his business with her. No one did, except Rob, when he gave her instructions about signing things for Finance ServiCo. And except for that bizarre dinner in Frankfurt when DiNiro had been so expansive. So drunk."

Adams continued. "Our attorneys are Strothers and Cole in New York. Archibold Strothers. You know him don't you?"

"Yes." She wondered why this revelation didn't surprise her.

"I know they would like to meet with you. They told me that they will be getting in touch. I thought I'd try to talk with you first. To give you some advance notice so you aren't caught off guard by all this. They don't know I'm talking with you. I'm not sure they would be happy with me if they did.

"But, Julia, if you talk with them, they'll see the relevance of whatever you might know. They might want you to..."

"Be a witness?" She couldn't begin to understand how this might affect her. Had she done anything wrong? Against the law, even? "Testify against Peter so that you can...?" Suddenly she was surprised to find that she was concerned, too, for the man whom she had once loved so strongly, in spite of all that had happened between them.

"Julia, we are not looking for anything more than we're entitled to. If we are right, and I'm sure now that we are—my partners caught on a lot sooner than I did—DiNiro lied to us in ways that led us into losing a great deal of money so that he could make a lot himself. He's our main target, but I'm afraid it looks as though Peter helped him. We think that Peter was working for him while he said he was on our side, acting as our representative. We think he may have known the truth all along, too. Or at least he set us up to be duped, which is almost as bad. That's it in a nutshell.

"Do you know anything that would support our case? Or even that would show us that we're wrong about Peter? What we need now is information. If it looks as though your testimony would be useful, we'll cross that bridge when we come to it. I promise we won't call on you if you decide you don't want to do it. Will you help us?"

"I can't do anything until after school lets out. Then I have a job at a children's camp. I'll have a little time in between."

"Then you'll meet with our attorneys?"

She pictured the earnest concern in Strothers' face when he had delivered his warning about her getting involved in Peter's business. Hurt, she had been blind to it at the time. Had he known then that he would be representing Adams? Had he already known about all this and not told her?

"I'll think about it."

"Thank you," Adams said. "We'll pay your expenses to New York, of course, or come to you if that would be better.

"One other thing. There could be criminal charges. Fraud, maybe. The securities laws. Strothers says that he has reason to believe (lawyer talk, I guess) that DiNiro may be the subject of a new Federal investigation. Julia, if it looks as though DiNiro used Peter, tricked him somehow, maybe we can at least find a way to help him with the authorities."

Not for the first time since she heard it she remembered Strothers' concern about DiNiro. That he could be "dangerous." Also, Strothers had told her about some earlier charges against DiNiro that had to be dropped because... She couldn't recall why. But it all seemed to have an ominous relevance to the dilemma that Adams and Strothers were creating for her now. Any way Julia turned, she reflected, she would be hurting someone. Her head was bowed over the table, her fingers still working at the cord of the telephone. But, she thought, the one person who is certain to be hurt in the end is me.

"As I said, I'll have to think about it."

"Of course, Julia. I'll tell the attorneys to wait."

"And now I have to go."

"Do you have my number?"

"Yes."

"And do think about it. Seriously."

She rose and walked to the counter.

"I will."

She replaced the receiver before he could say anything more.

39

IT WAS CURIOUS, JULIA thought, that after so many months of managing to maintain relative seclusion, her past should now begin to mount such a determined assault on her refuge.

The day after Adams' call she decided that she could work better at home than in a shared office preparing the last tests before final exams, so she returned from school earlier than usual. Clutching a brown paper bag of groceries and a canvas tote stuffed with books, notes and drafts of the tests, she struggled to enter the kitchen from the back porch. Her hip held an aggressive screen door at bay as she unlocked and opened the door to the house. When she pushed her way in with her shoulder, she was greeted by the silent red blinking signal of her answering machine.

She set the tote on the kitchen table. Then she pressed the "play" bar, and listened.

"Julia."

It was Peter. His no-nonsense voice, reserved for business calls. She sank to the closest of the chairs by the kitchen table, hugging the grocery bag to her like one of the stuffed animals she used to cling to for reassurance in times of anxiety when she was a little girl.

"I need to talk with you. We must get together. It hasn't been easy. Call me. You know the number."

No "hello," no "please," no "good-bye." Commanding. As if she had never left him, had not been gone for all this time. As if it *had* been easy for *her*. She felt a stab in the pit of her stomach, the kind of momentary pain that, if repeated over time, leads to ulcers. Then she smiled. Not any more, she thought. She lifted the bag, set it on a counter, and began to distribute its contents among the refrigerator and various cabinet shelves in the kitchen.

Earlier, after she left Peter, she had been overwhelmed by hurt. She was haunted by the things she had discovered about him and his life away from her, and by the strange meanness that seemed to have possessed him toward the end. Yet in spite of all the ways she felt he had hurt her, she harbored an unsettling feeling that in leaving him she had somehow admitted failure at an undertaking that was close to the core of her existence. Intellectually she was sure this self-blame was at least mostly undeserved. Still she carried it with her, an unwanted, immutable burden.

But recently, helped by the demands of teaching in a completely different context from what she was used to, she was able to banish virtually all conscious thought of these things. In the classroom and working at home, she responded to the requirements of the school and the needs of her students with a near-obsessive intensity that left no time or strength for such diversions. Being forced to meet all the challenges of setting up a new life in an entirely new environment helped as well. Then Josh Adams' call, and now this.

She knew she should get back to Peter right away to liberate her mind from the futile exercise of speculating on his purpose. She needed to dedicate herself completely to her work. It had to be ready by the next day.

Peter had always discouraged her from calling him on his cell phone. The same was true for his office, although it was still late afternoon and Peter should be there. In both cases he had said he did not want to be interrupted. For that reason, possibly, she had forgotten both numbers although she was sure they were written down somewhere. Besides, she did not want to deal with Brenda.

She remembered with distress her last, dramatic, encounter in person with Peter's secretary, who had been leaving the apartment with Peter's appointment books just as Julia had arrived after her hurried return from Frankfurt. She had been determined to see the story those very records might tell about what she had come on the plane to think of as his secret life: his life without her, outside of their marriage.

So now, sitting at her kitchen table, her telephone in front of her, Julia decided to leave him a message at home rather than trying to reach him at his office even if she could find the number somewhere. Before she picked up the receiver, she composed what she wanted to tell him on a pad next to the phone. She needed to be sure that she would not, in her confusion, fail to make any essential points as she fed the answering machine, in the short interval it allowed: essentially, that she did not want to speak with him unless he was calling to arrange for their divorce.

But to her surprise, when she called him at home, Peter answered.

"Julia." His voice had the same peremptory tone as in his message. "It's important that we get together as soon as possible."

Julia's quickly developed the edge of irritation she had been determined to avoid. "We haven't spoken for how many months?"

"I'm sorry. How are things going?"

"I'm teaching. Finally."

"If I'd known how important it was to you, of course, I..."

"Look, Peter, I've brought home a lot of work that has to be finished by tomorrow. There'll be more after that. It hasn't been easy starting in the middle of the school year. I don't have time to meet with you."

"I could come there if..."

"No."

"Some place near you? Philadelphia?"

By now, she knew, he would be pacing around the apartment, the portable telephone pressed to his ear, its stubby aerial thrust toward the ceiling.

"Why are you home?" she said. "You never came home this early when I was waiting for you. Who did you bring with you? Or was she there already?"

Julia herself stood and began to stride around the kitchen, extending her hand as she went to guide the long cord over the backs of the chairs and above a water glass filled with wildflowers that stood in the middle of the table.

"There's no one," Peter said. "But what if there were?"

"Why is it so important all of a sudden for you to see me?" Julia said. "You've managed without me quite nicely. And I without you, in case you're interested."

"Julia, please. I miss you for one thing."

"I missed you when we were married and living in the same place."

"We still are. Married. Remember that."

"I want to be un-married," she said. "Very much. Will you finally let me? Without a big fight? I won't ask for a lot, except my freedom. Lord knows I have grounds if I need to convince someone."

"That's something we could talk about."

She sat. Without direction from her, the fingers of her free hand began to work on the coils of the telephone cord. She willed them to stop, placing them in her lap. As soon as she started to talk, however, they resumed.

"On the telephone," she said. "We don't have to meet. Our lawyers can do that."

"Something else has come up. I can't talk about it on the phone. Don't worry, it won't be bad, the way it was before you left." He paused. Then his voice sounded brighter. "I'm a different person. I've changed."

She knew it wasn't so. She had heard that much in his tone when he left his message, and at the beginning of this conversation. His demand for attention, for submission.

"You can't be busy all the time," he said. She could hear annoyance working its way through the satiny veneer he had just now been trying to lay down.

Julia could not stifle a bitter laugh. He had been busy at least "all the time" when they were together, if you could believe what he said, although she had lost confidence in her knowledge of what it was he was doing, and with whom. And he was "busy" now too, with this call to her. So, what was his business?

"How about Sunday lunch. At Honneger's?"

Honneger's, in the countryside north and east of Philadelphia, was not, she had read, a "steaks, chops, and lobster" road house or an inn exuding rural quaintness. It was more like a French-style café catering to a sophisticated clientele that enjoyed classical music. She thought she remembered that it featured live ensembles on weekends. She had suggested excursions there to Peter, but he never felt he had the time. Once they even made a reservation which she was forced to cancel at the last minute. The restaurant was probably not much more than an hour-and-a-half drive from Ironton, not too different in length from the trip into Philadelphia.

"I don't think so, Peter."

He was silent.

"I would have to be back here before four."

"That shouldn't be a problem. I could pick you up."

"In a limousine? No thanks."

"Times aren't quite as good as they used to be. I'll be renting a car."

"Thanks anyway."

"So you'll meet me there?" Peter said. "At Honneger's. This Sunday. At eleven thirty, to give you plenty of time to get back when you want to."

"Yes."

Suddenly he sounded the way he did sometimes when she had overheard him cutting a deal on the telephone. "Are you sure? Then I'll count on you."

Julia stared out the kitchen window at the porch and the yard beyond. Her world. Her sanctuary. She would be leaving it, reluctantly, to meet with Peter. She wasn't at all sure why.

She felt the stabbing again in her gut.

"Look, Peter, you heard me. Don't press your luck."

"Thanks," he said, and hung up.

40

DESPITE HER MISGIVINGS ABOUT meeting Peter, Julia looked forward to the drive through the countryside in her mother's old Volvo sedan. Normally when she ventured away from Ironton, it was to take the state road to the Turnpike and then the interstate that cuts directly through suburbia to Philadelphia. Today she was going east, across the grain of main roads that fed from the north into the city. Although many intersections had already succumbed to commercial strip development, between them stretched miles of rolling hills checkered with green or plowed fields and tree-shaded clusters of farm buildings, punctuated by steeper wooded knolls and lines of low mountains. She had grown up not far from the area she would be passing through. She left early so that she could avoid the Turnpike in favor of this more leisurely, scenic series of two-lane roads she remembered from that time.

Low clouds hung just above the higher hills and clung to the tops of the mountains. Occasional drops of water spattered against the windshield, but not with enough frequency to require the wipers. It had rained during the night. The shoulders of the road were still dark with moisture. Standing water gathered in low spots in the pavement. The greens of the grasses and sparse young crops in the fields looked rich and succulent, the plowed earth almost black.

But before long the prospect of seeing Peter forced memories on her that in the end competed successfully with the charm of her scenic surroundings as she drove through the countryside. Her mind was assaulted by a kaleidoscope of disturbing images from before and during their marriage, many of which had come into focus only when circumstances required her, finally, to face their implications. She thought once more of the real meaning of Vicki Vardaman's message at the end of her first trip to St. Maarten, not intended for her ears, revealing to her that Vicki, not Rob, would be alone with Peter after she left. That, in turn, brought to mind her pain when she came to understand the source of Melanie Kingsley's proprietary manner with Peter during both of her trips there. She suffered even now from the jealousy she felt when she left Peter to be alone with Melanie after their second trip when Peter, supposedly, needed to stay longer to meet with

Denny DiNiro. She remembered her surprise, and distress, when she discovered Brenda's ticket to Chicago, triggering her suspicions, since found to be depressingly justified, of Brenda's role as sexual companion for Peter, both while he was in his office with her and on so-called business trips. In spite of her usually successful efforts to put it behind her, she was forced still again to relive her discovery of Vicki with Peter in Bonn and, later, Vicki's frank confession to Julia, near the end, of her intimate relations with Peter, and her revelations, presumably told to her by him, of many of his other liaisons. And all the time this was happening in front of her blind eyes, she had loved him so much!

The road to Honneger's had been climbing gradually, winding upward to a pass through a line of long ridges that would lead into the broad valley where she thought the restaurant must be. Wisps of cloud trailed among the tops of the taller trees. Without warning a hard rain began to clatter against the windshield, huge drops, almost like hail. She turned on the wipers and drifted to a slower speed as she peered in front of the car, trying to get used to the sudden restriction in her visibility. It didn't help that her eyes had filled. She blinked to clear them.

Ahead, on the other side of the road, she saw a widening in front of a low building. There were signs, not bright and glossy, but hand-done, faded: "Souvenirs! Coffee! Lunch! Gas!" She glanced to make sure no one was passing her, then for on-coming traffic, and swerved across at the last opportunity to pull into the parking area. The car bounced over a depression at the edge of the shoulder and skidded as she braked on the dirt and gravel, but slowed before any damage was done. She guided it to a spot at the edge of the woods, beyond the building and the gas pumps, out of the way of other cars that might come in. Almost before she turned off the ignition, she closed her eyes and rested her forehead on her arm on the steering wheel. Now her tears flowed freely.

In time, Julia sat back, took a deep breath, exhaled, and dried her face with tissues from the box in the glove compartment. She avoided looking at herself in the rearview mirror.

As suddenly as it had begun, the rain slowed to a light drizzle. She opened the car door and stood on the gravel, stretching and breathing in deeply. The musky sweetness of benign decay from the damp woods rushed through her nostrils and into her lungs, flushing out the stuffy air from the car. She walked across the rutted gravel to the store.

The old man behind the counter was thin and tall, with narrow, stooped shoulders. His hair was white and wispy. His smile, revealing an incomplete set of discolored teeth, was kindly.

"You don't look too good," he said.

His concern was genuine. His tone was not at all rude. He might have been speaking to his own granddaughter.

Both of Julia's grandfathers had died before she was old enough to remember them. When she was younger she had studied the few yellowed, black and white photographs that her parents had preserved. Neither man, she thought, looked like this man. Still, she could feel tears begin to well up again. She blinked, and smiled.

"I'm O.K., thanks. Some coffee would help."

"Where are you headed?" he asked while she fished for coins in the change pocket of her wallet.

"Well, I was about to turn around and go home. But I'm better, now." She presented him with two quarters, a nickel and five pennies. "Wish me luck."

"Thank you," he said. "Thanks for the pennies. We can always use those. And, my dear..."

While she pushed the top down on the Styrofoam cup, she rested one hand on the counter. He reached over and with long, delicate fingers gave it a reassuring pat. His touch was cool and dry.

"...good luck."

41

T HE STORM, APPARENTLY GONE now, had cleared the air, taking with it the sultriness that had seemed so oppressive just a short while before.

Honneger's Café occupied an old flour mill. Its weathered siding was stained dark by the rain but awash now in the bright midday sun that had broken through the clouds. When Peter strode up to her as she entered, she was relieved to find that her pulse did not quicken. She did not feel sudden regret at having deprived herself of this man to whom she once had been so attracted.

Rather, she looked at him with something approaching detached curiosity. He still carried himself as though he assumed that his presence would be highly regarded, but he was somehow less sleek than her mind's eye had fashioned him. He looked thinner, his face, never fleshy, seemed almost gaunt. She recognized his suit, but its fit now was less than precise, as if it had been bought off the rack instead of being, as she knew it was, custom-made. It was Sunday in the country, but this was a business suit, one that he wore to the office, to meetings, to closings of deals, when something important was to be bought or sold.

His smile did seem spontaneous, his eyes moist, even. He extended his arms. Julia offered her hand.

Peter had chosen a table at a window overlooking the narrow mill stream that flowed next to the restaurant and, beyond it, a large meadow on the side of a hill. A few horses kept each other company as they grazed in the same direction across the lush expanse that stretched from the brook and disappeared over a gentle rise, their progress hardly noticeable, like distant sailboats on a calm sea. It was sunny, but dark clouds lurked on the horizon above the meadow and the line of trees at its far margin.

Julia had determined in advance that she would hear him out before she reiterated her single desire from him, the promise of which had drawn her to this place. Yet uncharacteristically, he failed, she thought, to take the conversation forward. Instead he told her how well she looked, described how disorganized the apartment had been without her to straighten things out (she smiled as she recalled how little he had actually let her do), and talked about his work (something he had rarely done when, in times past, she would have hung on every word).

After a while, as he spoke, she caught herself glancing out at the horses. They had seemed to cover so little ground since she and Peter sat down. She turned back to look at the man across the table from her. Not a stranger. Not a friend.

"Peter," she broke in. "What do you want?"

A smile drifted across his mouth, lingering while he contemplated her question, but never reaching his eyes, which rested on her for this moment without expression. What Julia had taken once as innate mystery in them she now thought she recognized as an intentional effect—the drawing of a veil—and she found herself annoyed by it.

"You're right," he said.

Just then, the waiter brought their order and laid it out on the table with discreet ceremony. She had noticed musicians setting up in a corner of the room when she came in, had heard them tuning to the piano. Now she heard the piano lead a violin and cello into a Beethoven trio.

Peter's eyes fixed on hers and were strangely transformed to the focused magnets that had once drawn her to him with their intensity. She looked quickly down at her plate.

"Julia," he said, "I miss you."

Her head jerked back up. Her eyes widened.

"*That's* why you asked me here?" She noticed someone turn half toward them at the table behind Peter, and lowered her voice. "How could I have been so stupid!" She spoke to herself as much as to Peter as she continued to stare at him.

"Is it that bad?" he said, and smiled again, now bringing his eyes into the exercise.

Julia had spoken without thinking, in violation of her own resolve to wait him out, then to persuade. This time she did not answer.

"Please Julia, give me a chance."

She waited, and he talked. His words were those she had been afraid to hear: attempts to conjure up the feelings he had provoked in her before her disenchantment, the love she had felt for him. But as he was saying *Don't you remember that night coming back from the Algonquin Hotel? Our first kiss?* she wondered how long it had been since he himself had dwelt on such things, if ever. And when he said *I know I have to travel. I was neglectful. I can change. But don't you ever think of how good we were together?* she thought instead of how his absences had affected her before she suspected his infidelities. How lonely she had been those times, and how she had longed for him then.

"I need you!" he said, and reached for her hands, as he had so many times when she had shivered just in anticipation of his touch. She pulled them away, clutching her shoulders with them, her arms crossed in front of her.

She had meant to wait, but she spoke. Her voice dropped into a tense, harsh whisper.

"The last time I remember your saying 'I need you' was when you told me I should *grow up*! That yes you had seen Vicki from time to time, and Brenda, and Gina, and who knows who else. That you *'had* to'..." she mouthed "fuck" silently "...other women. That you guessed it was your nature. But, you said, to me, 'you are the only one I love. *I need you'.*"

As she talked she remembered how serious he had been. Sincere. As if he had just discovered a sure break-through strategy in some negotiations he was involved in, offering a simple solution to her dilemma. Incredulous, she had nevertheless kept her peace, determined not to let an emotional response give him the opportunity to show his scorn.

It had been morning. His proposition had begun over coffee after breakfast and moved to the living room. She was standing there when he said "You need me, too. Be practical. Don't be a child, Julia," and smiled.

Words had leapt from her mouth before she could stop them. "You goddamn shit!" she had shouted at him.

And he had hit her, in the face with the flat of his hand, with such force that she fell over the coffee table and cracked the side of her head against the arm of the chair next to the sofa. It was upholstered, but still hard enough that the blow made her ears ring afterward. He stood above her for a moment—she saw his legs flex under his trousers and the toes of his shoes crease as he shifted to the balls of his feet, nothing more—then he left.

In a few hours the angry hand print on her skin had become a nondescript red welt. It went down overnight and was gone by morning. Her neck stayed sore and stiff for a week. That night, not knowing when he might return and fearing what he might do if he did, she had slept on the couch, where she felt that she would be most likely to hear him when he came in. She slept lightly, reluctant to abandon the defense of consciousness, clothed in the dress she had been wearing since morning; but he did not come home until the next day. Then he was full of apologies. No word was spoken about what he had said, or where he had been.

Across the table from her, Peter's look dulled. His tone changed. Now it was flat. Weary.

"You couldn't have left me at a worse time."

"Why? Vicki's shut you off, too?"

He seemed to wince, and Julia found that in spite of the anger her thoughts had unleashed she was sorry she had spoken. The melody line of the trio drifted to her from the other side of the room through the clutter of lunchtime conversation. It had taken a hauntingly sad turn. Peter's hand held the side of the table, and she had to suppress an inexplicable urge to reach for it.

"I needed your support. I still do. More than ever. I told you. Business is lousy. My kind of thing has been slowing down everywhere, I guess, but it's been worse for me. It's been hard."

Her fingers had begun to play with the spoon that remained next to her plate on the table.

"What do you want me for?" she said. "What could I do for you?"

He hesitated in his reply. She picked up the spoon.

"Some of my contacts have deserted me. You could help..."

She banged the spoon smartly back in its place. "Damn you, Peter," she said, and looked away from him. She was surprised by a sudden urge to cry, but fiercely swallowed it back.

"It's not that, Julia. I need you to come home to, to..." He leaned toward her. "I'm under attack. That bastard Adams and his people have sued me. I haven't done anything to deserve what they're doing to me. Defending that fucking lawsuit is eating me alive. Accusations, depositions, prying into my confidential records. I need someone to be on *my* side."

"Peter," she sat back, looking at him again, her voice steady, "that 'fucking lawsuit,' as you call it, or at least what you did to bring it on, is one good reason for me to stay away from you. How could I live with myself, knowing those things?"

"What things?" Peter became attentive.

"I heard what you and DiNiro said in Frankfort about Adams. That you had 'taken care of him,' or whatever. And tell me, did you use me without my knowing it? Naïve, dumb little Julia, president of some company of yours that DiNiro had the hots for? Someone warned me about letting you get me involved. Were they too late?"

Peter's eyes narrowed. "What are you saying?"

She blushed. "Nothing," she said, and reached for her water glass. She took a long draft and stared for a moment at the rounded remnants of ice cubes that floated in the residue.

He leaned forward again. "I haven't done anything wrong to Adams or anyone else. Believe me. If DiNiro has, I don't know about it, but I'm sure he hasn't. There's nothing there. So that's not a reason for running out on me at the first sign of trouble, Julia." His voice softened. "Please come back. I'll change. I have already."

Julia laughed. Peter's look of surprise made her laugh harder. She could not help it, but she knew there was a danger. What had been a response to something she saw as being terribly funny began to verge on hysteria, dry heaving, almost like throwing up, because what was so funny was also so terribly sad. As suddenly as she had started, she forced herself to stop.

"What are you going to do about the Federal investigation?" she asked him.

"Damn it, Julia! Was that in the papers?" He clutched the edge of the table again.

"I don't know."

"Then how...?" He seemed to search his plate for an answer, the now-cold presentation of medallion of veal, with its bright sunburst of stubby young carrots, complemented by a fan of five or six slim string beans and the sprig of cilantro, all untouched. Then he looked up.

"Adams, of course. You didn't call him, I hope."

"I sent him my address and telephone number," Julia said. "He called me."

"The files. You copied them. It's more complicated than you think. Denny knows. I had to tell him because... Anyway, what did you..."

"Josh Adams wants me to talk with his lawyers," Julia said. "I didn't give him an answer."

She lowered her voice. "Peter, I want a divorce. I want it now. We've waited. No one could say we haven't had time to think about it. You say you want me back. The answer is simple. No. So wouldn't we all be happier if we just broke the ties completely? Make legally final something that's final anyway? Please."

He shifted his gaze away from her toward the window. "I can't. Not now. Can't you see?" He seemed to be looking into the distance.

"Why drag everything out?" she said. "Make me go to court, spend money on lawyers? It'll cost you, too. It seems so stupid."

He turned to her. "What are you going to say to Adams?"

"I don't know. He thinks you screwed him, Peter. Or at least you stood by while your dear friend Denny did. If not, then whatever I have to show Adams can't do any harm, can it? I don't know what to say."

"Some of the papers in those files are misleading," Peter said. "They could be taken the wrong way. What do I say to Denny?"

"Why should I care what you say to Denny?"

"Because they've sued him, and he's the one the Feds are really after, at least so far. And Denny doesn't like to have someone out there like you, a loose cannon, who knows too much and could hurt him."

"I haven't talked to anyone, or given anyone the files. But what if I did? What could he do about it?"

"Julia, you've got to understand. He'll assume that you'll be a witness against him. A damaging one. Since you left me, and now with the lawsuit and this investigation, as far as he's concerned, you're the enemy. And he'll do whatever it takes to keep you from hurting him. Unless you…"

"What? Come back? Be part of the 'team' again? Don't you see, Peter? It's too late for that. Much too late."

She realized that they were talking in circles, at least from her perspective. Frustrated, she looked away, out the window, at the meadow. The horses had gathered near a copse of trees that stood just on the other side of a fence that had stopped their progress. The clouds had grown in volume and piled up into a dark thunderhead that blotted out the sun, moving in her direction. Threatening.

Then Peter leaned toward Julia. "But whatever problems Denny might worry about, I have one thing going for me that he doesn't. You're my wife. My lawyer says that you can't testify against *me*, anyway. Can't nail *me* to the wall that way, damn it."

The musicians launched into one of Beethoven's spritely country dances to begin the last movement of the trio. Julia raised her voice to make sure she would be heard.

"I do not want to be your wife."

"My lawyer says that a divorce could weaken my protection, so I guess for the time being that's your problem. I can't help you."

"Won't."

"Have it your way, then. I won't help you."

"You bastard!" she hissed at him and rose from the table, pushed back her chair and gathered up her purse from the floor. Out of the corner of her eye, as she straightened and started to walk toward the door, she saw the glances of people near them shifting hurriedly away from her, returning to food or drink or to others in their party. Peter followed close behind.

The maître d' intercepted them smoothly as they filed past the other tables.

Peter nodded to him and muttered some assurance about the bill as he worked to keep up with Julia, who had broken free of the last table and was moving almost at a run for the door.

She had forgotten that her car had been whisked off to some unknown location by a valet parking attendant. She dove into her purse for the claim ticket and found the loose bill she had left there for this purpose. She thrust the ticket into the hand of an attendant and clutched the bill in her hand. As the attendant scurried off, she fled into the driveway, hoping somehow to distance herself from her tormentor. Her rapid footfalls crunched in the clean, thick gravel.

Peter followed her there. With no escape at her command, she stopped. He stood in front of her, his face close to hers. It was flushed. He grabbed for her wrists and held them both with enough force to detain her without causing her pain so long as she did not struggle. She stared at him with undisguised fury.

Out of breath even though he had not been running, his tone urgent, he spoke to her in a hoarse whisper. "Julia, please. Listen to me. I don't want you to get hurt." She glanced down at her imprisoned wrists. "I don't mean here. And not by me. But I warn you. The information you have must not get into anyone else's hands. Not Adams' lawyers, not..." he hesitated, "anyone's. Do you understand? Denny ..."

Julia's matronly blue Volvo scattered bits of gravel as it hurried around the circle and came to a halt a few feet from them in the driveway. The attendant hopped out and stood at ease by the open door. Peter loosened his grip and Julia jerked her arms away from him. She brushed past him and handed the crumpled bill to the young man at the car. He looked behind her at Peter.

"Everything O.K?" he said.

"Yes, thank you," she said as she settled into the driver's seat.

Peter strode to the side of the car, ignoring the attendant who turned as if to block his way but fell back quickly.

"For your own sake, Julia, please remember what I said."

She slammed the door.

For the first time in her life she stamped on the gas pedal and spun her tires as she started the car forward, barely aware that the rain had started again. Large drops exploded on the windshield as she drove away.

42

IN A FAR CORNER of the grounds of the Ironton High School, across an athletic field from the school building, a grove of maple trees had been planted to create a shaded picnic area. Next to them was a grill for outdoor cooking constructed of fieldstones with a flat flagstone counter space. The trees by now had reached a stately middle age and spread their branches generously to provide shelter from the sun. Underneath them, some gently decrepit wooden picnic tables stood well spaced at odd angles to each other. They were a favorite haven for the few students and teachers who chose to eat their sandwich lunches outdoors when the weather allowed.

Julia selected the table farthest from the grill and the school building, and deepest into the grove of trees. She carried a small brown bag and a paperback book—a collection of short stories she would be using with her seniors in the next few days, the last section of assignments before final exams.

She glanced around her. She had been the first to arrive and hoped that no one would join her until Rita came. She was early on purpose and wanted these few moments to herself.

She sat down, facing away from the school, and placed the bag on the seat next to her. Then she settled into reading the book, hunching slightly over it, her knuckles pressed against her cheeks.

The fragrance of the trees and the succulent new grass, and of the earth that was nurturing them, and a soft breeze that teased the wisps of hair that trailed over her temples, fought quietly with the book for her attention. After a quarter hour or so, she looked up.

She found herself gazing at a small gathering of lethargic cows crowded together on the other side of the fence marking the school's boundary, just under the reach of the trees at the edge of the picnic grove, seeking relief from the noonday sun. Across the lush green field where they stood, a small, weathered hay barn and an empty corn crib drew her eye. Behind these ranged the wooded hills that rimmed the valley. A hazy brightness paled the sky and kept them at a shimmering distance.

Julia's mind drifted back to the rural valley where she had grown up, to that other spring, when she first met Danny Johnson. She had been amazed then that he had known who she was. That he had thought about her at all, for that matter.

She remembered that afternoon, after school when she stood patiently at the pharmacy counter of the drug store waiting to pick up a prescription for her mother, who would be arriving soon to take her home. In a moment the pharmacist handed her the small, crisp white paper bag, with the receipt stapled to the top. As she turned to leave, she noticed Danny standing just a few feet away, in front of the magazine rack. She paused. He was talking with two girls in his class, a year ahead of her. It did not surprise her at all that he seemed not to notice her as she stood looking at him.

She had known of him since she had been going to high school. Yet from her perspective he inhabited an entirely different world. He was a jock. He starred in all the major sports and was captain of the football team. He was popular, particularly with the girls. Particularly with those she saw as being, compared to her, glamorous, or at least much more sophisticated in ways that would, she thought, be pleasing to him. She, like the other girls (she knew from their talk), was strongly aware of his broad shoulders, his athletic ease of movement, his engaging smile. But whenever she saw him, no matter how far or near he was from her, there seemed to her to be a hopeless distance between them.

She found herself inexorably drawn to the soda counter near where he stood. Before she could settle down she knew she had to justify her presence to the boy behind the counter, who stared at her from behind the cash register. For a moment she was lost in the dilemma of choosing what she should order.

"Hi." The voice behind her was soft and friendly, but very masculine.

She looked up into the mirror and saw Danny Johnson close behind her. She felt the heat of her blood rising in her neck and face.

"Hi." She twisted around toward him. He was looking down at her.

"May I sit here," he nudged the seat with his thigh, "next to you?"

"Sure."

"Can I get you a coke? I'll have one too."

"Yes," she said. "Thank you."

"You're Julia Davenport, aren't you? Where've you been hiding?"

"Hiding?"

As he talked, filling the silence between them, she tried desperately to concentrate on his words, to not be distracted by his mere presence. Then she heard him say, "I hear you want to go to Penn and that you're getting straight A's." Embarrassed, she looked down at her hands. They were damp with perspiration, clutched in her lap to still her nervous fingers. In passing, she caught sight of the liquid in the large glass he had ordered. There had been little enough ice to start with, and most of that was gone. No more bubbles fizzed merrily to the surface. It was the color of dirty motor oil, and dead flat. She took a sip. There was too much syrup. It was dark-tasting and heavy with sweetness. She hoped she hid her distress.

"What I really want to tell you," he started again, "is that I know it's not easy around here for someone who's serious about studying, like you. Kids don't understand."

For the first time, almost furtively, she looked directly into his eyes. In contrast to the light color of his hair, his eyebrows and eyelashes were dark. His irises seemed large. Blue, with rims that darkened at their edge, echoing the velvet blackness of the pupils in their center. They were arresting. Julia quickly looked back down at her drink.

"But you shouldn't let them get you down. You'll have your day."

She felt tears welling up. She tried to blink them back while she squeezed her fist, holding it under the counter top where she hoped he could not see, so that her nails dug into the palm of her hand until she felt a stab of pain.

She started once more for her glass, which was still two-thirds full.

"You know," he said, "you don't have to finish that." His face showed a flicker of suppressed amusement. "Where're you headed? Can I give you a lift?"

"Yes," she said. Then, "That is, no, thank you. I'd love to, but my mother is picking me up here. She's probably already waiting. I'd better go."

"I'll come with you." He got up and walked around her, reaching for her books.

205

She took the white paper bag from the top of the stack and slid off her seat. He was much taller than she had realized. He waited for her to lead, and followed her out the door.

The memory was bittersweet. Staring past the stolid cattle, at the picturesque barn standing in the distance across a rolling field of new spring grass, she was transported into the heady, languid pause between her own final exams and her graduation from high school and her disturbing encounter with Danny Johnson in the cool shadows of that other barn.

Even after so long an interval, her feelings for him then, the softness and warmth of their kiss, the thrill of his hands on her breasts and his fingers gently working her nipples, and his stroking of her, came to her in a rush. But so did the pain of his effort to force her to take their intimacies farther than she was willing, and the surprising strength of her rejection of that effort. She remembered still her confusion and despair at his retreat from her there and, she had thought at the time, forever. Her feeling of senseless loss.

"Julia?"

She turned toward Rita's voice.

"I'm late. Do you still have time for lunch? My feelings won't be hurt."

"Sure." Julia smiled at her friend. "I have more than half an hour until my next class."

They opened the lunch bags and began to consume their contents.

"You and Calvin have been so good to me ever since I moved in," Julia said.

Rita and her husband had ministered to her, having her over for meals, helping her move into the house she rented, and, in Rita's case, keeping her company from time to time when she needed that, too. Calvin, slim, and thoughtful, accommodating, and taciturn in manner, was a perfect foil for Rita's sturdy build and rambunctious personality.

"Don't be silly." Rita looked up. "We haven't done anything that anyone else wouldn't do for a friend."

Julia's eyes lowered.

"Do you remember Danny Johnson? From the conference."

"Sure. Drinks double bourbons. He couldn't take his eyes off you. You turned him down for dinner. How could I forget?"

"He called. He said he was going to be 'passing through' on his way back to his home, in Philadelphia, and wanted to see me."

Rita swallowed a mouthful of sandwich and looked at her. "Passing through *Ironton?*" She smiled.

"Anyway, at first I wasn't sure how I'd feel about seeing him again." When she had picked up the receiver the evening before her picnic lunch with Rita and heard Danny speak, she did not at first recognize his voice. As he identified himself, sounding slightly put off by the need to do so, it came to her that despite her feelings for him long ago, in most ways she hardly knew him. This was the first time ever that she had talked to him on the telephone.

His suggestion that he visit her had caught her completely by surprise. She had told Rita during their drive back from the reception that she was not yet ready to see any man, including Danny Johnson. That had been her honest reaction to the prospect of having dinner with him then. But now when she heard his voice she remembered again Danny's almost touching disappointment at her refusal of his last invitation, and pictured as he spoke the familiar presence she had once cherished so fondly, and her resistance softened. Also, that was before she learned from Joshua Adams about his lawsuit and his need for her help, and before Peter, at Honneger's, had worked hard to persuade her that the cost to her of providing that help could be improbably high. She began to contemplate the comfort, the support even, that the friendship of this man might provide her in the midst of her growing anxieties about these unintended consequences of her failed marriage.

Julia picked up the last piece of an apple she had cut into quarters and took a bite from it.

"You're crazy," Rita said. "Seriously."

"I don't think so." Julia popped the rest of the apple quarter into her mouth. When she was finished, she patted her lips with the paper towel she had brought as a napkin. "I asked him to dinner Saturday night."

"That's better!" Rita grinned.

Julia looked at her.

"Would you and Calvin come?"

"To dinner?"

"It's time for me to learn to entertain again. I want to be sociable. I have a grill I never use. I thought we could cook outside. Have some hamburgers or something like that. Besides, I owe you. Please?"

"While Danny is there?" Rita asked.

Julia's gaze moved once more to the barn in the distance. She hesitated.

"*Because* Danny will be there," she said.

"Are you sure?"

Julia turned back to Rita and moved her head in an almost imperceptible gesture.

"I'm sure."

43

THE WEATHERED CLAPBOARD HOUSE she rented in Ironton that had begun as Julia's refuge was fast becoming her real home—a place where she not only felt distanced from the fragmenting events of her recent past, but in which she now had begun to take some proprietary pride.

In spite of her heavy workload at the end of the school year, she took time during the day on Saturday to prepare for entertaining, a new experience in this setting. She cleaned thoroughly—the downstairs at least—even though she hoped that the clear, warm weather would allow them to stay outdoors. She dusted and polished the small collection of objects of her family's, some going back to her childhood, that had survived yard sales or the auction block during times of need before she married Peter. While she was with him, she had kept a few out, and the rest in a storage closet in the back of the apartment. She had taken all of these with her in the Volvo. Peter had shipped to her, at her request, her mother's cherished piano, which now stood in her living room.

Turning to the outdoors, when she moved in here she found two rickety aluminum folding chairs at the back of the garage, slung with strips of woven, bright green plastic, and a filthy, old barbecue grill. It was a flimsy affair with a warped wire grate and no cover. She washed them down as best she could. With a broom and a snaggletooth bamboo rake, also from the garage, she swept off the path leading to the driveway, and rid the back yard of dead leaves left over from the previous fall. She looked up at the large old apple tree whose blossoms had graced the yard earlier that spring. Now bright young leaves decorated its gnarled branches.

Rita and Calvin came early. They helped her haul out the kitchen chairs, set up a card table she had found in the attic and prepare the grill with charcoal briquettes contributed by them. They also brought the other essentials for outdoor cooking: lighter fluid, a fork and a spatula with long handles, and a bottle of water with a perforated stopper for dousing the fire to keep it from flaring up when the meat patties dripped fat on the flames.

Her back yard was narrow. Only six or ten feet separated her house on one side from her neighbor's wall. Still, the wall was high, covered with Virginia creeper that was beginning to fill out already, and the neighbor's house was set far enough away that only its roof was visible from where they would be sitting. Her garage and a six-foot wooden fence with narrow, closely spaced slats, like lathing, along the driveway beside the house defined the boundary on the other side. A privet hedge masking a cyclone fence that separated the yard from an overgrown vacant lot in the back marked the rear of her domain.

The effect was of seclusion, surprising to someone who approached from the front because there the shallow lawns of the irregular line of houses, reflecting differing degrees of care and attention, were completely open each to the other. The row of front yards along the street was broken only intermittently by the trunks of tall trees and clumps of bushes, punctuated by the occasional boat looming above a trailer or bus-like recreational vehicle parked beside a few of the driveways.

Danny arrived with a bottle of bourbon in one hand and a bouquet of dark red long-stemmed roses in the other. Julia found a glass vase that held water, despite a crack running down one side, for the flowers. The roses looked elegant but a little uncomfortable, arching above the bright red-checked tablecloth and standing among the paper plates she had purchased for the occasion and the assorted patterns of stainless steel flatware provided by the landlord, like an acquaintance who had misinterpreted an invitation and wore a cocktail dress to a neighborhood barbeque.

After Julia introduced Danny to Rita again, and to Calvin, they all settled in the chairs. In this retreat behind Julia's house it was quiet. The sun's rays imbued all they touched with the rich hues of an early evening in the late spring. Julia and her guests sat in the shadows, but the foliage on the higher boughs of the apple tree and the top of the vine-covered wall and a thin strip of back lawn not shaded by the house were bathed in this glow.

Calvin's contribution to the festivities was a couple of six-packs of beer, and he hefted a can while Rita and Julia contemplated their juice glasses of red wine. Danny stood, looked around the table at them and raised a tumbler in which a few cubes of ice were lost in a sea of bourbon. His voice seemed loud for the occasion. It projected well beyond the small group in front of him, disturbing for a moment the hushed tranquility of their sanctuary.

"To the most beautiful girl in the world," he announced, and smiled.

44

RITA AND CALVIN LEFT after dinner. Danny stayed.

The sky had darkened to full evening. Tree-toads chirped in the lot behind the hedge. Laughing voices drifted from a few houses away. A dog barked in the distance. Between the two of them, though, there was silence.

Julia had brought out a candle rather than turn on the bright porch light. Already burned down to a stump on some other occasion, it stood on a saucer in a clear glass hurricane shade to shield it from the drafts that moved fitfully in the still-warm air around them. The sinuous flame writhed toward the opening at the top of the glass enclosure, its point flicking at the precious air like a snake's tongue seeking the scent of its prey.

Danny looked across at her. She stared in rapt fascination at the distorted shadow of him cast by the light of the candle, wavering against the gnarled trunk and lower branches of the apple tree that stood behind him.

Earlier he had brought his bottle and a bowl of ice out to the table. Now he scooped the few, diminished cubes that were left into the remains of his drink and followed them with a healthy splash of bourbon.

"Well," Danny said, "here we are."

"Yes," Julia said.

Her eyes were fixed on his shadow image and its grotesque dance with the tree. In spite of her reason for inviting him, of the need she felt for his presence in her life as a friend, she could not help but dwell at this instant on the last time she was with him before their chance meeting at the reception in Philadelphia. On the events that had transpired in the barn that had thrust them apart so long ago.

Finally she looked directly at him.

"You said you were 'passing through' Ironton. I can't believe we're on the way to or from anywhere. Why…"

"It's true, I did make a diversion to get here," his brief smile seemed self-conscious, "to see you."

She looked away for a second, back at Danny's distorted image projected behind him, before her eyes settled again on his, which were dark in shadow, but still alive with an echo of the flickering candle. "You called me years ago, in college, and I didn't call you back. I've never felt right about that. But I was confused about how I felt then, and I guess I'm still confused."

Now it was his eyes that shifted away to a point somewhere behind her in the darkness. "Could I change the subject for a while? Do you mind if I ask about your marriage?"

"No."

He looked back at her.

"No children, I guess?"

"No."

"How long have you been..."

"Separated."

"And?"

"For months. It's over. Peter, my husband, seems to be having a hard time getting to the legal part. But it's over. Finished."

She thought she saw the fleeting trace of a thin smile on his lips. She was surprised at herself. She had not intended to get into this territory at all. He looked as though he was formulating a response. Quickly she broke into the momentary silence.

"How is your work?"

His shoulders visibly sagged. "Well," he said, "I'm having a hard time with, I guess you'd call it, direction." He looked at his hands closing around his glass. "From the beginning I envied you, with your sense of purpose, of plan. 'Here's where I want to go to college' and 'Here's what I want to do when I get out' and you worked for what you wanted, and got it, and that was that!"

"From the beginning?" Her eyes widened. For a moment she felt the same astonishment at his awareness of her existence then as she had when they first met, all those years ago.

Julia looked at the bottle standing in front of Danny. It was almost half empty.

"I'll make you a fresh pot of strong coffee."

She got up, and Danny followed her into the house. In the kitchen, Julia reached for the coffee that she kept in the refrigerator.

Danny wandered aimlessly around the kitchen, glancing surreptitiously at the reminder notes she had tucked in the frame of the glass door to the cupboard over the telephone, picking up a cup with a broken handle she used as a receptacle for stray paper clips and rubber bands, staring at the beginning of a grocery list that lay at the back of a counter. Julia was rinsing out the coffee maker when he finally came to rest, settling heavily into a chair at the kitchen table. Her back was to him as she worked to make the coffee.

Soon, though, she heard the chair scraping on the floor as he pushed it back, presumably to enable him to stand again. What was it about that sound, she wondered, that caught her attention with such force? Then it came to her. She closed her eyes for a moment to better recall the image of the two of them, Danny and Julia, in her family's kitchen, in the house where she had grown up, after the graduation dance. She smiled.

Danny Johnson had come back for his brother Billy's graduation—which was Julia's as well—and to her amazement, asked to take her to the Senior Prom. She remembered the drive home to the Colony—the small group of summer places in the hills, a good distance from town, where she lived. Her parents had bought one, winterized it and moved in, all the way from suburban New Jersey. From the outskirts of New York City.

Before they started from the school parking lot, Danny put the top down. He drove fast. The town seemed to disappear in an instant as they rushed away from it on the Valley Road in the darkness. The strangely warm air of the early summer night blasted against the windshield and sucked over and past them with a roar. Julia slid forward and pushed herself down in the seat, leaning her head back against it. She looked up at the vast gathering of stars that beckoned from the blackness in distant brilliance. She was a comet, streaking through the heavens, on the verge of joining them.

When they reached the house, Julia asked Danny in for scrambled eggs and coffee. Her parents had left the lights in the kitchen burning. The electric percolator was on the counter. Julia took the coffee from the refrigerator and spooned enough from the can to make four cups. Danny sat down on one of the white painted wooden chairs at the kitchen table.

"We love this big kitchen," Julia said. She poured in the right amount of water. "The windows look out at the woods, but even so it's sunny in the morning. We all eat breakfast here."

She continued her monologue, talking about her life in the Colony, as she plugged in the percolator, turned to the refrigerator next to her, and took out the container of eggs.

Danny had been silent as he watched her at her tasks across the kitchen. She took a stoneware bowl from the cupboard and closed the door carefully to avoid making unnecessary noise that might wake her parents. She cracked the eggs on the side of the bowl, trying to empty their contents without getting her hands sticky with the egg white. I have to stop talking, she thought. Her mouth was dry. She knew she must sound forced. She was not saying what was really on her mind, and she was running out of other things to say.

She was measuring a tablespoon of water to put into the eggs when she heard the scrape of Danny's chair moving on the linoleum floor. She did not look around. Instead, she tried to concentrate on shaking some pepper on the eggs and reaching into a drawer for a fork to stir them with. She opened the wrong drawer.

"How hard do you like your eggs?" she asked Danny. She knew she sounded flustered. She could feel herself blushing as she opened another drawer. "I like mine soft, but I can..."

"Julia." The proximity of Danny's voice surprised her.

"Yes?" She put down the fork and turned her head to look at him.

"You are beautiful." He reached up and touched her hair.

"I am?"

She started to move around to face him. He helped her with his left hand at her waist as if he were leading her in a slow dance. She looked up at him.

"I want to kiss you," he said. His right hand settled gently on the back of her neck. He was looking into her eyes.

"Yes," she said. Her field of vision had narrowed to encompass only his pupils, and the velvet darkness there pulled at her. She wanted to be lost in that darkness. She moved to him.

"Yes," she said, and their lips met.

She put her arms around him, under his, and held him as he held her. They kissed again, and his kiss was more than she had known to hope for, warm, and strong, and gentle all at once.

45

Now, with Danny again, this time in her own kitchen, these memories brought the heat of blood rushing to Julia's face as she plugged in the coffee maker and pushed the power button to "on." Worried that he would notice, she composed herself as best she could before she turned to face him. He was not there. Startled, she looked farther afield and spotted him moving carefully along the uncarpeted hall, walking toward the front of the house.

"Mind if I look around?" he called back to her.

"First door on the right, back in this direction," she said.

While the coffee brewed, she worked at finishing the loose ends of straightening things up that her guests, working under Rita's leadership, had begun. She put utensils, drinking glasses and pans that had been left to dry next to the sink into drawers and onto shelves. Danny returned and she poured coffee into two mugs and carried them back outside.

Danny followed her down the porch steps and over to the table, like a large, well-trained dog, but an old animal, walking with a stiff, shuffling gait. He steadied himself on the railing as he descended behind her into the yard, and held the seat of the chair with one hand when he sat down, as if he was afraid it might suddenly shy away from the prospect of bearing so much weight.

"Wow!" he said, shaking his head briskly from side to side.

"You all right?" she asked.

"Fine," he said.

She handed him his mug. He held it in both hands as he lifted it carefully to take a sip of coffee.

"I know what I told you back in high school, about my wanting to teach and all," he said, surprising Julia by picking up exactly where he had left off almost a half an hour earlier. "But I didn't really know what I wanted. Where I was going. The fact is, I was scared of the future. Just plain scared. That's why I always admired you so much, your sense of where you wanted to go. Your determination."

He raised his head.

"No kidding!"

She turned away.

"Look at me now." Her voice was small and distant. "What do I have to show for all that marvelous determination?"

"I'll tell you." He leaned toward her, holding the mug with one hand and clutching the side of the table with the other. "You're living in a place you've chosen for yourself, doing something you like and getting satisfaction from it, making friends like Rita and Calvin. And when you thought you'd found someone, you gave it your best shot. When you realized you'd decided on the wrong guy, that you'd blown it, you got out. Starting over is better than not starting at all."

He shook his head.

"No, that's not it," he said. "*You* start something and finish it, for better or worse. I just start and start and start."

He rose, walked slowly to the tree and leaned back against it, facing her. The candle's flame was low now, guttering as the wick burned down to the reservoir of liquid wax at its base. Its flickering light left dark hollows above his cheek bones. A speck of reflected fire still glimmered in his eyes. Lesser shadows played over his face, cast by his lips, the point of his chin. It was a dramatic transformation, as if he had stepped from the chair at the card table on her back lawn onto a stage, behind some bizarre, animated, but tragic, mask.

"I told you I taught for a couple of years. That was a lie. I just thought that's what you wanted to hear. I never even finished college. At least not all four years of it. After a year at State I began to get stir-crazy. I knew I had to get out as soon as I could. Into the world. To make money. So I switched to the two year business program. Accounting, marketing, whatever it took. I got my certificate, but did I get a decent job? Plan for the future? Oh no! That was for the plodders. Instead, I got hooked up with (maybe 'hooked by' would be a better way of putting it) great-looking deals that were going to make me rich. Since I didn't have any money for these guys, I worked for them for peanuts—gave them what they call sweat equity—looking for that pot of gold at the end of the rainbow. Which was never there. Finally, to be able to eat and keep a roof over my head, I started selling. One thing or another. Nothing much caught fire there either. So, a year ago I began selling these high school text books."

He stopped. Then he moved back to his chair.

"You asked why I came here."

"That's all right," Julia said. "I'm glad you did."

"No. It was a fair question, and I want to answer it. I came because, well, when I saw you at the reception in Philadelphia I found you very attractive. Again. I was at loose ends, restless. I wanted to see more of you right away. That night. And not just to have dinner.

"It was the same this time. I thought of how put-together you are, and good looking. And I thought, well, I blew it once, but she's been around some by now and I've learned a lot. So, maybe this time I'll make it with her. You know…"

"Danny, don't…"

Julia reached for him across the table, as if to arrest him physically from continuing. He did not move, and she stopped short of touching him.

"Of course when I got here I realized how dumb I'd been. For one thing I had to face a fact that I hadn't admitted to myself all along: I really like you. I think I liked you even before I talked to you that first time, in the drug store, years ago. See? I remember it all. You've probably forgotten everything, except what happened at the end.

"And because of that, I know it was wrong for me to come here thinking what I was thinking. Wanting what I was wanting. A big mistake."

She stared at Danny for a moment. Then she motioned to his mug.

"Half. Then I'll go. Get out of your way. Meanwhile, I have to," his eyes dropped, "look around the house again."

The candle was so low she had to extinguish it to keep tallow from running onto the table. Then she followed Danny into the house, carrying his empty mug. On her way back out with his coffee, and a glass of water for herself, she switched on the porch light. The harsh glare of the bare bulb purged the yard of its aura of mysterious intimacy.

Danny reappeared from the house.

"Sorry about the candle," Julia said.

He smiled weakly.

"It's probably better this way," he said.

"What do you mean?"

He worked his way down the porch steps, across the yard to the table and sat down.

"To say what I need to say."

He took a sip of coffee.

"That afternoon in the barn?" he said. "I was scared, Julia. Being with you there, all alone. It really turned me on. I wanted you. Badly. But I wanted you to like me, too. I had to have both. But I didn't know how to put all that together. You didn't act like the others. You seemed so, well, honest. Genuine. I got this crazy idea, that if I could just show you how great I could make you *feel*..."

"Please, Danny!"

"And I told you why I came here tonight—my real reason."

She got up from her chair.

Danny rose and stepped back, knocking his chair over.

"I don't know what I could have been thinking. You're out of my league. I've known that all along."

He righted the chair. His coat was wet from the dew on the grass where it had fallen. He shook the garment absently and pulled it on.

"I didn't come here for this, to apologize to you. I'm not even sure I felt it before. But the fact is, I'm very sorry, Julia. Sorry about what happened then—you probably don't care any more—and sorry for coming here. You've been great, but I know that however you feel now, tomorrow morning you'll wake up and be glad I'm gone, this time for good. And you'll be right."

He picked up his mug and the candle holder.

"The least I can do is help you finish putting things back together."

Julia took her glass, gathered up the tablecloth and the vase of flowers and led them once again to the kitchen. Then they wheeled the grill into the garage and carried the table and the rest of the chairs to the porch for shelter from the dew until the morning when she would wipe them off and redistribute them to their appropriate places.

Danny stood in the kitchen, near the door, while Julia wiped the counter next to the sink with a damp sponge.

"Now I do have to leave. I've got a long way to go."

Julia stopped.

"Thank you for having me," he said. "For putting up with me, I should say."

She walked to him. "Danny, won't you stay here and drive home when you're," she searched for the right word, "rested?" She was looking out through the screen door, conjuring in her mind the utter blackness that she knew lay beyond the reach of the light that gave the porch a glaring reality. "It's late. There's a bed that pulls out from a sofa in the room I work in upstairs. It was a guestroom before I took it over. I might as well put it to use."

She turned to him, but still avoided his eyes.

"I'm not suggesting...that is, what I *don't* mean is..."

For the second time that evening, she blushed.

"Thanks." Danny spoke quietly. "I know what you mean."

When Julia looked up, he was smiling down at her. At that moment, for the first time, his eyes and his smile, the shy amusement in them, were as she had remembered them. She felt then as though she had truly recognized him after a long absence.

"But I have to get back. Anyway, in my line of work I do a lot of late-night driving. I'll be fine."

Just then a thought came to her, a way to alleviate the frustration she felt when she had tried to understand the meaning of the papers she had copied from Peter Medea's files. Particularly daunting were the documents that seemed to be tracking the financial transactions of the company Finance ServiCo and how they related to various memoranda and minutes that were included in the files. She had pushed her concern about what information they might hold for her—about her, and about Peter and Marco DiNiro—to the back of her mind for months, but Adams' telephone call and her confrontation with Peter at Honneger's brought home to her the importance of understanding their content as soon as possible. Even more than before, she now suspected the worse: that they were damaging not only to Denny DiNiro, but also to Peter, and quite possibly to her.

From what Danny had told her of his education, he must know something about accounting and business practices—certainly a lot more than she did. Enough, possibly, to look all this stuff over and maybe make sense of it. And after seeing him again, and being with him tonight, she knew that he was her friend. Someone she could count on. If he told her he would help, then he would help, and if she asked him to keep whatever he found between the two of them, he would do that, too.

When he started past her for the door, she reached out with both hands and gently stopped his progress.

"Danny, I know you have to go, but I'm wondering, would you do a huge favor for me, when you have time?"

He looked at her again. "Of course. Anything."

She turned and started toward the closet where she had left the canvas carryall in which she had put all of the copied files, including the ledgers, which she had clamped together in sets that matched the original bound books, after looking them over herself. When she returned, she handed the heavy satchel to him.

"Here. These are some papers, accounts, whatever, from my past—with Peter. It's extremely important to me to understand what they say. I've tried, but they don't really speak to me. With your business courses, your experience, maybe you could do better. The ones that have to do with a company called Finance ServiCo should describe things that I was doing for Peter and his business friends. If it got into the hands of, say, Federal investigators, does it look like the information here could be harmful to a man named DiNiro, who Peter worked with? Or Peter? Or me? I'm not as worried about the other files, but maybe you could figure out the story they tell as well. We don't have time now, but call me if you need me to fill in whatever background I can."

"Sure." He smiled again and hefted what she had given him. "Pretty heavy stuff. And here I thought you were just a schoolteacher."

"I wish. But when I was with Peter, you'll see, I was into this, too, for better or worse."

Danny gestured toward the door with his free hand. "But now, I really have to..."

"I know." Julia interrupted him, and followed him out through the kitchen door. They went together around the house to the front.

The night air was cooler now, and silent, and carried in its folds the subtle scent, drawn out in the darkness by the dew, of grass and young leaves, and blooms in distant gardens. The moon was rising. Its pale glow, obscuring stars even before it emerged above the house in back of them, cast shadows across the front of the yard.

They stood together for a moment in silence. Julia looked around her.

The long-vacant lot across the street had grown into a weedy sort of woods. It was crowded with Locust trees with their frond-like leaves, tortured-looking vines climbing and twisting around their trunks and branches, tall sumacs and even bamboo. Even this early in the year it took on the incongruous aspect of a dense, exotic jungle, and seemed impenetrable in the dark. It was a favorite haunt of the more intrepid of the multitude of neighborhood children during the day, but its deep shadows and mysterious animal noises kept it clear of innocent human passage at night.

In front of it now, not quite opposite Julia's yard, shaded from the moon's cool illumination by the foliage of a tall tree on her side of the street, stood the dark bulk of a large low-slung car. It was alone. A ghostly intruder among the dim shapes of her small dominion and those of the surrounding neighborhood with which she was so familiar. She glanced along the line of yards in each direction and saw no cars in the street in front of the other houses. Just an occasional vehicle or two in a driveway, and a few lighted windows in the houses themselves. No one was having a late-night party that would lead a guest to choose such a place to park. She thought she saw someone inside, but could not be sure. Were teenagers using this dark but not really secluded spot as a hang-out? They never had before.

She did not feel close to any of the people who lived on this quiet street, but she recognized them all, and their children, and they waved and smiled in passing, as did she. She had come to feel secure here, unconsciously, the way it was when she was growing up. Unlike her neighbors, out of habit, she still locked her doors at night, and her car, even just to run into the store to pick up something. Otherwise she had gratefully tried to quit the defensive mindset she had learned by trial and costly error living in Philadelphia and New York City—her urban cunning and her suspicion. Her fear.

"Julia?" Danny said, "I have to go." He glanced in the direction of his car, parked in the driveway.

She turned her head to look at him in the gloom.

"I know," she said. "But Danny, before you leave, I want to take a better look at who, if anyone, is in that car over there. It doesn't fit in, somehow."

"Stay here," he said. "Let me."

He started before she could respond. The bracing air and the coffee must have had a good effect on him. Even lugging the heavy carryall, his strides across the lawn seemed strong and purposeful. Julia followed.

He stepped off the curb and into the road. Suddenly the car came to life. To ensure successful ignition, the driver must have kept the starting motor in play too long. The transmission protested for an instant with an agonized whine. Once in gear, its wheels spun as the driver's foot stamped down on the accelerator, the tires squealing while they sought traction. The heavy vehicle, low to the ground, lurched from repose into motion with a roar that might have belied a faulty muffler, then sped darkly, no lights, toward the center of town.

Startled, Danny leapt back to the sidewalk. Julia ran up beside him. She crouched for a better angle to look inside the car. Back-lighted by the illumination from distant streetlights, she thought she could make out the silhouette of the driver from behind: bulky and short, or hunched over the wheel, and someone in the passenger seat. Then it was gone.

"I wonder what the hell that was all about," Danny said.

"I don't know," Julia said. "Probably nothing, I guess. But I'm glad you were here."

As they walked back to his car, Julia reached out and touched the sleeve of his jacket.

"Thank you, Danny."

When they reached his car, he opened the door, and turned toward her.

"Thank *you*, for taking a chance on me. For letting me see you again. I hope you don't regret it, now." He offered his hand.

She shook it.

He climbed in, closing the door behind him, then started the engine and turned on the lights. He rolled down the window and looked out at her. "I'll call you when I've looked over your stuff."

"Danny," she said, "drive carefully. I'll worry."

"You must have more important things to worry about. Besides, I'll be fine." He began to ease the car backwards out of the driveway.

She walked beside the car, calling softly to him in the quiet of the night.

"Danny..."

He backed onto the pavement. The car's headlights caught her in their glare for an instant as he turned, then the beam passed over the driveway and her neighbor's lawn, like the beacon of a lighthouse sweeping across a darkened sea. By the time she reached the end of the drive, his car had pulled away. She stood there, arms crossed in front of her, hugging herself, suddenly aware of the evening's chill, looking down the road long after the taillights of Danny's car disappeared into the night.

At first her thoughts were of Danny. Then she remembered the strange car. So out of place, like an intruder from another world. So threatening. Just then, Peter's words about Denny DiNiro came back to her: that DiNiro would do "whatever it takes," she thought Peter had said, to keep her from disclosing the contents of the files Danny had taken with him to look over for her. Could there be a connection? It seemed almost too bizarre to contemplate. She shivered before she turned to walk back to the fragile haven of her home.

46

JULIA HAD INTENDED TO wait for a respectable period of time, a week maybe, before checking in with Danny to find out if he had looked at the files and had come to any conclusion about the information they contained. He was doing her a favor, and she didn't want to rush him when she knew that a thorough analysis by him could be time-consuming and would be intruding on the other commitments in his life.

Yet almost immediately, beginning with the fitful, nearly sleepless, night she spent after Danny left her at the curb in front of her house for his drive home, she was plagued with increasingly troubled thoughts born of Peter's words. He had warned her of Denny DiNiro's possibly extreme reaction to the likelihood, apparent to DiNiro it seemed, that she could be a source of information that would damage him. That this man had already seemed sinister to her, and had been characterized to her long before as being "dangerous," only added credibility to what Peter had said, to his stated concern that she not be "harmed."

The kind of threats that Peter had managed to conjure up in her imagination—physical intimidation, bodily injury, even death—all seemed strange, almost surreal, in the context of the prosaic, day-to-day life that she led. Her fondest wish was that it was all a bad dream, a troubling nightmare, that would evaporate to reveal only the realities and relatively humdrum concerns that she was used to coping with: whether she would be kept on as a permanent teacher in Ironton, how to ensure that the work she had committed to for the summer would be satisfying as well as providing her with sufficient income, when to clean up her garage. That was her emotional reaction to these disturbing intrusions into her life. But reason dictated that she had no choice but to take Peter's admonition at face value. It was surely heartfelt, albeit made, as it undoubtedly was, with self-serving intent. He had seemed deadly serious.

It was during that first night after she saw Danny, while she thought of her conversation with Peter, and pictured over and over again the large, low-slung car lurching from the far curb and speeding away in the dark, that she remembered her mother's compact .30 caliber pearl-handle automatic pistol. She soon realized that she could not sleep until she had retrieved it, if nothing else, to confirm that it had not been mislaid. She climbed out of bed, turned on the hall light and padded to the closet there that she used for storage. She reached to the back of the top drawer of a painted chest, behind some small boxes of trinkets from her high school days. She smiled when she felt the hard coldness of metal, the short barrel and body of the gun that her mother had bought long ago for protection when her father was away. With it were an instruction booklet and the box of cartridges she also had found among her mother's belongings.

When she and Julia were alone, her mother had worried about tramps or other marauders who might be a danger to them given the remote location of their house. It had been the only winterized, all-year-round residence in a colony of underused or abandoned summer cottages set at the edge of the woods, miles from town. As far as Julia knew, the gun had never been fired. She hadn't even remembered that she had saved it from her mother's possessions until she went through them when she moved to Peter's apartment. There it rested in a storage box until her move here, where, again, even though she kept it, she had seen no use for it whatsoever. But now might be different.

She took the gun, handling it gingerly, and the box of cartridges, and placed them in the drawer next to her bed. She was satisfied that she could wait until she awoke the next day to load it and make it ready for use. The following morning, as she read the instructions, she slotted cartridges into the clip, reseated the clip into the handle of the gun, loaded the first cartridge into the chamber by pulling back the slide mechanism, and made sure that the safety lever was on. For the first time since her anxieties had begun to overwhelm her, she had at her disposal a potent weapon for her own defense.

Logically, Julia felt, the presence in her house of this means for her self-protection should give her a greater sense of security and well-being. Perversely, though, it only served to increase the level of her apprehension and her sense of urgency to determine the level of risk that the information in the files was likely to subject her to, and ultimately, she hoped, what action she could take to eliminate that risk. The gun at her bedside, or in the kitchen drawer where she kept it before retiring, became to her more like a personification of the danger she feared than a source of reassurance and comfort. In her own home, she felt under siege.

So, in spite of her best intentions, it was only two days after she gave Danny the material that might hold a key to her peace of mind, if not her survival, that she decided she needed to speak with him as soon as possible.

It was Monday, so she had to wait until she arrived home after school. She had a premonition that finding him right away would be difficult. She remembered that he had said that the telephone number on his business card was an answering service. She tried it and immediately got a recorded answer soliciting a message from her, which she left, asking him to call her, telling him that it was urgent that he do so. Then she called the cell phone number on the card. Again she got his voicemail and left a message. Frustrated, she decided to search for a landline number that he might not disclose to business callers. She wasn't sure where he lived, so tracking down a home telephone number might be a challenge. There was nothing promising in the Philadelphia White Pages on the Internet. Then she tried the regional White Pages for the Philadelphia metro area. A Danny Johnson was listed in Camden, in New Jersey, across the Delaware River from Philadelphia. She smiled as she copied the number down.

She decided to wait to call him until it was late enough in the evening for him to be home if he had eaten out, but, she hoped, before he would have gone to bed. She filled the time by beginning her take-home school work. She heated up leftovers which she picked at as she leaned over the test booklets she was marking, her elbows on the kitchen table, glancing from time to time as she did so at the electric clock on the wall above the stove. Finally, she walked over to the telephone where it sat on the counter and picked up the receiver.

The phone seemed to purr into as it rang three or four times before someone picked up.

"Hello?"

It was a woman's voice, low and melodious. Julia was too stunned to hang up. Then she realized her mistake.

"I must have a wrong number," she said. "I'm sorry."

"That's O.K., honey," the languid voice said. "Who were you looking for?"

"A man. Danny Johnson. I'll try again."

"Hold on for a second," the voice said soothingly, "I'll get him for you."

Julia sought the support of the wall next to the phone as she waited.

"Hello?" His greeting was thick and slow, as if he had been sleeping.

"It's Julia." Her voice had lost its confidence.

"Julia? How did you find me?" He sounded suddenly alert. "This isn't the number I gave you."

"I was in a hurry to talk with you and I didn't want to wait for you to respond to my messages, so I found your home number."

She hesitated. The conversation was not developing as she had imagined it would when she decided to call him. Words were not coming to her. He was silent, too.

"Danny, I'm sorry. I didn't mean to interrupt..." Miles away from him, looking blankly out the window toward the apple tree which was dimly lit from inside the house, she blushed deeply.

"You mean Veronica?" he said. "She shares the apartment with me. I couldn't afford anything decent without splitting the expense and she answered my ad. Anyway, I don't do anything with Veronica that you *could* interrupt except talk, and not much of that. Usually she's working at this time of night. We don't see much of each other. She pays her rent, so I can't complain."

"Working?"

"Topless dancer, so-called. Sad to say, I've never seen her act. She seems very professional. No funny business. At least she's never brought anyone home."

"I thought you lived in Philadelphia." She sensed that an edge had crept into her voice.

"When you asked me, Philadelphia seemed like a better place to be."

"It doesn't matter," she said quickly.

She heard the clink of the neck of a bottle as it touched the edge of a glass, then, as the glass filled, ice cubes tinkling against its sides.

"Good thing this is a portable phone," he said.

She felt a sudden urge to escape. "I'd better go," she said. "I can call later. At a better time."

"Don't," he said. "Please. We can talk with or without her around, but in case you care, Veronica's gone to bed, in *her* bedroom." He laughed.

His laugh was again the way she had remembered it from long ago, confident, making gentle fun of her confusion, full of humor. And again she felt the warmth of recognition.

She stretched the long, coiled telephone cord and sat on the nearest chair at the kitchen table. "Danny, this isn't what I called you about, interrupted you for, but I was disturbed by the evening—when you were here—the way you talked about us, about what happened in the barn, the way it all came to an end for us. I just let you talk, even though what you said wasn't right. You made everything seem so simple, and maybe it was for you. But not for me. At all."

He said nothing.

"I didn't really know you very well when..." she paused, "...when we were in high school. In a way I guess I know you even less now. I'm sorry I wasn't very friendly at the teachers' reception. I'd pushed those memories, good and bad, to the back of my mind until I saw you there, standing across the room.

"And I admit that I was uncertain about how I should—did—feel about you. But even then I realized that... that I was glad that you're back in my life, no matter what happened in the past."

Finally he spoke. "I was obnoxious at the reception. And I told you after your party what was on my mind when I asked you out to dinner." His voice was flat. "Besides, what fond memories of me can you have from before, after what I did..." He stopped.

She could hear the ice cubes, restless in their prison of glass. She imagined them in their distress, their edges softening, dissolving into formless anonymity in the bourbon.

She leaned forward on her chair and tightened her grip on the receiver. "You are the person who came up to an intense, sad girl in the drugstore who was too shy to speak to you and told her that what she was doing in school was right. Your eyes told her she was pretty, something she hadn't even dreamed was possible. You carried her books for her.

"She didn't have a date to the graduation dance and you asked her. And when you took her, you stayed with her and held her as you danced with her. When you brought her home, you kissed her.

"When you came to the picnic, you didn't hang out with that girl with the long, blond hair and the terrific figure..."

"Gloria Enright," he said.

229

"Yes, Gloria Enright, or anyone else, but with me. You took me to the most romantic place you knew."

The ice cubes signaled sadly to her once more.

"Julia, I was..."

"You told me when you were here that back then you wanted me to like you," she said. "I thought I loved you. Maybe I did love you. And I wanted you to love me. We both wanted the same things. But we didn't know how to handle it. I didn't, anyway. I was so naïve..."

She *was* naïve, she thought as she groped for words. An innocent. He was not. He should have been thinking for both of them. That he was confused, or whatever, was not her fault. It was his. But did it matter any more?

"We were both just kids," she said, "and it shouldn't make any difference now, but what happened in the barn was as much my fault as yours, maybe more so."

She stopped. The phone was silent.

Then Danny cleared his throat. "That's bullshit, Julia," he said, finally, "but thank you."

She stood up and looked out once more at the old, bent tree, ghostly in the pale light from the kitchen, darkness lurking behind it. "And I don't want you to come back into my life for a moment, and then leave again, just like that." She snapped her fingers.

"But Danny?"

"Yes."

"That's not why I called," she said. "I want you to take as much time as you need to figure out what's in those papers, those files, that I gave you to look at. But it's been worrying me. Really worrying me. I can explain why sometime, but, well, I know you probably haven't had a chance to..."

"Actually I have." He paused for moment. "Finding time isn't one my problems." She heard a suppressed laugh. "Unfortunately, I don't think the news is good, if I understand what you're looking for. But I hate to tell you that without asking you some questions, to give me more context, to understand the players, including other companies that show up in these records."

Julia looked at a small calendar she had tacked to the wall in front of her. "Could you come here again, soon, so that we can talk about it? I may not know everything that I should to fill in the gaps for you, but at least I can try. And the more I think about it, the more important to me it seems to get. I'll give you supper. Could you make it tomorrow?"

He laughed again. "My business hours are flexible, to say the least. I wish I could say that selling textbooks was going so well for me that my schedule is crowded with appointments. Anyway, when?"

"I have some work to do at home. How about five?"

"Done. Don't cook. I'll bring some Chinese. We can heat it up later."

"You don't need to bother. I really can put something together." She wondered when she would have time to stop at the grocery store.

"My way'll give us more time," he said.

"O.K., I'd love it," she said. "And Danny?"

"Yes?"

"Thanks."

47

Julia's Tuesday afternoon classes were behind her, and Wednesday would be devoted to review. She would need little preparation for Wednesday or for administering Thursday's final exams. Even so, she lugged some year-end paperwork with her as she pushed down on the horizontal brass bar that unlatched the exit door at the back of the school building and trotted up the four or five concrete steps that took her to ground level.

The small teachers' parking lot with its rows of mostly aging but respectable-looking vehicles seemed glazed in the hot, metallic brightness, even though it was only the first week in June. The impact of the sun after the cool drabness of the basement corridor made her stop as she reached the square platform of concrete sidewalk at the top of the stairs. The heat seemed to press down on her.

She had been distracted when she arrived that morning and could not remember now where she had parked. She was tempted to lean for a second against the end of the pipe railing that ran next to the steps, or at least set her bulky briefcase on the ground. Instead, she shaded her eyes with the palm of her free hand, taking advantage of her slightly elevated position to scan the edges and tops of the sedans, vans and pickups.

That was when she first noticed a car standing at the far end of the aisle between the ragged lines of vehicles in front of her. It seemed out of place, a large, long relic of the last big car era: a Cadillac perhaps, two doors, a dull-coated faded green, rust-plagued, low-slung behemoth. Oddly, there was something about it that seemed familiar to her. Probably, she thought, because cars like this had cruised in a neighborhood not far from the apartment in Philadelphia that she and her mother had rented, and, of course, she had seen them in New York City. That is how it struck her as she reflected for an instant on its presence: as a city thing, out of place here in this quiet rural town. Neither parking nor leaving, was it waiting for someone? Who, she wondered, among the people who worked at the school—and she was at least on nodding terms with everyone—could be leaving in that car?

Then she spotted the Volvo, its boxy dark blue roof projecting a few inches higher than the other sedans near it, and stepped down from the curb, heading in its direction. Out of the corner of her eye she was aware that the city car, with its long shelves of hood and trunk had eased forward, on a course that converged with the line she had taken. She zigzagged between the parked cars, across the grain, angling directly to the Volvo, which she could still see when she stepped off the curb. The low-slung car was no longer visible.

She looked for it, though. Was alert to its presence. "Street smarts" is how she explained it. A product of the kind of fear you have to feel in order to survive in one piece in the city while you are waiting for a subway on an almost empty platform, or walking anywhere at night, or just strolling across town in the middle of the afternoon to the grocery store. Particularly if you are a woman. But, of course, you never really stroll, you make sure you look like you're going somewhere important and as you do you watch around you, note your surroundings, the man lounging in a doorway, a small group of teenagers gathered near an open fire hydrant. You look for something different from what you expect, for change, for movement, always ready to respond. She thought she had lost the habit from lack of apparent need over the time she had lived here, but, luckily, she was wrong.

As she emerged from behind a van that was parked in the line of cars before the aisle she was headed for and a couple of spaces short of her car, she saw that the strange car was facing her and standing directly in front of the Volvo, blocking its egress into the aisle. She stopped still and peered at it. The window was down, and inside, in the shadows, she could make out the passenger. Was he bald? His face was indistinct, his eyes shadow-sockets, his nose a bump. She could see no mouth.

For an instant he did not seem to see her, and the bulky-looking barrel of the gun he was holding in a gloved hand, just outside the car's open window, was pointed to the front, down the aisle she had been about to step into. As it swung around to aim at her she ducked back behind the van, turned, and ran. Still clutching her briefcase, her purse swinging behind her, she dodged in-between cars, racing diagonally through the open spaces, her heart pounding, back to the steps, and down them to the door.

"I crouched as low as I could. In fact," she said to Danny Johnson, "I tried to disappear."

233

He was sitting, once again, at her kitchen table, this time with a pile of manila file folders and clamped stacks of accounting records in front of him. Julia made coffee, which she poured into two china mugs. When she turned with the mugs in her hands she paused for a moment. As she took in the sight of him there, she was moved to smile by something more than her habitual desire to make a guest comfortable, and whatever that feeling was—she was not sure herself—it caused color to rise up her neck and into her face as she stood before him. His expression remained serious.

"I was close to it and I know it was a gun," she said. "I don't care what they say. All I could think of was the insidious darkness of the little hole at the end of the barrel. The menace. It must have been pointed right at me."

She handed him his coffee and sat down across the corner of the table from him.

"I only saw that car one more time," she said, "when I glanced back before I went down the stairs. It was turning in my direction. It must have come out of the aisle where I'd seen it, where my car was parked. I didn't wait to ask them why they were there!"

She laughed, but could not pull him along with her in her feigned amusement. They both sipped from the mugs.

"Of course the exit door to the school was locked—it always is—and I lost it. You should have seen me trying to find the key in my purse without spilling everything else out. But someone started to come out of the building. I hadn't seen him in the hall through the door. So I yanked the door open, pushed him back in (it was Carl, the chemistry teacher—he thought I'd gone bananas), and slammed the door behind us."

She remembered the startled look on Carl's face as she dragged him down the hall to the first office with a telephone. Her frantic call was answered by Marsha, Dave Concklin's assistant, the only secretary on the school staff, who was at the switchboard. Julia could hear her perfectly well, but still she shouted at her through the phone's receiver, telling her to call the security guard, Joe Jaspers, and 911 because Joe would never be able to cope with this.

When she ran upstairs to Dave's office, he tried to calm her by persuading her that nothing had really happened. Not that she was lying, of course, but maybe the bright sun had interfered with her vision or something. He did ask Carl, who was still tagging along, to go down and stand by the teachers' exit and warn people not to use it or go into the lower parking lot until the police arrived. Yet he allowed anyone to leave by the main entrance who wanted to, including students. "No use alarming everybody," he said, "and getting the parents up in arms." Julia had managed to keep her silence. She could not forget that she was provisional, and Dave was the Principal.

The police talked with her after they checked to make sure that no car like the one she described was on the school grounds or lurking at its boundaries. They found no trace of it in the teachers' lot. But they seemed to take her seriously. With coaxing by the detective from the county sheriff's office who questioned her, she realized that the man she saw in the car was wearing a stocking over his head and face, that the gun must have been a pistol with a silencer attached, and that the hood of the car was a darker shade of the sickly pale green than the rest of the body. She thought it had New York license plates, like hers until recently, but could not be sure.

No one could agree on why it had been there, but some sort of teenage gang or drug-related activity seemed to be the explanation that the detective liked most. Dave protested. He said that except for an occasional weapon showing up among the students over the last few years there had been no sign yet that the city's diseases had spread to Ironton's schools. The detective simply shrugged. They put a county bulletin out for the car. That was the best they could do, the detective said, without more information.

Dave's last words to her as she was released to leave, finally, nearly two hours later, had been "Are you *sure* about all this, Julia?"

"Why would gang members be laying for someone in the teachers' parking lot?" Danny looked up at the ceiling, then past her across the table. "All the way in the back of the school? Where do the kids park?"

"Opposite the front entrance. It's a big lot. That's where visitor parking is, too."

"See what I mean?" Danny turned back to Julia.

"I'm sure they weren't local people," she said, "with New York plates."

It was then, talking with Danny in her own kitchen, that she suddenly realized why the threatening car had seemed familiar to her. She sat up. "Wait. I just told you how I had this strange feeling that maybe I'd seen it before? Now I remember! It wasn't, like I said, because you see those kinds of cars all the time in some parts of any big city. Nothing like that. It was because I *had* seen it before! I wish you'd been there. You would have known right away. I guess I was just too panicky to think straight. You know that long, heavy-looking car that was standing outside my house that night. The one that ran away when we, that is when you, started to walk up to it. I know it was dark then, and hard to make out any details, but we did get a pretty good look at it when it went under the street lights, when it drove away. This was that car. The same one. I'm sure of it."

She stood abruptly, took the few steps to the nearest counter, and pounded her fist down on the Formica surface. She pivoted back to face Danny, both fists clenched. "How stupid not to recognize it," she said.

"I said I'd tell you why I was so worried. Why I need to know what you found as quickly as possible." Julia sat down again across the kitchen table from Danny. "Well, a week ago or so I drove to meet Peter at a restaurant out in the country where I hoped to persuade him to give me a divorce quickly. Instead, he gave me a warning. He as much as told me that unless I came back to him, to demonstrate to his business crony Marco DiNiro—whose name is all over the place in some of these files—that I'm still 'loyal,' DiNiro might take things into his own hands. That he might do whatever it takes to stop me from giving the information that is in these documents to people he's afraid of.

"After you left Saturday night I kept thinking about what Peter said, and about that car that you chased away, and whether there could be any connection. Now that I realize the car this morning was the same one, I'm sure there is. Once might have been chance, or a mistake, or maybe I overreacted to a coincidence, or something. But not after this repeat performance. That's really scary!

"Anyway," she reached over and patted the stack of material Danny had piled on the table in front of him, "now you know."

48

DANNY OPENED THE TOP file folder. It was his own, not one that Julia and the copy service had used to organize the copied documents. Inside was a lined writing pad with a loose sheet on top which he handed to her. On it he had written down a list of names. "Tell me what you can, what you think is relevant, about these people and companies. I picked them out of all the files, but I've spent most of my time on the Finance ServiCo stuff so far."

Julia did her best to summarize for Danny what she knew about Finance ServiCo and her role performing her duties, as its sole officer in accordance with Rob Vardaman's instructions. She told him about TryCo, Inc. and Adams, and his dissatisfaction with DiNiro and Grendel Holdings. In the end, she confessed, "When it comes down to it, though, I don't know very much. Peter didn't talk with me about his business unless he wanted me to approach a friend of my father's as a business contact. My father was an investment banker before we moved to Libertyville."

As Julia talked, Danny took just a few sips from his mug before he walked to one of the windowed cabinets, reached for a tall glass, scooped some cubes of ice from under the ice maker in the freezer, and poured himself a drink from the bottle he had brought with him. Then he returned to his chair.

Julia sighed. "I'm sorry. I haven't been much help. I forgot to tell you earlier, I was so worked up about that car, but a few days before I saw Peter, I got a call from Josh Adams, the TryCo guy, and he told me that he and his partners have sued DiNiro and Peter over the TryCo acquisition. The kind of stuff that Adams had told me about a long time ago—that DiNiro and Grendel had overvalued the Grendel stock that they used to pay for TryCo. Anyway, Josh also said that DiNiro was being investigated by a Federal agency for criminal violations. That was what Peter seemed to be really worried about. That's when he warned me about DiNiro, because DiNiro knows—Peter told him—about these files that I took and copied. There may be more, but they seem to be the main problem."

She looked away from Danny for a moment, out the window. "You know, at first, I thought that what I wanted most from you was to understand my involvement with this company. What it might mean to me. What, if anything, I was doing that could be held against me later in some way, in a lawsuit, or by the authorities. But now, I guess the most important thing is to find out why DiNiro would be so concerned that I have this information. Could it hurt him more now that he's being sued and investigated and all?

"What did you find?"

Danny took a sip of his drink.

"It's hard to know for sure. For one thing, at first I thought these ledgers were something like the official records of the company. Finance ServiCo. But they're not."

Julia broke in. "I guess that doesn't surprise me. Rob would probably have kept the formal books, if not DiNiro. Rob is the one who walked me through whatever I was to do."

"But," Danny continued, "they are still a sort of informal accounting record of transactions for whoever was keeping track."

"Peter. I'm sure these were his private files."

"Peter, then, recorded a bunch of transfers, withdrawals you might call them, from your company to DiNiro. Not that the checks say that, probably, and there aren't any check stubs, but after each entry to some seemingly legitimate business type of recipient, let's say, XYZ corporation, he has 'D' noted in parentheses."

"Where did the money come from?" Julia said. "I thought Finance ServiCo didn't really do much. At least that's what Peter told me."

"It must have done something," he said, "because Grendel paid it big bucks, although that money didn't stay around for long. It went out to these 'D' companies. I guess the question I have is what did those companies, or DiNiro, do to earn it?"

"Beats me."

"Of course," he said, "there may have been contracts, work orders, whatever. In the Finance ServiCo file there is a copy of a consulting agreement with DiNiro. You signed it."

"I did?"

"It was at the back of the stack of financial records. Maybe you missed it."

"I guess I didn't read over the financial stuff that carefully. Anyway, I don't remember the contract. What about the Adams and TryCo folders? Those memos from DiNiro? Peter's notes? Adams told me he thought that DiNiro had cheated him and the other TryCo owners when he gave them Grendel stock to purchase TryCo."

"Again, on the face of it they may or may not be a problem for DiNiro or Peter. It depends on two things. One is whether what Peter was directed to tell the TryCo stockholders was true. The other is the significance of the dates on those memos and notes that are dated. Are they before the acquisition? I guess those check marks and handwritten dates in the margins of some of them show that he did pass on the information DiNiro wanted him to, and when. But whether they lied about the value of the Grendel stock? That's something an accountant would have to tackle."

Julia remembered that some of the dates were well before the time she first met Peter at the party celebrating the acquisition.

"You asked me to tell you what I think," Danny said. "It's this. There's nothing here that you would call a 'smoking gun' necessarily, but there *could* be, depending. These could be pieces, maybe important pieces, of a bigger puzzle. If I had to describe what was going on with Finance ServiCo—and there could be other explanations that don't show up in these records—I'd say it was something called 'money laundering.' That Grendel's money was paid to DiNiro in a way that hid his identity, or at least the real reason for the payments, from Grendel's records. In other words, they may have thought that the payments were illegal or improper in some way, so they didn't want to disclose them to Grendel's accountants or stockholders, or the SEC. Securities and Exchange Commission. Instead they made it look as though they were made to a company, FinanceServiCo, and faked the reasons that the payments were made.

"Another thing. Finance ServiCo, is an off-shore company. I've got to think that its income is sheltered from U.S. taxes, and that it wouldn't be compelled to disclose payments it made to U.S. taxpayers, even though the taxpayers themselves would be required to report any income. If that's true, DiNiro might have been hiding taxable income from the IRS by using this money laundering scheme. He could get in serious trouble there, too.

"Remember, we can't be sure about any of this because we only have fragments of the story. There may be other, legitimate, explanations in some other documentation. If not, then it's easy to see why DiNiro, and Peter, would be concerned that you have this, even though you gave the originals back to Peter."

Restless, Julia stood and paced slowly in front of Danny. "I told you I saw Peter. He told me not to tell Adams and his lawyers anything. He told me that he couldn't be responsible for what DiNiro might do to protect himself. That's what makes me so concerned, so afraid, now. I can't be sure of his exact words. I was pretty agitated. Angry with him. But, Danny, just as I told you earlier, what he said definitely sounded threatening." The image of Peter came to her still again, holding her wrists in the parking lot of the restaurant, not quite hurting her, and the sound of his tense voice. "Not that he, Peter, would cause me 'harm,' but that DiNiro would."

"What did you say to Peter?"

"That I hadn't made up my mind what I'd do."

"What kind of person is this DiNiro, anyway?"

Julia thought for a moment. "Creepy." She laughed as the word came out. She hadn't thought of it before, but it suited the man so perfectly. Then she told Danny about the dinner in Frankfurt: what he said about Adams, how he drank to her joining the 'team' and talked about Finance ServiCo, his wet kiss at the end of the evening, which she had wiped off her mouth while he was talking with Peter, and that she had felt sorry for his female companion, regardless of what arrangement the young woman had entered into with him. And she told him what Archibold Strothers had said: that DiNiro could be ruthless if provoked, or words to that effect.

"When I hear that, and when I think about how you've been seeing this mysterious car that seems to be following you, or worse, and that it all started after Adams brought his lawsuit and DiNiro and Peter likely found out about the Federal investigation, and, of course, after you left Peter, I agree with you. It's time to worry. I'm wondering whether you shouldn't just send all this stuff to Adams' lawyers. Talk with them. Cooperate."

Julia looked down at her empty mug.

"I'm so confused. I don't know what to do."

Danny picked up his glass, absently swirling the ice cubes in the amber liquid. He took a sip.

She looked back up, into his eyes. "I don't want to stand in Josh Adams' way. I think he was cheated, and DiNiro should pay. But I do worry about myself, whether I did anything that can come back and hurt me. And I don't want to harm Peter, if I can help it."

At these words she noticed a momentary change in Danny's expression, but whatever it had been left no trace an instant later. His voice was not affected.

"It looks as though he may be too involved to avoid trouble, if trouble is there."

Julia saw that they needed more coffee. She stood up quickly and strode to the sink where she began to rinse the basket of the coffee maker, holding it under the tap. But as the water flowed into it, filled it, and cascaded down its sides into the drain, she stared out of the window at the play of the last rays of the sun on the tops of the apple tree and her garage.

"The only reason I met with Peter was to get a divorce as quickly as possible." She was looking away from Danny as she talked and had to raise her voice to be heard over the running water. "Seeing him didn't change that at all. He's holding off, which makes me mad. It seems so senseless."

She turned off the water and glanced over her shoulder. "Danny, it was so strange. I had no feeling for him at all when I saw him there, or when I left."

She felt tears beginning to fill her eyes. She let go of the basket and held onto the edge of the sink so tightly her hands began to ache. As she stood quietly, with her fingers pressing against the cold metal, she thought she had mastered herself. But words welled up from somewhere deep inside her. She tried to stifle a sob.

"Isn't that sad?"

She held her breath and bit her lip until it stung. Then she dabbed at her eyes and her face with a dish towel. She turned toward Danny. He was on his feet.

"Are you all right?"

"How silly." She managed the semblance of a smile. "I'm sorry."

Her voice still wasn't quite steady.

"You see, I wanted to make you understand that it's really over between Peter and me," her gaze shifted away from him again, "but now I don't know what you must be thinking."

When she looked up, Danny was standing in front of her. He moved his hands to her shoulders and searched her face with his eyes.

"Thinking?" he said. "About what?"

They sat on the front porch, on the rusted metal-framed couch with faded canvas cushions that came with the house. The sun had just set, but, beyond a few large trees that stood like dark sentinels, a pale radiance lingered, illuminating the lawn and the street itself and the open spaces in front of the other houses set back along its length.

They saw no one. Yet the tempting aroma of smoke from charcoal cooking and the squeals of children playing and the congenial mutter of backyard conversation floated to them through the stillness. Nearby, the hissing cadence of a sprinkler swished over a neighbor's lawn. A mockingbird began his evening concert with a reckless series of trills.

Danny tried to take another sip of his drink, but the glass only held the remnants of a few ice cubes. Julia had no wine in the house, so she had accepted a light bourbon and water in a glass that she filled with ice. She held it with both hands, staring up at the darkening strip of sky as evening enveloped the dusk.

"Peaceful," Danny said quietly. "Like another world. You must be happy here."

She sensed that he was looking at her.

"I've been in Ironton for more than half a year, and except for Rita and a few others at school, I really haven't made any friends. I hardly know who my neighbors are."

She rolled the cold glass, wet with condensation, against her cheek.

"I guess I kind of withdrew for a while. But now..."

She looked at Danny and smiled.

He got to his feet. "I'm going to get another drink." A neighbor's dog barked, playful but insistent, a few houses away. Danny turned and looked down at her. "Ready for a refill?"

"No, thank you," she said.

In a moment, Danny called from the kitchen. "Shouldn't I put our dinner in the oven to heat up?"

She turned her head toward his voice. "Not yet," she called back. "Let's wait a while."

She rose and walked down the front steps to the lawn. The bittersweet fragrance of linden trees in bloom, the tangy scent of sycamores, the smell of fresh-cut grass, stronger in the early falling dew, hovered around her, suspended in the soft air. Foliage lost substance in the gloom, and in mysterious shadows gathering where the light had fled, fireflies flashed urgent messages.

In a few minutes Danny reappeared. He put his glass down on the porch near the couch and moved to her side. He peered right and left into the darkness, which was not yet broken by the street light that remained unlit near the end of her driveway.

"No bad cars out tonight," he said.

Julia stepped in front of him and took his hands in hers.

"Danny..." she started.

Danny looked down at her. "I told you why I came here the first time. To your dinner party. Remember what I said? That's not why I'm here now. I'm here to help you. To try to be a friend. I want to make up for whatever I've done, or tried to do," he smiled faintly, "in the past."

"Danny, I want you to give me another chance."

"What do you mean?"

"In the barn. I've thought about it often. About you and me. I guess you were confused, but I was, too. I wasn't ready. It's different now. I know what I want."

Julia guided his hands behind her, and raised hers to the back of his neck to pull him down to her. She stood on her toes. For an instant she thought of Peter, only a few inches taller than she was, and so different from this man. Then she kissed Danny, her lips lingering until he warmed to her, and when he did, she gently forced access with her tongue. She closed her eyes and savored the experience—new and exciting to her now, but even after all these years, surprisingly familiar, too.

49

IN THE VELVET DARKNESS of the yard as they kissed, she had felt, she thought, like a starved animal that smelled food almost within reach. Her appetite for him had become overpowering. So, she was perplexed by his awkward reticence as they reached her bedroom.

She had kissed him, held him, and brought him there by the hand. With Peter, such seductive behavior by her had often been an important part of a ritual which he, nevertheless, had always led in the end. Foreplay with Peter was exciting for the very reason that she knew that he would carry it to its intended exhilarating conclusion.

But this man with her now, who had seemed so comfortable with women—with all of the Gloria Enrights that in the past had made Julia so uncomfortable—who minutes before had dodged out to his car to retrieve the small, foil condom packets which he just happened to have in his glove compartment, this man who had once sought her with an urgency that years later stirred her when she recognized him in a crowded room of school teachers, now seemed inexplicably detached.

She pulled him to her and kissed him again.

"Take me Danny," she whispered to him. "Please take me."

Danny extricated himself from her grasp and stepped back.

"I can't do it, Julia," he said.

He sat on the bed.

Her eyes flashed open. They showed an irritation born of impatience, but before she said anything she sensed his distress. She sat down next to him.

He took one of her fingers and worked the knuckle between his thumb and forefinger. He had touched her nipples this way in the barn, kneading them gently, and the remembered image from so long ago sent a shiver through her as if he was caressing her there again. But his gesture here was more one of reaching out to her, an appeal. He needed to stay in contact with her as he talked. His voice was low.

"I know this sounds crazy, but now that we're up here, in your bedroom, I feel somehow as if I'm returning to the scene of a crime." He smiled thinly, and she saw color rising in his face.

Julia looked around them. They were surrounded by tokens of Julia's childhood, objects that she, or her mother, had saved from the bedroom of the house in which she had grown from a girl to a young woman. The oval mirror with its painted border, the white spread, yellowed with age, sprinkled with printed sprigs of violets, her silver comb and brush set (too small, virtually useless now except as decoration), the ragged stuffed giraffe that stared at them from a chair in the corner.

"It's the room. All this girl stuff. I guess when I came here I was trying to get as far away from Peter as possible. Maybe this was a way to do it. Let's move somewhere else. Downstairs. We can make do."

"It's not the room, Julia," he said. "It's you, and me, together. I thought you would be bothered by it, but I guess I was wrong. I'm the one."

Julia's voice softened. "Danny, that was years ago. You've had other women. A lot, I imagine. Think of me as one of them."

His eyes lowered. They seemed to fix on his restless fingers.

"I can't. And you're not.

"It's hard to describe what I felt when I saw you with Rita in Philadelphia. You looked terrific, of course. But seeing you here, where we are now, doesn't just make me realize again how great you are. It reminds me how wrong I was." He looked up. "I don't mean forever, I guess, but just not now."

Julia looked at him for a moment.

"But you haven't *really* seen me yet," she said. "Wait here."

She ran downstairs and a moment later brought back the candles and holders that she kept in the dining room. She put them on the bedroom dresser, lit them, switched off the electric lights in the room and closed the door.

Standing before him, in the wavering yellow glow from the candles, she stooped to remove her shoes and kicked them aside.

She took a deep breath as she slowly unbuttoned her blouse and sloughed it off.

Julia remembered how when she was young she had practiced movement and expression before the full-length mirror downstairs when no one else was in the house, to try to gain the grace and poise she was sure she lacked. She imagined now that she was looking at her own reflection, appraising and guiding each gesture. That she was Danny, watching this woman that he thought he knew—first with curiosity, but soon, she hoped, with mounting desire.

Her bra unhooked at the front. She arched her shoulders back a little more than necessary to shrug off its straps, held the unpretentious garment at arm's length, and let it drop at his feet.

Danny started to rise. Gently, she pushed him back. When he looked up, his eyes moved to her small, firm breasts, soft in the soft light, with their dusky points of focus, themselves like dark, round eyes staring back, that had first drawn his attention once before.

She reached across to release her skirt at the side. The soft flesh under her arm grazed a nipple, setting off a small vibration of pleasure. She helped the skirt past her hips, wriggled it to her ankles, and cleared it away.

She slid a finger of each hand inside the waist band of her panties and pushed them down. Stepping out of them, she flicked them with a bare foot to join the bra in front of Danny.

Then she spread out her arms, palms open, and smiled.

"Julia."

Danny stood.

She moved to him, reaching toward the top button of his shirt. He fumbled to open the rest, pulled his arms awkwardly out of the sleeves, and let it fall behind him. She started for his belt buckle, but he leaned over to untie the laces of his moccasins, crouching to see them better in the dim light. Stepping back from her, he sat on the edge of the bed and pulled them off.

Finally, Danny got to his feet again, released his belt from its buckle and loosened his pants. Julia helped him ease his trousers and shorts down his legs to the floor, following them with her hands, moving her fingers over the outside of his limbs to his ankles.

Despite the utter casualness with which he must have shed his shirt during the time in high school when she first had been aware of him, displaying himself in the heat of exercise or sport, or to bake in the sun, or to swim, Julia had never seen so much as his chest unclothed. But when she stepped back to look at him she realized that she had built for herself a picture of him anyway, had assumed what he would look like, and that by now, after all the years since her infatuation for him then, this image had become her reality.

The thickening around his waist and the faded definition of his muscles did not match these expectations, but the extra fullness she had seen in his face and hands since they had been together again had prepared her. He was not in shape. Not tight, as Peter had kept himself. Peter had been compact and hard. Rather, this body was tall, rangy and smooth. Like a youth's, perhaps, before the toughening of manhood. Also like a youth, she supposed, no heavy mats of hair hid his skin. With only a thin, nearly transparent mist of blond fuzz covering his limbs, he seemed more naked than Peter ever did, and more vulnerable.

She brushed her fingers over his chest, circling his nipples lightly before her hands drifted downward. She followed them with her eyes to the darker blond thicket of hair that crowned the immediate object of her desire. Already heavy and standing apart, it was like a being separate from the hesitant person to which it was physically attached. One that empathized with her needs, and unambiguously shared them.

It responded to her touch.

50

AFTER A FINAL KISS, Danny rolled onto his side facing Julia, closing his eyes in sleep, a hand resting heavily on her leg to stay in touch. She pulled the sheet up over both of them and lay on her back, her eyes wide open, her mind like a pond in the woods. Clear and still.

Until she felt the pangs of a ravenous hunger. She spent a moment in the bathroom, put on the extra-large man's tee shirt that she wore around the house sometimes, and trotted down the back stairs to the kitchen. She emptied the takeout containers that Danny had brought into Pyrex dishes and placed them in the oven, setting it at a low temperature. Then she climbed back up the stairs at a run and shook Danny gently.

It was after ten. Before they sat down at the kitchen table, Danny, in his boxers, gathered the files they had been discussing earlier and put them back in the carryall.

"Okay if I keep these for a while longer? Now that I know more about the players I'd like to go over the Finance ServiCo papers again, and spend some time with the Adams files. I hope that's not a problem."

"Not for me. Let me know what you find out."

In a few minutes, Julia retrieved the Chinese food and doled out portions on two plates. She attacked their feast with chopsticks and her fingers. Danny ate with a fork and spoon. Between mouthfuls, she watched him. He consumed his dinner with enthusiasm.

She had made coffee and sipped it from a mug as they ate. Danny poured himself a new drink.

In a while, Danny looked up.

"That was great!" he said.

"What? The beef and bean sprouts?"

"No kidding," he grinned, "you were terrific."

She smiled.

He had seemed tentative. Very different from Peter. Not leading, but at the same time not used to being led. Once Danny was fully engaged, though, she knew he had been too eager. He began so quickly that she was not swept up on the wave she had longed to ride. And just as the swell was rising within her, and long before it could break, to throw her into the giddy free-fall she knew to expect, leaving her basking in the soothing caresses of its foam, Danny was through.

"You were great, too," she said.

She looked into his eyes. There was a depth there she was not used to. She remembered for an instant their effect on her when she had first dared to glance at them, years ago. Were they different now? She smiled again, shyly this time, and looked back at her food.

"I hate to, but I need to change the subject," he said, his tone altered. "We both agree that these people are obviously after you, and we have to assume that they don't just want to scare you. They're acting like they're much more serious than that. So what are you going to do to avoid them? To protect yourself."

She thought of the gun, still residing in her kitchen drawer.

"You can't just go on living your ordinary life, following your usual routines, can you?"

She put down her chopsticks. His question was troubling. She had thought a lot about what she should do, and had come up with no practical strategy at all.

"It's the end of the school year. I can't not go to work. Not now. I can't really go to the police about something as vague as this, when even I'm not sure what's going on. I just don't know what they could do, unless someone comes prowling around this place. Don't worry, I'll keep everything locked so that a patrol car will have time to get here if I call 911.

"I'll just have to be really careful. Really alert. The way I always was when I walked alone in New York at night."

She stood.

"That'll just have to make do for a few more days. Then maybe I can follow your advice and go to Adams' lawyers and see where that takes me. And I could go away for a while, like going into hiding, until everything gets sorted out. I don't know."

Danny started to speak, but she picked up her plate and interrupted him.

"I don't think I can eat any more."

"Me either," Danny said. "But Julia, please take care of yourself. If there's anything you think I can do to help, just ask."

Then he, too, rose. "Can't you save this stuff and have it again sometime?"

"Sure," Julia said. She reached for the coffee maker. "How about some coffee on the porch?"

She turned off the lights in the front of the house and reached into the closet for a sweater on the way to the door.

"You'd better put something on," she said. "It's going to be chilly out there."

"I'll be okay."

She followed him, carrying the mugs.

The moon had risen behind the house. Invisible to them, it bathed the objects of the night in a silvery luminescence, only hinting at their colors, distorted gray tints, in its mysterious reflected light, and cast deep shadows where its rays could not penetrate. The road in front of the vacant lot across from her yard and the wall of vegetation there were clearly illuminated, as was most of the street itself, except where it was shaded by the trunks of the tall trees along it. To Julia, moonlight always seemed like a sort of magic and she was quiet as she absorbed the scene around them. Danny spoke.

"Still no one out here. Maybe they saw my car in the driveway. Maybe they didn't like the moon."

He turned, silhouetted against the moonlit world beyond the porch. She smiled and settled onto the couch. He sat beside her.

"The car hasn't been back here since you frightened it away before," she said.

They sipped their coffee.

"I hope we're reading a lot more into this than there is," she said.

"I hope." He put his cup down on the floor at the foot of the sofa. "But I still worry about you."

"I said the same thing to you the last time you were here—that I worried about you. Do you remember what you said?"

"What did I say?"

"You told me not to. I remember it very well. You said that I 'must have more important things to worry about.'"

"And don't you? Like all this stuff going on with you now?" he spoke almost in a whisper.

"Nothing." she said. "I can't think of anything more important right now than you."

He turned to her. His voice was still low. "Really?"

She met his gaze. In the faint illumination she saw that his eyes were moist. She looked away.

"Why did you leave Peter?" he said.

Her stomach tightened. "I told you how he was with me toward the end. But that wasn't it, really. Or all of it. There were probably a lot of reasons. When I look back on it, which I don't do much any more, thankfully, I realize that it was a mistake from the beginning. But I did love him very much. No," she added quickly, "I don't any more."

She found that she had become relaxed while she talked about it, was even enjoying it as the words began to flow. For the first time. Without turning her head, she reached for his hand.

"It's funny. It all meant so much to me then, that last, awful, part. Everything that happened. You'd think that I'd remember every detail. That it would be etched in my mind. It's not that way, though. It all seems like a blur, somehow. Crazy, isn't it?"

"I don't know," he said. "I've never loved anyone that way. Never broken up. Never had anything *to* break up. Beginning in school. Until..." He stopped. "But, Julia, what did happen?"

"There were a lot of things, but in a word, he was unfaithful. Many times over."

He squeezed her hand.

"One of them was my best, maybe my only, close friend in the City. Of course, I should have known. In a way she came close to warning me. So did he. But, as they say," she sighed, "love is blind."

She knew she should have been crying by then, overcome with the pathos of Peter's transgressions, Vicki's treachery and her own mistakes, and the consequences of all of that. Instead, when she finished, she felt whole again, somehow, as if she had just retrieved a part of herself that had long been missing.

"You must be freezing," she said, and ran her hand up his arm to his shoulder. He put his arm around her back, under the sweater, and pulled her toward him.

"Maybe I should have put that jacket on after all," he said. He shifted to face her and pressed her against him, her side to his chest, stroking her hair. "But I think I know how to stay warm."

She closed her eyes and for an instant she saw herself with Peter. They were in Salzburg. It was after they had taken their continental breakfast on the little balcony. The air was balmy, and when they finished they brought the porcelain pot of rich, dark coffee and the pitcher of warm milk inside. The slanting rays of the early morning sun lingered on them as they lay on the elegant bed. A light breeze set the gauzy curtains which they had drawn across the doorway in motion, and an undulating diffusion of sunlight fell on them as they moved with each other, making their bodies seem to glow with the heat that they felt within, adding fire to fire. Adding fire, she had thought then, to their love.

She rubbed Danny's bare back with her hand. Then she turned to him. He reached behind her head. With his fingers laced through her hair, he pulled her gently to him, and kissed her. Lips parted, tongues engaged in their own sinuous dance. Surprisingly, their kissing again felt to her like returning home after a long trip. So peaceful, even as the excitement of her desire grew again.

She explored his chest, holding onto his flesh, kneading it. She let her hand settle onto his thigh. His muscles there tightened, then relaxed under the pressure of her fingers. She worked slowly up his leg. She found that he was ready again.

He rose and lifted her by the hands.

"I'll be better this time," he said. He was smiling. "I *can* control myself. You'll see."

He guided her back into the house and up the stairs.

51

AS SHE HAD PROMISED Danny she would, Julia took precautions. She made a point of parking in the student and visitor's lot. That, she thought, should confuse anyone who had studied her habits and might plan to waylay her based on her daily routine, as they had once before. She would try to leave when all the students did, so she would be difficult to spot in the confusion of the general exodus, and likely shielded from any direct assault. But this was the day before final exams were to begin and a faculty meeting had been called at the last minute, to start after the last class period, so she was forced to wait.

As she was walking out of the meeting with Rita, someone from the office handed her a pink telephone message slip. "Danny Johnson" it said and gave a number. She folded it and put it in her purse.

"Anyone I know?" Rita asked with a smile.

"I'll tell you about it later," Julia said. "I've got to get out of here if I'm going to beat the factory rush."

Rita said she would wait until later, when the worst of it should be over. Julia waved to her and walked briskly to her car. Relieved to see no suspicious activity in its vicinity, she climbed in and quickly drove off.

On a normal day, she would have been able to avoid the traffic from the shift change at the factory, but before long, she realized that she had not started home soon enough. The factory was letting out just as she approached it. A traffic patrolman stopped her to allow the exodus of a closely packed line of cars, pickups, vans and SUVs from the plant's huge parking lot. When he motioned her lane forward, she moved slowly up behind the vehicles he had let in. A mile or so further on, there would be relief. The road widened to two lanes on her side for a while before she turned off at the edge of town.

Her mind drifted. She had put in a full day reviewing the term's material in each class, with meetings in between with individual students. Even though she had started teaching these students in the middle of the year, it was an emotional day, too. She had grown fond of many of the seniors, whom she knew she would not be seeing in class again, and without permanent status, she might be saying goodbye for good to the others as well.

She was pleasantly tired. Driving so slowly, it was an effort to stay alert as the sun, still hot, fought for supremacy with the Volvo's elderly air conditioner. She had no idea when she had fallen asleep the night before, or more accurately, early that morning. She had set the clock a little later than the usual time, then plunged into a deep, seemingly dreamless slumber. Danny did not wake up at the alarm, which she shut off as quickly as possible. She left a clean towel for him on a chair, gathered her clothes and a toothbrush and tiptoed downstairs to use the small lavatory there before she dressed quietly for work.

Danny's worry, reinforcing hers, that Denny DiNiro was behind the threat to her in the parking lot as well as the earlier stalking car in front of her house, had totally disrupted her peace of mind at a time of year, with the end of school imminent, that was frantic enough already. While she was washing up and dressing she tried to sort out the few means she could identify to protect herself. Realistically, no place where she felt she needed to be—here at home, or at the school, where so many critical tasks cried for her attention—was safe. At the same time, she told herself again, staying away from work and running away altogether, were not options. That's when she decided on her tactics for approaching and leaving the school. And, of course, on her return she would check out her house, maybe cruise past at first to look for any signs of another presence there, before entering the driveway.

She worried that the aroma of coffee brewing and muffins toasting might rouse Danny, so she decided to pick up something on the way, or in the school cafeteria. Before she departed she set up the coffee maker, leaving it for Danny to turn on.

She wrote out a note to him. Pressed for time, she struggled with its wording. It started, "Thank you for a wonderful evening." She urged him to have breakfast. Her last paragraph was, "Call me if you learn anything more from the files. You can bring them back later." She hesitated, then signed it, simply, "Love, Julia." When she read it over she realized that it wasn't right at all; that it didn't say what she wanted to say, about him, about their time together. Worse, she wasn't sure, really, what she *did* want to say. She glanced at her watch and saw that it was too late for her to do anything about it, so she left the note under the salt shaker on the kitchen table, grabbed her purse and her work from school and hurried out the door.

Her car was in her garage. As she climbed into it and carefully backed into her driveway, she was visited by a vague feeling of apprehension that plagued her in spite of the measures she had decided on to foil anyone seeking to do her harm. With a conscious effort, though, she shook it off. She had to admit that her scheme to evade someone who might be after her was flawed and might not stand up to a determined enemy. But in spite of the anxiety born of her own interpretation of the recent disturbing events in her life, and Danny's, when it came down to it, she found it difficult to believe, truly, that there was an actual assassin out there dedicated to bringing her down, like a victim in a TV series. The concept just seemed too unreal, too much like grotesque fantasy. So distant from anything in her experience, or that of anyone she knew, or of anyone like her.

Besides, she had plenty of challenges just making her own way with her life in this new setting. She had to do whatever she could to win a permanent place as a teacher at Ironton High. She had to try her best to cultivate new friends, as much as she enjoyed and relied on Rita and Calvin, and now Danny. In short, it was difficult enough to achieve a normal existence, the kind she had craved ever since she had seen her life with Peter, the man she had thought her happiness was tied to, dissolve into nothing but heartache. There was no room in that picture for this other thing, whatever it was, or seemed to be.

Now, on her way home, Julia gripped the steering wheel and tried to concentrate on the road ahead and the heavy traffic, but at the thought of her note to Danny, she blushed.

Then she remembered again being with Danny, and smiled. The amazing thing was that despite getting only four or five hours of sleep, she felt terrific. She even enjoyed the faculty meeting. Reviving for a moment, she sang aloud, picking up a fragment from a song she had heard on the radio on the way to work that morning. "It feels so good," she sang, and then hummed part of the tune when she couldn't remember the rest of the lyrics.

As the road widened, the car in front of her speeded up. She followed its example. From experience, though, she knew that most people drove faster here than she would choose. Checking her rear view mirror, she signaled and edged into the right-hand lane. At that moment, for the first time, she focused on the car that had been behind her before she switched lanes. When she saw it, she started. It was the huge, dull-coated

Cadillac from the teachers' parking lot. She was certain of it. She could make out two people in the front seat. Exhaust fumes billowed behind it as it accelerated and began to come up on her, moving at the same time into her blind spot, out of sight to her left.

The chill of a grim reality she had tried so hard to ignore struck her to her core. Even in the stifling heat that had induced in her a languorous contentment only seconds earlier, she actually shivered as, in an instant, she traded her comfortable drowsiness for a state of high alert.

She glanced over her left shoulder. The Cadillac hovered there. Its progress was blocked by the car that had been in front of Julia before, which in turn had slowed because of the traffic. Julia, too, was hemmed in. She moved to within a car length behind a tall, wide van in her lane.

This part of the road was built as a precursor to development and was bordered with curbs and sidewalks. She steered close to the curb and leaned to the right to try to determine what lay ahead along the shoulder on her side, but the van's bulk made it impossible to see very far.

Just then, the left lane began to speed up again, and the low-slung Cadillac pulled alongside. Julia decided to ignore it and, with an effort, looked straight ahead.

Without sacrificing her full attention to any means she could find of evasion and escape, she developed a vain hope that the occupants of the other car, when they had sought her in the parking lot, might not have known which of the many cars there had been hers. Could their presence here just be a horribly unlucky coincidence? With her window rolled up might they fail to recognize her as their target unless they saw her face head-on? Or could they simply be mistaken and be after someone else? Maybe it really did have something to do with drugs, as the police had speculated.

Movement on her left caught her attention. Instinctively, she turned toward it. The windows of the cumbersome-looking vehicle were heavily tinted, almost opaque. They seemed incongruous against its faded pastel green paint, and sinister. The front one was opening slowly. Despite her resolve, she found herself consumed for a long moment by an effort to distinguish objects in the gloom behind it.

She glanced forward quickly. The van had pulled away a little. She must have been drifting off its pace. Gently she accelerated. On the right now, ahead of the van, she noticed a break in the curbing, as if for an intersecting street. She turned back to the car beside her. It was then that she saw the thick barrel of what looked like the parking lot gun pointed at her from inside the Cadillac's partially opened front window, a few inches above its edge, not extended into the light. Visible to no one but herself. Behind it, the blurred face.

She stamped her foot on the brake pedal. There was no time to check for cars behind her, so she yanked the wheel to the right and swerved off the main road and into the side street she had seen ahead to avoid being piled into from the rear. As she did, she heard a muffled explosion in her left ear. With everything else she had to cope with to avoid losing control of her car, she was barely aware of the sting she felt at the same time on her forehead.

The car careened as it skidded in its turn. Then it stabilized for an instant and she eased up on the brakes. But what had looked like a side street intersecting her road had not been finished more than a few yards beyond the width of the sidewalk. It led immediately into a graded dirt field, an incipient housing tract of some sort. A wooden barrier marked the end of the pavement. On impact with her car it flew into the air in front of her. Frantically she thrust her foot down again, jamming the brake pedal to the floor. The steering wheel jerked out of her hands, one way, then the other. The car bumped over low obstacles she could not see. Then it lurched to a sudden halt.

52

Tap. Tap. Tap.
Julia sensed as much as heard the sound, and, reflexively, opened her eyes. But she quickly closed them again without looking up. She knew it must be someone outside the car. *Them!* If she stayed still, they might think she was unconscious, or better yet, dead. It shouldn't take long for someone else to stop and frighten them away.

Tap. Tap. Tap.

Then she heard a muffled voice.

"Julia! If you're awake, unlock the door before we have to break the window!"

She looked up to see Rita peering at her anxiously. A few people stood behind Rita, one with a good-sized rock in his hand. More had gathered on the other side of the car, which was in a ditch of some kind, and tilted.

She could feel nothing but a painful headache. She touched her forehead. When she brought her hand down, there was blood on her fingers. She opened the door. Approaching sirens had been wailing to a crescendo in the background. Abruptly, one after the other, the sirens groaned to a halt nearby.

"There's no smoke. Can't smell gasoline. You can stay right where you are." It was the man who had brandished the rock, leaning in front of Rita. "You shouldn't get out until you really feel like it. Here," he handed Julia a folded handkerchief, "you might need this."

Julia did feel fragile. Faint. She was aware of cold perspiration on her face and patted her skin with the handkerchief. She looked at the fabric in her hand. Blood. She looked down. Her skirt showed dark blotches of stain. Her blouse was streaked with red.

"You'd better hold it against that cut to slow the bleeding." It was the man again.

"I must have hit my head when the car stopped," Julia said.

"That gash looks awful," Rita said.

Two men in black jackets, pants and boots—from the fire department?—appeared and walked in opposite directions around the car. One crouched to look underneath.

"How do you feel?" A burly man in a light blue shirt that looked like part of a uniform had taken over the space at the open door. His voice was quiet but businesslike. "Hurt anywhere—except your head?"

"I don't think so. I feel awfully weak."

The man reached in with a gauze pad and dabbed at her forehead. He stared directly into her eyes for a moment, then put something under her nose. "Sniff," he said.

Julia did and jerked back. Ammonia. She blinked. In that instant her mind felt clear. Her head still ached badly.

"Now, how about moving around to the side of the seat so we can work on you while you're sitting up," the man said. He and a companion reached in to help her, but she unfastened the seat belt, swung her legs over on her own, and faced them.

He cleaned the wound on her forehead, placed a large medicated pad over it and held it in place with a few turns of some kind of wrapping that fastened at the back of her head. Then he squirted a clear liquid from a plastic bottle on a small towel and washed the blood from her face. His hands were gentle but firm, his movements deft.

"You were pretty lucky," he said. "Another fraction of an inch and you'd be in bad shape."

"What do you mean?" she said.

"The bullet just grazed you. You'll have a headache for quite a while, but probably nothing worse."

"Bullet?"

The man gestured toward the window of the open door. A tight intricate pattern of spider web fractures radiated from the small circular hole in the glass.

"Before you can go with us, the cops want to talk with you. I'll tell them to be quick. I want you on the way to the hospital as soon as possible."

"Hospital?"

"They'll need to do some work on your head. Then they'll want to check you out. They'll probably spring you in a few hours, unless they find something else."

Julia stared at him without expression.

"I'll follow you there." Rita had been hovering in the background. "You won't be alone."

A uniformed policeman appeared.

"What about my car?" For the first time, Julia was close to tears.

"We'll need to take a look at it here," the policeman said. He glanced in the direction of the hole in the window. "Then we'll have it towed to a safe place." He crouched in front of her as he was talking and pulled a note pad from his back pocket. He spoke with calm authority. "One of the fenders is pushed in. It's not in bad shape. You'll be driving it in no time. Once we release it."

He stopped to flip through the pad. When he reached the place he was apparently searching for he looked up at her.

"Now," he said. "may I please see your driver's license and your registration, Ma'am?"

Julia sat in a room in the emergency department of the regional hospital, on the edge of an examination table. It had been lowered to allow her feet to reach a portable step that a nurse had positioned to help her climb off when she felt up to it. A short, heavyset man in a suit jacket and tie stood facing her. Rumpled trousers that didn't match the coat sagged below the bulge of his ample belly. It was the same detective from the County Sheriff's office who had questioned her after she had seen the person in the stocking mask with a gun in the teacher's parking lot. She had forgotten his name. He flipped open a plastic case to allow her to inspect his badge, handed her a calling card and introduced himself again.

"Herman Crane," he announced.

Without getting up, she shook the beefy hand that he offered her.

His gray hair was clipped close in a military type of cut that left his large head and thick features to fend for themselves, with, she thought, unfortunate results. His complexion was light, his face florid with blotches that might, in a farmer, have resulted from excessive exposure to the sun, but in him, she guessed, betrayed a weakness for the bottle. He seemed to be surveying her, taking her in with a meticulous curiosity that would have been embarrassing under other circumstances. Then he lowered himself into a plain wooden chair that he had positioned in front of her and looked up, straight into her eyes.

Two days before he had been solicitous and concerned. Now he seemed different. He led her back over the events as she remembered them, again taking notes on a steno pad. And again he encouraged her: "Yes, yes," he sprinkled through her narrative. But before long, this time, she realized that it was an automatic response, a habit, and it became distracting, even annoying, to her as she tried to recall and relate the details that he said were of interest to him. As before, he asked her questions, interrupting her sometimes, politely enough, but with an edge in his voice now that seemed somehow to imply doubt about the soundness of her answers or the effort she was expending in reconstructing the elements he seemed to feel were necessary to make the picture as complete as possible.

When she was finished, he put down his notebook and looked at her.

"Doesn't this all seem unusual to you, Mrs. Medea?"

"I would say so." A nervous laugh burst through her attempt to stay calm after having to re-live her encounter for his benefit. "Yes. Unusual." She ended with an uncomfortable smile that faded quickly.

He picked up his note pad and thumbed through it slowly, glancing for a moment at one or another page, then let it settle once more in his lap.

"No one at the scene saw what was happening, it seems. Certainly not the stuff you say you saw."

"*Say* I saw?"

"We can only go by what witnesses tell us."

"I am a witness," she said, looking at him steadily. "But if the others are anything like Rita, they all came up afterward when they found me in a ditch beside the road. How could they have seen anything?"

"Maybe," he said. Then, after a moment of silence, "What's unusual is this. We get our share of violence around here, of course. Break-ins sometimes. Fights in bars. Domestic stuff. But not drive-bys. Not attempted assassinations." He paused again. "You say this was the same car that you saw in the parking lot, right?"

"Yes. I'm certain it was!"

"Well, we decided then that they were there because of drugs, didn't we?"

"Did we?"

"And it sure looks like they know you, doesn't it?"

Julia did not respond.

"So the sixty-four thousand dollar question, Mrs. Medea, is why? Why do they know you?"

Throughout what seemed to her to have become her interrogation by this man, Julia had thought to relate to him what she strongly suspected was the real reason this attempt had been made on her life. But how could she explain the sinister motives of Marco DiNiro, as identified to her by Peter, her husband, and their complex origins and be believed? Besides, the story would be too long and too complicated, and too nuanced, for him to comprehend. She was convinced, now, herself, but there was certainly nothing she could prove. Then she thought of Peter. She didn't believe that he was involved, but if they were to take her seriously about the rest, would they believe her about him? And she still worried about her own culpability, without knowing exactly what her transgressions may have been.

Crane looked up at her. "I was thinking maybe you would help us find the answer."

Again Julia was silent, staring at the face of her inquisitor with what she hoped were expressionless eyes.

Crane rose with surprising athletic ease and stood over Julia.

"Look," his voice was flat and heavy, "we've got no place for this shit around here."

Her eyes widened and the knuckles of her hands whitened as they gripped the edge of the cot.

"What exactly are you saying?"

"I don't have anything on you," he continued in the same tone. "Your car is clean. I have no probable cause to search your house..."

"Me?" She jumped to her feet and immediately, despite the pain killers and sedatives, her head began to throb. She was almost shouting. "You think I shot myself? What kind of a policeman *are* you?"

Crane stood his ground. Still he did not raise his voice.

"I'll do what I can to find these bozos and put them away. But you are a newcomer around here, Mrs. Medea, and you brought them into my back yard. What am I supposed to do? Thank you?" He extended his arms, palms out, in a gesture of helplessness or frustration.

Julia sat down.

"We're impounding your car for a day or two," he said, "to gather evidence. The County Attorney'll have to O.K. its release. You're not planning any trips are you? Keep us informed of your whereabouts. You are a material witness. If you remember anything more, call me. My extension is on the card."

Detective Crane did not offer his hand to her again. He turned on his heel and walked out of the room.

53

AFTER JULIA'S DISCHARGE FROM the hospital, Rita and Calvin took her into their home and care. She felt much better when she had eaten the dinner Rita prepared, even though the ache in her head had begun to sharpen again as the medication, which she was to renew when she went to bed, began to wear off. While her friends were cleaning up in the kitchen, she found a comfortable chair for herself in their living room.

She had called her own answering machine and retrieved two more messages from Danny but had put off responding. When she thought about it, she realized that she was reluctant to admit to him that his concern had been justified, that her efforts at evasion of the threat that they had both identified as real, even urgent, had been pitifully inadequate. Moreover, she did not want him to worry about her now. She had been shot, but had been lucky. It was just, as they told her, a flesh wound. And, for a while, at least, she would not be going home, where the occupants of the stalking car, now the attack car, had seen her, and him, in the front yard. In a while, though, she began to feel guilty about her reticence. She had, after all, asked him to call her. Despite the hour—it was after ten—she held the telephone receiver in front of her, and with the pink message slip from the school switchboard in her other hand for reference, she entered his number.

Danny answered on the second ring.

"Julia!" His voice was alert.

"I'm sorry I missed your friend," Julia said.

"She's at work," Danny said. "Where have you been?"

She hesitated. "I should have called earlier. Is this a bad time?"

"No, no. Not at all. Is everything all right?"

"Yes. Sort of. They shot at me..."

"At you?"

"Well, they missed. Almost. The bullet just grazed me. But I'm totally fine. Really."

"Fine? You've been shot! Where are you?"

"At Rita and Calvin's. Please, Danny, don't worry about me. I'm safe here. Just a little shaken up. That's all. Do you have any more ideas about the stuff I gave you?" she said.

"The files?"

"Wasn't that why you called?"

She had to wait a moment for his reply.

"Yes, I suppose so," he said. There was another pause. "I'm sorry I missed you this morning. About the note..."

"Did you get yourself some breakfast?"

"No, I mean *my* note," he said. "There was so much I wanted to say—should have told you—that I..."

"I'm sorry, but I haven't been home yet. I haven't seen it."

"Maybe just as well." He laughed quietly. "Anyway, I did look over everything again—some of the Adams and TryCo stuff for the first time. We can talk about it later, but all it did was make me even more certain about what we already know, I guess. It's easy to see that if DiNiro is the kind of person he seems to be, why he could be after you. Is after you."

"Oh Danny, I wish I'd done a better job with *my* note, telling you..." Julia started to stand, but her head reacted to the sudden movement, forcing her back into the chair. She groaned without realizing it.

"Is something the matter?"

Rita appeared in the doorway, pointed upstairs and tilted her head against her hands, palms together, in a sleeping gesture. Julia nodded.

"I'm sorry, but I've got to go. I'm exhausted and I really have to get to bed, to get some sleep."

"Julia, when you get home..."

"I'm not going home. I'm staying here for while, with Rita and Calvin."

"You are? Good." He paused for a moment. "Look, Julia, since," he paused again, "last night, I've thought about you a lot. It was much more, to me, than just another..."

"I know, Danny. If that weren't true for me, I wouldn't have been there." She knew that sounded so weak. It didn't come close to expressing how she felt about him. About them. But at the same time, she wasn't sure exactly what she did want to say just now, and whatever that was, she didn't want to tell it to him over the telephone. The instrument she held in her hand suddenly felt so impersonal, and her voice, alone, so inadequate.

"But Julia..."

"I'm really dead on my feet. I'm sorry. I'll call you tomorrow, I promise. Thanks. For everything. Good night, Danny."

"You're sure you're all right?"

"I'm sure."

"Okay. Good night then," he said. His voice was hoarse and low. She put down the receiver.

At dinner, she had accepted Rita's and Calvin's suggestion that she stay with them for a few days. At first she insisted over Rita's objections that she herself administer the final examinations for her students, but in the end welcomed Rita's offer to make arrangements for Rita or another teacher, or a substitute, to handle them for her instead. She did persuade Rita that she needed to stop by the house before Rita left for work to change and pack an overnight bag. Rita would drive. They set their alarms for earlier than usual.

In bed, before the sedative began its work, she thought of Danny and what he had wanted to say to her, what he may have already said in his note. She pondered her own failure to organize her thoughts, to tell him what she hadn't been able to put in the note she had left for him.

Then she thought of Peter. Could he possibly be involved in the events that had nearly led to her death?

54

J ULIA WOKE UP TO the sound of knocking.

Rita's voice was muffled as it reached her through the bedroom door and the fog of sleep. "If you want me to help you before I go to work today, you'd better get up."

Julia looked at the clock. She had slept through the alarm. Ripples of dull soreness moved through her brain.

"Are you awake in there?" Rita knocked again, harder this time.

A few minutes later, after coffee and rolls, they cautiously ventured out. Calvin had made a circuit of Julia's neighborhood in his large sedan and returned to report that he could see nothing unusual.

As they approached Julia's house, Rita and Julia were as circumspect, Julia thought, as a mother bird flying to her nest of hatchlings. They paused down the street to look for danger, drove past the end of the driveway, peering down it as they did, turned around to head for the house again, quickly collected the contents of the mailbox at the curb in front, and finally darted down the driveway to the back of the house. Julia planned to be there for less than half an hour. Still, they parked Rita's small sedan in the garage, with the door closed.

They had seen no one, suspicious or otherwise, in the vicinity, and no car, other than a familiar jalopy, more or less maintained by a neighbor's teenager, that was parked down the street. Even so, Julia was apprehensive as she opened the screen and reached for the knob of the back door. It turned before she could insert her key, and the unlocked door swung into the house. Quickly but gently she pulled the door back, turning the knob so that the latch would not click noisily when it closed. They looked at each other.

Rita whispered, but her tone was emphatic. "Didn't you say that you always lock your door? Someone could be in there! We've got to call the police. Maybe there are fingerprints or something that'll help them find those thugs that shot at you. Anyway, it's dangerous. We shouldn't go in."

At first Julia was as alarmed as Rita. Then she remembered her hurried departure from the house yesterday morning when she was rushing to get to the school on time. Had she stopped to check whether the kitchen door was locked? She was sure, now that she thought about it, that she hadn't turned the deadbolt with her key. Over time, she had gotten out of the habit in this quiet, small town suburban setting. Would Danny have thought to set the lock on the door when he left?

"There aren't any cars around," she said. "Anyone breaking in would have driven here, wouldn't they? Besides, it's broad daylight. If someone was here, they would have left by now."

She pushed the door open again, and stepped inside.

What she saw in the kitchen made her uneasy. Drawers were left open that she hadn't remembered using. The same with cupboard doors. Would Danny have been so careless? He had left the coffee maker clean, next to the sink. And she spied a sheet of lined yellow paper on the kitchen table, held down by the sugar bowl. Quickly she reached for it, folded it, and stuffed it into her pocket. A sidelong glance at Rita was reassuring: it was clear that she hadn't seen Julia pick up the note, and her friend had already started slowly down the hall to survey the rest of the first floor, so it should be easy enough for Julia to check out the second floor alone.

She called to Rita to wait for her and ran up the back stairs. At the sight of the disarray in her bedroom she stopped, surprised again by the same anxiety she had felt when she found the kitchen door unlocked. Then she remembered. The second time she had come to this room with Danny. How good it had been with him. She sat on the edge of the bed and let her hand smooth the place where they had lain. She picked up the pillow his head had rested on afterward and buried her face in it.

Distracted by these memories, it took a few moments before she realized that something was wrong here, too. Her dresser drawers were open, some of their contents strewn on the floor in front of it. She heard Rita calling from downstairs, and found her at the entrance to the living room from the hall.

"Julia, someone *did* break in, unless a tornado's been through here."

And it was true. Drawers and cabinets were open, some of their contents scattered on the floor. The small guest room that she used as an office was in the same condition. It flashed through her mind that Danny had kept the copies of Peter's files, so if that's what they were looking for, they must have been disappointed. It was impossible to know if anything had been taken, but clearly these had not been ordinary thieves. She checked to find her family's silver flatware still in the sideboard in the dining room, and the few decorative pieces she had displayed in the first floor rooms that might have had any value were left in their places.

As they looked around at the evidence of an intrusive, if not destructive, presence in what had been Julia's sanctuary, she felt violated, almost as if whoever had been there had touched her and forced her open instead of the drawers and doors in her house. And, in spite of the lack of any appearance of an immediate threat to either of them, she sensed that they each still felt in the grasp of an almost disabling fear.

Rita spoke first. "You could have been here, enjoying the sleep of the innocent in your own bed, when these guys showed up. Maybe they were even looking for you, in addition to whatever they were rifling through all these drawers for. We should call the police."

"No!" Julia responded in a sharper tone than she had intended. The thought had crossed her mind, too, but she worried about her relationship with the police already, after the implied accusations of Detective Crane the day before, and it wasn't clear what good they could do, anyway. "It'll take them ages to get here, and longer to look at everything. And what good will it do? I can't believe that whoever did this didn't use gloves so as not to leave finger prints. Nothing seems to be missing, so all they did was break in, and all the police will do is write up some kind of report and file it somewhere."

"Well…" Rita sounded doubtful. "It's your house, and your life, so if you don't want to report this, it's okay with me. It'll save us a lot of time not to."

"You wait here for a minute while I get my things together." Julia started for the stairs. "It isn't as bad in my bedroom, so it shouldn't take me long to find stuff and pack. I'll be right down."

There was a reason she discouraged Rita from following her beyond not wanting her, with her sixth sense for mischief, to be exposed to any remnants of Danny's visit. On her way through the kitchen to the back stairs, she looked in the drawer where she had kept her mother's gun. Miraculously, the drawer had not been opened—it was under the ledge of the table top, with a plain wooden pull, so maybe they hadn't even seen it—and the pearl-handled automatic weapon lay there, untouched. She picked it up and went quickly to and up the stairs to her room. There she found the box of cartridges in the back of the open drawer of the bedside table, also apparently unnoticed by the intruders. She knew the gun was loaded, but she picked up the box anyway, along with the thin manual of instructions that lay underneath it. Once she found her overnight suitcase in the hall closet, she placed the gun and its accessories on the bottom. Then, on top of them, she quickly stuffed her nightgown, a couple of simple changes of clothing, walking shoes, underwear, and her toilet kit with its toothbrush, comb and other personal articles—the minimum of what she thought she would need for her stay with Rita and Calvin. She changed into jeans and a pullover before trotting down the stairs, suitcase in hand.

When she reached the bottom, she found Rita in the kitchen. She started for the back door, but paused in front of her friend. "I don't need anything more here. And we don't have time to get this mess back in order. So let's go."

"Wait a second." Rita held up her hand. "Don't you think that first we'd better see if your friends have come around?"

Julia put down her load and stood for a moment. Incredibly, she had forgotten.

Together the two women looked through the kitchen windows, searching the back yard and the area in front of the garage. Then they walked to the front of the house to check the street and the neighbors' yards. Without venturing outside, their view in both directions down the block was obstructed.

Julia found herself whispering. "It's my house, and I ought to be here anyway, so I'll walk out to the sidewalk and see what's going on."

"Maybe you're right. We don't want anyone to know that you're with me," Rita whispered back. Then she said in full voice, "For heaven's sake, be careful."

"Nothing can happen," Julia said, her voice normal, too, but not strong.

As she opened the front door, she had a fleeting image once again of the threatening gun, this time as it had looked in the parking lot, swinging in her direction. She forced her mind to the mundane, noticing the door mat so she would not trip over it, watching the porch stairs as she moved quietly down them. She stepped off the path where it turned across the front of the house to the driveway, and set out across the lawn toward the street.

She reached the sidewalk quickly and looked in both directions, past the trunks of the great trees that lined the street and the bushes and hedges in neighbors' yards. The same jalopy sat as it had been, at a slight angle to the curb. A car backed out of a driveway many houses down, straightened, and drove away toward town. Otherwise, nothing.

As her gaze swept back in the other direction, her eyes stopped. She peered intently into the shadows beyond the outer shell of vegetation, stalks and tree trunks that crowded the vacant lot directly across the street from her. It was impossible to see in there, to penetrate its darkness. The swath of early morning sunlight seemed almost to glare back from the dense clutter of leaves and branches at the edge of the woods, serving to make the gloom behind them even more obscure in contrast.

As she stared, she thought she saw movement among the leaves of a low sumac tree entwined with some kind of vine toward the bottom of the weedy wall. She remembered how the window of the low-slung death car had caught her attention as it was being rolled down while the car had pulled up beside her. But then, at least, she could make out the instrument designed for her destruction, aimed at her from the depths inside the vehicle. Here she could see nothing. Or could she?

Abruptly, Julia turned and ran, stumbling at first, then with frantic agility, back across the lawn. She took the porch stairs in two leaping strides and plunged through the open door, slamming it shut as she came to a breathless halt in front of Rita.

"What was it?" Rita held her by the shoulders. She was almost shouting.

"Nothing, I guess," said Julia between gasps as she tried to catch her breath. "But Rita," she said as her friend took her in her arms, "I'm so scared!"

55

AFTER RITA RETURNED FROM school, Julia and Rita picked up Julia's car, released by the County Attorney, from the police holding lot. The fender would need to be bent back into shape, but did not impede her driving. The front window on the driver's side was still functional. There was a gash just above the passenger door where Julia guessed the police must have retrieved the guilty bullet. She followed Rita back to the Craigs' house. They parked her car off the street, behind the Craigs' garage. Calvin had come home early, and they joined him, sitting with drinks in comfortable outdoor chairs around a table under a large canvas umbrella that stood near the pool in the manicured backyard. Calvin and Rita nursed beers and Julia, against the doctor's advice while she was on the medicine for her headache, sipped from a tall glass of bourbon and ice heavily diluted with water.

As they had planned, Julia stayed at the Craigs' all day and Rita arranged for her and another teacher to monitor Julia's students while they took their final exams. Now Rita related how well it had gone. The other teacher, along with Dave Conklin, the principal, were told that Julia was still recovering from her automobile accident. Rita brought the completed exams home with her, and Julia planned to mark them and develop grades for her students working from here. She had until the following Monday.

Julia knew she was in hiding, so to speak, under Rita's and Calvin's wing, and therefore protected, but she could not shake a lurking feeling of apprehension. She remained silent while Rita and Calvin chatted, trying their best to bring her into their conversation. She looked across the table at them. They were shaded by the umbrella. Behind them were the pool and a corner of the brick house and elaborate planting in the space between, the bright colors intensified by a strong afternoon sun— elements of their domain, of which they were justly proud. Julia felt a surge of warmth for both of them, and a comfort in their presence.

Oddly, though, at the same time, the setting reminded her for an instant of the terrace next to the pool, washed by a gentle ocean breeze, where she and Peter had sat at just such a table with Vicki and Rob Vardaman, on St. Maarten. She had agreed, then, to sign the papers

Rob had handed to her later, pointing out the signature lines, that had been the cause, in part at least, of the trouble she was in now. She had thought of them as friends, too. The contrast made her smile.

"That's more like it," Calvin said. "Maybe my whiskey is finally doing its thing."

It was true that for the first time in the twenty-four hours or so since she had spotted the killers' car in her rear view mirror she thought she might come close to relaxing. She took another sip from her glass.

"I'm glad you can still smile," he said, smiling himself, "and I'm sorry to introduce a topic that might bring up less happy thoughts, but what are we going to do to get you out of this predicament?"

"What do you mean, honey?" Rita's voice sounded contentious. "Julia can stay here as long as she wants."

Julia blushed.

"Of course she can," Calvin said. "That's not what I mean. What I mean is that staying with us is not a permanent solution, if it's a solution at all. Besides, if she'd really wanted to stay with us she'd have moved in a long time ago." He chuckled. "Right Julia?"

"He thinks he's funny." Rita looked at her husband and laughed.

"Seriously," he said, "I wish we had a better idea of what this is all about. What do the police say?"

"I told you," Rita broke in, "they think Julia is a drug dealer or something. Fat lot of help they'll be."

"You got any ideas, Julia?" Calvin stood up.

These people were going out of their way for her, no questions asked, and might even be putting themselves in danger on her behalf. It was time, Julia decided, to tell them what she knew, or suspected about her situation, and her and Danny's conclusion, based on those facts: that she was being hunted down by professional killers hired by a sinister man who was trying to save himself from embarrassment, financial loss, and possibly prison.

"I've thought about it a lot. At first I kept hoping that someone simply made a terrible mistake, and once they understood," Julia gazed up at the sky for a moment, "they'd just go away. But now it looks as though it isn't as simple as that. By a long shot."

She then held her intimate audience in rapt attention while she told them her story.

When she had finished, Calvin shook his head. "So what it amounts to is that the guys who are after you know what they're doing, and what they want. They just haven't gotten it. Yet. And your staying away from home, and work, is the only protection you have at the moment. That is a real cause for concern." He gestured toward the house. "And on that happy note, why don't I get another round for everybody."

Julia surprised herself by letting him take her glass.

"I'd like a bourbon, if there's any extra available."

It was Danny's voice. Julia turned toward it. He had walked from the front yard and was standing by the corner of the house, a sheepish grin across his face, carrying at his side the canvas bag containing the files she had given him. After he waved at the group, he did not move.

"Hey there!" Calvin called to him. He had forgotten Danny's name. "This is a surprise."

"Danny!" Julia grinned broadly, and rose. The movement brought a low wave of new pain, and unconsciously she reached up to the bandage on her forehead.

"How did you find us?" Calvin said.

"Julia told me who she was with, and I did a little research. It wasn't hard."

Calvin looked back to Rita and Julia. "See why I worry? I was in the army, and I can tell you, our defense perimeter here is like a sieve."

Danny turned to Julia. "You didn't call today, and I began to worry again. I hope you don't mind."

Rita motioned Danny to join them. "Come on in. Don't be bashful."

Danny walked quickly through the open gate in the fence around the pool and up to the table. "Julia! That's worse than I imagined. How could you tell me you were 'fine'?"

Rita was on her feet before Danny reached the table.

"If you'll excuse us for a few minutes, while Calvin is getting your drinks, I'll look after dinner."

"Dinner?" Calvin said. "It isn't even six!"

He had hardly finished speaking, though, before Rita was guiding him by the arm up the path, through the French doors that faced the pool, and into the house.

56

DANNY SET THE FILES on the table and held Julia in front of him by the shoulders.

"Now I'm right here looking at you, so you've got to be honest. Are you really all right?"

She felt strength in his touch. He seemed to search in her eyes for a response without waiting for her words. She returned his gaze for a moment before she spoke.

"I'm sorry I didn't call again."

She had not realized how close to the edge she was. Or maybe it was the concern in Danny's face, or his eyes. She began to cry. As she did, she felt a great release of tension that she had not suspected was still in her, that must have been lurking just below the surface. A worm eating out the insides of an apple without touching the blush on its skin. She closed her eyes, but tears welled up in them, brimming over and down her cheeks, like the waters of a healing spring.

Danny hesitated before he put his arms around her. He kissed her eyelids, then her mouth. She returned the soft pressure of his lips without thinking. At some point—not, necessarily the night she had spent with him, she thought, but possibly just at this moment—her feeling for him seemed to her to have passed a kind of boundary. Through some unseen, quiet transformation he had joined a very small circle close around her, like her mother and father had been, like Rita and Calvin, too, now. It struck her that Peter, as much as she had loved him, had never been in that circle.

She pulled away from Danny, wiped her cheeks with the sides of her hands.

"I'd better sit down."

He drew up one of the other chairs near hers, and they looked into each other's eyes. In a moment she was smiling again. So was he.

Calvin returned with their drinks, and Rita drifted back out after him.

Danny tilted his glass for a deep draft. "Is it okay to talk about those files you gave me to look over?" he said to Julia.

She looked into his eyes again and nodded.

"As I told you yesterday on the phone, I went over all of this stuff again." Danny put his hand on the files that lay on the table. "Still no 'smoking gun,' as they say, but I'm convinced more than ever that DiNiro was up to something shady and that the material here, along with other corroborating records, would go a long way toward making a case against him. The TryCo files still aren't as clear. There are notes and correspondence and the like that show some of the things that Peter and DiNiro told the TryCo owners about Grendel, but the key there would be proof that the things they told them about Grendel's financial status, its value, the amount of cash it would have available to help TryCo, weren't true. That they were lies. And the answers to those questions would have to come from an audit of some kind by accountants, I guess. Still, these records would be important if that other proof became available, which it could in a lawsuit or criminal investigation. One thing I'll bet they didn't tell Adams and his people, or the Grendel public stockholders, is that DiNiro was skimming money from Grendel's till through your company."

He leaned back in his chair. "Again, as I said on the phone, I didn't find anything totally new. But more of the same just confirms what we already decided, given your talk with Adams, and then Peter's threat..."

"What are you guys talking about?" Calvin said. "I feel like I just tuned in to the middle of the episode."

"I'm sorry," Julia said. "Danny's been analyzing the files that I told you about, the ones that have caused all the trouble, and I haven't talked with him about it since yesterday. We're just catching each other up."

Then she turned back to Danny. "It was a warning by Peter, not a threat. I don't think he would be part of this. I'm sure he isn't."

Calvin wagged his finger at her. "I'm not what you would call a man of the world, but just from reading the newspapers I can tell you that you don't really know what Peter would do if he felt he had to for some reason. Kids murder old ladies for pocket change."

"Or each other for Philadelphia Eagle warm-up jackets, or basketball shoes," Danny said.

"But he loves..." She stopped. "We were in love."

Calvin's eyes dropped. For a moment he stared at the flagstone pavement in front of her. Then he looked upward before his eyes settled on her again. He smiled.

"It'll be time to eat soon," he said.

She followed his glance. The sky was still bright enough, but the shadows had lengthened and the light had deepened, laying richer colors on the objects around them.

"I thought I'd put a few steaks on the barbecue over there," he waved toward a niche in the fence where the elaborate, shiny black symbol of suburban masculinity stood. He turned to Danny. "You're staying, I hope." Then back to Julia. "But first, we've got to give you some advice. We've all got to work out a plan to help you get out of this mess."

"One thing we know," said Rita, "is that the cops won't be much help."

"But, to be fair," Julia broke in, "I didn't tell them about all this."

Danny stood. "The problem is, if you told them everything you know about why someone might be after you—about DiNiro and Peter—they probably wouldn't buy the connection."

"Not Peter!" Julia said quickly.

"And even if they believed you," Danny said, "they would have no way to get to DiNiro, and they wouldn't turn around and provide twenty-four hour protection for you."

Calvin took it up. "My point before was that protection or hiding might help for awhile, but it isn't really a solution for Julia anyway, is it?

"And there's another problem. Just suppose, Julia, that you decided *not* to disclose to anyone whatever it is that's making this DiNiro person so nervous. What do you do then? Send him a nice letter promising that you won't do it? Enclose whatever you have that might be evidence? How can he be certain? How can he know that you haven't made more copies? I say that you can't count on convincing him. Now that he's got this idea in his head, you will never be really safe until whatever it is he's afraid of is completely settled.

"One more thing. Let's face it, if he's after you, he and his hired thugs are way out of our league—and I'm sure that includes our local cops, too.

"So my advice is this." Calvin looked at Rita, then back to Julia. "Settle everything by going to this Adams guy and his lawyers right away. Take everything you have, all the papers. Tell them everything you know on the condition that they don't wait a second before they go to the right authorities with any evidence that might have to do with the criminal charges against DiNiro.

"It's true that your cooperating with Adams, and going to the police, or FBI, or whoever deals with crimes like this is likely to stir up the hornet's nest even worse, but once the New York police, or the Feds, think they have a case against DiNiro, then maybe you'll have some status. Then they should take your well-being seriously. You'll be a potential witness. Anyway, once they nail DiNiro for good, you'll be safe. Plus, Julia, given all the harm this guy seems to have done, it's just the right thing to do. Until then, stay with us."

"But what about Peter?"

"Either he's a sparrow in a flock of crows," Calvin glanced again at Rita, "or he's one of the crows. He may be in trouble. You can't help that either way. If he's not guilty of anything, then nothing'll happen to him in the long run."

"Danny?" Julia looked at him. He was sitting again, staring at his hands lying on the table in front of him.

"Well," Rita got up, "let's go find those steaks, Calvin. I'll get a salad together. Maybe Danny will think of something. Whatever happens, we've got to eat."

Calvin followed her into the house.

"I don't know," Danny said. "That is, I agree with most of what Calvin says, and I'm sure it's the right thing to do apart from everything else. Only I'm thinking about how heating things up that way could make it even more dangerous for you, for a while at least."

He fixed his eyes on hers.

"Julia," he said, "would you come and live with me in Camden? I have a sofa with a pull-out bed I can sleep on."

Her eyes shifted away from him. She thought of what he had written at the end of his note to her: "I miss you already. When can I see you again? Love, D." She picked up her drink, which she had hardly touched, and rubbed the icy glass, wet with condensation, against the side of her face and her forehead, and put it down slowly.

Danny stood and moved close to her to where she was sitting. "If you want to hide, Camden is the place to do it, and my neighborhood more than most. It's something they'll never think of." He dropped to a crouch in front of her and took her hands in his. "Besides," he said, his voice almost crooning to her, "it'll be fun. Not fun. More than that. Much more. I dream of being with you, Julia. You're my obsession. And don't think it's some kind of passing fancy. Some infatuation. I've already told you. I felt that way in high school. I just was too stupid then to recognize it for what it was."

Julia squeezed his hands. "Oh, Danny," she said, then pulled hers back, gently forcing him to release his hold. "I am fond of you. I think you're very special..."

"As a friend," Danny said. He rose and returned to his chair.

"No," Julia said quickly. "That's not it at all." She reached a hand across the table to him. "Danny, what we've shared together...I hope you don't think that I would do that with someone—anyone—who is just a friend. It's that it comes as such a surprise. I'll have to think about it. I guess I'm not sure I'm ready. Not right now." She extended her other hand, too, and smiled weakly. "I'm not saying it very well, am I?"

He laid his hands over hers. Color rose in his face.

"I understand," he said slowly. "I came on too strong anyway. You seem to do that to me." Then he laughed. So did she.

But he stopped abruptly. "The thing is, it's important to think about it soon. I worry about you here." He gestured as he spoke. "The same town, the same streets. They're probably laying low now, but if they want to try again, all they have to do is wait someplace and you're bound to come by sooner or later."

He picked up her hands and held them. "Look," he said. "Veronica..."

"The go-go dancer." She couldn't suppress a smile.

"Yes. She can stay. It'll just be like having another roommate. Everyone does it now. Guys and chicks...girls. Who didn't even know each other before. Like Veronica and me. We're living in the same apartment, but we aren't even friends. She can be your chaperon. Not that you'll need one, because...

"Anyway, Julia, please consider it. Seriously. The most important thing is that it's safe."

"What's safe?" Rita had walked up without their noticing. Calvin was puttering with the grill behind her. The aroma that rose with the smoke from steak grease spattering on the flame-heated bed of the grill drifted to them on a cooling draft in the still light of early evening.

Danny looked at Julia.

"Danny asked if I would like to share his apartment, with him and his roommate, for awhile," she said, "Until this blows over."

"In Camden? That's a great idea." Rita looked at Danny and back to Julia. "They'll never find you there."

"I said I'd think about it and let him know."

"Think?" Rita's eyes widened.

Calvin joined them.

"One other thing," Danny said. "When you go to New York to see Adams, please let me come with you. I just need a little advance notice."

"Thank you, Danny," Julia said, "but I still haven't decided exactly what I should do. I'm going to sleep on it. I should wait until after the exams are marked and after I've given out grades for the year, so I've got a couple of days, anyway, to make up my mind."

"Don't wait too long, Julia." Calvin waved a forefinger at her again. "This is like war. Serious business. I mean it."

"I won't," she said.

57

THAT NIGHT, AS SHE lay in bed in Rita's and Calvin's guestroom, Julia knew she should feel safe, and after the turmoil of the last two days, she desperately sought the numbing comfort of sleep. Instead she remained wide awake, troubled as she was by an insistent, almost painful anxiety about her predicament. Danger seemed to stalk her no matter where she turned, a stifling, merciless presence. She could not escape the feeling that she was cowering in a hiding place that, as Danny and Calvin pointed out, could only be effective for a short period of time. She had no idea how long—how many days, how many hours—it would remain secure.

She craved relief, but found herself still conflicted about the solution that both men had urged upon her as her best means of escape: going right away to Adams, Strothers and the authorities. Mostly, she worried about its consequences to Peter, and to herself. Finally, though, she focused on Calvin's pronouncement that, in effect, it was the only morally correct thing she could do, and admitted to herself that he was really just reinforcing a conclusion that she had already faced up to herself, when she was with Danny, the evening before the attack on her in her car. So before long she was compelled to recognize that she did not have the luxury of weighing and choosing among possible solutions. There was no real alternative. It was at that moment that she at last decided on a plan of action.

The first step was to talk with Joshua Adams. When she confided her intention to Rita at breakfast, Rita encouraged her to get it out of the way then and there, before she could change her mind. To Julia's surprise, Adams answered in person—no recorded voice mail—even though it was before five a.m. in Chicago. By the time she put down the receiver less than five minutes later, she had agreed to meet him the next day, Saturday, in New York City, at Archibold Strothers' home, which Adams said was a formal-looking brownstone near Park Avenue. She realized that it was not far from Peter's building. She told him she would be sending the copies of the files, to be delivered by the time she, herself, arrived. That way, she reasoned to herself, she would not need to carry the heavy burden with her on her journey there, and if she were delayed, or had to postpone her trip for any reason, she still would have set the wheels of her deliverance from DiNiro's relentless pursuit in motion.

But her plan had two parts. She knew that neither the Craigs nor Danny would approve, so she did not tell Rita about the second call she needed to make: to Peter. In spite of Calvin's concern to the contrary, she was certain in her heart that Peter was not involved in DiNiro's effort to harm her, and she was determined to see Peter before her meeting with Adams and Strothers. She needed to warn him of what she was about to do, if for no other reason than to let him be prepared for, if necessary to protect himself against, DeNiro's inevitable, violent, reaction. She waited to call Peter until after Rita and Calvin had both left for work, but early enough that he should still be in the apartment. She used a phone card so that no charge would show on their statement.

"Where are you?" he said. "At home?"

"I need to talk with you, Peter," she said.

"Have you changed your mind? About us?"

"No."

She knew she should get on with it. She had rehearsed what she wanted to say. She must tell Peter in advance that she needed to see him, but without revealing what she intended to do next until she got there. But she could not find the words now that she was on stage. Before she could reconstruct her presentation, he spoke.

"I was hoping you'd call before now." She sensed tension in his voice despite his effort at self-control. "Have you thought about what I told you? About the information you have? You haven't," he paused, "done anything foolish with it, have you?"

"Nothing," she said. "Foolish or otherwise. In fact that's what I need to talk with you about. The files I borrowed."

"Julia," he continued the studied evenness, "we should not talk about that now." He gave each of the last few words separate weight.

"Oh?"

"I would really like to talk with you in person." Again the unusual emphasis.

That, in fact, was what she wanted, too, but she sensed he had a special reason of some kind for not wanting to talk about it in this conversation, over the telephone. What was he afraid of?

Then his tone changed. "Honneger's, our time there, left me feeling a little dissatisfied."

"That's one way of putting it."

"Are you mad at me?" Peter said. "Still? It's been a long time. You never used to hold a grudge."

"Peter, you always try to make things seem so simple. Anyway, I still want a divorce as soon as possible, if that's what you mean. But that's not why I called."

"If you want to talk," he said, "why don't you come to New York?"

"Actually…"

"School must be over soon," Peter said. "Take a vacation. Do a little shopping or something. And see me. We can do better than we did at Honneger's."

"Tomorrow? Saturday? In the morning?" she said.

"I can work it out."

"Why don't we go somewhere for lunch? Some place that will bring back congenial memories."

"I'm not sure that's possible," she said, "but I can't, anyway."

"Why not? Shopping can't be that important."

"Peter, I can't shop. I don't have any money."

"I told you at Honneger's, and you must believe me. Things have been really tight for me. Business has fallen apart. Just the existence of that fucking law suit. Otherwise…"

"I don't want anything from you. I just can't shop, that's all. I don't *want* to shop."

"You're coming all the way up here to see me for only a few minutes and turning right around to go back home?"

"I have to see a cousin. She's sick." Julia marveled at her own ingenuity. At her casual tone as she lied to him.

"I didn't know you had relatives in the City? You never mentioned…"

"We lost touch, but she reappeared. In New York."

"My good fortune. I'm sorry she's ailing. What about later? She'll want to sleep or something. After you see her, come back here."

Julia lied again. "No. Then I have to leave. Graduation is that night."

"Saturday night?"

"I know," she said. "Crazy, isn't it?"

282

She did not want to be with Peter longer than necessary for her purpose. She was supposed to be at Strothers' sometime before mid-day. "So, how about between nine and ten."

"That's fine," he said. "Great. I'm looking forward to it."

Early that afternoon, after Rita's return from school, Julia borrowed her car, to confuse anyone who might be on the lookout for her, and drove to the post office. There she mailed a package containing the copies of the files, Express Mail, overnight delivery, to Archibold Strothers' home address.

She decided it would best to make it a day trip by train. She would carry nothing but a purse and her canvas carryall with a sweater and a book to read on the train. Then she remembered her mother's gun, which she had loaded and kept at hand in her house after the threat of attack in the teachers' parking lot. Should she take it with her? It was not large, but not small enough to fit comfortably in her purse. Besides, why would there be any danger? She was sure that DiNiro's thugs didn't know where she was hiding, so there wasn't any way for them to follow her from the house, or find her to attack her en route, or when she arrived in the vicinity of her destination. She could tell from the way he spoke to her that Peter had been concerned that the Federal authorities might be listening in on his phone calls, but even if they were, they weren't the enemy. Besides, she had never fired a gun of any kind before. She had no clue how to use the weapon her mother had kept for protection other than the steps described in the instructions, which she would have no opportunity to practice, or what she might have gleaned from the movies or television. Should the occasion arise, which realistically seemed highly improbable, if she managed to discharge the weapon at all, she was just as likely to hurt herself or some innocent bystander as she was her target. With almost no misgivings about her decision to do so, she left her mother's automatic pistol in hiding, in her suitcase.

Of course, Rita, and therefore Calvin, were aware that she planned to see Adams and Strothers, but she knew that they would not approve of her plan to see Peter first. And they, and Danny, would insist that Danny accompany her, making her stop at Peter's awkward if not impossible. So, to avoid confrontation with her friends, she set off in her car for the North Philadelphia Station early Saturday morning, undetected, while they were both still asleep. She left them a note to inform them of her ultimate destination, with no mention of her intention to make her intermediary stop. She would have to call Danny later.

In spite of his directive to the contrary, she did not notify Detective Crane that she was leaving his jurisdiction. It would only be a short trip. With luck she would be back by early evening.

PART 4

58

A RUSH OF COOL, damp air greeted Julia as she climbed the steep steps out of the subway. It smelled of rain. She found the sidewalks stained with moisture. The desultory residue of what had been a heavy shower dimpled puddles that lay in the gutters and low spots in the blacktop street. The darkened sky grumbled with distant menace. The storm was not over.

It had been sunny and clear when she left Ironton early that morning and she had not thought to bring a raincoat or an umbrella. She pulled a scarf from her canvas tote, knotted it under her chin babushka-style, and walked briskly across town.

She had been prepared for a flood of memories of the time just two years before when she had traveled this same route in the oppressive August heat, lugging her heavy suitcase to the hotel near Peter's apartment. Instead, she was surprised by the memory of Peter's first wife, Gina, blond and voluptuous, and Julia's encounter with her on another wet day. As she crossed Madison Avenue, she remembered her walk on the same street down to her aerobics exercise class, leaning against the slanting rain. She had been attracted to Gina in many ways, but Gina was apparently anxious to avoid Julia. She came to believe that it was because Gina was seeing Peter then, or at least wanted to without the baggage of friendship with his wife. All of the women who serviced Peter must have known that there were others except, of course, his wife. Julia wondered at their tolerance.

There was something about Peter, Julia mused wryly, an energy of his, that none of them could resist. Even she, herself, for a while.

Then she was surprised by a more recent image: Danny Johnson appearing in the Craig's backyard, like a miraculous fulfillment of a wish, but one she hadn't had the confidence to know to make in the first place. He had offered to come here with her. She knew she could not do what she had to do with him as her escort, but still she missed his comforting presence.

Now, as she walked up Fifth Avenue toward her meeting with Peter, Julia forced her mind back to the present and lengthened her stride. She wanted to get to Peter's before the next downpour, and then away as soon as possible. Even in a city where rushing from one place to another is a way of life, her pace drew a few quizzical looks. But when Peter's building finally came into sight, her progress slowed. The last time she had seen that view—and from roughly the same vantage point, too, although then the trees planted along the street were bare and a cutting wind had buffeted her car—was a glimpse in the rear view mirror of her Volvo as she headed for Philadelphia, and refuge.

She came to a stop. Her confidence seemed to drain. The doorman, who might recognize her if she came closer, was facing away, talking with a man who was walking a dog. It was not too late to turn back, to call Peter and say she had not been able to make it. To scurry to the Metropolitan Museum nearby, or the labyrinthine paths of Central Park, and wait until the appropriate time for her appearance at Archibold Strothers' townhouse six or ten blocks away.

Instead, just as the doorman turned in her direction, she started toward him.

The doorman was Eduardo. She noticed that after almost a year since he started there he still looked uncomfortable in his elegant uniform.

"It's good to see you again, Mrs. Medea."

Julia knew Eduardo's words were a form of flattery born of professional necessity, but still they warmed her as she walked up to him. He smiled as he held the door for her, then passed her on to the care of the elevator operator, whom she did not recognize.

When the familiar elevator reached his floor, Peter was not waiting for her in the small vestibule. She glanced in the mirror there while she pulled off her scarf and ran her fingers through her hair, shaking her head to loosen it. He answered her ring promptly.

"No one announced you."

He motioned her inside.

"Maybe he thought I belonged." She laughed nervously as she walked past him.

"Maybe he was right..."

"He's wrong," she said quickly, then turned and looked at him. As before, at the restaurant, she was struck that seeing him, being near him, had so little emotional impact on her, one way or another. "The whole thing was wrong. We weren't right for each other—something you knew all along, maybe, but I didn't catch onto until you, and your girlfriends, made it impossible for me to keep lying to myself." She turned away from him and started toward the living room. "I'm sorry. I didn't mean to get into all that. It's just that I can't understand why you won't let go. I've got to get on with my life. Don't you feel the same way?"

"Would you like some coffee?" He seemed unfazed by her outburst.

"Thank you."

Instead of following him to help, she strolled around the living room, then the study. She walked through the dining room and peered through the door to the terrace before retracing her steps, passing the kitchen without looking in. Having been away for so long, it seemed strange all over again that nothing in his apartment ever changed. She had not altered things much herself when she had been living there, but what she had done—moved a floor lamp or two, added a few pictures from a local print shop, rearranged displays on the tops of the sideboard in the dining room and a small chest in the living room—remained exactly as she had left it. She managed a thin smile when she noted that the crystal ashtray they had received as a wedding present, that she had meant to take with her but had forgotten in the confusion of her departure, still stood at its post near a corner of the coffee table in front of the sofa.

Once the impersonality of it all had reminded her of a stage set of some kind, but that was when she had envisioned herself as a protagonist in a romantic drama that would unfold there. Now she decided that the entire apartment was more like a luxury hotel suite in which Peter was a guest. A businessman making do on the road. Indeed she now remembered how the study, his office at home, was the only place, except for his bedroom, that showed more than a faint imprint of his presence.

Even the bedroom had given little insight into this man beyond, when the overhead mirror had been there, betraying the urgency of his sexual appetite. Had he put it back now that she was gone? She did not try the door.

"How does it look?" He returned with two large cups and saucers. "You don't take anything in it, do you?" He set them on the coffee table, near the ashtray. She picked hers up and sat in the chair at the end of the sofa furthest from the entrance to the room. He remained standing.

"Nothing's changed."

"Should it?"

"I guess not. Of course." She took a sip of her coffee. It was bitterly strong. She put her cup down and raised her eyes.

"Peter, I'm worried about you."

"Really. Well, I guess I'm worried about myself, and about the files you stole from me. You said you wanted to talk. I assume it's about them. I thought that to keep it between ourselves, we should talk in person. You know, with that Federal investigation going on, and with me as one of its subjects, I can never be sure who might be listening, and where."

"That's one thing..."

"*One* thing? I'd say that's a lot. And then there's Adams' blasted lawsuit..."

"Anyway," she interrupted him, "I stole nothing. I borrowed. Everything I took had to do with me, or I thought it might at the time, and you have all the originals back, safe and sound. Of course, I did read them..."

"And copy them."

"Yes, I copied them," she said. "But Peter, what is it about them that has everyone so stirred up? There are some things there that might put DiNiro in a bad light, and maybe you, too, but not by themselves. At least that's the way I see it. So, should I just assume that all the missing pieces to the puzzle are bad news for DiNiro? And that you were working with him or for him or whatever in all this so that anything he did rubs off on you, too?"

"Don't assume anything," he said. "It's none of your business. Just give me whatever copies you have and stay out of the way. Don't talk with Adams, or anyone else who may get in touch with you. Anything short of that could do me a great deal of harm. Or is that what you want?"

Julia stood and began to walk around the room.

"No. I don't want harm to come to you. But if DiNiro has broken the law, or if he has cheated Adams, or anyone else, don't you think it's wrong for him not to pay for that? If I knew something important about what he might have done, wouldn't it be wrong not to tell the authorities, or Adams, or whomever? If you weren't involved, then no harm should come to you in the long run, should it?"

"No harm?" Now Peter began to pace the carpet of the living room himself, gesturing for emphasis as he spoke. "Damn it, Julia, that lawsuit is already ruining me and it hasn't even gone to trial yet. My business depends on people trusting me. How can I persuade them to deal with me when that kind of thing is poisoning the air?"

Peter stopped. "And what do you know about right and wrong? You're sitting on your ass making easy judgments while I'm in the arena, fighting. I'm a gladiator. For me, right is winning. Wrong is getting killed."

He glared at Julia across the room. She stopped as well. They stood facing each other.

"But Peter," she said, "suppose what you do to win hurts a lot of other people?"

"Other gladiators, Julia. Not other people. No one is a babe in the woods in my business, believe me. They'd all screw me to the wall if they got a chance, Adams included."

"DiNiro's company has stockholders, Peter. People like my mother after my father died. Like me."

"I don't have anything to do with that side of things. I can't control what Denny does or doesn't do."

Julia sat down again, but stayed on the edge of her chair. She leaned toward Peter and pointed at her forehead.

"Do you know what this is?"

"I noticed it when you came in. I should have said something. You bumped your head. I'm sorry."

"This," she said, "is why I worry about you."

"What?"

"Someone shot at me while I was driving home from work. Luckily they were a little off, but not by much. The creeps that tried to kill me on the road had already pointed a gun at me in the school parking lot. Before that, they—it must have been the same people—were stalking me at home. Parking and watching. It began after Honneger's, where you gave me your 'advice,' I guess you'd call it, about talking with Adams." She knew her anger was rising. It felt good. "And your warning." Her voice grew louder. "Remember? About not wanting me to 'get hurt?' I believe that's the way you put it."

"I had no idea..." Peter took a step toward her. Then he sat down. "You don't think that I..."

"I know I'm incredibly naïve," she looked down for a moment, then back at Peter, "but no. I don't think it was you. If I did, I wouldn't be here. I do think it was DiNiro. People he hired. I'm sure of it. And he could just as easily turn on you."

"You're wrong about DiNiro," Peter said. "I work with him all the time. I know him. He's a tough dealer. That's how he's been able to get as much as he has for himself. How he wins most of the time. I admire him. He's like me that way.

"But when I talked with you at Honneger's? Those were just words. I guess I was trying to scare you a little, to make you realize how important those files are. Denny wouldn't physically harm anybody. Not that kind of thing. Impossible."

"Impossible?"

"Anything's possible, but I've never seen a sign of it. He's never talked to me about going around bumping people off."

Julia sat back. "Who then?"

"How would I know? Crazy things are always happening. Drive-by shootings. Things that gangsters used to do. Now it's kids."

"But they were following me," she said. "Stalking. And why would they try twice, maybe three times? I'm not in a gang, you know. I'm not dealing drugs.

"Peter, it had to be DiNiro. That's what I think. That's what my friends think."

"Your friends?" Now Peter's voice began to rise.

Julia's remained steady. "And the only way I can be out of harm's way and stay that way is to get the facts out in the open. If DiNiro has done something bad enough that he thinks he has to kill me to keep me quiet, then I'll only be safe when he's in jail."

"What are you talking about?"

"I'm going to Adams as soon as I leave you."

Peter leapt to his feet. Julia rose, too, and moved quickly behind her chair, so that it and the coffee table were between them.

"I have to do it, Peter," she said. "It's the right thing to do. But it's also the only way I can see to save my own peace of mind. Maybe my life."

Julia grasped the back of the chair in front of her with both hands and leaned toward Peter. "I wanted you to know first. That's why I came here. So that you can do whatever you need to protect yourself."

"Shit, Julia!" he shouted. The veins on his forehead and his neck were engorged, his face florid. He clenched his fists. But his voice subsided to the painfully controlled tone with which Julia had become familiar. It made her wary.

"It's not too late to change your mind." He moved slowly around the side of the table and stopped. "Forget DiNiro. He's an asshole anyway. But it'll ruin *me*. If Adams gets that stuff, when he's done with me, he'll take it to the feds. It would be the end. You said you didn't want that. And afterwards, I'll never be able to do anything for you. I'll be finished."

Peter passed the low table and angled toward her. Instinctively, she stepped back. He crossed in front of the chair she was standing behind before she realized what he had in mind. She had left her purse and the canvas bag on the sofa, leaning against the arm nearest her.

"Where is that stuff from my files? The copies?" he said. He picked up the bag and looked inside. Then he threw it down and reached for the purse.

"It's no use, Peter..."

Julia's words were interrupted by a buzzing sound.

"Damn!" Peter said. She knew he was debating whether he wanted to appear at the front door with a woman's pocketbook in his hand. He let it drop.

"What the fuck is wrong with the doorman. I never know who the hell is coming up here any more." He turned to Julia. "Wait. I'll be right back."

She had no choice. But she was grateful for the break in the rhythm of his rage. She had expected something like this from him, and was confident he would cool down before long. Maybe the lull would speed that return to reason. In the meantime, she gathered up her belongings and moved to the corner of the room farthest from its entrance to gain a better angle for looking into the hall, to try to get a sense of Peter's mood upon his return, and to give her more time to react to it when he did.

Carpets and curtains and upholstery muffled noises in Peter's apartment, but she thought she heard the sound of a short scuffle. Then Peter appeared, straightening his jacket. He was walking in front of two men. One of them was crowding in behind him.

"We have visitors." Peter made the announcement, his voice loud and strained, while he was still in the hallway.

A short, beefy man bustled into the room past Peter. She saw tight black pants and a cheap quality black and tan plaid jacket stretched over a pastel shirt that was open at the collar. His eyes were small. Shiny black beads, they fixed on her as soon as he entered.

Behind both of them, walking more slowly, completely at ease it seemed, was a large man with smooth, black hair not unlike Peter's. His conservatively cut dark business suit, white shirt and floral-patterned necktie looked at home on him despite his bulk, stylish without being flamboyant. When he smiled at Julia, his eyes retreated mysteriously into the flesh around them.

59

"I**T'S BEEN TOO LONG.**"

Denny DiNiro's tone was smooth and cordial, but he stopped his forward progress short of where she stood and did not offer his hand in greeting. She was surprised, as she had been when she first met him, by the flat, gray eyes that stared at her without apparent emotion through the smile and the pleasant words. They looked as if they had been pasted on his olive-tan face by a child playing with cutouts of human features. And they were cold.

"Denny!" Julia felt her legs weaken but she was still able to force a thin smile.

"And this is Paolo, my, uh, business associate." He waved in the other man's direction. "Paolo and Pete are already acquainted."

Julia strode toward DiNiro. "I was leaving. Saying goodbye." She held out her hand. "Sorry I can't stay. To talk with you. To catch up."

DiNiro stepped back, moving more directly between Julia and the entrance to the front hall from which he had come. "But Julia," he held out his arms in evident dismay, "we came all the way over here just to see you."

Julia stopped and looked at Peter. Peter caught her glance as he turned to face DiNiro.

"What the hell's going on here?" he said.

At Peter's words, Paolo moved toward him, but DiNiro motioned to the chunky man and he pulled up short, glaring at Peter. He was poised eagerly, leaning forward like an overweight attack dog, barely restrained by training but frustrated nevertheless.

DiNiro's impersonal gaze remained fixed on Julia. His voice was soothing. "Pete's not to blame, if that would be your word for it. Our visit is, I'm sure, as unexpected by him as it is by you. He as much as told us so when we came in," he glanced at his companion, "didn't he Paulie? Except that anyone who does business with me, like Pete," he nodded across the room, "must know that I like to keep tabs on my friends. Know what they're doing. Who they're seeing, if it comes to that."

"The telephone," Julia said. "My call."

DiNiro smiled.

"Jesus!" Peter sat down on the sofa.

"Of course, we had to take care of the man downstairs to make our little surprise complete."

"Eduardo?" Julia started forward, then checked herself.

"Don't worry," DiNiro said. "He's a little richer than he was a few minutes ago, that's all. Besides, he's a friend, too, you might say, Eduardo is."

Julia looked again at Peter. He was slumped back, staring at DiNiro, and silent.

DiNiro continued. "Well, now, why don't we have a little talk before you leave us, Julia? You can do that, can't you?"

"Please." He gestured toward the chair on the opposite side of the low table in front of the sofa, the one she had been sitting in when she was alone with Peter.

Instead she backed up, reaching behind her for the one in the far corner of the room where she had been standing when DiNiro came in. She settled tentatively on its front edge. She felt like a wary bird perched there, ready at the slightest disturbance to fly. But to where?

She sat with her purse in her lap and the canvas bag still hanging at her side. Her eyes remained locked on DiNiro's, drawn, she was vaguely aware, by the same uneasy fascination that must overcome a small victim, a field mouse or a vole, looking at a snake that is poised to devour it. At the same time, she sensed that the man he called Paulie had shifted his attention from Peter to her as well.

DiNiro began to stroll around his end of the room. After a while he stood gazing at one of the two large, heavily-framed prints that hung there. They depicted graceful long-legged birds. Then he turned back to Julia.

"Tell me, why are you here? Why did you come to the big city? Not just to look at these lovely works by John J. Audubon, I assume."

"You know why I'm here, in this apartment." Julia felt anger begin to rise in her despite her fear. "You heard me. On Peter's phone. Which I guess is why *you* are here, isn't it?"

"You came all the way to New York to talk with him?" DiNiro nodded at Peter. "Are you still such good friends? Besides, just a few minutes ago you were leaving. That's not much of a tête-à-tête for such a long trip, is it?"

She continued to meet his gaze. "What difference does it make to you? Anyway, why should I sit here and satisfy your curiosity about my private life?"

"My, my." DiNiro clucked his tongue. He walked to the table in front of where Peter was sitting. He leaned down and picked up the heavy crystal ashtray, hefting it and running his fingers over its smooth edges before he replaced it on the polished wood surface. His eyes moved to Julia again.

"What in the world happened to your head? That bandage looks like it might cover something nasty. I hope it doesn't hurt." He smiled. "You should take better care of yourself."

While Julia was moved to lash out at this man, she sensed that his verbal jabs at her were intended to induce just such a response. When she spoke this time, she hoped her voice sounded more composed.

"I came to New York to visit a sick cousin. I have to be there before noon. I need to get some flowers for her first, so I really must be going. I'm sorry."

A glance showed her that Peter's expression remained unchanged. He said nothing. She rose to her feet.

"So you said to Peter, and so you say now. I'm afraid I can't believe you, my dear, but it doesn't really matter in the end."

DiNiro reached behind his back, underneath his suit jacket, and in an instant, as in a sleight-of-hand trick, he was holding a snub-nose black revolver, pointing it at her. Seeing a gun emerge so quickly seemed almost surreal to Julia, but she knew it was not some kind of illusion, and that it embodied for her a true, tangible menace.

"Fuck!" Peter said without moving.

DiNiro walked toward her. "What do you have in that bag?"

"Nothing you're looking for." Julia pulled the canvas satchel closer to her. As she did, its strap fell from her shoulder.

Swiftly DiNiro reached out with his free hand and swept it away from her. He emptied it on the floor. After a glance at the contents, he looked up.

"Then where?"

Julia took a deep breath. "I mailed everything to...to a safe place."

DiNiro's expression froze.

"It doesn't amount to much anyway, does it?"

"I'll be the judge of that." He sighed audibly. "You pose a difficult dilemma for me, Julia. I'd hoped we could tie up all the loose ends with you before now. But we lost you for a while and we can't afford to let you get away again in the hope that you'll retrieve those copies for us, and we can't take the time to go around with you. Besides, how do I know you don't have another set someplace? More important, how do I know what you might tell someone about something you know, something you may have heard, that isn't even in those files?" He nodded toward the entrance to the hall and the front of the apartment, and motioned in that direction with the gun. "Let's go."

"What the hell is this all about?" It was Peter, still sitting on the sofa. He leaned toward DiNiro.

"It's simple, Pete. She knows too much. Part of it's my fault. That dinner in Frankfurt. And I have no idea what she might have learned from you."

"We never talked about business, Denny. She doesn't know a thing. I told you that before. Besides, we're married. I thought your legal guy said she couldn't testify..."

"Against you, Pete. Besides, we can't trust that kind of thing, anyway, I'm afraid. In fact, if you weren't so deep into this with me, I wouldn't even know if I could trust you, my friend." DiNiro smiled again. "And then there are the all-important files."

Peter sat back a little, but she could tell from the new intensity in his look as he glared at DiNiro that whatever state of lassitude he might have lapsed into was past.

In apparent compliance with DiNiro's command, Julia stood, shifting her gaze back to the barrel of the gun that was pointed at her middle. Surprisingly her mind had left fear, and anger, both, behind as it ranged over the meager collection of alternative means she could think of that might be available to save her. She picked one.

"I lied to you, Denny." She forced her attention, with an effort, away from the lethal instrument and toward the man who was holding it.

"Yes?"

"I don't have a cousin in New York City, sick or otherwise."

"That's more like it, Julia."

"And the real reason I made the trip was to meet with Joshua Adams and Archibold Strothers, his lawyer. They are expecting me in less than an hour." She glanced at Peter. "They know I was coming here first. If I don't show up..."

"Well, well!" DiNiro started another tour of the portion of the room nearest the entrance and the hall. "If that indeed is where you are headed, it *may* be that they know where you are." He paused. "But I doubt it. Would you have told them that you were going to consort with the enemy before you cooperated with them? I'm sure they would have advised you strongly against doing so if you had.

"Besides, you don't give us enough credit. We're not going to leave road signs behind us. No one but friends knows we are here, or will know how you left. I'm sure our imagination is up to helping Pete with an explanation, if that becomes necessary."

As DiNiro finished, he halted at the entrance to the room from the hall, facing Julia. Paolo stood near him, but with the chair at that end of the sofa between him and his boss, his eyes shifting between Julia and Peter. Peter sat in the middle of the sofa, the coffee table in front of him. He was not far from either of them.

Julia stood in the far corner of the room facing the three men. She felt a wave of nausea rise from her gut to her throat. Her legs threatened collapse. She stepped behind the chair where she had been sitting and steadied herself on its back. She took a deep breath. Then she looked straight into the cold eyes of Denny DiNiro. The inside of her mouth seemed as dry as talcum powder, so she was pleased at the strength in her voice.

"I mailed the files to Archibold Strothers. Yesterday. Express mail. Saturday delivery. They should be opening them up by now."

She managed a smile.

A dark flush stained DiNiro's face. His thick lips pressed tightly together in his fury.

"You bitch!" he shouted at her. He had let the gun drop to his side while he had been pacing the room, and as she had been speaking. Suddenly he brought it up and in a fit of rage, without taking careful aim, he pulled the trigger.

The explosion was loud enough that it nearly deafened her, but she was not conscious of the noise so much as the force of the concussion from the blast. At the same instant she felt the heat of pain in her right arm. Sharp, but not the vital kind. More like a wasp stinging. Without thinking she ducked down, partially behind the chair she was still holding onto, keeping her eyes on the scene that was quickly playing out before her.

DiNiro seemed crazed, and almost to lose sight of her in the confusion of the noise and recoil of on the gun in his premature effort. In an instant, though he started to bring the gun back under deadly control, leveling it and pointing it once again at Julia. He took a step to the side as if to gain a better field of fire. Julia moved in the opposite direction, farther behind the chair, but she knew that it would provide scant protection. Instinctively she crouched more, to dodge, somehow, from her tormentor.

That was when she saw Peter reach for the huge crystal ashtray on the low table in front of him. He grasped it in his powerful hand and cocked his arm. Paolo's hand was moving toward the inside the front of his jacket. But before he could find what he seemed to be searching for, Peter stood and snapped his arm forward.

The missile flew at DiNiro's head. He must have seen the movement out of the corner of his eye, because he whirled toward Peter and fired at him just as the ashtray cracked into the middle of his face.

Still clutching her purse, Julia leapt around the chair and ran across the room toward the entranceway from the hall. To reach her goal she had to pass behind DiNiro. He had dropped the gun and was reaching with both hands for the place where the blow had been struck. Blood was already part of the picture. It was like a still frame of a movie. A splash of crimson stained the flesh of his face below his crumpled nose.

Peter's expression was new to her. His lips parted to form a perfect "o," his eyes opened wide. She had never seen him showing such surprise before. He was falling back on the sofa.

Paolo now held a gun in his hand and was pointing it in her direction, but the chair next to him, and DiNiro himself, stood between Paolo and her route of escape. As added insurance, she shoved DiNiro from the side, toward Paolo, with a strength born of desperation as she tore past him.

Her last impression from the chaos that had erupted around her was of Denny DiNiro lurching over the arm of the chair and into the way of his thwarted associate. Paolo seemed to be trying to dodge around the big man, still seeking a clear line of fire toward her. As she darted out from the room, eyes fixed on her route of escape, she heard another explosion. Now, she realized, it was Paolo who was trying to shoot her.

60

JULIA'S MIND RACED AS she left the living room behind her. She started at first toward the front door, but recognized her error in an instant: that route led only to the vestibule and the elevator. She veered toward the kitchen and the service door at its back. She burst through it to the landing—where during happier times she had pushed carefully tied dark green bags of trash through a covered hatch into the chute to the basement far below—and fled down the stairs.

Ten floors. The steps were concrete and metal and reverberated as she settled into a rhythm, eight or ten steps in each flight, jumping over the last two to each landing, one landing between and one at each floor. She swung around the cylindrical steel column supporting the staircase at each switchback to speed her turn into the next flight.

Luckily she had worn practical low-heeled shoes for walking in the city, but it still took her full concentration in the dim lighting to keep her footing. She lost count of the landings in front of the sets of white doors at each floor and in her haste she could not see where they were marked to show the number of the floor. She had never before descended these stairs, but assumed the lobby door would be announced by a sign and she looked for it each time she turned on a middle landing. She knew that the other doors would be locked. Would the one to the lobby be open?

Soon pain began to shoot through her knees and her thighs. Her legs felt heavy and unmanageable. Her ankles ached. She knew that she could not have been in the stairwell for more than half a minute, but despaired of reaching the bottom before her body failed her. Had she somehow missed the street level? Would she end up running down into some sub-basement she had not known of, and a dead end? Finally she saw a brown door with a brass placard next to it. She leapt the last two stairs and reached for its handle.

Before she could pull it, the door to the lobby swung toward her. Startled, she tried to stop, but her momentum carried her through, and into the grasp of a pair of strong, unyielding hands. Eduardo. As she struggled to wrench herself free, she felt his fingers dig into her upper arms. She caught her breath in what came out as a single, grating sob.

"Stop!" he whispered, his face next to hers, his mouth at her ear. She was almost overwhelmed by the heavy scent of sweet-smelling men's cologne, and garlic. "Paulie's behind you." Her ears were still ringing from the report of both guns, and in his excitement Eduardo's accent grew intrusive. She struggled to understand him. "Go down to basement. No noise! Hide under stairs—quiet—'til Paulie's gone. You'll know. Then out back door. Run like hell. Sorry."

He held the door against its spring with his hip, spun her around so that she was facing back into the stairwell and gave her a helping push across the landing toward the stairs. Their encounter ended in a moment of stillness broken only by Paolo's heavy tread echoing in the stairwell above them. He was closing fast. With the thumps of his footfalls in her ears, Julia pulled off her shoes and dashed down the final two sets of stairs as quietly as she could.

At the end, was the last step higher than the others? Was the light different? Was she distracted by Paolo's pursuit? She stumbled and fell. A pulse of pain snapped a signal to her from her ankle as she went down. She crawled along the wall, back and under the stairs.

"She went out here."

Eduardo's voice was clear and close by. It gave her a start. He could have been standing in the basement in front of her.

"How did you let that happen, you dumbass wetback?" Paolo sounded out of breath. "I called you. Why didn't you stop her?"

"I was just opening the door when..." Eduardo's tone dropped into the cadence of the ignorant, exploited immigrant, ingratiating and servile. Julia had to smile.

Paolo broke in. "Get out of my way, asshole." His voice faded as he ran into the lobby.

So did Eduardo's. "I tried..." he was whining as the door to the stairwell slammed shut, cutting him off and leaving Julia in utter silence, and alone.

Only then, crouched below the stairs, did she notice the dark stain on the side of her black skirt, and feel the pulsing of a dull pain in her right arm. When she pulled the arm in front of her with her left hand and peered at it in the shadows she saw above her elbow the furrow made by the bullet fired in her direction when DiNiro had first tried to shoot her. It was like a rip across her flesh, matted with mostly clotted blood, but with some still oozing out. The blood had run down, over her forearm and the back of her hand, as if she had spilled dark red paint there and not bothered to clean it up.

Quickly she crawled out and stood, holding onto the railing of the steps to test her ankle. It hurt, but, she thought, was not so stiff that she couldn't use it. Clutching her purse and her shoes, she staggered for her first few steps, then hobbled down the short, gloomy basement hallway to the door at the end. It was solid metal, a fire door, operated by a bar that she pushed, exactly like the basement door at the high school. It moved with difficulty.

DiNiro, she thought, must have gone down by the elevator. He and Paolo would have looked for her out the front door of the building. Could they have circled around and be waiting for her on the other side?

She eased the heavy door open.

61

INSTEAD OF MARCO DINIRO or Paolo, Julia was greeted by the loud grumble of thunder, and by rain. Water cascaded in sheets from the small roof that sheltered the basement entrance to Peter's apartment building and blew into the doorway. It flowed down the short flight of stairs from the alley behind the building into the flooded stairwell. The drain was backed up and water had risen almost to the level of the step on which she stood.

She hesitated for only an instant before plunging across to the stairs, splashing deep in the cool, murky liquid, then pulling herself up them by the railing to favor her sore ankle. She sat on the top step to put her on her shoes. The runoff from the downpour coursed around her, gurgling into the stairwell.

They must already be searching for her, she thought, trying to find where she had fled to. She was fearful of appearing on the street too close to the front of the building, so when she was ready, she pulled herself up using the rail again, turned away from the open end of the alley, where she could see cars passing, and limped further back.

Some of these alleys, she knew, opened onto more than one street. She found that this was not one of them. Straight back she saw a second building, and soon she found that around a corner, instead of an outlet to the street, was a cul-de-sac in back of a third. There, at least, she was able to pause out of sight of the street, and she rested against a wall, away from the full force of the storm.

Most of the blood had been washed from her arm and hand by the cloudburst but the clotting over the wound had been loosened, too, and it was starting to flow again. Her hair hung in strings against her forehead and her ears, as if she was standing in the shower. Her stylish blouse (dark green silk, dry clean only) was soaked through and plastered coldly against her skin. She felt a chill beginning to penetrate, exploiting the weariness of her battered and abused body.

She was like a water rat that had abandoned a sinking ship, she thought, clinging to a scrap of wood, unable to orient itself toward dry land and a place to rest and recoup. Adrift. Worse, it was only a matter of time, and probably not much of that, before her pursuers' search would bring them here, where she would be caught with no place to flee, or even to hide.

In front of her a lone, square-looking truck was backed up to a large, metal door facing onto a low loading dock. The vehicle was a dingy white and unmarked, except for scrapes along its side where it had been maneuvered without finesse into narrow docking spaces. No one was in the cab, and the door into the building seemed to be closed. Still, that door was her only chance.

Julia took a step and found that her ankle had stiffened, but as she hobbled back across the alley, the pain settled into a manageable throb. When she approached the truck, she realized with a start of hope that the door to the apartment building was not seated flush in its metal frame. She smelled cigarette smoke as she climbed the few steps, reached for the handle and pulled. Slowly it opened.

"Hold it lady!"

A young man with a dirty blond pony tail, his physique bulging through a torn T-shirt, stepped in front of her. Another, smaller and older, remained sitting on a straight-back wooden chair inside the entrance. A cigarette bobbed from between the first man's lips as he talked. "You can't come in here," he said. "This door ain't even supposed to be open, for chrissake."

"Take it easy, Harry," the other said, flipping his smoke to the floor and rising. "She looks cold." His eyes flicked over her. "We could warm you up real quick, baby," he said to her. He laughed as he grasped for her arm.

Julia stepped aside and away from them, but stayed inside the door, which swung back against the piece of wood the two men had jammed it with.

"I live here," she said, her tone indignant and annoyed. "Apartment 5A. I've had an accident and I need help, but not from you, thanks." She glared at the first man and he stepped aside. The second backed away. As she brushed past them she turned to look over her shoulder. "Are you supposed to be smoking in this building?"

"It's raining," the younger one said plaintively.

By then Julia was turning a corner into a hallway that she thought should lead to the front of the building. Out of sight, she stopped long enough to take the handkerchief she carried in her purse and blot the blood from around the gash in her arm. Then she straightened her shoulders, pulled open the door at the end of the corridor, and walked with as little eccentricity as she could manage into the softly-lit, carpeted lobby of the building.

She saw that it faced Fifth Avenue. She recognized the old-fashioned green awning that stretched from the entrance toward the street. She realized that she was only one door uptown from the apartment house she had left just a few minutes before.

The doorman was leaning against one of the marble columns that flanked the entrance on the inside, staring out at the rain, which seemed to have slowed a little. When he heard her approaching he straightened up abruptly—he was a tall man—then turned to greet her. He looked elegant in his uniform, totally at ease and self-assured. And, he looked familiar.

At the sight of Julia, his face shifted from a controlled non-expression of complete composure to surprise, and back again. Then he spoke.

"Can I help you, Miss?"

She was sure he could, but was having trouble focusing on how. She continued to walk from the back of the lobby toward him, scanning the fragment of sidewalk and street she could see from her vantage point.

"Is someone expecting you?"

From his manner she sensed the care he was taking in dealing with this surprising apparition that had emerged from the forbidden area behind the back door, and, in spite of her circumstances, she was amused. She stopped in front of him.

His expression changed again.

"Excuse me, but I've seen you before, haven't I?" His voice was altered, too. It had relaxed to a still-guarded, but almost conversational tone. "Don't you live down the street?"

"Not any more. But I did. I used to walk by here a lot, remember?"

"Yes, Miss, I do. I'm Mike. Is everything all right?" He had begun to take in her bedraggled appearance in a different light, to ponder its possible significance with empathy. His eyes moved from the bandage on her forehead to stop at the red-stained handkerchief that, without thinking, she was holding against her arm. "Have you been hurt?"

"Yes," Julia said, "and I need to take a taxi to the hospital. Do you suppose you would be able to find one for me?"

"Of course, Miss. It'll be hard to hail one in this weather, but I'll do the best I can. I'll give a call to a limo company some of our tenants use, too. Then, whichever gets here first wins."

He gave her a wave as he strode to a telephone on the wall just inside the entrance, flicked a switch next to it which she assumed activated a flashing light at the top of the green awning, and picked up the receiver. In a moment, after a brief conversation on the phone, he went out with an umbrella in hand and began to blow a whistle he took from his pocket and to wave at passing taxicabs. Julia waited behind the same column that Mike had been leaning against, partially hidden from the street. She peered around it to keep watch.

Fifth Avenue was one-way, and all the traffic moved to the left, downtown, toward Peter's building. Soon a large, black sedan pulled up to the curb. Mike spoke to the driver and came inside.

"This is your man. Ernest. I know him. He's good. Most of our tenants who use this company have an account with them, but you can pay with a credit card. That okay?"

"Perfect," said Julia. "One other thing, Mike. Would you mind if I use your phone for a quick local call?"

"Be my guest," Mike said, and discreetly moved just outside the entrance. He motioned to the car to wait.

She found the number in her purse and got Archibold Strothers after two rings.

"Julia? Where are you?"

"I'm going to be there in a few minutes," she said. "By cab. A limousine, sort of. I can't explain now, but it's important for someone to be at the door when I get there."

"Fine," Strothers said.

"I know the number of the house. But what block is it in? I don't want to be cruising around there for long."

Strothers gave her the directions.

"One more thing," she said. "Peter Medea has been shot. It happened in his own apartment. I know because I was there. It was DiNiro and someone he brought with him named Paolo." She gave Strothers the address. "It's apartment 10A. Please call the police and tell them to get up there quickly. DiNiro and Paolo will be gone, but Peter may still be alive."

When she was finished she walked to the entrance door and called to Mike, motioning for him to come to her.

"Could you help me to the car?" she said. "My ankle is a little sore and my arm is cut. Would you let me lean on you?"

"Of course," Mike said. "I do it all the time with my older tenants. Here." He offered her his right arm.

Shielded by Mike from the area in front of Peter's building, Julia limped out to the limousine. Mike raised the umbrella over her when they left the cover of the awning and opened the door to the car.

The driver was a huge man. As she climbed into the back seat she saw that his knees rose on both sides of the steering wheel. It looked insignificant in his large hands. When she sat down, his broad shoulders and thick neck nearly blocked her view to the front. His head was practically touching the roof of the car and seemed, up there, not quite in scale with his monumental body. His skin was the color of rich, dark chocolate.

He turned to look down at her. "I'm Ernest," he said, and grinned. "Where can I take you? Mt. Sinai Hospital is back uptown aways. Lenox Hill is a few blocks down, over near Park Avenue."

"Hello, Ernest," she said, "I'm Julia," and smiled back. His significant presence and his good humor were reassuring. Relief coursed through her like a flood. She relaxed a little for the first time since she had walked up to Peter's apartment house, an eon ago, it seemed now. Out of the woods at last, she thought.

"I've changed my mind," she said. "Instead, please head downtown for a few blocks and then I'll let you know where we go next. But first I want to say goodbye to Mike."

She lowered her window and motioned for Mike to come back to the car. Then she reached into her purse to find her wallet. Mike put his hand over the opened purse, then touched hers lightly.

"Please, Miss," he said, and smiled. "You'd do the same for me, I know."

"Thank you, Mike. You may have saved my life."

He looked startled as the car pulled away from the curb, but waved, and Julia waved back.

She had planned to hunch down in her seat to hide until the car was well past Peter's entrance, but preoccupied with closing her purse and their slow progress in the midday traffic, even on Saturday, she forgot.

Without thinking, she turned in that direction and found herself, even at the distance of the ten or so yards that separated her from the front of the building, looking into the eyes of Paolo, who was standing there as if he had been waiting for her to appear. He ran toward her. At the same time, the car began to slow to a halt.

"Ernest," she said, trying not to shout, "we need to go faster."

"This is a red light," he said. The car slowed to a stop.

"That man," she tapped the driver on the shoulder and pointed out the window, "wants to hurt me."

Paolo was already approaching the curb.

Ernest pushed a switch that locked her door.

"I ain't goin' to run that light," he said, "but they ain't no one goin' to hurt one a my passengers." With surprising quickness, he sprang out of the car, which was not far from the curb, and stood at full height in the path of the other man's charge.

"He has a gun!" Julia called after him, but Ernest either didn't hear or didn't care as he took a step toward the running figure.

Paolo's head did not come to Ernest's chest as he pulled up in front of him, then nearly disappeared behind the other's sheer bulk. Julia shifted her position to get a better view. No one spoke. Ernest took another step toward the smaller man. Paolo seemed to hesitate. He glanced at the stopped cars backed up close behind the limousine on Fifth Avenue, and then once more at the formidable obstacle that blocked his way, before he turned on his heel and walked away at a measured pace. Julia expected him to whirl at any moment with his deadly little black pistol in his hand, but he did not.

Ernest crossed his arms and stood, apparently oblivious to the rain, the green light and the honking from the traffic jam he was creating, until Paolo reached the entrance to Peter's building. Then he made his stately way back to the door of the limo which he had left open in his haste. He folded himself back into the driver's seat and the cramped space allotted him there with, Julia thought, the dexterity of a hermit crab retreating into its shell.

Julia laughed at the sight, letting out her breath in a rush, and laughed again at his broad grin as he looked over his shoulder and shook his head.

"Some people jus' don' know how to act, now, do they?" he said, moving the car through the intersection just as the light started to change.

"Thank you, Ernest," she said. She sat back, holding her own smile. As she felt the limousine picking up speed, she heard through its closed windows the sirens and horns of police and emergency vehicles approaching. Then the limo moved smoothly downtown, away from the place where she had just been, the place she knew to be their destination. She shut her eyes and let out her breath.

"Thank you!"

62

THE RAIN HAD DIMINISHED to a steady drizzle, more like a heavy mist. It glossed the leaves of the elegant, and fragrant, gardenias standing in ceramic pots at the front corners of the second story veranda where Julia sat. It slid in droplets from the tall ferns bowing under its weight and the clumps of red and white impatiens, all arrayed in luxuriant display before her. Beyond, the lacy top of a mimosa tree told of the small courtyard garden from which it sprang. Earlier, leaning over the cast-iron railing, she had seen the gatherings of ferns, hosta and boxwood set among narrow pea-gravel paths, quietly soaking up the nurturing moisture. The trunk of the tree at its center was encircled by a stone bench.

With the open French doors to the living room behind her, she was sheltered by a striped canvas awning. It only extended part way over the terrace, leaving the pots and planters at the balcony's edge exposed to the weather. Wrapped in Amelia Strothers' soft terrycloth robe, she reclined in a nest of fluffy cushions piled into an oversized wicker arm chair. She sipped tea from a large Victorian Chinese cup inhabited by a fierce, orange dragon that glared at her from the bottom, inside the bowl, when she tipped it up to drink.

Her strained ankle was propped in front of her on still another cushion set on a squat wicker stool. It was wrapped in an elastic bandage that threatened her circulation while she was inactive, and she wiggled her bare toes as a precaution from time to time. The white dressing over the row of stitches on her arm was bulky and ugly, but she felt no pain there unless she tried to stretch. The doctor in the emergency ward of Lennox Hill Hospital had replaced the bandage over the wound on her forehead, too. "You've had your share of luck," he said as he released her.

By five in the evening she had finally met the demands made on her at the hospital to treat her injuries, and by the police. Amelia Strothers had loaned her a simple dress while her clothes were being cleaned at a neighborhood place that did work on the premises. They would have them ready before the end of the day. Archibold Strothers, whom Julia learned again to address by his first name, had accompanied her for the afternoon. Earlier, Amelia called Rita Craig in Ironton to tell her of Julia's whereabouts: that she had been hurt but was all right, and would not be back in Ironton that day as she had planned. On Julia's instructions, Amelia also gave Danny Johnson's telephone number to Rita and asked Rita to pass along the same information to him. She promised a call from Julia to Rita and Calvin, and to Danny, when Julia was feeling stronger.

Julia was exhausted, but she could not sleep. Closing her eyes simply served to conjure up a whirlwind of stormy images in her brain despite her calm surroundings.

She saw Peter fixed in an instant of time, a photograph in her mind, in the act of falling back toward the sofa, but suspended over it, his expression open and wondering, like a boy in a schoolyard tussle who has had the wind knocked out of him by someone half his size. But she knew from the police that he was dead.

Responding to Archibold Strothers' call while Ernest was delivering her to the brownstone townhouse, the police had found Peter lying there, presumably where she had seen him propelled by the bullet from DiNiro's gun. But she was surprised to learn from them that there had been a second body—a tall, heavy man in a business suit, who had suffered a blow to the face, but more important had been shot in the body at almost point-blank range. He was breathing when the paramedics arrived, but they could not save him. He died in the ambulance without regaining consciousness.

Julia tried, with the police detectives, to reconstruct how Marco DiNiro could have met his fate. They came to the conclusion that Paolo, in his haste to shoot Julia, had accidentally shot DiNiro instead. She remembered that Paolo had been trying to get around DiNiro, when she heard the report of the gun, and realized then that she must, in effect, have pushed DiNiro into the path of Paolo's bullet, the one that had been intended for her. Now she understood why Paolo was delayed for a critical few seconds from his pursuit of her. He must have known when he started after Julia again that his boss was injured, and stayed with him for just a moment before leaving him to resume his chase. DiNiro's fate also could explain why Julia had been given enough time in the ally behind Peter's building to find sanctuary and a means of escape.

Although there was ample documentation on their persons, the police needed someone to give them positive identification of the dead men. To save his parents the agony, Julia agreed to provide it for Peter as well as DiNiro. She explained that she was not related to the other man in any way, although she did know what he had looked like. All of that would take place tomorrow, Sunday, with the coroner, at the morgue. The police would need to talk with her again as well.

She was surprised at the depth of her sadness when she contemplated Peter's death.

The last two times she saw him she could identify in herself no spark of affection or desire for him. It had been this very lack of feeling that had both reassured and disturbed her then. True, she had been mourning the year of her life spent with him as wasted with someone who was using her in some way she still did not fully understand, and chastising herself for her naïveté in allowing it to happen. But in spite of it all, she knew that she had loved him, even though she had been driven away from that love by him, and that he must have loved her, in his way. And that without that love the time they were together would, in retrospect, have been unbearably demeaning, as well as lost.

Again she recalled the look of him when he was shot. Studied it.

At that moment, his face was like a child's. And like a child, Peter was, after all, vulnerable. Perhaps all along. She had guessed as much, secretly wanted it she supposed, but he would never let her know, had never expressed it—until the bullet, exploding away his life force, tore off his mask.

How much had he loved her? Of what kind of love was he capable?

He made love to her as if he were in love. She knew that wasn't enough. But maybe it was all she should have expected. All that he could give.

Yet, in the end, for her, he risked his life. And lost it.

She became aware again of the dripping and trickling of water from the mist whispering in her ears, a hushed, soothing cadence. From the meager patches of moist earth offered by the garden below, and the blossoms and leaves of the plants, a dark, vital fragrance spoke to her of the awakening of the redolent, Spring-dampened woods behind the house where she grew up. Her woods.

And so her thoughts shifted, and she remembered again how she had retreated there long ago to contemplate the surprising prospect of being taken to a dance by the first man with whom she was sure she had fallen in love.

"Julia?"

His voice drifted to her as in a dream.

"I think they're having dinner soon."

She opened her eyes and turned toward him. It was almost dark now, but no lights had been turned on. He was standing to the side, well inside the house, and at first, in the twilight of the living room, she had trouble making him out.

"Danny?"

He moved a chair to where he could watch her from a discreet distance, and called to her again from there, leaning forward out of the darkness as he spoke.

"I'm sorry I woke you up."

Julia rubbed her eyes, and stretched. Her stitches pulled and she started with the stab of pain. Traces of sleep thickened her voice.

"What are you doing here?"

She had curled up, taking her ankle from the stool, and it throbbed when she moved it gingerly back to its proper place. As her mind cleared she rephrased her question.

"Why are you so far away?" She held out a hand for him.

Danny stood and walked to her. "Rita called. Luckily I wasn't on the road, so I came right away. I hope you don't mind. I drove. It's less than three hours." He took her hand, touched her hair. "We... I was worried to death." He dropped to a crouch in front of her.

"So, here you are again." She smiled. "I'm glad."

"Why didn't you call me before you left? Why didn't you let me help?" He brushed her hand with his lips and looked at her for an answer.

Julia's eyes began to glisten. She managed a crooked smile as she blinked back unexpected tears, but did not trust herself to speak.

63

"IT'S MY FAULT, I know." Joshua Adams' voice was low, almost as if he were talking to himself.

Amelia Strothers had included Danny for dinner. Now they were back on the veranda. Archibold offered after-dinner drinks to his guests. Adams and Julia declined, Danny asked for a bourbon and ice, and Strothers poured himself a brandy. Amelia brought out coffee on a tray.

The rain had stopped completely. The small group was gathered in front of Julia, who was settled once more among the cushions in the commodious arm chair, her foot again elevated to rest her ankle and ease the swelling. The tree growing in the garden below, its rain-darkened trunk and its branches with their fern-like leaves, was illuminated by the wavering yellow-ochre glow from kerosene torches in holders placed on the terrace beyond the awning, as well as subdued light from the shaded lamps in the living room.

Adams was perched on a wicker stool. His feet were pressed against its base with his knees jutting out. His large head was thrust forward, his generous ears much in evidence, his hands braced on the edge of his seat. His bushy eyebrows were knit with concern. To Julia he looked for a moment like a crouching gargoyle, an anachronistic illusion dramatized by the backdrop of the flickering shadows cast by the torches. He had not touched his coffee.

"I feel responsible," he continued, his voice stronger, his eyes, gleaming from shadowy recesses, fixed on Julia. "I had no idea what my partners and I were setting in motion." He looked down at the tiled floor and shook his head.

"But how could you?" Archibold Strothers' hand moved in a tight but leisurely circular motion, sending a small wave of brandy around the sides of the snifter cradled in his palm. "Who could have known how bad the man really was?" He glanced in Julia's direction. "I remember telling you that his reputation was pretty grim."

"A long time ago. I know." Julia was gazing at the tree: exotic, almost tropical looking in the light of the flames. Her mind drifted back to the weedy jungle of the vacant lot across the street from her own house. To the dark bulk of the low-slung automobile lurking in front of that wall of unruly vegetation the night she had seen Danny off after her dinner party. How, when Danny walked toward it the car had sped away. She closed her eyes. A prickly feeling deep inside sent a shiver along her spine.

She turned to face Strothers. "I think I know why those files might have been important to DiNiro. But what could possibly make anyone want to..."

Strothers broke in. "No normal person would. But DiNiro was obviously not normal. He was in a world of his own, with his own standards. His own rules. Anyway, part of it was undoubtedly our lawsuit. We allege that DiNiro committed some pretty bad misdeeds. There was a lot at stake for him. Significant damages. His reputation, such as it was. Your files can no doubt help us still, against Grendel, if it's worth anything any more. I'm sure Peter was concerned about them because they could have damaged *him*. DiNiro must have found out about them from Peter."

"He did." Julia said. "Peter told me that when I met with him."

"In any event," Strothers continued, "DiNiro must have suspected, not without justification I would say, that Peter was down-playing the whole thing to avoid DiNiro's considerable wrath. As important, perhaps, DiNiro didn't know what Peter might have told you about this business, either."

"But was just the chance that he might lose a lawsuit enough to make him try to kill me?" Julia heard her voice taking on an edge and felt her color rising.

"It may have been," Strothers said, "but there were other things at stake for DiNiro, and for Peter as well."

Amelia rose. "Can I pour anyone some more coffee?" She looked around the group. Danny tilted his head back, swallowed the last of his bourbon and started to get up, the empty glass in his hand. Julia touched his sleeve and their eyes met for an instant. Instead of rising, Danny shifted in his chair and put the empty glass on the floor.

"I'd like a cup," he said. "Thank you."

Strothers continued. "On top of the lawsuit, there is the Federal investigation, by the Securities and Exchange Commission. The SEC. It could have had some disastrous consequences for him, too. I'm not privy to it, of course, but the type of thing they'd be looking for would be lies he might have used to help sell Grendel stock, or information he might have withheld from his shareholders and bondholders about the TryCo deal or the acquisition of the second company, both of which they voted to approve.

"Then there is his sale of a large number of his own Grendel shares just before the bottom fell out of their price. Given his relationship to the company, and depending on what he knew when he sold them, he would probably be found guilty of insider trading. Peter, too. People have gone to jail for just that sort of violation."

"But I didn't know anything about that," Julia said. "How could I?"

"Isn't there more?" It was Danny. "Julia asked me to read over the papers in the files, and it looked to me as if there were a lot of payments to DiNiro from an off-shore company that Julia says she was involved with, but nothing about what he did to earn them."

"It was called Finance ServiCo," Julia said. "I was made an officer, its only officer they said, when it was started. Peter and I were with Rob and Vicki Vardaman on St. Maarten at the time. Later I signed papers, checks even. Rob Vardaman told me what to do. It was stupid of me, but it was hard for me not to. I felt Peter was counting on me. I was in love…" Her voice faltered. After a short pause she gathered herself together. "Back then. It seems so long ago."

Danny drank down the coffee Amelia had served him in a gulp.

"If that money originally came to Julia's company from Grendel," he said, "and Julia's company didn't do anything to earn it, and then it was paid to DiNiro, and he didn't do anything to earn it, isn't DiNiro sort of stealing the money from Grendel?"

"It's not my company." Julia's voice rose plaintively.

"You're right," Strothers said, "in effect, it would be stealing. Theft. And then he did what he could to cover it up. Money laundering. Bigger players than DiNiro have spent a lot of time in jail for that type of thing, too. Another thing: if it was an off-shore company, he might have been using it to avoid paying taxes that should have been paid on income generated in the U.S. That could add tax evasion to the list."

Julia glanced at Adams, then turned back to Strothers. "There is something more that I was going to tell both of you, when I got a chance. Danny knows. I only went on one trip with Peter—well, two, counting the one to St. Maarten I just told you about—during the year we were married." She looked away, into the darkness beyond the flickering torches. "Part of it was supposed to be a vacation for both of us. It didn't end very well, and I left him a few months later. But that's another story. Anyway, we landed in Frankfurt and had dinner with Denny DiNiro and a friend, I guess you'd call her, before we drove to Salzburg.

"DiNiro seemed to be on a high of some kind. Champagne before dinner. Then he had quite a lot of gin. After, while we were still at the table, DiNiro and Peter talked business. DiNiro's girlfriend was German and didn't speak English, so I couldn't carry on a conversation with her. I didn't have any choice, really, but to listen to what they were saying."

"And?" It was Strothers.

"Well, I remember some of it, but certainly not everything, mainly because I couldn't tie it all together. It didn't make a lot of sense to me..."

"Out of context..." Strothers offered.

"Exactly." She looked over at Adams. "For instance, they both were irritated by your complaints. Peter said that he thought you were on to something. DiNiro said you 'didn't know the half of it.' Those were his words, I think. They laughed about that. In fact, DiNiro said he wished he'd 'gotten rid' of you, or something like that, a long time ago."

Adams laughed uneasily. "I guess we know what he meant by that, now."

Julia continued. "They did talk about Finance ServiCo, too, and how much it had helped DiNiro. I don't remember what else.

"But isn't all that talk still too vague to hurt DiNiro?"

"It depends," Strothers said, "but the important thing is that DiNiro probably remembered a feeling he had at the time that he may have said too much in front of you. He couldn't recall exactly what he did say, probably because he'd been drinking so much. So he was running scared, just the way he was running scared about the documents in the files you copied. And, as I said, he couldn't be sure what Peter might have told you over time. It looks as though he was right to be worried, but beyond that he'd probably built it all up way out of proportion in his own imagination. Which was anything but good for you."

Strothers stood. "Well," he looked around at all of them with a thin smile, "he won't be worrying about any of that any more, will he?"

"I'm wondering," Julia's voice was subdued, "what the government investigators will say about all of those things that I did that ended up helping DiNiro do some of the stuff that you're saying would have gotten him into so much trouble. What kind of trouble will *I* get into?" She remembered how at first she had hesitated to come to Adams and Strothers in part because of the fear that she, herself, had done something wrong, maybe even against the law. Embarrassed, she looked away from both of them.

Adams spoke up before Strothers could answer her. "Don't worry about our lawsuit. At all. If there's anything that might involve you, which I doubt, we'll just drop it. Period."

Strothers walked to Julia's chair and put a hand on her shoulder. She looked up at him as he spoke. "Of course Federal investigators will want to talk with you, and maybe even take your deposition. It depends on the subject of the charges they decide to bring how involved you would have to be. With DiNiro dead, it may not amount to much. But I'm sure we can persuade them that you were that man's victim, not his associate in crime. All of your actions later, taking the files, coming to us, work in your favor. As far as I can see, you have nothing to worry about." He patted her before stepping away.

Julia became aware that Amelia was looking at her intently from behind her husband while he had been speaking. "You must be close to collapse, my dear," Amy said. She looked around at all of them. "We should be getting a good night's sleep. It doesn't look like tomorrow will be a day of rest for any of you, does it?" Her eyes settled on Danny. "We would like very much to be able to ask you to stay with us tonight, but we're full up, I'm afraid. Maybe the couch…"

Danny smiled. "I've already managed to mooch a terrific dinner from you. That's plenty. I'll find something nearby."

Josh Adams got to his feet. "Danny, please stay with me. I have plenty of extra room in my hotel suite. This will finally put it to good use."

"Thanks, Mr. Adams. That'd be great," Danny said. He looked down at Julia. "I'd like to stop by here tomorrow, though."

"Of course," Strothers said. "We'll be setting out shortly after noon. Why don't you join us for a late breakfast. Around ten?" He glanced at his wife for confirmation.

"I'll be here," Danny said. Then he leaned down to kiss Julia's cheek and squeeze her shoulders. He crouched in front of her, looking into her eyes. "See you...," he said softly, almost in a whisper. Then he joined Adams and Strothers took them toward the front door.

After they left, Amelia helped Julia up. "Forgive me for asking," the older woman said, "but what is your relationship with that young man? No, that's not what I mean." She laughed self-consciously. "I mean, how do you feel about him?"

Julia was surprised.

"Why do you ask?"

"Oh. Well, I don't know. He seems so concerned about you and so supportive. He seems like a really good person. But a little uncertain with you."

Amelia paused. She looked earnestly into Julia's eyes.

"I want you to know, my dear—I hope you don't mind my telling you this—that we, Archibold and I, think he is..."—for a wild moment, Julia thought she was going to say 'acceptable.'—"...well, very nice. We both like him a great deal."

"But you've only just met him."

"We can tell." Amelia said. "And he cares very much for you. We can tell that, too."

Julia smiled while she searched for an appropriate reply. But suddenly, she felt overcome with fatigue. She reached for the doorframe for support as she started into her room. Her hostess moved toward her.

Julia waved her back and smiled. "I'm sure I'll be all right," she said.

Amelia Strothers lowered her voice, as if she were sharing an important confidence.

"You will, my dear." She touched Julia's arm. "I know you will."

64

ANNY DROVE NORTH ON Riverside Drive. Across the Hudson River, the sun was poised to settle behind the ridge that crowned the cliffs of the Palisades. In its glow, the George Washington Bridge stood out ahead of them with startling clarity. Julia was mesmerized. Graceful and almost delicate at a distance, as they drew nearer the great structure loomed higher and larger above them, finally taking on an aspect of force and energy that bordered on intimidation.

Her day had been difficult and tiring. Hobbling on crutches and accompanied by Archibold Strothers, she began at the City Morgue, with the strangeness of confronting Peter's remains in that terribly mundane, and yet surreal, setting. Pale and waxy-looking, the face—all that she was forced to view—was a shoddy likeness at best of the vital, complex human being who had existed in that shell less than a day earlier. An object, not a person. Sad.

She was surprised that she felt no satisfaction, or repulsion, in seeing the injured face of her dead adversary, Marco DiNiro. It was hard to imagine that what was left of him had once been the living person whom she had detested, and ended up fearing, so much. She had, of course, experienced profound relief when she learned of his death, but in its actual presence, she felt only numbness and a desire to get away.

Next she faced the seemingly endless questioning by the police. It was some consolation that this time, unlike her experience with the detective in Ironton, no one was questioning whose side she was on. But they were determined to extract from her memory every detail about the very events that she wanted to forget, or if that was impossible, at least to avoid revisiting with such persistence. When they were finished, she agreed to make herself available to them later at their request. She also promised Strothers that she would help him with Adams' lawsuit in any way she could, and that she would cooperate fully with the Federal investigation, both of which were still on-going in spite of DiNiro's demise.

With her immediate obligations in the city behind her, she had returned with Strothers to the now-familiar brownstone. Danny and Josh Adams were already there. Amelia Strothers brought them sandwiches and iced tea, and joined them. They all sat together in a corner of the room overlooking the garden. Strothers spoke to Julia.

"I know that all of this has been a tremendous strain for you emotionally, not to mention your wounds and your ankle. Amelia and I," he nodded in his wife's direction, "hope that you will consider staying with us for some rest and rehabilitation. Once you're physically stronger, and you're no longer in any pain, I'm sure your mind will be more at ease. None of that can happen overnight, and we want to help."

Surprised, Julia hesitated. "Thank you." She glanced down. "You have been—are—so kind to me, and you've done so much for me already. I know I'd thrive here." Then she looked up again. "But I have exams I still have to grade. When I left Ironton I thought I was taking a day trip here. That's hard to believe now. And I have a summer job lined up at a local camp that I really can't afford not to take advantage of. I still have to pay the rent. So I guess I might as well take the leap now." Then she accepted Danny's offer to drive her back, and after an early dinner, they left.

Now, as Danny's car ascended the spiral ramp to the top level of the bridge, both its passengers were silent. Julia looked over at Danny. His attention was consumed by the task of following the curved lane without straying into the path of cars that were merging from the Cross-Bronx Expressway. She realized again that his features were fuller in maturity, the lines softened, but still she saw there, in essence, the same face that she had been drawn to so intensely long ago.

The ramp leveled off and merged with the road of the bridge itself, and they found they were facing directly into the sun. Danny squinted and pulled down the sun shade in front of him. Julia let her eyes drift back so that she was looking behind and beyond him, through the blur of vertical cables that held the roadbed from plunging into the river, past the cars that rushed in the opposite direction on the other side of the bridge, and off into the distance.

There, the elements had played a trick above the lower half of the island of Manhattan. The molten light from the not-quite-setting sun had transformed the smog that wallowed in the canyons of the streets, swallowing up smaller buildings with its acrid-blue fumes, into an ethereal cloud that lay golden and gleaming over the city. It seemed to lift countless skyscrapers upward: tall, vertical crystals glinting in the distance against the sky, like clumps of glistening stalagmites rising from the misty floor of a vast, magical cavern.

Julia was fascinated. Could that be the same place where a man she had once cherished had been murdered in front of her eyes? Where the same gun had been turned on her? Where her tormentor had met a violent death at the hands of his own hired thug? Where she had shed her blood? Had fled for her life?

She touched Danny's shoulder and pointed at the fleeting sight. "Look!"

He turned his head for an instant. "Nice," he said before fixing his eyes back on the road. And by the time he did, they were across the river and the concrete buttress of the bridge, and the wall of the cliff through which it cut, had risen abruptly next to them. The miraculous vision had passed from view.

Soon they reached the New Jersey Turnpike and angled more to the south so that the glare of the setting sun became bearable.

"Julia?" Danny glanced across at her before turning back to concentrate on the road ahead.

"Yes?"

"Remember when I asked you whether you would stay in my apartment to hide from the people who were after you? You said you'd think about it."

"Yes."

"Well, I've been thinking about it myself. There's nothing for you to hide from any more. I know it's selfish of me but in a way I'm kind of sorry to see that excuse get blown out of the water." He smiled. "But I'm wondering if you might feel a little uncomfortable for a while alone in that house of yours, after everything that's gone on, that you've been living through."

He seemed to wait for a moment, for a response that didn't materialize.

"I'm sorry I got a little over-enthusiastic when I pitched it the first time. It would only be for when you need it. You move back to your house as soon as you want, of course. As soon as you feel like it. That's all I really had in mind in the first place."

Out of the corner of her eye she saw him turn toward her again for a moment, but she did not speak.

"There's been one development," he said. "Veronica..."

"The topless dancer." She grinned.

"I talked to her about staying if you were going to be there. She said no. Nothing personal, she said, but it would be too crowded. Too confusing. But that's good news in a way. That means there will be a free bedroom."

"Is that fair?"

"She doesn't have a lease, but she can stay as long as she wants while she's looking. Anyway, I can't believe she'll have any trouble finding another roommate." He laughed.

"I'd make a contribution if I were staying there, with you, of course."

"You'd lose your chaperon." Danny looked at her again for a moment and spoke earnestly. "But you can trust me. Really."

"I know that, Danny." Julia reached across the seat and rested her hand on his knee. She slid it toward him, a stroking motion along his thigh, before she patted him and withdrew. "But can you trust me?"

The glowing red ball of the sun disappeared slowly behind the hills that ranged beyond the flatlands where the road lay. They drove past Newark, an island of towers. Then they sped beside a runway of the airport, racing a plane, huge and lumbering, its running lights blinking with silent urgency, until it lifted into the sky with sudden grace.

She remembered her thoughts as she had sipped champagne, gazing from the window of the airplane on the way to St. Maarten, near the beginning of her eventful journey with Peter Medea. He had been dozing in the seat beside her. Now, here in the car with Danny, so different from Peter, rushing into the half-light of dusk, she felt the same shiver of excitement at the possibilities of the unknown, with him, about to unfold before her, hovering in wait just beyond the horizon toward which they sped.

About the Author

William W. Blunt graduated from Yale University and Harvard Law School. He interrupted his corporate legal practice in New York City to serve in Washington, D.C., as Assistant Secretary of Commerce. Today he lives with his wife, Blair, in Irving, Texas. He has written numerous short stories. This is his first novel.